The Iron Edge

THE IRON EDGE

by
Lexa Luthor

Luthor Publishing
2023

The Iron Edge
© **2023 By Lexa Luthor. All Rights Reserved.**
Luthor Publishing
www.LexaLuthor.com

Editors:
RJ Creamer
Lila LaBine

Cover Artist:
May Dawney of May Dawney Designs
maydawneydesigns.com

ISBN-13 (paperback):
978-1-952993-14-5

ISBN-13 (ebook):
978-1-952993-13-8

First Edition – March 2023 – 01 02

CONTENTS

ACKNOWLEDGEMENTS

Four years ago, this was a historical book about half the size—and half of the story. There was so much left untold, until now. I'm thrilled to have a second chance to retell Thora and Halcyon's love story the way it was meant to be.

Thank you to my alpha reader and beta readers for their input. Without them, the book would be a few thousand words shorter (haha). Love to Alex, Dani, Hazel, Heiður, and Terry.

VILLA HONOR THE BELOVED

1. Bathing Room
2. Store Room
3. Kitchen
4. Master's Suite
5. Mistress's Suite
6. Guestroom
7. Master Bedroom
8. Chamber Pot Room
9. Slaves' Quarters
10. Stable
11. Tool shed
12. Farm field

PROLOGUE
Halcyon

Apollo's burning yellow chariot hung in the western horizon and continued to travel across the arid summer sky. In the northern district of Sparta, the strongest-known female Omega, Halcyon, marched through the streets on a mission. Many stepped aside for her, knowing to trifle with her meant risking their lives. Halcyon was an accomplished businesswoman, a landowner, and a well-decorated hoplite in the king's guard. She was the only Omega hoplite in Sparta's military. None came before her, and she doubted any would come after.

Behind Halcyon, her elder slave, Cesare, trailed her at a respectful distance. He understood her better than anyone after so long. Halcyon loathed the idea of his future passing, so she ensured he stayed healthy. Cesare had known her since she was a pup, after her sire purchased him from another family in Athens. When Halcyon's father moved them to Sparta, Cesare was registered with Sparta's slave books and received a new slave iron on his wrist.

Crossing a street, Halcyon approached the gates of a large villa and pulled on the chain to ring the iron bell. The Greek symbol on the gate indicated that it was Telamon's residence. Telamon was a prominent figure in Spartan society and known for his ability to smuggle in private slaves for purchase. With a huff, she peered over her shoulder and confirmed that Cesare was still with her.

Cesare stood a few steps back. His expression was unreadable, but that was normal for him. In recent years, Cesare had developed gray streaks through his dark hair, and his brown eyes were slightly cloudy. Time made his skin form soft rolls, and his shoulders fell forward rather than remained square. Cesare's speed in the house had become slower each year, which concerned Halcyon.

A soft commotion caught Halcyon's ear, so she looked beyond the gate's iron bars. She was pleased when a scraggly slave unlatched the bolt and allowed her to enter the villa. With a neutral gaze, she stole a glance at the courtyard, which measured one's wealthy stature in Greek life.

The slave sealed the gate after Cesare joined his owner. He bowed to them, then darted off without a word.

The wait was brief. A portly man in a soft blue chiton strolled out from one of the ground-floor rooms. He had the same slave with him and ordered him to fetch more slaves. "You are Halcyon." He crossed the courtyard to his guest. "Your mate, Euclid, mentioned you would be here today." He offered his hand. From one sniff, it was obvious that Telamon was a Beta.

"I am Halcyon."

"And I am Telamon." For a beat, Telamon raked his eyes over Halcyon's muscular figure, then stared into her golden eyes.

Halcyon was well aware of the gossip about her attractive features despite a few minor scars from training and battle. Most Omegas were soft and delicate, but she was well padded with muscles. Her ornate lilac peplos accentuated her built figure. Many were enthralled by her unusual, masculine beauty, and Telamon was no different from the rest.

"I'm looking for a slave," Halcyon said in an attempt to refocus him. "Two of mine died this past winter." She released his meaty hand from their clasp. "I was informed you're the best source."

"Yes." Telamon stepped to his side and indicated the line of eight slaves behind him, deeper in the courtyard. "I have the finest slaves." He studied Halcyon's exposed neckline. Halcyon wore a beautiful golden necklace, which was a family heirloom.

Like Halcyon, there were a handful of secret clients in Sparta who purchased personal slaves. To own a personal slave was looked upon as a sign of wealth in Sparta. Many of the clients had amassed their private fortunes outside of Sparta's reach because all types of commerce were illegal in the city and nearby territories. After her sire's passing, Halcyon inherited her father's land and estate, the personal slaves, and the revered horse-racing business, but that was located in Athens.

The majority of slaves were owned by the government and were provided to the Spartan citizens at no cost. Daily and common chores were for the slaves so that citizens could focus on the military. The government-owned slaves were known as helots, who tended to be Gammas. A Gamma was at the bottom of the pecking order, even subservient to Omegas. To be born a Gamma was to be cursed by the gods for life.

Today Halcyon continued the tradition her sire had set and preferred to choose a qualified slave rather than an assigned one from the government. Citizens were often infuriated by the helots, who lacked the proper skills for chores and were unhealthy due to poor diet. On principle Halcyon refused to have a Gamma in her villa—they were unpredictable and a strange lot.

Halcyon approached the available slaves and studied each face. Three slaves were foreigners. Their distinct features, such as a lighter skin tone, brown hair, or hazel eyes, indicated they came from outside Greece. They were perhaps victims of war, then traded to Greece. Each of the slaves was a Beta or an Omega, easy to keep in line. It was uncommon to find a male Alpha slave, and a female Alpha was beyond rare. In general, Alphas tended to be more hassle than they were worth. As a result, Alphas captured during wars were often killed rather than enslaved.

"I require a cook."

Cesare shadowed his owner and Halcyon noted Cesare's own concerns about the lineup of slaves. Each slave was built rather similar, close to Halcyon's height but scrawny, especially in comparison to her. They required nutrition and a thorough bath. Halcyon wanted a young, healthy slave in the household. Many of the daily chores included upkeep of the home, courtyard, stable, horses, and surrounding lands, and Cesare was a terrible cook.

"A female cook." Halcyon turned to Telamon, who toyed with the ring on his finger.

Telamon pointed to the female slave near the end. "This one is a fine cook and Illyrian. Her Greek is strong."

Halcyon glowered. The indicated slave was weathered with time. "Far too old." Cesare was old enough, and adding another senior slave concerned Halcyon. "I need a young one." She studied the other available slaves.

Telamon pointed at the one young female Omega in the lineup. "Glauce has not learned to cook, but she is excellent at weaving."

Halcyon was further displeased by the news. Cesare could teach weaving to a new slave. She considered leaving Telamon's residence, as it appeared he had no young slave to suit her needs.

"Perhaps you could purchase both slaves." Telamon smiled at the brilliant idea. "The elder can teach the younger to cook." His idea sounded closer to a sales pitch rather than a logical solution.

Uninterested in hearing any more of his commentary, Halcyon walked away from the lineup of slaves that displeased her. Telamon had wasted her time, and there were other private slavers in the city who may have a better selection. As she crossed the courtyard toward the gate, Telamon bustled alongside her and continued his sales pitch. Halcyon was close to growling at him, but she slowed upon seeing an unusual young female. As she drew closer, she was mesmerized by her distinct features.

The unusual female was crouched by a few plants, which she watered with a clay jug. Her long, straight hair curtained around her face. When she lifted her head, the strands fell back to reveal her pale cheeks and light-colored eyebrows. From this angle, Halcyon spotted a faint scar on the slave's upper lip. She was younger than Halcyon; possibly by ten years. As the slave rose from her crouched position, her long legs seemed endless. She wore a dirty, oversize chiton that failed to hide her athletic build, indicating the physical labor she'd done. With a glance at the female Alpha's wrist, Halcyon confirmed her slave status.

Halcyon was fascinated by her and couldn't ignore the warm burn growing between her legs. The Alpha slave's spicy, warm scent had drifted under Halcyon's nose. She had to have her.

Telamon shuffled over, stiffened, and opened his mouth but was cut off.

"How much for her?"

Telamon shook his head and rested his linked hands on his rotund belly. "She is not for sale."

"How much?" Halcyon demanded. She had yet to tear her gaze away from the gorgeous slave. At first, it had been the golden hair that captured Halcyon's attention. But drawing closer, she inhaled the distinct scent that rested heavy on her tongue. "She is an Alpha," she whispered with a measure of awe.

"Y-Yes." Telamon cleared his throat, then he straightened and spoke with firmness. "You may purchase any but her." Halcyon suspected Telamon regarded the slave as a trophy piece in his household and paraded the female Alpha at his symposiums.

Halcyon was lost in her admiration and wondered if the color of sky had been painted in the slave's eyes by the gods. There were myths about female Alphas existing, but Halcyon had never seen one. She marveled at the rare find before her until Telamon's words sank in. Glaring, she tested him with an offer. "A hundred drachmas."

Telamon balked and sputtered at the weak offer.

"Three hundred drachmas." Halcyon smirked at his developing hesitation, which was promising for her. Everyone had a price, especially Telamon.

"She is quite the Cerberus, stubborn and troublesome."

Halcyon's lips pulled into a small grin at the slave being compared to Hades's three-headed dog. With a deep stare, she watched the storm inside the golden-haired Alpha. To have this gorgeous Alpha enslaved felt like a crime. Halcyon wanted to learn everything about her. "Four hundred drachmas."

Again, Telamon played with the gold signet ring on his pinky. He narrowed his gaze at the slave. His pheromones started to shift, hinting at his wavering resolve. "She speaks little Greek."

Halcyon considered whether Telamon was trying to discourage her or himself. She refused defeat, like all Spartan hoplites, and had to own the unique slave. In Telamon's hands, the slave would suffer, then be given to the government when he tired of her. As a helot, she would be murdered due to her unique features and Alpha nature. Halcyon's heart rate doubled at the horrible thought of the Alpha slave being killed. She shoved aside the instant attraction she had for the slave, not wanting Telamon to use it against her.

"Five hundred drachmas." Halcyon turned to Telamon. "And I will purchase another slave in one to two months." Both of her offers were outlandish, but it could do the trick.

Telamon's features showed the war within himself. After a long minute, he sighed and held out his hand. "I accept."

Halcyon clasped his arm in final agreement.

"She does cook," Telamon said after the shake.

Reaching between her peplos, Halcyon fished out a pouch. "There are ten owls." She handed the coins to him. "The rest will be brought to you by tomorrow's sunset." Much of her coin came from Athens and had Athena's owl stamped on the face. Her Athenian coins were far more valuable than Sparta's worthless iron discs.

Halcyon turned to Cesare. "See to her."

"Yes, mistress." Cesare bowed his head to his owner, then neared the tall slave.

Telamon signaled the same scraggly slave to help organize the sold slave. He then escorted Halcyon back to the gate.

"Tell me her history."

Cradling the pouch in his hands, Telamon paused beside the black gate and said, "I purchased her from an Athenian some time ago. Like myself, he had trouble handling her. He received her as a payment from a Phoenician merchant." He paused, then mentioned, "I believe she is from Gaul."

Halcyon considered the information for a moment. People from Gaul lived in the northern lands that the Romans found of interest. "Her age?" she asked.

"Perhaps twenty or so." Telamon shrugged but smirked and added, "She is in her prime"—he unlatched the gate—"if you prefer a body slave."

Halcyon curled her upper lip, flashing her canines at him for what he insinuated. "Her name, Telamon?"

Telamon glanced at the approaching slaves and huffed as if he were, in fact, happy to be rid of her. "Makistia." Frowning, Halcyon knew that was only a slave's name, which meant "tallest" in Greek. It was clear that Telamon knew nothing about the slave's birth name, but perhaps she could learn it in time. What mattered was that Halcyon now owned a rare female Alpha from faraway lands.

CHAPTER 1
Thora

A few firm bangs on the door echoed through the small room. With a groan, she sat up and rubbed away the sleep from her face. Over a fortnight had passed since she joined Halcyon's household and she'd yet to adjust to the early mornings. Tossing the thin sheet aside, she stood and crossed the short distance with one step. Cracking open the door, she was met by the elder slave's displeased features.

"It is a new day, Makistia," Cesare told her, similar to yesterday and all the days before. Even though she understood only bits and pieces of Greek, she knew the drill. "Meet me downstairs," he added before he hurried off without another word or glance.

She listened for the slap of his sandals against the stone floor to become faint, then she muttered, "Thora." Her name was Thora, not Makistia. But early on in her enslavement, she had learned to keep her mouth shut. Even now the harsh memory of a wooden stick across her back reminded her why. For a moment Thora toyed with the metal bracelet around her wrist. The slave iron was fitted to her when she was first brought to Greece. Everyone in Greece was familiar with the distinct bracelet that marked her as a slave. In her homelands there were some slaves, who were called thralls, but they weren't marked or mistreated.

With a frown, Thora shut the door, leaned her back against it, and stared at her tiny square confines. The walls were bright, like snow from her homelands. Only a single window, with a mat covering to block the night's cooler air, broke up the whitewashed interior. On the floor, a bedroll and a ruffled blanket called to her. However, Thora had to prepare for the day, although Sunna had yet to appear above the eastern horizon to draw her chariot with the sun in it.

While readying herself, she considered her past. Thora's previous owner had been cruel, much like the slave trader, Telamon, who sold her. Her previous owner was an Athenian, living in the city. He was an Alpha determined to dominate a female Alpha by any means possible. Thora learned when to stand her ground and when not to fight. She found a measure of relief when Telamon purchased her. He was a Beta and easier to handle than an Alpha master. Her current owner intrigued her in different ways—she expected an Omega owner to be the easiest of all. However, when Halcyon stood before her, Thora became confused by Halcyon's Alpha-like personality mixed with Omega pheromones.

On the first day, Thora had received a long bath and then a detailed tour of the two-story villa that was called Villa Honor the Beloved. She had been impressed by Halcyon's home and lands, which stood on the eastern side of the Greek city at the end of a twisty street. Like many Greek homes, it was made from a combination of wood, stone, and clay. A classic rustic tile had been used on the roof. When visitors arrived, they entered through the front gate and were greeted by a beautiful courtyard with a water fountain and a marble bench, and draping plants from the second floor.

There were two floors to the home, which divided work from pleasure. The downstairs had several important rooms for supplies, bathing, and weaving or potting. Additionally, the kitchen was tucked into the rear and was accessible from the outside as well as from the courtyard. The most important room, however, was the master's social suite. The upstairs had several living quarters for slaves and guests, as well as the masters. One room upstairs was dedicated for the mistress's use, but Halcyon was rarely seen in it, preferring the traditional male-only master suite. Thora often wondered why her owner was missing from the house. Most females in Greece were tied to their homes, but not Halcyon. However, she was aware that Sparta was different from the other cities in Greece.

Beyond the villa, the lands were vast. Beside the house was a stable with twelve stalls for Halcyon's horses. Alongside the stable was an open grassy field, but Thora noticed strange wooden posts. She was unsure of their purpose. Farther beyond the open grasses was a rolling field that the government used their helots to farm.

The helots were an unusual bunch themselves. Upon her arrival in Sparta, Thora had noticed that helots had no scent, then later she learned they were a different breed from Alphas, Betas, and Omegas. They were called Gammas. She suspected the Spartans saw the Gammas as inferior for not having any scent and had decided to enslave them. Thora frowned at the strange existence of Gammas and wondered why the Spartans were cruel. Back in her homelands, there were no Gammas.

With a shake of her head, she hastened from her room. For the first fortnight, Thora had spent most of her time cleaning the stable stalls. The task had been arduous, even for her. Growing up on a farm, she was accustomed to constant labor, but the stable's needs were beyond the norm for one person. Much of her time was spent mucking stall after stall, then cleaning and oiling tack. Each day began in stench and ended in soreness. As soon as a job was done, she was required to repeat the task the next day. Thora decided the labor was meant to break her thunderous spirit. She resolved to play by the owner's rules, for now. If nothing else, her duty to clean the stalls took off a load from Cesare, who was cheerier than when she first arrived.

Once downstairs, Thora found Cesare and was shown the kitchen in detail. The kitchen was large and spacious compared to Telamon's old one. But it was rather disorganized and messy, which irked Thora. Before sun high, Cesare took Thora to the market where she would need to go often for supplies. Thora tried keeping track of the lengthy list of items. Most days would require food for the house and, occasionally, textiles for clothing, reeds for weaving baskets, or clay to make new cups, plates, and such. Cesare always handled the supplies for the stable. Thora suspected Halcyon was particular about her horses' diet. Cesare seemed well trained on how to care for them.

Cesare had conversations with the merchants and pointed at Thora several times. The merchants smiled and nodded at her. It was obvious they were informed about her lack of the Greek tongue. They seemed too curious about her rare features, which Thora had become accustomed to since she was torn from her homelands.

Thora helped Cesare put away the purchased goods when they returned to the villa. Then they started to prepare the midday meal. Thora expected to see Halcyon at some point. She had seen her on the first day, but since then, Halcyon had been elusive. She sensed that Cesare was curious about her skills in the kitchen. Perhaps he expected her to make something from her homelands rather than a classic Greek dish. Since her time in Athens, Thora had learned to cook many traditional Greek meals.

Cesare appeared pleased with Thora's skills in the kitchen. Together, they carried the tray of food, a jug full of diluted wine, and a cup through the villa. They located Halcyon enjoying the sunlight in the courtyard. As a team, they organized the meal on a table, then stepped aside and waited for any orders.

Halcyon finished reading a scroll and rolled it up. She set the scroll on the bench to her left, then stood and went to the table. She hummed low, and Thora could scent the hint of complexity in Halcyon's pheromones. Her golden eyes leveled on Thora.

"Is this her first attempt?" Halcyon asked Cesare, who had been handling basic meals for Halcyon. He seemed to know enough, and she wondered where Cesare had learned to cook. It was strange for males to be in a kitchen. Thora admired Cesare's skills.

Cesare kept his hands behind his back. "Yes, mistress." He remained neutral in his expression while his Beta pheromones were calm. In a few days, Thora had concluded that Cesare held a special place with their owner. Halcyon's interactions with Cesare were different from the interactions between any owner and slave Thora had seen in the past.

"A bit of an Athenian flare to it." Halcyon slid into the stone seat at the round table and studied each of the food dishes. A slight grin pulled at the corner of her lips, but she remained quiet. Thora attempted to remain indifferent despite the obvious scrutiny from her owner. Part of her considered whether her selection of dishes was in poor choice. Sparta seemed different from Athens, much like different regions of Thora's homelands.

After a silent moment, Halcyon ate from each dish, using her hands. She said nothing, but her scent had grown a little warmer. Thora held back a relieved sigh and reflected on how different her life was now compared to when she was at home with her mate. At thoughts of her former mate, she grew distressed, which triggered Cesare to shift on his feet. Thora reeled in her emotions and cleared her throat.

"Cesare, excuse us." Halcyon peered up from the food and watched him leave.

Remaining still, Thora wondered what Halcyon wanted from her, as they could hardly speak in a common tongue. Although there was a constant pull she felt toward Halcyon. The sensation was more than pleasant; it was hot and created a soft throb between Thora's legs.

Halcyon tore a piece of bread and hummed after each bite. After swallowing, she cleared her throat and focused on Thora. "We can exchange only a few words."

Thora held her owner's gaze, unsure what was said to her.

"I will learn who you are," Halcyon said in a determined tone. She raised an eyebrow, and curiosity colored her features. "How you came to be here. Where you came from. Who you once were."

Thora sighed, disliking how Greeks spoke at her rather than to her, regardless of the barrier.

"And I will find out." Halcyon picked up the clay cup of wine that Cesare had filled earlier. She rested the cup in her lap. "First, you can tell me your name." She sipped the sweet wine.

Thora clenched her hands behind her back. Halcyon's eyes held expectations that were lost on her.

Halcyon set the drink on the table. After a tilt of her head, she placed her hand against her chest and said, "My name is Halcyon." Then her hand traveled to Thora's arm, which burned in automatic response. Thora resisted the urge to yank it away. "Your name is?"

Thora narrowed her eyes at Halcyon. It was clear that Halcyon was asking her something, but she failed to translate the request. Her Alpha pheromones started to roil in the space between.

Halcyon gave a soft sigh, then rose and stood in front of Thora. Again, she rested her hand on her own chest. "Halcyon." Then she touched Thora's shoulder. The heat from her palm brought a slight tremble to Thora's knees. How could an Omega have such power over her?

Glancing at the hand on her shoulder, Thora studied Halcyon's cool features again and replied, "Makistia." She hoped her answer would end their odd conversation. She needed space and fresh air.

Halcyon shook her head in disapproval. "Your birth name." She narrowed her eyes and added, "Makistia is your slave name."

Thora had a thin furrow across her brow, but she understood the Greek words for slave and name. For some reason, her reply was insufficient even though it was true. Then it occurred to Thora that her owner wanted her actual name from birth. She pursed her lips, unsure about her owner's interest in her former name. Was it a trick to test her? Any other slave owner would relish the chance to punish her for such a minor mistake. However, the earnestness in Halcyon's scent was strong. She bit her lip and studied Halcyon's eyes, which were enchanting and different from the eye color of Thora's people. There was curiosity burning in Halcyon's eyes. With a deep breath, she gave in but also braced for a nasty response.

"Thora," she stated, her voice tinged with dignity. To her relief, she was rewarded with a thin smile.

"Th-or-ah," Halcyon said with a hesitant and broken voice, then she released Thora. The contact on Thora's shoulder remained charred in Thora's memory.

Thora shook her head and drew out her name. "Ttthhhooorrraaa." From Halcyon's expression, she repeated it slower. "Th-or-a."

Halcyon was confused by the first two letters, attempting it again. "Thhhoraaa." After Thora's nod, she tried it again at a normal pace. "Thora."

Thora had a small smile and nodded. "Yes," she agreed in the Greek tongue. For an instant, she caught a quick smile that broke Halcyon's hard features. However, Thora was certain it was her imagination. Her mate had often told her that she had an overactive one.

Returning to her seat, Halcyon nodded to herself and ordered, "Go see Cesare."

Thora pursed her lips at the returned coolness between them, but she dipped her head and then left her owner. When she passed the entrance between the courtyard and the home, she paused and sneaked a glance at Halcyon. Unlike any other Omega, Halcyon presented as an Alpha and continued to bewilder Thora to a degree. If it weren't for scents and pheromones, Thora would have assumed Halcyon was an Alpha, like her. However, Halcyon's frozen exterior was softened by the undeniable scent of an Omega. There was nothing anyone could do to hide their true nature, not even Halcyon.

* * *

The next day, Thora was required to prepare a morning meal for her owner. Cesare assisted her, giving her suggestions. After an initial yawn, Thora set to work and put together a hearty meal. She carried the two bowls in her hands while Cesare brought a cup of apple juice.

"Good morning, mistress," Cesare greeted after he and Thora arrived in the master's suite.

"Good morning." Halcyon placed a quill in an inkwell and set aside the scroll. The overhead lamp illuminated much of the space since the sun had yet to rise.

"I directed Thora on what items you like for the morning meal." Cesare set the cup on the desk, then stepped aside.

Thora had placed one bowl in front of her owner, but she paused upon hearing her birth name from Cesare. Had he overheard their conversation in the courtyard yesterday? Or had Halcyon instructed him to use her proper name? She wanted to believe that Halcyon had spoken to Cesare and even taught him how to pronounce her name.

"Excellent." Halcyon picked up the bread from one of the bowls and used it to scoop up a large amount of the oxygala. After her first taste, a delicate sound started at the back of her throat.

Thora contained her rumble after hearing her owner's pleasure. She took a step back and glanced at Cesare, who offered a discreet nod. It was time for them to depart.

"Wait."

Both slaves paused by the open door.

"Thora, I wish to speak with you further."

Cesare grazed his fingertips against the outside of Thora's hand. In recent days, he and Thora had developed a certain comfort level and ability to communicate through touch. He left without a word.

"Come," Halcyon ordered and rose from the desk chair. She took the second bowl, which was filled with fruits. She popped pieces into her mouth and directed them over to a long chair. Resting in the middle of the lounger was a rolled-up scroll.

"Sit." Halcyon took the space to the right side of the scroll and placed the fruit bowl near the edge of the chair. She picked up the scroll, untied the ribbon, and opened it. The parchment contained more than Greek words; it also had a large drawing.

Thora accepted one end of the scroll when Halcyon handed it over. She helped spread out the parchment between their laps. The beats it took organize the scroll gave her a chance to steal glances at her owner. Halcyon had a distinct jaw line, a straight nose, and eyes that glowed like the sun on a hot summer day. With a closer glance, Thora confirmed the few fine strands of gray hair hidden in the black strands along Halcyon's temple. She wanted to know Halcyon's age. But Halcyon's voice forced her to avert her eyes to the smoothed-out parchment between them.

"This is a map of Greece and the lands to the north."

Staring at the drawing, Thora attempted to understand what the image was and why her owner wanted to share it with her. There was wording on it, but it was in Greek. She studied the bold lines, thin ones, and dots. A few spots had other icons and symbols.

"I suspect you are from the north." Halcyon continued to speak, but Thora was transfixed by the illustration. After a moment, Halcyon touched Thora's forearm and called her name.

Gasping, Thora jerked her attention from the scroll to her owner. "Sorry." Her Greek vocabulary was minor, but she knew a few basics. Her apology seemed to be unnecessary though.

Halcyon withdrew her touch and tapped at the drawing. "This is Sparta."

Thora blinked and regarded the entire scroll, which her owner said was Sparta. The scroll was a map, and she smiled in realization. She had heard of formal maps back in her homelands. Their clan leaders had one or two, sometimes more. They were scratched into leather hide and used to record a clan's territory along with neighbors' lands. With a smile, she marveled at the drawing of the city, but her features tightened the longer she stared at it. So little of it made sense if it was Sparta.

"Sparta?" Thora raised her hand and waved it over the entire parchment.

"No." Halcyon shook her head, then pointed one spot on the map and said, "This is Sparta." She moved her pointer finger to another dot with wording next to it. "This is Athens."

Thora leaned forward and studied the dot above her owner's finger. "Athens." She'd been sold to an Alpha in Athens. The city had been her initial pseudo home after her enslavement. Scanning lower on the map, she pointed at the earlier dot and said, "Sparta?" She met her owner's gaze, finding it warm and inviting for once.

"Yes." Halcyon's lips curled with a slight smile. She placed her hand on top of Thora's larger one and started to guide Thora's hand in a particular direction along the map. "All of this is Greece."

Thora's breath hitched in her throat from the firm grip around her hand. She tried to ignore the speed of her heartbeat, but it was a little loud in her ears. A single line of heat raced down her arm and sparked an arousing jolt between her legs. She prayed to her gods that her scent remained neutral rather than give away her attraction.

With a quiet but deep inhale, Thora forced her mind to concentrate on where her fingertip was tracing on the map. Gradually the dark outline for Greece's borders started to stand out before her. As they made their return to Athens, Thora could see Greece and the waters surrounding it.

"This is Rome." Halcyon moved their joined hands to a dot on a strange boot-shaped piece of land.

"Rome." Thora had heard of the city and their people. "Romans."

"Yes." Halcyon brightened, while the heat from her palm started to burn against Thora's skin. Thora was certain she could feel Halcyon's pulse. Then there was a slight roughness along the pads of Halcyon's palms, which brushed against Thora's knuckles.

Thora swallowed against the growing dryness in her throat. She forced herself to remain focused on the map rather than Halcyon's hand molded to hers. Moving their hands north, she grazed all of her fingertips under a rather large Greek word etched into an open area. "What?"

"Gaul," Halcyon replied. "Are you from Gaul?" She raised her head but sighed upon seeing Thora's confused expression.

"Gaul," Thora repeated, having heard the name before. She hadn't heard it in her homelands, but rather during her enslavement and transport from her homelands to Greece.

"Yes, Gaul." Halcyon touched her slave's forearm and asked, "Are you from Gaul?"

Thora was unsure about her owner's question and looked at the map again. Halcyon wanted to know about Gaul, which she knew nothing about other than brief glimpses between a wagon's bars.

Halcyon grumbled, and a sharpness entered her scent. After a breath, she pointed at Sparta and said, "Sparta. We are here. Yes?"

Thora chewed on her lip and looked between Sparta on the map and her owner. "We Sparta." They were in Sparta.

"Where are you from?" Halcyon tapped Sparta several times and said, "I from Sparta."

"From?" Thora considered the new Greek word.

Halcyon nodded, touched her chest, and said, "I from Sparta." She placed her same finger back on Sparta. "You from?" She moved her hand and pressed her palm against Thora's chest. "You from Gaul?" She pointed at the huge area labeled as Gaul.

After a huff, Thora shook her head. "I no from Gaul." She puffed up her chest and looked at her owner. "No Gaul."

She took in Halcyon's pleased scent, causing Thora to smile a bit.

"From?" Halcyon pointed at the entirety of the map.

With better understanding of both the map and her owner's wishes, Thora studied the map and then glowered at Gaul. She remembered that the sun rose to her left when they traveled toward Greece in the wagon. But before Gaul, there had been a dreadful ride on a ship across an angry sea. At the memory of the voyage, her stomach pitched and forced her to take a deep breath. She wasn't fond of ships or water, at least seas and oceans. It helped to refocus on the map, which didn't depict that body of water that was above Gaul. Regardless, Thora had a sense of where her homelands may rest.

Without thought, Thora clasped the top of her owner's hand and threaded her fingers through smaller ones. She guided their hands higher until they were above the map, then she circled their joined hands through the air north of Gaul. "I from." After she indicated her homelands in the imaginary area, she looked at her owner and declared, "I Norsk."

Halcyon stared at their hands hanging in the empty space beyond the parchment. Her jaw grew loose, then she let out a strange but soft sound until she snapped her mouth shut. She turned her bewildered features toward Thora. The overhead light glowed in her golden eyes. "Norsk."

Thora felt her heart stutter upon hearing someone else speak her nationality after several years. "Yes, Norsk." She swelled with pride. She was in Greece, but her homelands still resided inside her. She forced herself to separate their hands, ignoring her Alpha's internal protest.

"I see," Halcyon murmured and stared at the unseen lands north of Gaul.

For a beat, Thora marveled over how well their hands and fingers fitted together, as if designed in such a manner. She wondered what else about their bodies was natural. Halcyon was muscular, more so than Thora. But the contours of Halcyon's body were perhaps the perfect shape to match Thora's longer curves.

Halcyon yanked her hand free, as if recalling herself. She flexed her hand once before she took Thora's end of the scroll. "You may go, Thora." At some point, they'd managed to press their sides and legs against each other until Halcyon scooted to her left.

Thora heeded the command and stood once the scroll was off her lap. Her inner Alpha pulled at her, encouraging her to stay. However, she was a slave, and punishments were never far from disobedience. Halcyon was a kinder owner than Thora's last two, but Thora didn't mistake her kindness for weakness. Halcyon held power and control, which she executed when necessary. Once out of the suite, Thora grinned at Halcyon's reaction at the end. Thora wasn't alone when it came to attraction.

Halcyon was also being pulled in by the primal and basic urges brought on by their true natures.

* * *

After the map lesson, Thora didn't see Halcyon until the next day, about an hour after sunrise. At first, she had assumed Halcyon disappeared to a solitary spot in the villa or outside the villa each day. But her theory was disproven when she spotted Halcyon leaving yesterday morning at sunrise after the morning meal. Halcyon had been clad in shiny bronze armor, which reflected in the early sunlight. Later Cesare explained that their owner was a type of warrior, revered in Sparta's ranks. Cesare had called Halcyon a hoplite, Thora reminded herself.

But this morning was different. Halcyon didn't take her morning meal before dawn, nor did she leave for duty at first light. Instead, she rose from bed an hour later, bathed, and took her morning meal in the courtyard once the sun was high enough. Perhaps today was a day off.

Thora busied herself with cleaning up in the kitchen after feeding everyone. She dried off the various dishes and plates after Cesare had helped her wash them. Once finished, she considered the midday meal and the light evening meal. There were a few items she needed from the market. Using a shattered piece of clay and a reed pen, she jotted down what items she needed. They were also low on wine, which was often delivered to the villa after Thora made a request from the merchant.

For a beat, Thora admired the reed pen that Halcyon had given her. With her previous owners, she had to memorize lists of items and often forgot at least two or three things. The reed pen itself was old, but it was much nicer than using ash from a fire pit back on her family's farm. She also had a small inkwell and spare blocks of ink to refill it. The writing tools were kept in a tiny drawer on the kitchen table. The list itself was written in Norsk. Even though she was a farm girl, her mate had once taught her how to read and write their native tongue.

Thora headed out of the kitchen, snatching the carrying satchel from the peg on the wall by the door. She put it across her shoulder and slipped the clay shard inside it. Stepping out into the courtyard, she admired Halcyon seated on the bench and reading a scroll.

"Thora?"

Halfway to the gate, Thora did an about-face and went to her owner. "Yes, mistress?"

"You are going to the market." Halcyon pointed at the satchel. "I shall join you." She started to roll up the scroll.

Thora shifted on her feet, uneasy about her owner's company. Only Cesare had gone with her in the past, and now she was allowed to go alone. Did Halcyon not trust her? The trips to the market were nice and different especially after being confined to Telamon's villa.

Halcyon left the scroll on the bench and started the journey to the market. Thora made sure to close the villa's gate. The day was humid but less so than in recent days. In the coming months, the summer would become more unbearable. On the twisty streets, other Spartans greeted Halcyon by name or with a simple nod. Helots hastened to make room for them. Thora had taken note that helots even steered away from her.

The market was heard before seen. People chatted, wares clanked, and wagons squeaked. Then the sweet, floral smell of fruits and vegetables drifted under Thora's nose. Halcyon seemed to have a particular destination in mind when they entered the busy streets.

"Stay close," Halcyon ordered, peering over her shoulder.

Thora closed the gap between them but remained behind her owner. To walk alongside or in front of Halcyon would be deemed a crime. In this situation, she didn't mind taking residence close to her owner's right shoulder. With hawkish intent, Thora studied the crowd and ensured no one bothered them. Thora's towering presence and rare features captivated those who walked past them. She had grown accustomed to the stares.

"This way." Halcyon directed them to a stand that had the familiar scent of leather. There were several stacks of sandals that created a makeshift wall on the table. A merchant popped out from the end of the table and greeted Halcyon. "I require a pair of sandals for my slave."

After several nods, the merchant turned to Thora and spoke faster than a strike of lightning. Thora frowned at him, then growled when he grabbed her arm. He ignored her threat and dragged her to the stool nearby.

"Thora," Halcyon warned in a cool tone.

Thora cut her growl short and sighed. The merchant knelt in front of her and removed the tattered sandals on her feet. Off he went to the stacks, searching through them. It then occurred to Thora that she was receiving new footwear. She snapped her attention to Halcyon, who stood with crossed arms and a stern expression.

The merchant slid the sandals onto Thora's feet, adjusted them, and stood up. He beamed at Halcyon, as if his first attempt was perfect. With great doubt, Thora rose and took a few steps within the confines of the stall. She paused and stared at the leather sandals that felt as if they were made for her feet. Muttering a Norsk curse word, she looked at her owner.

Halcyon raised an eyebrow in silent question.

Thora nodded and wiggled her toes, which were freer in these sandals. The old ones were too small, but her feet had stretched them out enough. The new ones were much more comfortable and would ease the strain from her daily chores.

The merchant rested his hands on his hips. "Your name for the records?"

"It is Halcyon of Villa Honor the Beloved," Halcyon replied and signaled for Thora to exit the stall space.

Thora watched the merchant scribe Halcyon's information onto a wax-coated tablet. Once on the street, she stared at her feet and smiled at her owner's consideration. A light touch to the back of her arm redirected her attention to Halcyon.

"What do you require from the market?" Halcyon tugged on Thora's satchel.

Thora retrieved her list and replied, "Fruit, vegetable, wine." The specific details of the list were different, but the generic Greek words were enough.

Halcyon took the clay shard and stared at the foreign words. She ran her thumb over the dried ink on the clay, then returned the list to Thora. Without further conversation, she led the way to the stands that Thora mentioned. At each one, she stepped aside and allowed Thora to shop for the supplies. Their last stop was the wine stall, which was owned by a jeering

Beta who often attempted to corner Thora. Today he wore a yellow chiton that matched the color of his teeth.

"Hello, golden barbar," the winemaker greeted when Thora approached him.

Thora raised her chin and ignored his hungry smile. "Two sweet. One dry," she told him. Later today, someone from the winemaker's stall would deliver the tall teardrop-shaped containers and place them in the supply room. The delivery person would also take the empty ones.

The winemaker scratched down the order. He stepped out of his stall, entering Thora's personal space. Holding out the tablet and reed pen, he waited for her to sign.

Thora gritted her teeth and took the pen. Next to Halcyon's villa name, she signed her name in Norsk and noted the drastic difference between Greek and Norsk. She held out the pen, but the winemaker snared her wrist and tugged her closer.

"When your owner tires of you, I'll have you on my vineyard," he promised her and breathed in her scent. Thora prepared to retaliate with her Alpha scent, knowing hers would crush his in a heartbeat.

"Release *my* property," Halcyon ordered, emerging around another customer. Her lips curled on a dangerous snarl that forced the winemaker back. He stumbled into his stand and used the tablet as a shield against her. Halcyon's heated pheromones swirled in the air.

Thora's head spun from the rich, protective scent pouring from her owner. Between her and the winemaker was one furious Omega.

"M-My apologies, Iron Edge. I d-didn't realize the barbar was y-yours."

Halcyon growled deeper and pointed at the tablet. "Liar. Everyone in this city is aware of who is Villa Honor the Beloved." She closed the gap between them, leaned into him, and whispered a final warning or threat that was too soft for Thora's ear.

Thora reversed a step when Halcyon spun around and revealed her irate features. Behind her, the winemaker was a trembling mess that brought on Thora's smirk.

"Thora," Halcyon called upon her departure.

Thora raised her chin at the winemaker and cursed, "*Bacraut.*" Even though he couldn't understand her, she was satisfied that the asshole wouldn't bother her in the future. She followed Halcyon's heated pheromone wake. She caught up and went with her owner to the outskirts of the market.

Halcyon took a seat on a bench and let out a huff. She patted the empty spot next to her when Thora stood nearby.

Thora glanced about the area and worried over being seen seated next to a Spartan citizen. However, Halcyon was her owner and had given her a silent order. After a sigh, she sat next to Halcyon and waited to be struck down by a Greek god. Nothing happened to her, but Halcyon's grab for the satchel startled her. "Mistress?"

After rooting through the goods, Halcyon produced two plums and handed one to Thora. She sank her teeth into the fruit and hummed from the first mouthful.

Thora turned the plum through her fingers and smiled at the fruit that had become one of her favorites in Greece.

Such a fruit didn't grow in her homelands. The sweet and juicy nature of the purplish flesh was a delight.

"I hate that slimy winemaker. He makes Alphas look passive," Halcyon said, then took another bite of the fruit.

Thora was unsure of the conversation, but Halcyon's fiery scent indicated the topic might be about the winemaker. She suspected Halcyon didn't expect a response, nor was it her place. And yet, she wished she could offer a reply. For once, her inability to converse brought an ache to her heart rather than frustration. She and Halcyon were from two separate worlds, walled off by language.

Halcyon tossed away the remnants of the plum and met Thora's regard. There was a different light in her eyes, almost delicate and affectionate. She parted her lips, as if prepared to speak, but she exhaled low and stood from the bench.

Popping up, Thora took a last bite of the plum and rid of it. They journeyed through the busy city and returned to the villa without exchanging another word or command. Thora went about her duties for the rest of the day and stayed as busy as her mind was. Her trip to the market with Halcyon had been exciting and memorable. She hoped it wasn't the last time they went together.

CHAPTER 2
Thora

After yesterday's eventful trip to the market, Thora doubted today's would be quite as fun. She went alone as normal, and much earlier. When she passed the sandal merchant's stall, he waved at her in a friendly manner. Thora halted in the middle of the street and stared at him, but his smile was genuine. She returned his wave, then went on her way. There was much she needed for tonight's meal including fresh fish.

Halcyon was on duty today but had forewarned Thora and Cesare that her special guest would be coming tonight. By now, Thora should have been accustomed to her owner's special guest, who was snobbish. On top of it, Halcyon wanted the evening handled in a particular way. Thora clamped down on her frustration over the situation.

Rushing back to the villa, Thora hastened to prep all the food and dishes. Cesare helped her neaten up the suite. Then they worked together to decant yesterday's wine delivery. The wine was mixed with an appropriate amount of water, then poured into jugs for serving later. Only so much was opened and mixed at a time.

By late midafternoon, Halcyon returned from duty and requested a bath. The slaves worked together to draw water and fill the pool in the bathing room. About an hour after Halcyon was done, the special guest arrived at the villa. Thora retreated to the kitchen and started to slice the flatbread. Her wandering thoughts disrupted her focus, and the knife's blade ran down her thumb. She cursed and dropped the knife. After inspecting her bleeding thumb, she clamped down on the wound with the towel from her girdle.

Cesare entered with a flustered expression. "Thora, hurry!" With an overbearing wake, he pointed at the half-cut bread but paused upon seeing Thora clutching her hand. He came to her side and tried to inspect her hand for the problem, but she refused him. Cesare swatted away Thora's uninjured hand. "Cesare."

Thora followed the command from her superior and lowered her good hand to her side.

Cesare's fiery pheromones settled. He removed the towel, only to sigh at the minor cut. Ripping a piece of towel, he tied it over the bleeding wound, then handed her the torn piece while pointing at the bread again. "Hurry."

Thora nodded and returned to her task. She saw Cesare picking up a filled wine jug from the counter and heading out of the kitchen. She stilled her knife and called, "Cesare?"

Cesare paused next to the entrance.

"Thank you."

For once, Cesare traded a smile and then dashed out of the kitchen without another word. Soon Thora placed the cut flatbread onto a wooden board. The board already held a large bowl of herbed olive oil, feta, and another bowl of grapes. She hoisted the substantial board off the counter, then left the kitchen.

Thora entered the courtyard, cut across it, and walked into a large room. The suite was reserved for the master and his other Alpha guests. Spartans continued many strange Greek traditions, even though Spartan Omegas held full control of the house because their mates were often in the barracks or at war. Thora thought the Greek home's segregation was strange in comparison to her homelands' customs. However, Halcyon seemed to overlook the tradition.

Thora hurried into the room and found Cesare pouring wine for the guest. She wondered if he knew of her disdain for Halcyon's guest named Selene. The female was an Omega who was infatuated with Halcyon. Or it might be an obsession considering the slathering of extra sweet Omega pheromones Selene attempted to use on Halcyon. Thora often enjoyed an Omega's scent, but Selene's left a bitter taste on her tongue; there was a fake element to it.

Halcyon seemed pleased by Thora's arrival. "Thora," she said and pointed at her guest, who was sprawled out on a comfortable long chair.

Thora contained both a sigh and an eyeroll. She went over and lowered the tray while the guest took her time selecting the food. Thora's patience was strained by her growing irritation.

Selene dipped a piece of flatbread in the oil and chomped down on it. "When does Euclid return home from the barracks?"

Halcyon finished sipping her wine, then lowered the cup onto the long chair's soft linen. "Not for another month." Her fingers tangled in one of the cup's handles.

Selene chuckled and dipped her bread again. "Pity for him," she said in a husky tone.

Halcyon grinned in response. Selene took a few pieces of feta, and then she waved at Thora to leave her. Thora crossed over to Halcyon and lowered the tray. After eating a piece of feta, Halcyon took a vine of grapes from the bowl and inspected the other items. The long pause gave Thora a chance to visually trace the valley of Halcyon's petite cleavage and admire the definition of Halcyon's bicep. But it was her owner's bare neck that made Thora's canines feel longer. She fought off the urge to taste such delicate flesh. Her clitoris pulsed with a bit of neediness.

Halcyon finished and peered up at Thora. Their stares locked, and Thora attempted to school her features. Her owner may punish her if she caught on to Thora's desire, which crept into her pheromones. Thora swallowed and waited for a negative outcome, especially when Halcyon rumbled at her.

After a few more tense heartbeats, Halcyon pointed to the low table that was between her and Selene.

Bowing her head, Thora moved to the table and placed the board on it, then joined Cesare, who stood by the door, holding a wine jug that had an ornate design on it. She freed a heavy breath that she'd been holding earlier.

Selene turned and regarded her with heavy scrutiny. "The barbar seems to have improved." Her insult about Thora's status as a foreign barbarian was not lost on any.

"The stables appear to have helped her disposition."

Selene laughed at Halcyon. "Your training is always effective." There was dark amusement in her eyes.

"I have been well taught," Halcyon said. Like her voice, her features were distant for a beat. Thora considered how far into the past Halcyon went before she refocused on Selene.

"Yes," Selene said. "Only the champion of the Heraea Games could do such." Again, her scent strengthened with a sickening sweetness, trying to bait Halcyon.

With a narrowed gaze, Halcyon crossed her legs, which caused the slit in her chiton to reveal muscular calves. "The Heraea Games were pups' games."

Selene chuckled and said, "Perhaps to you, but many Omegas struggle in those games."

"We fare well in those games."

"Maybe one day, you will find yourself in Olympia." Selene's grin was wide.

Halcyon remained neutral, although her scent took on a harsh note. Thora bit her lower lip and wondered what they were conversing about that annoyed Halcyon. After a heavy sigh, Halcyon said, "Not even upon the death of Zeus would they allow female Omegas to compete."

Selene wagged an index finger. "Never doubt your fate."

Halcyon waved off Selene.

Selene sobered after a strange expression. "When do you return to the barracks for rotation?"

"A little more than a fortnight."

"There is much talk about the Persian force in northern Greece."

Halcyon chuffed, then her scent developed a richness that caught Thora's attention. "King Xerxes is foolish. He will fail like his father, and he's too foolish to realize it."

"They say it's a large force," Selene said between draws from her cup. "A million soldiers."

Halcyon rolled her eyes. "I suspect it's a quarter of that."

"Plus a naval force." Selene played with her cup and stared into it. "It's hard to imagine King Xerxes was able to have such a large force cross the Hellespont."

"With the right engineers, anything is possible," Halcyon argued.

Selene peered up from her cup, revealing her somber features. "Will you go?"

Halcyon pursed her lips, then blew out a soft string of air. "If our kings declare war, then I am certain I will march with King Leonidas."

Selene remained quiet, then her scent strengthened with the sickening sweetness again. She regarded Thora and asked, "Have you been successful in seeking out a translator?"

Halcyon sipped her wine first. "I've found one who may assist me. He's due to arrive from Athens any day now."

Selene dipped her head and played with the rim of her wine cup. "It seems an awful waste of coin to hire him simply so he can teach your helot to speak our native tongue." Upon hearing the familiar term for the government's slaves, Thora considered why Selene thought she was owned by the government rather than Halcyon. She concluded that Telamon's business was a secret or at least not advertised.

Halcyon tilted her head at Selene. "Indeed." She set down her wine and plucked several grapes from the food board. "I am curious to learn her history."

"She is a helot," Selene said in a harsh tone. "What matters is that she's skilled enough to cook."

Halcyon remained silent and waved Cesare over for a refill. After he approached, she held out a hand to the food. "Eat, Selene. Do not let my feta go to waste."

Selene obliged and took a handful of the feta cubes. She curled back up on the long chair.

Halcyon smiled and asked, "Can you stay tonight, Selene?"

Selene revealed a wicked grin that was emphasized by the thick black eyeliner under her brown eyes. "Of course." In a beat, her pheromones grew heady and caught Thora's attention. However, Selene wasn't calling out to Thora, who was an Alpha. Instead, Selene was bidding for Halcyon's attention. Thora bowed her head and frowned at the strange situation that was unheard of in her homelands. Two female Omegas didn't mate with each other, at least not without an Alpha or Beta with them.

Halcyon turned to the slaves. "Cesare, see that Thora begins preparing our meal."

"Yes, mistress." Cesare bowed, grabbed Thora's wrist, and left with her. In the kitchen, he assisted Thora with making the food.

After serving the prepared meal, Thora observed the pair while they were immersed in their dinner and chatter. Over the years, Thora had learned a few techniques of proper Greek dining etiquette by studying her various owners. She first watched Halcyon, who was more dignified while dining. Then there was Selene, whom Thora had nicknamed Linnr in her own tongue. Like the linnr in her homelands, Selene was a monster that slithered and hissed—often at her.

With a careful eye, Thora assessed Selene, who was short compared to Thora and closer to Halcyon's height. Selene's eyes were a dark brown and were nearly lost by her mammoth nose. Her hair was a typical mousy color with tight wavy locks. She often wore her hair up in a bun with a few curly strands falling about her shoulders and nape. Similar to last time, Selene wore a soft yellow chiton, but Thora imagined she owned more than one set. Selene was close to Thora's age, unmated, and seeking a mate.

From what Thora gleaned, the traditions were different in Sparta than in Athens. The Athenian females mated in their fifteenth year. The Spartan females mated closer to eighteen or even as late as twenty-two. Thora recalled being mated after her sixteenth birthday. She pushed away her old memories of home and her mate after Halcyon called to her. She hastened and collected the empty plates.

"What a daydreamer," Selene accused. "I can't imagine what her barbaric mind is thinking up." She glared up at Thora when she came to collect the empty plate from the table.

Not understanding the words but sensing Selene's harsh judgment, Thora contained her natural response to growl and collected the dirty plates. She released a sigh once she was gone from the room, and went to the kitchen to rid of the dishes in the wash tub. In a hurry, she organized the strange but sweet dessert and returned to the suite with it and a full wine jug.

She went back to her spot by the door and watched the Omegas dine. The food's smells made her stomach rumble, but memories from her homelands helped divert her attention.

"Thora!"

Thora jumped from Halcyon's shout and hastened to fill their empty cups. She started with Selene, who gave her a condescending smile.

"Perhaps she requires another punishment to get her out of her daydreams." Selene's gaze went cold while she watched Thora.

Curbing her Alpha, Thora finished, refilled Halcyon's cup, and then grabbed the dessert plate before leaving the room. The brief trip to the kitchen helped cool Thora's irritation. This time, she went slow and refilled the container with fresh wine. Calmer now, she returned to the suite and noted that Halcyon had moved to Selene's long chair. Selene leaned against the back of the chair, legs curled up, and Halcyon was seated at the far end of the chair. Thora glued herself to the wall and looked to Cesare, who entered next and claimed the spot next to her.

Selene laughed at Halcyon's remark, set her cup on the table, and placed her left hand on Halcyon's knee. "I cannot imagine."

Halcyon moved her drink from her lips and revealed a grin. "Hopefully, I will never upstage my mate, though, in such a manner."

Selene rolled her eyes. "How the people would talk. An Alpha's Omega mate bested him in fair combat."

"I'm not sure it would bode well in the barracks."

Selene shook her head. "I hear the Alphas talk about you. The tales about the Iron Edge. They say the kings, especially King Leonidas, are enamored by you." She leaned in until her lips grazed Halcyon's cheek. "I cannot blame them."

"Seleeene," Halcyon drew out. She set her wine down beside the other one. "This will not be going on for much longer."

Selene frowned, but it changed to smugness. "Yes, soon *I* will be the mated Omega seeking the affections of a young Omega." She chuckled at her lover's seductive smile.

"I pray yours is as fine as mine has been," Halcyon said with a new husk to her voice. She leaned toward Selene.

Selene touched Halcyon's left cheek, then her lips met the soft ones above hers. Her eyes closed, and she hummed into the long kiss.

Thora struggled with a sharp twinge in her chest when Selene kissed Halcyon. It grew into a growl that threatened to break free. She lowered her head, locked her jaw, and willed her developing snarl to undo itself. With a deep inhale, she wrangled in her Alpha and considered her unexpected response to seeing them kiss. She blew out a low breath and continued to stare at the floor rather than risk looking at them.

Over the years, a few slaves had offered to share a bed with her, but Thora's Alpha was uninterested in those particular slaves. Their scents were unappealing, even wrong. Nor was Thora interested in being bedded by another Alpha.

She glanced at Cesare, who appeared unfazed by Selene's romance with Halcyon. All his attention was focused on them. He was born and raised in the Greek culture, if not Greek himself. Perhaps he was accustomed to two Omegas being together.

"Thora?"

After raising her head, Thora spotted Selene waving her empty cup. She neared Selene and tilted the clay jug over Linnr's cup.

Halcyon watched her slave with open appreciation that Thora noticed and attempted to ignore. Selene caught Halcyon's interest in Thora and leaned in for another warm kiss. Thora clenched her teeth at the purposeful kiss meant to incite her. Her Alpha loosened her chest and snapped: *Mine.* With a spark of defiance, she moved the tipped jug forward until the red wine spilled all over a yellow lap.

Selene jerked away and cried out in horror. "By all the gods!" The chilled liquid soaked through her lap. She stood with the overflowing cup splashing over her chest.

Thora stepped back with a satisfied smirk, then a flash of her teeth. Her earlier growl returned, but it ended when Halcyon jumped to her feet. After a glance at Selene, Halcyon narrowed her eyes at Thora while her features darkened.

"Get some rags, Cesare!"

Cesare had neared the group earlier, but he rushed out to handle the request.

Halcyon stepped around her cursing guest and approached her. She was shorter than Thora, but it didn't matter. Halcyon's muscular build and surging, hot pheromones made her bigger than life.

Selene turned her ire on Thora. "She purposely did that." She started toward Thora until Halcyon halted her.

"She is *my* slave. Now sit."

Selene froze and swallowed loud enough for each of them to hear it. She sank down onto the chair and waited for Cesare.

Halcyon centered her fury on Thora, who held her ground. Thora's lip gave a slight curl at the obvious challenge set before her by an Omega. All her slave training was forgotten in the moment until Halcyon matched her. Thora lost her soft snarl when Halcyon's heavy pheromones crashed against Thora, who was forced back a step. Halcyon advanced and used her powerful pheromones to crush Thora's Alpha with ease.

Panting, Thora dropped the container of wine, which painted itself across the floor. Unable to hold her strength, she crumbled to her knee and bowed her head. Her inferiority grew more apparent as she twisted her head to the side, exposing her neck to Halcyon. For a moment, Thora was certain her heart would burst from her chest.

Halcyon bared her teeth at her kneeling slave while her growl carried through the room. In that moment, she redefined herself as the Alpha despite her true nature as an Omega. Her pheromones crushed Thora with great ease and reminded them all who was the slave owner and who was the slave. After a loud exhale, her snarl ended, then she pivoted toward Cesare and barked out her next order in a gruff voice. "Clean up the mess and remove her."

"Yes, mistress." Cesare bolted forward, went around the table, and came to Thora's side. He hooked underneath Thora's arm and drew her to her feet. Thora gulped for air and stumbled one step toward Cesare, who grappled with her weight and height. His Beta pheromones soothed enough of Thora's muddled mind, then she was directed out of the room with his help. When they stepped out of the suite, she distantly heard Halcyon.

"I apologize, Selene. It's obvious she still requires a heavy hand."

"Let us forget it now," Selene replied back, then their voices faded.

Thora was guided downstairs to the courtyard, where the fresh air cleared her head. She leaned against a pillar when Cesare released her. Gulping air, she regained control of her pounding heart, but the arousal between her legs was another matter. How could an Omega bring her to heel and excite her so?

"Are you mad?" Cesare asked. His gaze burned against her already flushed features.

Thora wished she could explain herself, but it was pointless. After all, she was guilty. She turned her head away and clenched her jaw, holding down her growl. But a soft rumble made its way free.

Cesare sighed, then his shoulders drooped. "You are finished for the night." He pointed toward the upper level of the villa. "Go," he ordered in a gentler manner.

Nodding, Thora pushed off the pillar and said, "Thank you." She hoped her sincerity meant something to Cesare. He returned the nod, then went toward the master's suite. Thora dragged her fingers through her golden hair and took another deep breath that rid the last of her tension.

She returned to her room and prepared for bed. Stretched out on her bedroll, Thora replayed the events of her defiance and Halcyon's responding dominance. Halcyon may be an Omega, but she was bred to be a warrior. When Halcyon stood over Thora, she had been stunning and powerful, stirring the heat in Thora's veins. The memory rekindled the soft burn between Thora's legs. She groaned and considered rolling to her side rather than face the temptation Halcyon brought on.

The temptation was greater than Thora.

After ridding of the blanket, Thora exposed her nude form in the warm moonlight from the open window. She propped up one leg, spreading herself wider. Already droplets of slick had slipped past her pussy and coated her thighs. After muttering a curse in her native tongue, she touched her clitoris that ached with certain need. For a moment, Thora ran her fingertips over the swollen head, and each lazy stroke encouraged a groan from deep in her chest.

Halcyon was a willful and strong Omega, who excited Thora's Alpha in new ways. Thora kept a grip on her Alpha, but it was becoming impossible around Halcyon. Thora sensed that Halcyon's warrior training had locked up her Omega nature. Until tonight when Halcyon used her rich pheromones to bring Thora to her knees. Even now, Thora continued to taste the residual heady sweetness that was Halcyon.

Thora reached behind her head and balled up part of the sleeping roll under it. She tucked her hand under her head and admired the glistening of her fingers. Like any female breed, she had a sensitive clitoris, but as an Alpha, hers was a bit larger than a female Omega's or Beta's. As an Alpha, she could enter into a rut, which would trigger her clitoris to grow and lengthen until it was a penis. Then she would be able to knot and impregnate any female breed or a male Omega. However, Thora hadn't experienced a rut since her first normal one during puberty. She had a faint memory of what her cock looked like when she was a teen. But since then, no one had triggered a rut inside her, including her mate when they were together.

Thora pictured her clit swelling to its full length during a rut, so that she could please Halcyon. With a groan, Thora cut off the fantasy of rutting into Halcyon, who was a free and wealthy woman, certainly not willing to bed a slave. Yet, Thora needed to handle the growing fire deep in her gut. She focused her touch on the perfect spot against her clit.

"Oooh." Thora let out another moan and returned to her daydream about knotting her owner. While she massaged her swollen clit, she was certain it had grown a little. She pushed aside her intrigue and drowned herself in the pleasurable jolts in her body. Her moans grew louder, but she tamped them down. Thankfully her room was at the end of the second floor's walkway.

"*Fukka,*" she muttered and rubbed harder, faster even. Thora clenched her teeth against a rising growl when the hot pleasure swept over her. She didn't let up, forcing a second orgasm within a minute. Thora bucked and clawed the wooden floor.

Slumped against the bedroll, she panted and moaned after the release cooled her Alpha, for now. Thora was well aware that her owner would arouse her again. Playing with her vulva, she groaned from the amount of slick compared to earlier. There had to be a large wet spot on the sleep roll.

Leaving the blanket off, Thora closed her eyes and attempted to relax her mind now that she'd handled her body. The night was plenty warm, and the breeze from the window offered the last bit of relief she needed. Tomorrow she would bathe and wash her sleep roll, after she handled her punishment for insulting Halcyon and Selene. With a huff, Thora already accepted the unknown price because Selene was a linnr.

CHAPTER 3
Thora

Taking a break from the punishment, Thora slumped against the pitchfork in her hands and scowled at the stinky stall. Last night had ended on an ugly moment after Thora had dumped wine on her owner's lover. Her punishment had begun last night after a short period of rest. To Thora, the horse manure was a more welcoming smell than the chamber pots this morning. The human waste had made Thora nauseous compared to the horse manure. Several other straining chores were given to her until first light when she was sent to the stable.

As a pup, she had received several different punishments on the family farm for being a troublemaker. Her sire was the one to dole them out rather than her gentle mother. Her eight siblings were less troublesome, but they tended toward their mother's personality. Thora was more like her sire, even when it came to physical appearances. She hoped her surviving family members were well and safe. She missed all of them.

After a heavy exhale, Thora shifted and leaned against a post, wiping the sweat off her brow. She kept the pitchfork away from her face, arm stretched out in front of her. After the short break, she resumed mucking the horse's stall. The stable was about halfway done. Resuming her normal chores after the short break would be a relief.

Due to her weariness, Thora registered the approaching footsteps too late, prompting her to spin around with the pitchfork. Her old fighting senses were ready against the bronze-covered intruder.

"Steady." Halcyon's voice rumbled behind the bronze helmet, the red plume on top making her appear taller. Her right hand rested on a sword hilt. Thora had learned that Halcyon wore her armor on days she was on duty.

Thora lowered the pitchfork and leaned it against a wall. For the first time, she was dazzled by the rich amber orbs that burned under the shiny helmet. Halcyon reached up and removed her helmet, the cheek plates brushing her temples.

Stepping back, Thora put space between her and Halcyon. Her eyes darted down to the sheathed short sword at Halcyon's side. She parted her lips, but her foreign words hung silent on her tongue. In her culture it was common practice for an Omega to know enough about weapons that she could defend herself and her pups. Some Omegas even became warriors. However, in Greece, Thora doubted Omegas even knew how to hold a kitchen knife. She thought perhaps it was illegal for an Omega to wield a weapon or wear armor, but it appeared to be legal in Sparta.

Halcyon stretched out her hand, brushed her fingertips across Thora's cheek, and locked their gazes. There were few words they could exchange, but Halcyon's eyes were filled with questions. Defiance stormed across Thora's features, which seemed to amuse Halcyon. They both were well aware now that Halcyon held power over Thora and her Alpha nature.

Thora held her ground, unapologetic about last night. In her homelands, Thora would have done the same to any Omega or Alpha who scorned her like Selene had. Although Thora was a slave in Greece, her heart and spirit were still that of a free person.

Halcyon released a frustrated breath when Thora remained rigid. Last night's incident had been a step back for them both. Thora refused to be truly tamed, but her Alpha was another matter when it came to Halcyon's Omega. Thora was annoyed at her Alpha for caving into her owner. In the end, their roles as owner and slave had been tested last night.

Halcyon withdrew her touch, which left a lingering afterglow against Thora's skin. She instead held out the bronze helmet from under her arm. It appeared to be a type of peace offering or at least an attempt to undo Thora's stubbornness.

Gazing down, Thora accepted the helmet, turning and inspecting every part of its shiny surface, then running her fingers through the red plume. The helmet had once been a perfect piece from the smith, but it had since collected wounds from fights, battles, and maybe even wars. A faint dent on the once smooth top caught Thora's eyes. Several times she ran her fingertip over various scratches, including one heavy gouge over the right temple. Her fingernail passed through it, and she imagined it was from a sword blade. From the front, Thora admired the craftsmanship, such as the details given to the eye slits, nose guard, and the fine metal etching that followed the helmet's edge line all the way around to the back.

Thora returned the helmet and grew bold about the rest of her owner's uniform. For a beat, she glanced at the sword hilt and stretched out her hand to touch it. Her wrist was snatched and held in the space between. Thora's attention snapped to her owner.

"No." Halcyon redirected Thora's hand to rest on her bronze cuirass that went down to her lower waist. She set Thora's hand against her bronze-clad stomach. "Yes." She then lifted Thora's hand and placed it against her helmet. "Yes." She pointed at her bronze greaves and nodded. She placed Thora's hand near the sword's hilt. "No."

Thora's hand was freed after the simple instructions. Halcyon tilted her head while Thora started to explore the uniform. Thora took the earlier invitation to the cuirass and touched the stomach area. It was firm and warm, like the helmet. There were ribbed spots that mimicked muscles and a belly button. Higher up, the cuirass was crafted for Halcyon's upper body, including a pair of nipples that matched her male counterparts' cuirasses. At the top, two small bronze rings allowed for the red cape to be hooked to them. Again, Thora was impressed by the craftsmanship and even the fact that a smith would accommodate a female. It was obvious that her owner was held in high esteem by her male counterparts.

Thora withdrew her hand after she released one of the decorative leather straps that was attached to the base of the cuirass. She lifted her gaze to Halcyon, then took a step back to signal she was done. For a moment, neither of them moved or spoke but rather studied each other, using their pheromones to communicate. Halcyon was calm and at ease, less guarded than usual, which seemed strange considering Halcyon's bronze armor.

Halcyon broke their trance first and said, "Come with me." She stepped around Thora and went deeper into the stable, passing a few stalls. The second-to-last one on the right had the most beautiful horse. He was bay color with a black mane and tail. Halcyon opened the door and closed it after Thora entered. "This is Cheimon," she told Thora and patted the horse on the rump.

In her homelands, horses were plentiful and excellent helpers on farms. Thora had worked with one or two on her parents' farm, borrowing ones from the clan when necessary. Horses were a community livestock. Thora had never seen one person owning multiple horses for their sole pleasure. From the first day, the stable told Thora how wealthy her owner was.

Coming to Halcyon's side, Thora admired the horse who seemed to have Halcyon's love. She smiled when the horse breathed in Thora's familiar scent. A few of the horses in the stable were skittish but not this one.

Halcyon took Thora's hand and brought it to Cheimon's cheekbone. "He's friendly."

Thora pursed her lips and drew their joined hands up, touching the base of the horse's ear. "Cheimon?"

Halcyon nodded and appeared stoic, but the light in her eyes was unmistakable. She withdrew her hand and ran her palm down Cheimon's neck.

Thora smiled at how Cheimon nudged into her hand. She looked to her owner and asked, "Favorite?"

Tilting her head, Halcyon revealed the slight upturn of her lips. "Yes." She rubbed Cheimon's shoulder. "Can you ride?" Her question was lost on Thora, who sighed at their language barrier. Halcyon remained patient and pointed at the horse tack, then at Cheimon. "Ride?" She pointed at Thora, then to the horse's back.

Brightening, Thora pointed at the horse's back and shook her head. "No." She blew out a breath and imagined what it might be like to ride one. She had only walked, watered, and fed horses back at home. One day she hoped to learn, but now it was too late. "I no ride."

Halcyon shifted closer to Thora while she ran her hand over Cheimon's neck and shoulder. "One day I will teach you." She regarded Thora. What words she'd spoken were lost on Thora, but a promise lingered in her golden eyes. Halcyon grazed her fingertips across Thora's hand, then whispered, "If you're a good Alpha." She brushed past Thora, unlatching the stall door.

Thora grumbled at her inability to understand and reply. She withdrew from Cheimon while Halcyon's touch lingered against her skin. They left the stall and returned to where Thora had been working earlier.

Halcyon gave a soft hum, turned toward Thora, and asked, "What were you thinking last night, Thora?"

Thora frowned at the question, but she suspected the topic. "Selene?" She was unsure if she was allowed to speak Linnr's proper name. Yet she didn't care if it was impolite, because Linnr was ill-mannered.

"Yes, Selene."

Thora caught on to what bewildered her owner. Her annoyed expression grew as she thought more about the obnoxious Omega who bedded Halcyon. "*Selene is a serpent,*" she replied in her native tongue. After Halcyon shook her head, Thora sighed and ran her fingers through her long, straight hair as she considered how to explain it. She stared at the packed dirt under her feet as she pictured a linnr, then she straightened. She grabbed her pitchfork from the wall.

Halcyon tensed until Thora used it as a drawing tool.

Thora wasn't an artist, but she drew a linnr in the dirt. Its long serpent body told most of its origin and Thora's meaning behind the nickname. Halcyon bent over and studied the childlike image scratched into the dirt. She flashed a perplexed look to Thora, who pointed at the picture. "Selene." For emphasis, she hissed in example. "Selene… linnr." Perhaps it was in poor taste to explain a linnr, due to the simple fact that Thora was depicting Halcyon's lover as such a wretched creature.

Halcyon stared for another beat before snapping shut her jaw. "Lenrm?"

Thora shook her head and enunciated, "Lin-nr."

"Linnr," Halcyon said with more confidence.

"*Já*," Thora agreed in her native tongue. She set the pitchfork aside again.

Halcyon stared at the drawing, then lifted her gaze to Thora's smiling features. She raised a dark eyebrow and pointed at the linnr. "Selene?"

Thora's smile faded against her owner's stern features. She dipped her head in silent confirmation.

Halcyon remained stoic other than pursing her lips. Her scent grew in strength, circling them both.

Thora fisted her right hand at her side and waited for certain reprimand from her owner, who was an armed warrior at the moment. She did her best not to snare the pitchfork and use it as a weapon. Thora lifted her chin, sniffed the air, and analyzed Halcyon's growing pheromones, which were heady yet unthreatening. She was unsure whether to be relieved or remain prepared for Halcyon to become hostile.

Halcyon bowed her head as she lifted her helmet. She slid it on and allowed it to cover her face. Her eyes pierced through the darkness of the helmet's slits once she lifted her head. She said nothing and turned on her heels. Her red cape floated behind her as she exited the stable.

Startled by her owner's departure, Thora canted her head and watched Halcyon vanish beyond the stable's entrance. Any explanation of what transpired between them left her baffled. She expected Halcyon to at least impose herself upon Thora for such an insult about Selene. Instead, Halcyon walked away without a look or remark.

After a confused huff, Thora grabbed the pitchfork and went to the next dirty stall but paused after she thought she heard a laugh. She had to be mistaken, so she brushed it off. She needed to finish so she could prepare the next meal for Halcyon, but only after a quick bath. The gods knew she needed one.

* * *

Later that afternoon, Thora returned to the quiet villa. She had a quick cold bath and then went to the supply room. After a scan of the room, it was clear that Cesare had gone to the market for food and drawn today's water. She sent him a silent thank-you.

Thora gathered the items she needed and went to the kitchen. She prepared a meal for Halcyon, who would expect it soon. Right on the mark, Cesare barged into the kitchen.

"Finished?" He pointed at the tray full of food.

"*Já.*"

Cesare went over to the wine jug. He pointed at the food and said, "Master's suite."

Thora nodded and glowered at the news. Halcyon tended to use the master's suite when she had a guest, like Selene. If Halcyon was alone, she would take her meal in the courtyard and enjoy the evening sun.

From the first day in Greece, Thora was taught that any female was forbidden to enter the master's suite, a social room only for males. On occasion, female slaves could go to the restricted suite, but that was only with the master's permission. However, Thora had not met Halcyon's mate, who was the master of the house. Thora took the board of food and went to the master's suite, settling her gaze on Halcyon, who was stretched out in a long chair.

Halcyon wore a soft purple chiton, sandals, and a necklace. She appeared much less threatening in her regular attire than her warrior uniform. She signaled for Thora to come to her.

Once in the room, Thora noted the young male seated on a long chair to the left of Halcyon. She noted his Beta scent. She averted her eyes to Halcyon and set the tray of food down on the low table between her owner and the stranger. Unable to help herself, Thora studied Halcyon's guest, who had warm brown eyes and wore a slight grin. He was young, but his thin beard added the appearance of age.

"Thora?" Halcyon frowned when Thora ignored her. She leaned forward and snared Thora's wrist. Thora startled from Halcyon's warm touch.

"*It okay*," the male Beta said in Thora's native tongue.

Thora went still, and her attention jerked to the stranger. She must have imagined he spoke in her native tongue, or at least something similar. "*You know my language?*" Halcyon released her.

"*I know… tiny.*"

Even though his tongue was imperfect, Thora's lips tugged with a smile. She opened her mouth to say more but was cut off by Halcyon's thick voice.

"Stop."

Thora faltered, snapped her jaw shut, and glanced at Halcyon. She rumbled, yet her curiosity was leveled on the newcomer. Her body grew tenser the longer she had to wait for an explanation about him. How could he speak her language? From his appearance, he wasn't from her homelands. He could be another slave trader who wanted to purchase her. She fought back a growl, but her scent increased a fraction.

"I'm already impressed, Vitus."

Vitus bowed his head, then smiled at her. "I spent many years with a merchant. He had a keen interest in the lands to the north. I picked up some of their words for trade."

"Did you travel to those lands?" Halcyon asked.

Vitus nodded. "We traveled into parts of Germania within Gaul but no farther. They are dangerous lands, dangerous people."

Halcyon regarded Thora with interest and hummed low. She pointed at the tray of food. "Would you like anything?"

"I'm fine, but thank you." Vitus folded his hands in his lap. "Has she learned any Greek?"

"Only simple words." Halcyon paused. "She is good at deciphering body language and tones."

"I imagine so." Vitus lifted his attention to Thora.

As Halcyon reached for the grape bowl, she asked, "Have you seen Germanics similar to her in your travels?"

Vitus studied Thora, who had golden hair and a milky complexion. He rubbed his chin and shook his head. "Similar," he replied after a beat.

Halcyon took a drink of wine. "What is different?"

"Germanics do not have hair as light as hers. Her skin is also rather pale for a Germanic." Vitus tilted his head. "You say her name is Thora?"

Halcyon gave a nod. "And she told me she is Norsk. Her lands are farther north than Gaul or Germania."

"Norsk? I have heard this once or twice." Vitus bit his lower lip for a beat. "Would you like me to question her about where she is from while you eat?"

Halcyon's stoic expression cracked under the slightest of smiles. A pleasant warmth entered her pheromones and intrigued Thora. "Yes."

Vitus smiled and nodded before he focused on Thora. Like most Betas, he had a gentle nature about him that disarmed her. "*Is name Thora?*"

Thora considered the stranger's odd dialect. She had heard it after she was taken from her homelands and was shipped across the strait. "*Já.*"

"*I, Vitus.*"

Thora nodded and was certain the name was Greek or Roman.

"*You Norsk?*" Vitus asked.

Thora narrowed her eyes at the choppy tongue and shook her head. She wished to communicate with him, but she could tell it would take patience for them both. His presence was unexpected yet also refreshing after years of being barred from fully communicating with others. With a glance at Halcyon, Thora wondered why her owner had brought Vitus here.

"*I am Norsk.*" Again, pride swelled in her chest.

Vitus rubbed his stubbly beard and said, "*Your home.*"

Thora understood the most important word. "*My home is far north of here.*"

Vitus appeared to grasp fragments of Thora's reply and gave a faint nod. Their conversation was a bit stilted but it was enough. He gave pause before tilting his head. "*From Germania?*"

Thora had heard the name Germania for the people south of her homelands. From Halcyon's map, it seemed liked Germania was located within Gaul. She shook her head and replied, "*Much farther north.*" She raised her left fist level to her chest. "*Germania*." She then lifted her right hand above her head. "Norselands."

"Norselands?" Vitus repeated with slight awe. He tapped his chin and developed a thoughtful expression.

"Is that not Scandia?"

Vitus looked at Halcyon and smiled at her. "Scandia is farther north than Germania." He gazed upon the unusual Alpha slave. "I have not journeyed there," he muttered, then his eyes grew distant as if he was revisiting the northern lands.

Thora looked from Vitus to Halcyon. "No Scandia. No Germania. No Gaul."

Halcyon popped a grape into her mouth. Her grin appeared after Thora's proud correction. "I imagine the Norselands are cold lands." She grinned wider at Vitus. "She carries a fire within her that keeps her warm."

Chuckling, Vitus nodded and folded his hands in his lap. "Yes, I imagine so. Those from Germania are rather proud and strong. It's as if they're forged from iron."

Halcyon grunted, set down the bowl of grapes, and focused on her guest. "I am pleased, Vitus. I heard you were fluent in several languages." She crossed her legs and placed her hands in her lap. "Can you teach her Greek?"

"Yes, I believe so."

Halcyon nodded and gave a pleased rumble. Thora shifted on her feet when Halcyon glanced at her with a thin smile. "And what of your other employer?"

"I completed my duties with Tyre after we arrived in Athens." Vitus paused, bowed his head, and said, "I am at your service."

"I'll have my slave Cesare bring your belongings to a room. You'll have your own quarters here." Halcyon sipped more wine, then asked, "How much coin do you require per month for your services?"

Vitus nibbled on his lip and was quiet for a moment before he spoke his price. "Fifteen drachmas."

Halcyon had a stern expression and remarked, "A hoplite's wage is one drachma per day."

"I am not a hoplite," Vitus reminded and shifted under Halcyon's scrutiny.

"No, but you are a skilled translator." Halcyon tilted her head, then declared, "Twenty drachmas a month." Her scent deepened and indicated the seriousness of her decision.

Vitus smiled, and his eyes glowed in appreciation. He agreed to Halcyon's wonderful proposition of room, board, food, and twenty drachmas a month. He murmured his gratitude to the Greek gods.

Halcyon appeared content with the arrangement. Her attention cut to Thora, who had been quiet but curious about what transpired. "We will speak soon," she promised Thora.

Holding Halcyon's eyes, Thora failed to understand the promise, but she was certain her owner had made an arrangement with Vitus. She hoped that Vitus was here to teach her Greek. The idea seemed outlandish because slave owners viewed their slaves as property. However, Thora believed there was something different about Halcyon. From the first day, Thora was drawn to Halcyon, and she strangely trusted her. Only the Norns knew Thora's future.

CHAPTER 4
Thora

Thora stood over a three-legged stone basin located in the far corner of the kitchen. She had spent much of her late morning grinding barley with a stone but paused when a new presence entered the room.

Halcyon rested her hands on her hips and watched Thora with a curious expression. To her right stood Vitus, and behind her was a female whom Halcyon turned to and ordered, "Come."

Once the young female stepped around Halcyon, Thora's eyes lit up upon seeing the familiar face. "Glauce." She had forged a friendship with Glauce when she was in Telamon's household. Glauce had been nice to Thora even though they couldn't communicate much. A few other slaves assumed that Thora and Glauce had mated, which prompted Thora to roll her eyes. She looked upon Glauce as a younger sister more than anything.

Halcyon turned to Vitus and ordered, "Please explain to Thora that she will train this new slave."

Vitus nodded and did his best to explain it to Thora. After an exchange, Thora understood that Glauce was her responsibility. She was unsure if Glauce's purchase was a sign of her weakness in the house. "*Is Glauce replacing me?*" she asked in her native tongue.

Vitus had a befuddled expression, so Thora explained the question. "Ah." He shook his head in response, then said, "*Show Greek you.*"

Thora opened her mouth to ask more, but she faltered. Her question was too complex for Vitus's meager skills in a strange dialect. She read Halcyon's features and concluded that Halcyon showed no signs of displeasure with her. Glauce was not a threat to her place in the household but rather someone to assist her.

Glauce remained quiet with her head down. Her short brown curls curtained around her face. She continued being as small as possible even if her pheromones were calm. Thora made a silent promise to help Glauce with her self-confidence now that they would work together.

"Glauce—kitchen." Thora pointed at Glauce and then at the kitchen. She nodded, confirming her understanding of the new arrangement.

"*Thak,*" Vitus said but frowned as if sensing his own error.

Thora shook her head, smiled, and corrected him. "*Þakka fyrir.*" His attempt to thank her meant something to her. Vitus was easy to like.

Vitus smiled at Thora and repeated, "*Þakka fyrir.*"

Thora beamed at his quick ability to learn. "*Ekki at þakka.*"

Vitus chuckled and nodded, then noticed Halcyon had watched their exchange. He straightened his back.

Halcyon pursed her lips and focused on Thora. Her expression was passive, but her pheromones told everyone that she was pleased. "Selene. Tonight." She raised an eyebrow at the annoyed spark on Thora's face. Without comment, she departed the kitchen.

Vitus waited until Halcyon was gone, then he said, "*Greek first light.*"

"*Já.*" Thora was thrilled to learn Greek tomorrow. She had quickly learned the basic phrases and had a rudimentary idea of the people and their language, but having the chance to become fluent was an asset she would never squander. She bid goodbye to Vitus, then touched Glauce's shoulder and smiled, watching how her comfort eased Glauce. "You cook."

After a shy nod, Glauce shadowed her teacher in the kitchen for the day. Together, they made fresh barley bread for the upcoming three days. Next, they began to prepare the evening meal for everyone, which included Selene. Thora battled with her frustration that Linnr was in the house tonight. It had only been two nights ago that she spilled wine on Selene. The subsequent punishment was also fresh on her mind and reminded her why she needed to wrangle in her Alpha.

Later, Cesare arrived in the kitchen and announced that Selene was in the courtyard with Halcyon. There were at least three hours until sunset. A nice meal in the courtyard was common for Greeks. Cesare assisted Glauce with taking the first dishes to the courtyard. Thora noticed that Glauce had forgotten the wine, so she hastened out of the kitchen with the filled jug.

In the courtyard, Halcyon sat beside Selene on a bench. In front of them was the table that normally was used with the chairs. Halcyon took a handful of olives and half opened her mouth until Thora approached them. She gave a contented rumble while Thora filled their cups.

"Go to Selene," Halcyon said to Glauce.

Glauce bowed her head after Thora assisted with the wine. Her cheeks were dusted with a soft pink hue, but Thora gave her a compassionate glance. Glauce offered the board of finger foods to Selene.

Thora picked up the next empty cup from the marble table. She filled it and held it out to Halcyon. She expected Halcyon to take it without any regard for her. Much to her surprise, Halcyon held her gaze.

"*Þakka fyrir*," Halcyon said.

Pausing, Thora wondered if she had misheard Halcyon's appreciation in the Norsk tongue. Had her owner paid attention to Thora's brief lesson to Vitus about how to say "thank you" in Norsk? On top of it, Halcyon was the first of Thora's owners to say such kind words.

"Serve Linnr." Halcyon was stern, but a glint shown in her eyes.

Thora bit her smirk. "*Já*, mistress."

Selene frowned and looked between the pair before she asked, "Liner?"

Halcyon shook her head. "Linnr."

Thora poured wine in the remaining empty cup, then offered it to Selene. She held her tongue and kept her mouth closed while a slight laugh rolled inside her chest. For once, she attempted her best neutral expression so that Selene wouldn't react. Halcyon had turned Thora's nickname into a joke between them.

"What is Linnr?"

Halcyon shrugged, but amusement laced her tone. "That is your name in her native tongue."

"Oh." Selene accepted the cup from Thora. "It sounds different from Selene."

"Well, you know that barbaric tongue," Halcyon said with a degree of mockery.

Thora suspected that her owner muddled the truth about what Linnr meant. If she hadn't, Selene would be irate at the moment. Thora backed away. Selene and Halcyon were comfortable in their chairs, and Glauce or Cesare could care for them. Thora left for the kitchen but paused after ducking through the doorway, intent on trying to figure out what they were saying.

"Why do you waste your time, Halcyon?"

"A good mistress can communicate with her slaves."

"Next time, select one that speaks Greek."

Thora rolled her eyes at Selene's condescending tone, knowing it was about her. After a huff, she muttered, "Linnr." She cupped the underside of the wine jug and continued to eavesdrop.

"Your new slave speaks Greek," Selene argued.

After a pause, Halcyon spoke in a perturbed tone. "A slave that is forgetful is not an efficient slave."

Thora flinched for Glauce's sake. She suspected that Glauce was flushed with embarrassment again. In time, Glauce would settle in, but until then, Thora would do her best to shield Glauce from their owner's temper. Halcyon was intimidating and could make it difficult for any young slave.

"It seems such a waste of time and coin," Selene said in a flippant manner.

"You are still bitter about the wine, Selene."

Thora shook her head and continued to the kitchen. The conversation's details were lost on her, but she translated enough key words to understand that Linnr harbored hatred toward her. She concluded it was mutual. Thora prepared the main meal and considered her earlier interactions with Halcyon and Selene. This evening had a slight difference compared to two nights ago. Halcyon had used Thora's nickname for Selene and also thanked her in Norsk. Both of Halcyon's actions encouraged a spot of warmth in her chest.

Cesare arrived in time to help Thora. She was dazzled by his perfect timing each evening and was grateful for the help. Together, they carried out the platters of food and jug of wine. Glauce had a relieved look when they rejoined her.

"Has your sire selected a mate?" Halcyon asked but studied the different items of food Thora and Cesare put on the table.

Selene brightened. "I am preparing for the pretrial union."

"I see your hair has not been cut," Halcyon said with a wicked smile. "So I must have a few nights left with you." Her pheromones shifted and deepened, catching more than Selene's attention. Thora did her best not to inhale too much of her owner's alluring scent.

"A couple of months. My sire is preparing the dowry."

Halcyon grinned at the news. "Does he follow my sire's example?"

Selene laughed and shook her head. "No sire has followed yours in a while, because you have not given your mate these lands."

Thora finished organizing the dishes on the table, then she went to Glauce. "Linen?" She hoped her prompt worked and encouraged Glauce to leave for a moment to search for linens, and gather herself. Thora had purposely left behind the linens so that Glauce could leave.

"Y-Yes." Glauce widened her eyes, but nodded and dashed off without hesitation.

"And why should I?" Halcyon countered in a rumbly tone, catching Thora's attention. "My mate is never here." She held out her hands toward the villa around them. "I am the master of my home." She lowered her hands to her lap.

"Yes, as many other Omegas, but they have all signed over their lands to their mates. That is the agreement of the union."

Halcyon shook her head. "Over two-thirds of the Omegas in Sparta own the lands. And why?" She crossed her legs under her chiton. "It is because our Alpha mates are busy in the barracks."

Selene inhaled, then released it with a strained note. "They must sire our sons." For once, she went quiet, then Thora noticed Halcyon's pheromones held a hint of warning in them. Selene had pushed Halcyon a bit too far. "Fortunately, Euclid has never seen it fit to loan you to another."

Halcyon grunted and took a long drink of her wine. She leaned forward and placed the cup on the table. "Euclid wishes I become pregnant, so he can have a son."

"Why have you not?" Selene asked.

"Pregnancy eludes me," Halcyon replied, then she turned to the meal. She handed a clean clay dish to Selene.

"You must time it more properly." Selene frowned. "Soon you will lose all chance to bear an Alpha for Sparta." There was a bewildered note in her voice, as if she was confused by Halcyon herself.

"I let the Fates decide." Halcyon's voice was tight, indicating she wished to conclude the discussion. She placed different items of food onto her dish and ordered, "Eat, Selene."

Selene huffed low but leaned forward and started to fill her plate. She seemed to have accepted that the topic of conversation was over.

Thora remained next to Cesare, standing on the edge of the courtyard close to the kitchen entrance. Glauce rushed out and handed out the linens that Thora had left behind on the kitchen counter. Once Glauce joined them, Cesare exchanged a nod with Thora and left them. In the evenings, he had to attend to his other chores in the stable before dark. For the most part, the dinner went by in relative silence. Thora suspected that Selene had agitated Halcyon more than normal.

After the meal, Halcyon left to relieve herself. Selene signaled for Glauce to refill her wine. With a full cup, Selene reclined across the bench and sipped her drink. When Glauce returned to Thora's side, she touched Glauce's forearm and gave a silent question. Glauce understood and nodded that she would be okay. Thora rumbled low and used her Alpha pheromones to soothe away the last of Glauce's uneasiness. Glauce smiled in appreciation, then Thora was on her way.

In the kitchen again, Thora sliced the sweet bread and lined up the pieces on a long, narrow wooden board. Pleased with the simple presentation, she carried out the dessert to the courtyard and frowned at Halcyon's continued absence. Thora tightened her grip on the board and approached the table in front of Selene. There was enough space to slip the board onto the side closest to Selene. Thora did her best to ignore Selene rather than prompt a reaction. Before Thora could straighten, Selene snared her wrist. Selene was on her feet and jerked Thora forward, causing her to bump into the table.

Thora balanced herself and yanked her arm free. She straightened with power and pride, then a growl started deep in her chest. Selene seethed at Thora. "You owe me for your insult from last time, barbar."

"*Go to Hel, serpent,*" Thora snarled in her native tongue.

Selene breathed in the venom that rolled off Thora. Rather than back away, Selene raised her other hand and slapped Thora across the cheek. Thora gritted her teeth and touched the stinging spot. She fisted her own hand in a fierce attempt to restrain her Alpha.

"You Cerberus!" Selene sneered and continued her rant. "You are jealous of me. But you will never be anything, you worthless horseshit!" She raised her hand.

Thora narrowed her eyes and willed Selene to try again. She would retaliate if Selene struck her again, unable to contain her Alpha anymore. Selene's attempt to belittle her would fail every time.

Selene's hand came to an abrupt halt a breath from Thora's cheek. A strong hand was latched around her wrist hard enough to make Selene whine. Turning her head to the left, she gaped at Halcyon, who loomed over her.

Thora smirked at Linnr's shocked expression. She was relieved when she first spotted Halcyon return from behind Selene.

"Never touch my slaves, Selene." Halcyon growled and yanked Selene against her body. "Thora already paid her debt for what she did that night."

"To you—not to me." Selene pulled on her trapped arm, but Halcyon's grip was iron. "You are too easy on her, Halcyon."

"This is my home." Halcyon lowered her head closer to Selene's own. "And you are not fit for it right now." She shoved away Selene and ordered, "Leave."

Selene gawked for a beat, then gathered her wits and walked around her lover but glared at Halcyon standing in front of her slave. "I hear what they call you, Halcyon. They call you an Amazon. You are unnatural like the Amazons." Her eyes narrowed, and her tone gained acid. "How fitting that you should have such a barbaric slave!"

Halcyon grew quite smug. "If I recall correctly, it is this body"—she signaled her own—"that you often fantasize about. A pity you will not find a mate or a maiden who will match me." She waved off Selene and turned her back on her former lover.

Selene trembled and stormed out of the courtyard. She slammed the iron gate open, in final protest to Halcyon and her barbarian. Halcyon faced Thora and inspected Thora's cheek, hissing in disapproval. Her genuine concern for Thora's well-being sparked a variety of sensations inside her that slowly settled into a needy burn between her legs. Last time she was able to satiate herself of the arousal, but now Glauce was her roommate. She may have to wait until she had a bath to have any privacy. Thora contained a groan but decided Halcyon could be her ending.

Thora gathered Halcyon's hand into her own. "It okay."

Halcyon revealed a sad smile at Thora's attempt to speak to her. "Selene is a linnr." Her words caused Thora to grin, and she squeezed the larger hand that was inside hers.

"Thank you."

Halcyon frowned at the praise for intervening with Selene. She shook her head and ended their contact. "Please clean up." She indicated the dishes around the table.

Glauce hurried over to assist. Thora pivoted when Halcyon departed, but she snatched the board of sweet bread and called, "Mistress?" Halcyon paused near the steps that would go to the second level. Thora crossed the distance with a few wide strides and held out the tasty bread in silent gratitude for earlier. Halcyon eyed the sweet bread, peered up at Thora, and sighed before taking a slice. Without another word, she climbed the steps and munched on the bread. Thora released a pleased thrum after regaining a part of her owner's trust. They were at least on the mend.

CHAPTER 5
Thora

"Okay?" Thora asked Glauce in concern. She set down a sack of grain on a table in the supply room. She and Glauce had returned from the market with rather heavy satchels.

Glauce shoved her sack that contained a mix of meats, vegetables, and fruits. "Yes." She smiled and dusted her hands. Similar to other days, she remained attached to Thora's side and was attentive to everything Thora showed her. Despite their inability to have lengthy conversations, they were able to communicate what needed to be done.

Over the past fortnight, Thora's duties were reduced so that she could learn Greek. She often handled making meals as per Halcyon's request. Halcyon seemed to enjoy Thora's cooking style, which was Greek with a flair of Norsk now. Vitus had informed Thora that Halcyon liked the Norsk-style dishes added into her diet. Thora was happy to make food from her homelands and be able to eat some of it. She had also learned what made up a more Spartan diet compared to an Athenian one.

Thora patted Glauce's shoulder and considered the time. Glauce would be fine on her own, prepping for tonight's meal. While Glauce readied the food, Thora went in search of Vitus for her lesson, but the courtyard was empty and quiet.

Beyond the villa, she heard a yell followed by a low thud. Thora followed the noise behind the house and past the stable. She came to a grass clearing between the stable and the fields where the helots worked the summer crop. Thora thanked her gods she was a house slave rather than a government one. Her thoughts were cut short by the sight of her owner's prowess.

Halcyon wore a simple white tunic and a short skirt. She hefted a long spear closer to the spiked end with the pointed tip faced forward. With honed skill, she slashed and attacked the large wooden post with the weapon's spearhead.

Staring in amazement, Thora stood to one side while Halcyon practiced several types of thrusts. She better understood why Halcyon was muscular. From prior village raids in Thora's past, she could imagine the strength and endurance it took to constantly drive such a long weapon at an enemy.

Cesare was near Halcyon and stood at attention. To the right of his foot were two damaged spears. The heads had probably been snapped off from Halcyon's practices. Vitus stood behind but off to the side, observing Halcyon's intense hoplite training. Thora neared her tutor and joined him, captivated by her owner's skills.

Halcyon stole a glance at her slave but remained focused on her training. After numerous attacks, she snapped the spearhead. Halcyon spun the spear and used the counterbalance spiked end for a weapon. She drove it into the wood and slashed her wooden opponent.

Thora was impressed by Halcyon's prowess as a warrior. "*Beautiful,*" she whispered in Norsk. Then a sudden blush dusted her cheeks.

Vitus glanced at Thora, but his bemused expression indicated his inability to translate her soft praise of Halcyon's physique. He tilted his head at Thora for a beat before he turned back to admiring Halcyon.

Completing the drill, Halcyon tossed the broken spear by the other two and approached Cesare, who gave her the sheathed sword. Halcyon accepted it, then went over to Vitus and Thora. "Are you going to practice today?" She wiped sweat from her brow, using her forearm.

Vitus nodded. "We will be in the courtyard."

Halcyon's cool features were broken by a thin smile. "Is Thora learning quickly?"

"She is efficient." Vitus smiled at Thora but turned back to Halcyon. "The languages are quite different, especially certain sounds."

Halcyon rumbled and leaned the flat of the blade against her shoulder. "Yes, I noticed, but Thora seems to be up to the challenge."

Vitus grinned, nodded, and then turned to Thora. "Let us start."

Thora left with her tutor. One time she glanced over her shoulder at Halcyon, who practiced with the short blade. In the future, she might be allowed to ask Halcyon about her life as a warrior. She was fascinated by Halcyon's unusual position as a warrior in a society that didn't condone Omegas being more than breeders. In Thora's homelands, Omegas were revered for both their ability to breed as well as their readiness for battle if their home and pups came under threat during raids. Thora doubted a Greek Omega could protect herself much less her pups. However, the Spartan Omegas appeared to be more resilient and resourceful than those in Athens.

* * *

From sun high to sunset, Vitus and Thora sat in the courtyard on the warm day and practiced Thora's Greek.

When there was an hour of sunlight left, the lessons came to an end. Thora was exhausted, yet she needed to prepare dinner even if she was behind on her routine. Glauce could cook the meal, if necessary, but Thora wanted to spend more time teaching her the basics. After thanking Vitus, Thora hurried to the kitchen and estimated how much time they had until Halcyon expected dinner.

With her back to Thora, Glauce stirred the contents of a pot over an open fire. Thora glanced at the central table, taking stock of tonight's dinner, but she was unsure what Glauce was cooking. As Glauce poured a container's contents into the pot, Thora approached her from behind and greeted her.

Glauce squealed and dropped the pitcher into the fire. A roar of flames flared up and lapped at her hand. As the container crashed into the pot, the smell of burning fat filled the air. The fatty liquid fed the fire, which roared like the fabled wolf Fenrir she'd been taught about as a pup. The flames jumped onto Glauce's chiton.

"Glauce!" In two wide steps, Thora knocked Glauce to the ground and smothered the flames on her chiton. She then hauled them both to their feet as the thick smoke filled the room. "Up!"

With watery eyes, she stared in horror at the thick gray smoke that twisted up from the fire and billowed across the white ceiling. Her attention snapped to the left when Cesare barged in from the outside door. Already smoke piped out of the kitchen's single open window.

Cesare stared wide-eyed when Thora attempted to get near the fire. He looked to Glauce and ordered, "Tell mistress!"

Glauce raced out to the courtyard.

"Thora, here!" Cesare indicated the washtub full of water.

Thora coughed several times but hurried over to Cesare. Together, they hefted the basin from its stand and carried it to the uncontrollable fire. With synchronized strength, they poured the water over the fireplace.

Blinking against the irritating smoke, Thora expected the fire to be extinguished, but instead, it stretched out to the walls and the ceiling with eagerness. Feeling the full weight of the basin pull her down, she looked over at Cesare, who was toppling headfirst toward the stone floor. Her heart leaped into her throat.

"Cesare?" Thora hollered. She launched over the flames that had spread over the floor despite the water. Kneeling, she touched his face and damp shoulders, but he was unconscious. "*Skit*," she cursed in her native tongue.

Only Cesare's soft moan gave Thora the strength to act fast. It would take too long to reach the entrance that led to the courtyard. Instead, she climbed to her feet with Cesare in her arms. She carried him through the back door and was overwhelmed by the fresh air. After setting him down, she reentered the kitchen in hopes to stop the fire.

The blaze had become a mindless creature that raced down the adjacent wall, which held countless wooden shelves for all the cookware. Similarly, the ceiling was consumed by red-hot tendrils, and the wood beams glowed bright, but it was the dense smoke that filled Thora's lungs.

Each one of Thora's thoughts whited out as her mind clouded and sweat coated her skin. She wanted to save the kitchen for Halcyon, but it was hopeless. As she turned to leave, an overhead cracking noise made her peer up. The overhead timber collapsed and blocked the back door to the outside, forcing Thora into the center of the kitchen where the fire raged. Coughing and teary-eyed from the smoke, she lowered herself to the floor for fresh air. The courtyard entrance was only steps away, but now it was a crawl through *Hel*.

Urging her weakened body, Thora crept across the damp floor but slumped when her deprived lungs tightened and made her light-headed. Her slow thoughts turned into weak prayers to her gods. Then in the distance, she heard her gods call her name, again and again.

"Thora!"

Thora forced her eyes open after realizing it was her owner's voice. She worked her hands under her body and tried to lift herself. Thora struggled, and tears pooled in her eyes while she fought to move toward the sound of her name.

Halcyon rushed through the courtyard entrance. "Thora!" Her voice trembled for the first time that Thora could recall. "Thora!" Halcyon dropped to her knees, slipped her arms under Thora, and hauled her to her feet.

Another deafening snap overhead, and Halcyon raced them outside. The burning timber crashed down and nearly swiped their backs, but they made it through the doorway and collapsed in the courtyard.

Thora gave a low moan when her body collided with the floor and rolled out of Halcyon's strong arms.

Halcyon coughed and patted her chest, then wiped her eyes. Behind them, the smoke billowed out of the kitchen. She reached for Thora and continued to move her farther from the danger, but with the villa needing to be cleared out, Thora knew Halcyon would reenter the home. Thora grunted and did her best to hold on to her owner as she dragged her away.

Vitus was beyond the gate at the front of the house. He rushed to Halcyon, who settled Thora on the stone street. "Are you... is Thora?"

Halcyon cleared her throat, swallowed, and murmured, "She is breathing and a little aware."

Thora moaned and rolled her head toward the pair. "Glau—" She was cut off by a coughing fit.

Vitus patted her back. "I'll get her water." He dashed off.

Halcyon remained beside her slave and said, "Glauce and Cesare are safe." Her attention was drawn away by the commotion sounding from beyond the iron gate. Neighbors had formed a bucket brigade that stretched from the well in the courtyard to the kitchen's door.

Thora began to move, prepared to assist with putting out the fire.

"No." Halcyon coughed once, then pushed on Thora's shoulder to hold her down. She looked to Vitus, who dropped to his knees with a clay cup. She helped Thora drink from it, then ordered, "Stay with her. A healer will arrive soon." Without another word, she hurried off and went into the villa.

After several minutes, Vitus helped Thora to a different spot, away from the line of neighbors. She remained propped up against a tree, facing the villa. No longer could she feel the heat, but the smoke was all around them. Several times she replayed what had happened in the kitchen and worried her lip. Halcyon would be very displeased later.

"*How feel?*" Vitus asked. He was seated next to her.

Thora cleared her throat and replied, "Better." She used Greek instead and received a smile from Vitus for her attempt. They both spotted Glauce coming toward them with a male in tow. She appeared unharmed thanks to Thora's swift actions in the kitchen. Glauce introduced the stranger, and then Vitus explained to Thora that the male Beta was a healer named Giles. Glauce stood by, playing with the charred ends of her chiton.

"Can you bring Cesare here?" Giles asked, regarding Glauce.

"Yes, of course." Glauce hurried off.

Giles first looked over Thora, doing his best to inspect as much as he could in the fading sunlight and dark smoke. He clicked his tongue twice, shook his head a few times, and used a salve on her burns. By the time he was done, Glauce had returned with Cesare, who leaned on her. By the time Giles finished checking over Cesare and Glauce, Halcyon arrived and revealed her soot-covered face.

Giles approached Halcyon, who waved him off.

"I'm fine."

Giles frowned and tried again.

"I am fine." Halcyon's tone held no room for argument. She turned to Vitus and asked, "Do you need the healer?"

Vitus shook his head.

After a sigh, Giles gave his report to Halcyon, even warning her that Cesare and Thora would need rest for several days. He also promised Halcyon he would bring more salve for them soon. Halcyon insisted the healer return tomorrow for further checks.

"Thank you for your service." She gripped the healer's shoulder.

"Of course, Iron Edge." Giles took his leave.

Halcyon studied her three slaves and Vitus. Even though she reeked of smoke, her pheromones still managed to drift through the air. Thora was soothed by her owner's strong presence. "See to them, Vitus."

"I will." Vitus received an appreciative pat on his shoulder, then they watched Halcyon march back to the villa. The villa's front was safe, but the right rear roof over the kitchen was smoking. The earlier flames were already gone, contained by the brigade.

Thora slumped against the tree and let out a few mild coughs. She cleared her throat and closed her eyes.

"*You fortunate slave,*" Vitus said to Thora, who opened an eye.

Thora grunted and met Vitus's gaze. Even in the approaching darkness, she could read the concern in his eyes. But she was certain she would recover. Her fears rested with Glauce and what Halcyon may do if she learned how the fire started in the first place. Looking to her right, she frowned at Glauce's constant fidgeting and tearing at the grass. Thora clasped Glauce's hand and squeezed it. Glauce peered up and went still when Thora smiled at her.

She swore to Glauce that everything would be fine. Thora hoped her promise was conveyed in her eyes. Glauce's scent softened from Thora's reassurance and Alpha pheromones. As Thora looked toward the damaged villa, she realized how grateful she was that they all were alive.

CHAPTER 6

Thora

A very low moan escaped from Thora's dry lips. She coughed and tried to open her aching eyes. Her body hurt, although her surroundings were comfortable. The air was fresh from the open window, but the smell of medicine wafted under her nose.

"Thora?"

The familiar voice pushed Thora to blink a few times. She smiled at Vitus and his concerned face. "*Am I dead?*" The memories from yesterday evening returned to her. She was unsure how she made it to her room. Maybe someone had carried her here.

From his spot in a chair, Vitus tilted his head with a bemused expression, then he sighed and shook his head. "*Nei.*"

Thora was relieved to be alive despite the pain in her body. Vitus stood and left, steps fading away. After a moment she realized the room was not her and Glauce's usual one; it was one normally reserved for a guest. She slept on the floor in her room, but in the guest room she was on a comfortable bed. She attempted moving but was too sore. From the open window, Thora could see it was late afternoon and assumed the fire was last night.

After a few minutes, Halcyon appeared in the bedroom and took the wooden chair by the bed. Thora attempted sitting upright until a firm hand made her lie down again.

"*Nei*," Halcyon ordered in Norsk, then crossed her legs. "How do you feel?"

Thora considered the Greek words she could use to reply. "Tired... hurt."

"I know." Halcyon canted her head while her scent started to fill the room. There was a distinct warmth to Halcyon's scent that reminded Thora of an Omega. It was the first time that Halcyon had used her pheromones in such a manner. The inviting comfort helped Thora ignore the dull pain that radiated through her body.

"How long?" Thora asked. Her rough accent cut into each word.

"A day and a half."

Thora groaned and rubbed her brow, which was a bit damp. Her assumption that the fire had been last night was wrong. She felt filthy after the fire in the kitchen and being in bed for this long. The amount of time had passed in a heartbeat and Thora had many chores to handle. However, it was clear that Halcyon would deny her. Their stalemate was broken by movement at the door. Glauce entered without a word and served bread, wine, and feta to Thora.

"Cesare?"

Halcyon nodded. "Cesare is okay."

Glauce stood at the foot of the bed. She kept her head down and waited until Thora was finished eating or Halcyon gave her instructions. Halcyon glanced at Glauce, who was avoiding eye contact with everyone. She whined low, turned back to Thora, and removed the cup from the tray.

"Glauce?" Thora asked.

Glauce flinched. Her pheromones registered with Thora and held a sour clue to them.

Halcyon frowned after Thora's failed attempt to reach Glauce. With a curt tone, Halcyon ordered, "Leave us."

Glauce turned on her sandals and departed the room. Thora tracked Glauce's departure and frowned when the door squeaked shut. She lifted her distraught features to Halcyon. "Why?" She pointed at the door as if it were Glauce.

Halcyon exhaled and replied, "Glauce is upset."

"Up... set?" Thora asked and shook her head.

Halcyon tried another approach. "She is not happy."

"Why?" Thora was confused. "Everybody okay." She ran her fingers through her golden hair. The kitchen fire had happened fast and had become out of control in moments. There was little anyone could have done to stop it.

Halcyon made no comment, held out a bowl of cheese, and said, "Eat."

Thora sat up and accepted the bowl. After a spoonful or two of the soup, she realized how famished she was. Her last meal had been about two days ago. Her thoughts about the kitchen fire returned, and she wondered how Halcyon was handling it. Even though Halcyon appeared calm on the exterior, she could be brewing with a firestorm on the inside. There was no doubt that Halcyon would do her best to research what happened and then seek retribution. In the end, it was a horrible accident and would cost Halcyon more money than she and Glauce combined were worth.

"You are to rest. Tomorrow you may be able to work," Halcyon said after a while.

Thora pursed her lips between mouthfuls. Even though she couldn't translate everything, she picked out important words. She was forbidden to work today and had to wait. From the hardness in her owner's features, she wouldn't attempt arguing. In reality, she was exhausted and not ready to tackle any of her duties. But it did little to take away the guilt she felt for Glauce handling all the chores alone, since she assumed Cesare was immobile too. Tomorrow she would do her best to be back on her feet.

Halcyon took the empty bowl from Thora and placed it on the tray. She handed over the bread, which would settle heavy in Thora's stomach. Reaching down she picked up a clay jar, removed its lid, and tilted the opening toward Thora. "This is for your arms." She pointed at Thora's injuries.

Thora paused midbite and raised her bandaged left arm. She grumbled and realized she hadn't noticed it earlier. The substance in the small jar was white and smelled of various herbs. It was a salve that would assist her skin in healing. She gave a faint nod.

"Good." Halcyon placed the salve on the table. She appeared stoic, but her scent was comforting, more like an Omega. "I must go." She climbed to her feet and pointed at the last few food items on the tray. "Eat." Without another glance, she was gone, leaving Thora bewildered.

Thora grinned at the thought of Halcyon's Omega stirring inside her. Her smirk softened to a smile once it became clear to her that she wasn't the only one being affected by the unusual attraction between them.

They were, after all, an Alpha and an Omega.

* * *

By the next day, Thora was out of bed and moving through the villa. The burns on her arm were healing. Her chores had been reduced and were being handled by Glauce. Several times she attempted to help, until caught by Halcyon, who somehow had a maddening talent of popping up the instant Thora started working.

Thora spent her time visiting Cesare. He was healing well but hadn't recovered his strength quite yet. They spoke little, but she was glad to see his beautiful brown eyes, his smile, and his salt-and-pepper hair. Since before the fire, he had slipped into her heart. She missed her family, but Cesare was becoming a sire to her.

About a week after the fire, she resumed her lessons with Vitus and cooking for Halcyon, at least as best as possible. A temporary kitchen had been set up in the supply room. Then one afternoon Halcyon ordered Thora, Cesare, Glauce, and Vitus into the master's suite. Halcyon sat at the main long chair, legs crossed and features stern. She had the slaves stand while Vitus sat on another long chair.

"Cesare, you were in the kitchen with Glauce?"

Cesare nodded. "Not at first, mistress. I was finishing up at the stable. As I neared the back door to the kitchen, I saw smoke coming from the window and rushed in. Glauce and Thora were fighting the fire."

Thora attempted to translate the discussion, head tilted and eyes narrowed. Next to her, Glauce fidgeted like a pup, and Thora was tempted to do the same. Shoving the urge down, she straightened further and watched her owner's features for any clues.

"I told Glauce to find you," Cesare said but paused and sneaked a glance at Thora and Glauce. Cesare had been in Halcyon's service for decades and understood Halcyon the best. Thora suspected he already knew what Halcyon may do once she learned about the events.

"Go on," Halcyon encouraged him.

"Then Thora and I tried to throw the water from the washtub onto the fire. It seemed to make it worse, because the fire exploded. I fell, hit my head, and went unconscious."

Halcyon nodded, then her eyes flickered over to Thora. "What can you tell me, Thora?" She indicated for Vitus to translate for them.

Breaking from the memories, Thora composed her thoughts and assumed her words would be relayed to her owner. She looked at Halcyon while she spoke slow enough for Vitus.

"Thora finished her lesson with me, then helped Glauce with cooking." Vitus paused and listened to the next part of Thora's story. He turned to Halcyon and translated it. "Glauce was accidently scared by Thora's arrival. Glauce dropped a pot into the fire." He looked to Thora, who explained what happened next.

Halcyon rumbled and folded her hands against her stomach.

"Glauce was burning, so Thora pushed her to the ground. Cesare arrived and helped Thora throw water on the fire." Vitus sighed and shook his head. "It made the fire worse. Cesare fainted, so Thora dragged him out, then she went back in to stop the fire." Vitus rubbed his chin while Thora continued the story. "Thora couldn't breathe well and collapsed to the floor, started crawling like a pup. That's when you arrived." He looked to Halcyon.

After a nod, Halcyon said, "Yes, I helped you escape the kitchen." Vitus translated her response.

Thora had been close to unconsciousness from inhaling the smoke. The flames or the falling beam would have finished her off, but instead Halcyon arrived and saved her. She cleared her throat and said, "Thank you."

Halcyon dipped her head in acknowledgment.

Thora asked, "I work?"

Halcyon weighed the request, now that her two older slaves were well again. After a long moment, she released a heavy breath and replied, "You may start tomorrow."

Thora was relieved. She enjoyed her lessons with Vitus but was also ready to continue her duties. There was a certain comfort in having a routine and schedule. "The kitchen?"

Halcyon arched an eyebrow at Thora, then traded a glance with Vitus, who had an amused expression.

"You wished for her to learn Greek," Vitus reminded and held out his hands as if innocent.

Huffing, Halcyon turned her attention back to Thora. "It will be rebuilt."

Thora glanced at her teacher. "Rebuilt?"

"*New kitchen,*" Vitus replied in Thora's language.

Thora nodded. She wanted to speak more, defend Glauce. However, Halcyon excused them from the suite. As Thora exited after the other two slaves, she caught a whiff of raw heat under Halcyon's scent in the air. Under different circumstances, Thora would have been aroused by it, but this situation was serious. Her owner had the truth about the accident. But she suspected Halcyon would think through the chain of events, then decide the next steps. Cesare had once warned her that their owner may seem quiet but her mind was always busy.

* * *

The next morning, Thora started her normal routine, including grinding the grain for the evening. She asked Cesare whether Glauce had left to go to the market for grain, vegetables, and meats. He replied that Glauce was still drawing water from the well in the courtyard. A moment later, Glauce emerged in the temporary kitchen in the supply room. She gathered the empty satchel for the trip to the market.

"Glauce," Cesare said.

Glauce paused and looked at Cesare.

"Our mistress wishes to see you before you go."

Paling, Glauce returned the satchel and exited without a word. However, she left behind a stormy scent in the air that stirred Thora's Alpha.

Thora was confused until Cesare explained that Halcyon required Glauce in the master's suite. Thora's stomach pitched low and drove her out of the room. Cesare's yell went ignored until he snared her wrist. She whirled around and pinned him with a glare.

Cesare sighed at Thora's rebellious nature and then her growing Alpha scent. He parted his lips a little, but he remained silent and instead allowed her arm to slide free. As a Beta, he was a step below Thora on the breed ladder, even as slaves.

Thora marched around the courtyard's fountain and approached the sealed doors of the master's suite. It was strange to see them closed, but she peered through the thin crack. Already Glauce's scent poured through the sliver of an opening and rallied Thora's Alpha.

Glauce stood in the center of the room, wringing her hands together. To her left, Halcyon glared at her, then approached and circled Glauce as if she were prey. "It is because of your foolishness that I have lost my kitchen." She paused, and the venom seeped into her voice. "I must rebuild the kitchen." She stood behind her trembling slave. "You endangered two of my slaves." She returned to pacing around Glauce until she was in front of her again. "Thora and I nearly died."

Glauce closed her eyes, and tears trickled down her cheeks.

"Do not cry, slave," Halcyon barked. "If you make a mistake in life, you must pay a price." She walked behind Glauce, then snarled at her. "Yours will be returning to that disgusting slave trader, whom I purchased you from."

"No, mistress, please!" Glauce collapsed to her knees. Her panting turned into panicked breaths. "Please, no! H-He will rape me again and—"

"*Nei!*" Thora burst into the room, unable to stand by any longer. Glauce's confession about Telamon further fueled her Alpha's need to protect Glauce from harm. She took a firm stance between Glauce and her furious owner. "No return Glauce." She was less muscular than Halcyon, but she towered over her owner. "My punishment." There was a brief silence other than Glauce's whimpers.

Halcyon, jaw clenched and knuckles white, sneered at Thora's disobedience and fisted her hands but didn't strike. Thora held her position and, using her intense pheromones, willed Halcyon to listen. Even though Glauce was at fault, the fire was an accident. Thora was certain Halcyon could be reasoned with, but for now her Alpha scent filled the room and held Halcyon at bay.

"I fail. Glauce not cook. I do. I late. She help." Thora pointed at the suffering Omega behind her. Glauce was gentle and kind, not a criminal who torched the kitchen. "You not punish." She held her owner's burning gaze and searched for any signs of reasonable thought. The loss of the kitchen was ugly and expensive, but such a harsh punishment wasn't warranted. Halcyon acted as if someone had died in the fire when in fact Halcyon saved Thora. Then she was blindsided by the truth behind Halcyon's reaction, but it made sense to Thora. With a huff, she whispered, "I alive."

Halcyon breathed heavier, then she jerked back after Thora's last words. She recoiled one step even though her scent remained fiery. Their last argument had ended with Halcyon dominating Thora, but this time, she heeled to Thora once the truth came to light.

Thora gave a faint nod after she confirmed why Halcyon was overreacting. Omegas were the most protective breed and would strike down threats at any cost. "Send me back Telamon," Thora declared. Unlike Glauce, Telamon held no power over Thora due to her Alpha nature. He was curious about her breed and seemed gratified by owning her. But he was often apprehensive toward her whenever they were alone or near each other. Perhaps the idea that an Alpha slave could best him, especially in bed, instilled fear in him.

Halcyon's fury crumbled after the surprising demand. Every single punishment she gave to Thora did little to smother her slave's thunderous nature. She growled low and narrowed her eyes, top lip curling up. "Leave, Thora." She cut her attention to Glauce on the floor and hissed through her clenched teeth. "Take Glauce with you." After a moment of stillness, she snapped, "Now!"

Thora broke from the stalemate, turned, and hooked her friend's arms. In soft murmurs, she coaxed Glauce to her feet and hurried them from the room. She used her body to shield Glauce from their owner until they were in the courtyard. Glauce held on to her, sobbing on the walk upstairs to their shared room.

Glauce tumbled onto her bedroll in the room and attempted to hide her tear-streaked face in her knees and arms. Thora sat next to and rubbed her friend's back, which shook from her soft whimpers. She used her pheromones to ease

Glauce's distress about what happened, but her mind returned to what Glauce said earlier about Telamon. She was unaware of him attacking Glauce, and it encouraged a slight tremble deep in her gut. Thora wanted to find him and tear off his cock for harming Glauce and any other slaves.

"You safe," Thora whispered and earned a sideways glance from Glauce. She hoped that Glauce believed her.

"Th-Thank you," Glauce managed between sniffles and tears, her face between her knees.

Thora hopped onto her feet after hearing a loud boom. "I return," she said to Glauce before hastening from their room.

"Clean the suite by the time I return!" Halcyon ordered to everyone. Cesare darted out from the supply room, and he and Thora watched their master storm out of Villa Honor the Beloved through the iron gates.

Silence lingered for a moment before Cesare looked up at Thora by the railing of the second floor and shrugged. "She will ride her horse and return with a cooler head."

Thora felt a frown tug along her features, but she refrained from worrying too much about Halcyon, who needed space and time. If nothing else, Thora was grateful that Vitus was away from the villa this morning rather than witnessing their owner's rage.

CHAPTER 7
Thora

The days after Halcyon's outburst were long and edgy for the entire villa. Even though Vitus had been gone that morning, he learned from Thora what had happened between Halcyon, Thora, and Glauce. In a soft voice, he recommended to Thora that she keep her head down rather than confront Halcyon again. His suggestion was easy considering Halcyon had remained quiet during the passing days. Her features were devoid of emotions and her eyes distant.

Glauce steered away from their owner while Thora and Cesare handled Halcyon. Thora was thankful that Halcyon made no further attempts to corner Glauce. But Halcyon also ignored Thora, which she thought was her punishment for defending Glauce. Regardless of the reason, Glauce wasn't returned to Telamon.

Otherwise the days continued as normal. Halcyon rotated between her duties as a hoplite and her responsibilities to her villa. About a fortnight after the fire, strangers came and went from the villa and inspected the ruined kitchen. Each one left, then returned a few days later to speak to Halcyon. The last one earned a hearty handshake from Halcyon.

About a month after the fire, Thora rose one morning to the predawn and prepared for the day. She did her best to be silent and allow Glauce to rest longer. Glauce stayed up later at night, handling the villa's closing. After dressing, Thora went downstairs and noticed Cesare was working early rather than enjoying his one day of the week to sleep in.

"Good morning, Thora."

Thora smiled at him. "You early."

Cesare nodded and said, "I helped Halcyon prepare before dawn."

Thora paused, then her brow knitted together while she deciphered what Cesare meant. "She left?" At Cesare's nod, she glowered further. "I not say bye." There had been chatter among them that Halcyon was expected to spend a couple of weeks at the barracks, part of her requirement as a hoplite.

Cesare neared her. "Halcyon does not require farewells." He then touched her stiff shoulder. "She will be back in a month's time."

Thora was bothered that Halcyon left with their silence intact. They exchanged few words, which were often commands and agreements. A dark cloud from their last dispute lingered between them, but Thora had hoped to resolve it before Halcyon went to the barracks.

"Do not worry, Thora." Cesare offered an assuring expression, then released her shoulder after a soft squeeze. "We must hurry. We have a lot of work to do today."

Thora shook her head. "What work?"

Cesare came closer and said, "Our master returns tomorrow. Euclid must not know that our mistress goes into his side of the villa."

Thora huffed at the Greek home's segregation compared to her homelands. "Why?"

Cesare gave pause before he sighed and shook his head. "Things will happen in this house that should not if our master learns of Halcyon's lifestyle." He edged closer to Thora and held one of her hands, squeezing it. "You care for Halcyon?"

"*Já.*"

Cesare gave a pleased noise at her affirmation. "Then we must hurry." He took Thora's hand and guided her to the master's suite. He explained that they needed to return things to how Euclid would have them. The desk was already tidied up, perhaps by Halcyon. The long chairs were reset to their normal arrangement, the tables returned to their original spots, and the master's favorite sculpture of Ares was brought back into the room. According to Cesare, Halcyon favored Athena over Ares, so she tucked the sculpture of Ares into the corner once Euclid left home.

Vitus assisted the slaves until it was time for Thora's lesson. Thora sensed that Vitus was a bit on edge about the master's pending arrival. But for now, they had a lesson or two to focus on.

As expected, Euclid arrived late the next morning in full uniform. His entrance was loud, his gear crashing into the master bedroom upstairs. Cesare welcomed Euclid first and then introduced Thora and Glauce to him. He also handed Euclid a scroll, which was from Halcyon. Euclid untied it, read it, and stomped off to the ground floor. Once he checked over the latest changes to the villa and the status of the kitchen, he toured the stable with Cesare.

Later, Euclid stripped off his tunic and took a bath that Thora and Glauce had prepared for him. Thora poured the last bucket of steaming water into the in-ground stone bath and went over to Cesare, who gathered Euclid's armor. With a raised eyebrow, she held out a hand to her friend. Cesare huffed and eyed Thora's open palm. Without a word, he slipped the greaves into Thora's hand and marched off. Thora grinned to herself and followed him out of the bathing room. Once far enough away from the bathing room, Cesare turned to Thora.

"It is best if you remain quiet around him."

"Yes." Thora glanced toward the doorway of the bathing room. "He all Alpha."

Cesare snorted, then grinned at Thora. "Yes." However, his grin slipped and he whispered, "He is not as forgiving or as understanding as our mistress."

Thora had no plans to challenge Euclid, not as one Alpha to another. She was the slave after all. However, she perceived Halcyon as her owner, not Euclid. Still, Cesare had a strong point that it was best to hold the peace by being a ghost. "I understand."

Cesare opened his mouth but was cut off by a throaty and gratified moan that echoed from the bathing room. Thora snapped her head in the direction and rumbled low before she looked at Cesare with a smirk. Shaking his head, Cesare muttered, "It is only the beginning." He nodded toward his right and Thora followed him. After they deposited the armor and weapons, Thora went to the supply room, rid of the bucket, and started to make a light midday meal along with prepping for dinner. Glauce arrived a little later to assist her.

Thora was about to slice bread for the midday meal, but paused when she heard Euclid talking to Vitus. Curious about the ongoings, Thora told Glauce to slice the bread, then went to the doorway.

"Yes, my mate informed me that you are here to teach the barbar some Greek."

"Yes," Vitus replied in a neutral tone. He had taken a seat in the opposite chair from Euclid at the courtyard table.

Euclid gave a grunt. "What a waste of coin." He waved his hand and said, "But the slaves are her duty." After a pause, he asked, "Do you wish to share a meal?" From his tone, it was clear that Vitus had little choice.

"Certainly."

Thora pivoted and said, "Vitus eat too."

Glauce nodded and collected another plate, cup, and linen. "What are they discussing?"

Thora sighed and came over to help Glauce gather everything for the food. "Euclid ask me learn Greek." She fought to keep the growliness from her voice. "They talk Vitus's travels."

Glauce had picked up a few plates of food, one balanced on her forearm. "You must be careful about speaking the master's name." She spoke softer than a breeze, but her suggestion rang in Thora's ears.

After a sigh, Thora conceded to Glauce's recommendation. She might not see Euclid as her owner, but he would see himself as the master of the villa and of her. If she slipped up by using his proper name, then it was within his right to punish her. "Yes." She snared a jug of wine. "Thank you."

Glauce beamed for a moment and nodded. Together they headed to the courtyard to deliver the food. Thora remained in attendance while she shoed away Glauce to keep her away from Euclid. Glauce would handle the rest of the prep work for dinner this evening. None of them wished to fall behind on the meal schedule. Famished Alphas never boded well for anyone as Thora knew. While Thora remained silent off to the side, she thought of her owner and wished for Halcyon's return.

* * *

By the third day, workers had arrived at the villa and started the reconstruction of the kitchen. There was hope that the new kitchen would be ready before the autumn equinox. Euclid worked alongside the hired workers, as he was quite good with physical labor and construction. By sunset, Euclid was worn out and retired to his room, taking his meal there. However, he announced that he would host a symposium before he returned to the barracks. Cesare explained to Thora that the social gathering would garner him political popularity in Sparta.

The symposium required extensive planning and prep work for Cesare, Thora, and Glauce. They worked from sunup to sundown to ready for the symposium, which would commence in a few days' time in the evening. Thora had to minimize her lessons with Vitus so she could manage the extra workload. The temporary kitchen in the supply room caused additional trouble with its tighter space, older equipment, and small oven, which was meant for firing clay pieces rather than cooking.

The night of the political party, Glauce, Cesare, and Thora were exhausted, but they pushed through it. Glauce and Thora were permitted to enter the male side of the villa under Euclid's instruction so that they could serve his guests. She and Glauce pretended it was new to them, even though they went into the master's suite when Halcyon was home. Thora was surprised at how many people were in attendance at the symposium. Most of the guests were males, both Alphas and Betas. There were a few female Omegas and Betas, but they were entertainers of different sorts. Musicians and a bard also arrived to entertain Euclid's guests. In the center of the room, two large hand-painted metal pots were filled with wine. They were drained several times by the guests.

Thora slipped out of the room with two large empty bowls that needed to be filled with more cheeses. She disappeared into the supply room to retrieve the precut cheese cubes and place them in the linen cloth. Once organized, she hurried out but slowed upon seeing Euclid in the quiet courtyard. In silence, Thora went past him and ensured a certain amount of space between them. From his scent, he was drunk and aggressive, which ruffled Thora's Alpha.

Euclid turned in place, then snared Thora's shoulder. "You ignore me, slave."

Thora ground her teeth and held the bowls tighter to keep them from falling out of her hands. She turned around to face him, breaking their physical contact. The redness around his eyes confirmed what her nose already knew. With gritted teeth, she kept her attention to the side in hopes the submissive posture would satisfy his Alpha. Over the past three years of her captivity, she had submitted one too many times, but she had promised Cesare and Vitus that she would keep the peace.

Euclid was shorter than Thora, but he was much bulkier, and advanced on her. "I was told you set the fire in the kitchen."

Thora clenched her jaw harder and kept her eyes off him. However, she held her position rather than shrink back like he expected her to do. She refrained from using her pheromones, even with his growing scent crashing into her.

"Answer me." Euclid yanked her closer.

With strained wrinkles across her brow, Thora held his cold stare and willed him to release her before it was too late. For some silly reason, Euclid seemed to be under the impression that she could speak Greek well, even though he'd heard her practicing with Vitus.

Euclid narrowed his eyes at Thora. "I know you understand me." He tightened his grip further, sending a mild pain through her arm. "Vitus teaches you day and night. I have heard you speak my tongue." He then growled and showed off his canines. "Did you set my kitchen on fire?"

Thora inhaled a deep breath and narrowed her gaze at him. "Yes, start fire." She would protect Glauce and stand against their master for Glauce's sake.

Euclid smirked in triumph. "I knew you understood me." Then his features slipped toward darkness, and he shoved

Thora backward. "You have cost me a lot of coin!" He cut his eyes to the bowl that had shattered on the floor.

Ignoring the clay shards and scattered cheese, Thora placed the other bowl on the bench next to the pool. She fisted her hands, ready to defend herself against Euclid, who was the master of the villa but not of her. Like a snake uncoiling, Thora's Alpha awoke and prepared to strike back.

"You may not have the coin to pay me, but you do have something else."

Thora missed most of his words, yet she caught the intent in his pheromones and read the hunger on his face. With her teeth now bare, she dared him to attack her. If he was used to Beta and Omega slaves falling to him, then he would learn how different an Alpha slave was.

Euclid launched at Thora, and with his bulky weight he took them both down. He attempted to grab her hands, but she landed a punch to his side. "Be still!" With a hand around her throat, he tried to choke her into submission.

Thora snarled, unfazed by the actions of a typical male Alpha. In the distance, a chorus of laughter echoed into the empty courtyard around them.

"Let us see if you have what I have," Euclid breathed into her face, then hiked up her chiton and reached between her lower thighs. His sexual remark freed the heat of Thora's Alpha, which caused her to release a dangerous blanket of pheromones. Euclid stiffened and went still, seeming to take in Thora's brief warning.

Thora seized Euclid by his hair, yanking his head back. She rammed her knee into his side, which forced him to loosen his grip on her throat. With a deep growl, she rolled them until she was on top and then batted his hand from her throat. His shocked expression was a small victory, but Thora wasn't foolish to think she'd won anything. He was a male Alpha and a trained warrior. Her main advantage at the moment was that he was drunk, making him weaker and uncoordinated.

Euclid's features hardened, then his pheromones strengthened to match his power. Thora challenged him back and unfurled her own scent. He went for her throat again, but she grappled with him and increased her pheromones. Euclid should have beaten her, except her suppressed will was greater than his. She was from a long line of successful warriors and had trained herself to battle anyone who wanted to dominate her. Euclid jerked underneath her, then his pupils started to constrict as Thora's heavy pheromones weighed on him.

Thora sensed his fight start to wane, and his pheromones withdrew. She growled at him and continued to force her superiority over him. On the outside, she appeared to be a slave, but she was an Alpha, and she would battle any unworthy Alpha. Slavery did nothing to halt the natural order among Alphas.

After a soft curse, Euclid dropped his hand away from Thora's face, then released her hip. He became slack underneath her yet continued to emit a slight growl that softened to a dejected rumble. Thora had defeated him on an equal battleground that only Alphas met on. Satisfied with his surrender, she climbed off him and took a step back.

Panting hard, Euclid struggled to get to his feet. He glared at Thora but also kept a certain amount of space between them. Their new understanding of each other was enough to keep him back. Thora would respect his orders as the master if he respected her in turn. But their attention jerked toward a newcomer.

Vitus stood on the other side of the water fountain's pool. He appeared calm, but his scent drifted on the breeze and caught Thora's nose. Vitus was leery of Euclid. With a tilt of his head, he studied Euclid's tense and hunched posture, then said, "A dead or pregnant slave is a worthless slave."

Euclid groused before glaring at Thora, seeming to weigh Vitus's suggestion.

Thora returned Euclid's glower and better understood what drove him—she was just another piece of property to him.

Euclid huffed, then pointed at the broken bowl and ordered, "Clean this mess and continue your duties." He went around the pool and met Vitus.

Vitus tore his attention from Thora and met Euclid's murderous features.

"You speak to me again, and I will run you through." Euclid left the courtyard and returned to his guests.

Thora contained a heated snarl after Euclid's vicious promise to Vitus, who had found a place in Thora's heart. Once Euclid was gone, she released a shaky breath and rubbed her brow.

Vitus approached her and touched her shoulder. "Are you okay?" His fingers curled against her and cooled her Alpha. His warm scent cleared her mind.

"Yes." Thora rubbed her brow and worked the knots from her temple. "Halcyon be anger." She had defied Euclid, and so had Vitus.

Vitus was quiet for a moment, then shrugged and asked, "Can you still work?"

"I must," Thora replied. She cleared her throat, hearing the roughness in her own voice. Like any Alpha, she rumbled often and growled on occasion, but it had been years since she last clashed against another Alpha.

"I will find Cesare or Glauce to clean this." Vitus pointed toward the gathering. "They need the cheese."

Thora nodded and went to the supply room first, hoping there was another bowl she could use for the cheese. Vitus had retrieved Glauce, who handled the mess in the courtyard. Thora thanked her on her way to the symposium. Glauce seemed prepared to ask what had happened, but Thora shook her head and continued to the party. Slipping into the large room, Thora placed the two bowls of cheese in their spots and checked that the wine containers were full.

Cesare was off to one side, watching everything from his quiet spot. A bard was telling a dramatic story about the gods. Cesare's attention was disrupted when Thora joined his side. Thora stayed close to him. He tilted his head toward her, and she sensed his rise of concern, but she shook her head.

"Thora," Cesare said in haste, eyes big.

"It fine," Thora assured and waved him off. She indicated the bard, hoping his tale would distract them both. Now that she understood Greek better, she enjoyed the story and could perhaps learn more about the Greeks and their religion.

Cesare let out a low but frustrated sigh and stared at her for another beat. After a grumble, he turned his attention toward the bard but shifted closer to Thora, as if he could protect her better than she had already protected herself. Still, she found she loved him for it.

CHAPTER 8
Halcyon

After a full month of training at the barracks, Halcyon was ready to return to her regular duty as King Leonidas's guard. The training was necessary and kept Halcyon at her best, but she lived to protect her ruler. Coming to her villa's stable, she halted Cheimon and dismounted beside the familiar stable, her armor clanking when her sandals hit the dirt. She wiped the sweat from her brow, but her body was boiling from the inside out. The hot weather over the past few days was tiresome. Once she had the reins, she guided Cheimon into the stable to a clean stall and enjoyed untacking and brushing her horse. Sunset was in a couple of hours, giving her enough time to settle back into her home.

The brief time alone with Cheimon gave her a chance to reflect on the past two fortnights at the barracks with her comrades. She was always torn between her two lives as a hoplite and as a guard for the king. With a heavy sigh, she shifted her mindset to her duties at home and her pending visit with Euclid before he returned to the barracks tomorrow. Near the end of her care, she smiled at the approaching and familiar footfall.

"Good afternoon, Cesare."

Bowing his head, Cesare had a smile and offered, "Welcome back, mistress." He admired Halcyon in her hoplite armor.

"You sound as if you missed me," Halcyon said with good nature.

Cesare chuckled and put his hands behind his back, which made his soft brown chiton sway. "We've been busy. The master is still here and waits for you."

"I'm unsurprised," Halcyon said. "And busy with what?" She stilled the brush over Cheimon's rump and glanced at Cesare. "I see work began on the kitchen as I instructed."

"Yes, mistress. They work every day. I believe they will finish soon." Cesare paused. "The master had a symposium last night while you were gone."

Halcyon's lips thinned at the news. "Strange, considering we have no kitchen."

Cesare bit his lower lip, then replied, "It didn't deter him."

"I see." After setting the brush in the wall rack, Halcyon patted the horse, then pointed at the saddlebags. Her hoplite helmet was lashed to one side of it. Cesare would take care of polishing it and her armor.

Cesare stepped forward and plucked the saddlebags from off the stall door. He took extra care with the helmet that was tied to the side.

"Did the symposium fare well?" Halcyon asked. It was uncommon for her mate to hold a political party, especially without her name behind it. Many in Sparta were well aware of Halcyon's wealth and prestige. Much of her fortunes were handed down to her from her sire, who was once an Athenian. He had moved his daughter, his ailing mate, and his fortunes to Sparta. In his late life, he taught Halcyon how to train slaves, run a house, and operate a business.

"We managed."

Halcyon nodded, then stepped out of the stall with the rest of the horse tack. She went to the end of the stable and hung up the tack, which would be cleaned later. She stood by the doorway. "How does Vitus fare?"

"He is well, mistress. He's currently at the market." Cesare followed her out of the stable. He carried the saddlebags, then took them to the master bedroom once in the villa.

Halcyon gazed about the courtyard after passing the open gate, finding everything much the same. However, she avoided the male's side of the house since Euclid was home and instead wandered toward the kitchen that was no longer a darkened, ashen mess but well on its way to being rebuilt. She toured the inside and was pleased by the progress the workers had made during her absence.

Halcyon's head snapped to the left after something was dropped on the other side of the villa. As she crossed the courtyard, she heard low curses in another tongue. She entered the supply room, which had been adjusted for a temporary kitchen. Little to her surprise, Thora was dealing with a broken clay jug.

"Let us not start another fire, shall we?"

Thora had her back to the supply room's entrance but whirled around with shards of clay in her hand. Thora's perturbed features were broken by a smile once she focused on Halcyon, who was still in full hoplite uniform.

"Welcome home, mistress."

Halcyon hesitated and studied her slave for a beat. "Thank you." She cleared her throat and pointed at the broken jug. "Are there any left?" She didn't expect to receive an answer.

Thora glanced at the clay fragments on the floor, holding up a large piece in her hand. "Six or eight."

Halcyon sighed. Her two female slaves, Thora and Glauce, could be clumsy at times. Glauce was far worse than Thora. "We will need to make more soon." Cesare was decent at making clay cups, and the oven in the supply room was designed for firing and hardening clay objects for the villa. But she was unsure whether Thora or Glauce were skilled with clay.

"Once kitchen done." Thora spoke as if she held the authority over the villa. Halcyon would have reminded a slave of their standing in life, but she felt no desire to do so with Thora. After setting the shards on the table, Thora indicated the bronze armor. "Your training good?" Even though her Greek had improved, she had developed a distinct accent.

"Yes." Halcyon was having a regular conversation with Thora for the first time thanks to Vitus's teachings. She was more impressed with Thora's Greek tongue than the kitchen's near completeness. "Have you been busy?" Halcyon moved closer to her slave, drawn in by their normal conversation.

"Yes." Thora leaned against the table, her hip on the edge.

"Cesare mentioned my mate had a symposium." Halcyon rested her hand on the sword's hilt. She always admired the blue of Thora's eyes and the gold of her hair. Many times at the barracks, Halcyon had looked at the sun in the clear sky and thought of Thora.

"Yes, went well."

"Did you manage without the kitchen?" Halcyon expected Thora to become confused by her words. However, Thora's Greek tongue was much stronger. The coin she was spending on Vitus's teaching was well worth it.

"Yes. It took more time."

Halcyon nodded, but she hesitated to ask more when the faint marks on Thora's neck caught her attention. She stepped into Thora's space and removed her hand from the hilt. Halcyon smelled Thora's tension, but she allowed Halcyon to look over her. Upon closer inspection, it was clear that the marks came from something being around her neck, such as a rope or fingers. The idea that someone could manage to put anything around Thora's neck seemed impossible. Thora may be a slave, but she was an Alpha first.

"What is this?"

Thora rumbled and narrowed her fiery blue eyes at Halcyon. "It is nothing."

"Ares's balls," Halcyon snapped, then took a step back. "You *will* tell me who touched you." The sudden stiffness in Thora's posture set off alarms in Halcyon's head. She was determined to find out the truth about what happened to Thora. With each passing beat, her Omega rallied harder in her chest. The idea that her Alpha slave was harmed incited her

Omega. On a hunch, she reached and pushed the chiton off Thora's shoulders. Once the chiton pooled on the floor, she was able to see the bruising over Thora's now bare side.

Thora clenched her hands, keeping her eyes straight forward. Her pheromones grew stronger, taunting Halcyon, who struggled to remain in control of herself. It was the first time that Halcyon had seen Thora without any clothes. Halcyon started to withdraw, but her gaze dropped and caught a brief glimpse of the patch of blond between Thora's thighs, which left Halcyon with a slight flush. She turned her back on her slave, giving Thora unspoken permission to dress. The humid air became thicker, causing Halcyon to sweat more.

"Tell me now why my mate touched you." Halcyon neared the temporary kitchen table and took stock of the prepped food. She peered over her shoulder toward her slave and warned, "Before he tells me."

Thora adjusted the sleeves of her attire. "He fought me about fire."

Halcyon gripped the edge of the table and growled low. "It was not your fault." She spun on her boots and returned a hand to her sword.

"He believe different." Thora hesitated and bit her bottom lip. "I want him attack me. Not Glauce." She brushed the front of her clothes, as if attempting to hide the slight arousal they were both aware of.

Halcyon narrowed her eyes and gripped the hilt harder. The kitchen fire was old business, and none of the slaves required punishment, especially Thora, who had saved Cesare. Glauce had caused the fire, by accident. Even though Halcyon had been blinded by her initial rage, she conceded to Thora rather than send Glauce back to Telamon. Unbeknownst to her, Telamon was more than a slave trader; he was a rapist too. It wasn't unheard of for slave owners to abuse their property, but to rape them was another matter. Many considered a pregnant slave useless. In Halcyon's opinion, Telamon deserved to be sent to Tartarus alongside all rapists.

Without another word, Halcyon marched out of the supply room and entered the courtyard. She called for Cesare, who appeared from the work room on the other side.

"I need you to draw a warm bath for me, and have Thora assist you." Halcyon started to the steps to go upstairs. "And I want Glauce to prepare the meal." From the corner of her eye, she spotted Thora emerging from the supply room and heading toward her, but Cesare stepped into Thora's path. Halcyon was grateful for Cesare's ability to understand her needs.

With quick movements, Halcyon climbed the steps to the second floor and went to the master bedroom. The drumming of her heart echoed in her ears with each step she took closer to the entrance of the bedroom. As she approached the doorway, Euclid's familiar moans caught her attention. Halcyon huffed at her mate's obvious activity, but it did nothing to slow her down.

Euclid was nude and seated upright in the middle of the bed. He was propped up against the wall, legs spread, and his cock in his fist. With his head back against the wall, he didn't hesitate when his mate entered the room.

Halcyon remained poised a few steps into the room and watched her mate finish himself off. She imagined he pictured his young lover, Tycho, who, like other youthful male Alphas, took on an older male Alpha. Halcyon was well aware of the tradition among the hoplites and had accepted Tycho's place in Euclid's life. Her and Euclid's time in bed was strictly for breeding purposes, even though every attempt was a failure.

With a few more strokes, Euclid was done and slouched against the wall, panting hard. He kept his eyes closed, but he seemed aware of Halcyon's presence. Opening one eye, he glanced at his mate and whispered, "You have returned."

"Yes." Halcyon studied the glisten of her mate's muscular body. In her youth, she had felt a measure of attraction toward him, but it became diluted over the years. Now she bred with him out of a sense of required duty for her people. Many gossiped about her inability to become pregnant. Halcyon despised the gossip as much as the idea of being pregnant. A pup would take her away from her position as the king's guard. The one saving grace was that she no longer had heats, which would ensure a pup.

"How was your monthly training at the barracks?" Euclid asked while he wiped himself clean with a towel nearby.

With a raise of her eyebrow, Halcyon replied, "It was satisfying." She sensed how her word choice piqued her mate's Alpha. He tossed the towel over his shoulder and scooted off the bed, giving Halcyon a full view of his semihard shaft. However, she was not interested in mating with him this time.

She flexed her grip on the sword hilt and said, "You attacked my slave."

Euclid donned a simple linen chiton that had been resting at the end of the bed. "I confronted her for destroying our kitchen."

Halcyon rumbled and straightened further as her mate approached her. He was taller and bulkier than her, even though she was well built for an Omega. "She has bruising on her throat."

Euclid grunted and studied Halcyon. "She's fortunate that is all that happened to her." With a sharp inhale, he started to rumble deep, then his eyes became blown and his pheromones thick in the room. "You are going into heat."

Halcyon's attention snapped, and her heart lurched inside her chest. How could it be possible that she was approaching a heat? Her last heat was at least ten years ago. She felt no loss when they ended and became more empowered by the change. The sheer idea that she was capable of having heats again was ludicrous. Even if it was true, there had to be a trigger rather than the gods playing a random joke on her. But a heat would explain her steady rise in body temperature and the developing itch under her skin. Her focus recentered on her mate, who latched onto her biceps.

"Come to bed with me," Euclid ordered and guided her forward. He smiled with raw hunger. Already his cock was hard and stood at attention between them. The depth of his pheromones had once enticed Halcyon years ago, but it did the reverse tonight.

Halcyon took a half step, then shook her head and held her position. Her Omega rebelled against the posturing of her Alpha mate, who wanted nothing more than to mount and breed her all night. Halcyon flexed her grip on her sword hilt and dared him to pressure her.

"It's been ages since you last went into a heat for me." Euclid canted his head and studied her with more regard than lust. "We should not squander our chance." For a beat, his words hit a thin chord with Halcyon's Omega.

However, Halcyon took a step back from him and raised her chin. Her Omega may have stirred under his touch, but she wasn't drawn to him. Her heat wasn't for him. "No." Halcyon's single word of rejection brought a dark wave across Euclid's features. Bristling, Halcyon prepared for an argument with him.

"Halcyon, if you are in heat, then…" Euclid faltered, and his attention lifted from his mate, going past her shoulder.

Without a single glance back, Halcyon was well aware of Thora's commanding presence behind her. A layer of tension receded from her shoulders when Thora took a towering position. She watched her mate's warring expression as he and Thora locked eyes on each other. They were Alphas battling over her, and the incoming tide of Thora's stronger pheromones caused Halcyon's Omega to swoon. She fisted her empty hand and regained a margin of control before she sought out Thora's touch that very moment.

As she gazed upon Euclid, she became aware of his inability to push back against Thora. Halcyon had assumed Thora lost that battle after seeing the bruising on her neck.

Now it appeared her assumption was wrong. Euclid broke his eye contact with Thora and took a side step around Halcyon but paused next to Halcyon's side.

"See that you drink the infertilis herb," Euclid ordered in a rough voice. Their eyes met for an instant, then he looked over at Thora before looking at his mate again. "You'd embarrass us both with a bastard pup." He ignored Thora's rising snarl and departed the room.

"Be silent," Halcyon commanded her slave, who bit back her growl. She reached for the collar of her bronze cuirass and tugged on it, finding its weight stifling now. Putting space between her and Thora, she approached a closed trunk that she stored her armor in. "Why are you here?"

Thora shifted on her feet and replied, "I came because bath ready."

Halcyon freed her sheathed sword and placed it on top of the trunk. Cesare would have announced that the bath was ready. It was the first time Thora had taken it upon herself to inform Halcyon. The change could be because Thora could speak in Greek better. Or it was because Thora's Alpha drew her upstairs to check on Halcyon. The idea that Thora's Alpha was protective over her sent a shock deep into her gut.

"I see." Halcyon had long ago removed her helmet, which Cesare took for polishing. For a beat, she stared at her weapon that rested on the trunk and considered her options. She could dismiss Thora and have Cesare help her out of her armor. However, Cesare was a Beta, and his pheromones were inferior against Euclid. Halcyon held a measure of concern that her mate would make more attempts to bend her over and breed her. Once the process started, she would be at the mercy of her heat's control over her mind.

Thora, on the other hand, was an Alpha and had outmatched Euclid's dominance.

Thora's movement toward the doorway drew Halcyon from her thoughts. She failed to realize how much time had passed since she last spoke aloud. "Stop." When Thora paused, Halcyon turned her head toward her slave, decision made. "I need assistance removing my armor."

"*Já*, mistress." Thora neared her owner, bringing along her attractive scent.

Halcyon clutched the collar of her armor after Thora reverted to her native tongue. Weeks ago, she realized how much she enjoyed hearing the language of Thora's people. The language was rugged but strong and beautiful. It was far different from Greek. In just the month she'd been gone, Thora's command over Greek had increased enough for them to communicate. Halcyon admired Thora's natural talent with learning a new language at such a fast pace. For a moment, Halcyon considered whether Thora rested her head on Vitus's scrolls and absorbed Greek overnight. She let out a low, amused huff.

Thora faltered a step away from her owner and studied Halcyon's profile. "You laugh."

Halcyon hardened her features before she met Thora's curious gaze. She opted to ignore the insightful remark and said, "First you have to loosen the straps here." She indicated her sides. "Then the ones on my shoulders."

Thora nodded and started with the leather strap on Halcyon's left side. She went slow, as if concerned she would damage the straps. Halcyon allowed her to learn. After Thora had loosened all four straps, she waited for the next instruction.

With a rumble, Halcyon ordered, "Next you can lift the plates off me." She assisted Thora and raised her arms when Thora hefted the armor without any effort. While Thora placed the armor on the trunk, Halcyon propped up a booted foot on the trunk and leaned forward to undo the strapping for the greave.

"I do." Thora pushed her owner's hand away, knelt, and worked the two straps free.

Halcyon swallowed against the dryness in her throat while she watched her slave kneel for her. Thora placed the first greave onto the trunk and waited for Halcyon to offer her other leg. With her left leg now propped against the trunk, she again admired Thora below her. Every tiny bit of Thora's wonderful, warm Alpha pheromones drifted under Halcyon's nose. Thora's scent held a protective note that had never been there in the past. Halcyon's Omega wanted to submerge in it, breathe and live in it. But Halcyon grappled with her natural instincts that were invoked by her strange heat. She cleared her throat when Thora stood.

"What next?"

Narrowing her eyes, Halcyon read the tension lines that had formed across Thora's brow. Her Alpha slave seemed to be in a similar predicament with her self-control. At least Halcyon wasn't the only one suffering this evening. "I will bathe." She faced Thora and stepped in closer, but she was forced to tilt her head back. "You forced my mate to submit to you."

Thora's breathing grew a bit more irregular, but she remained still and quiet. The blueness of her eyes was replaced little by little with the raw intent of an Alpha. It brought a measure of comfort to Halcyon's earlier concerns about Euclid, Thora, and her developing heat.

But did this mean Thora would go into a rut? The unexpected thought sent a thrill through Halcyon's entire being. She grappled with her emerging Omega rather than tumble into a heat-induced state of mind.

Halcyon grinned at her slave's lack of response. "Telamon's remark about you being a problem makes more sense now if you're capable of forcing others to submit." She canted her head and asked, "How did you learn to make other Alphas submit to you?" Upon Thora's continued silence, she leaned in and used her honey-like pheromones to tantalize Thora. "Were you a warrior once? Tell me."

Thora rumbled, deep and heavy. A bead of sweat had formed on the right side of her brow, then her jaw loosened. "*Já*," she whispered in a rough voice. Now that they could speak better, Halcyon wished to ask every question she had saved in the back of her mind. However, it would have to wait until after Halcyon's heat passed.

"Until you were captured," Halcyon whispered and frowned at the possible events that played out in her imagination. Thora's silence returned, so Halcyon allowed her to have it, for now. She took a step back and ordered, "You'll stay close by me for the rest of the night."

"Yes, mistress."

Halcyon pursed her lips and continued to breath in Thora's scent that soothed the uneasiness of her Omega. "Do you understand why?"

"Yes." Thora flexed her jaw a few times, and the hardness in her features amplified. "Euclid not harm you."

Somehow Halcyon placed a hand on Thora's stomach. But she was unsure whether it was out of instinct or by accident. The heat that radiated from Thora's body was tempting Halcyon. "Do not speak his name," she ordered but without any bite. If her mate heard a slave use his name, then Halcyon would have a losing fight on her hands.

After a sigh, Thora nodded and said, "Sorry, mistress."

Halcyon held her slave's gaze, then stepped around her and said, "Come." She led the way from the bedroom and back downstairs to the small bathing chamber next door to the supply room. Glauce was busy preparing a meal for them all, but it was the floral scent from the bath that called to her. She entered the bathing room and saw Cesare pour another bucket of hot water.

"Mistress," Cesare greeted and neared them by the open doors. "What else do you require?" He glanced at Thora, who stood behind Halcyon.

"Can you retrieve a fresh chiton for me?"

"Of course." Cesare left the bucket with the stack of other ones. He went around his owner and Thora. Halcyon disrobed from her dirty tunic, then descended the stone steps into the small bath that was large enough for three or four people. She moaned as the warm water soothed her tense, strained muscles. Slowly, the lilac scent eased her mind.

Collecting Halcyon's favorite soap, Thora sat beside the edge of the bath, next to her owner, and placed the soap on top of the drying linen. She had assisted Halcyon a few other times, but today's bath carried a new undertone to it. Halcyon's scent was headier, and Thora's own attempted to match hers.

"Your Greek has improved," Halcyon said. She closed her eyes and leaned her head against the stone wall of the bath, near Thora. A moment later she heard Cesare drop off the chiton for her.

"Yes. Thank you." Thora fell silent and caused Halcyon to open her eyes. Thora released a soft thrum that sung to Halcyon's Omega. "Vitus wishes I learn read and write."

Halcyon twisted her head and peered up at Thora. It was unheard of that a slave could read, much less write. "Has he taught you how?" She had yet to see Vitus, but she suspected he was heeding her advice about keeping his interactions with Euclid to a minimum.

Thora shook her head. "No." She toyed with the hem of her chiton. "He not tell teach me." There was a subtle weakness in her response that prompted Halcyon's interest. It was plausible that Vitus had already started to teach reading and writing to Thora. If her slave was so apt with learning the verbal parts of Greek, then she may be as speedy with the other parts.

"Do you wish to learn?" Halcyon posed. She had been schooled at a young age on how to read and write. Rarely did females learn such skills, but Halcyon's sire had deemed it necessary after his mate passed away so early and was unable to produce anymore pups. Halcyon stood to inherit her sire's fortune, and the skills behooved her. Furthermore, Sparta encouraged a female's education.

Thora gave a low nod. "*Já.*"

Halcyon turned her gaze away, hiding her smile at Thora's habit to switch between Norsk and Greek tongue. Gradually, the smile fell away as she thought about the request. In truth, if Thora could read and write, it would integrate her further into Spartan society. "Then, if that is what you wish, Vitus shall teach you."

Thora jerked her head up and stared in awe at her owner. "Thank you."

"*Ekki at þakka,*" Halcyon replied in Thora's native tongue.

Thora revealed a wistful smile at Halcyon's attempt to use her language. After a pleased rumble, she reached for the soap and held it out to Halcyon.

Opening her eyes, Halcyon sniffed the soap's distinct scent and took it. She lathered her body, then returned the soap to Thora's larger hand.

Thora wet her hands and waited until Halcyon was seated in the bath again. It took nearly two months after Halcyon purchased her for them to garner enough trust that Halcyon allowed Thora to clean her hair. Halcyon put her head underwater for a moment and came up again, then long fingers worked the soap through her black tresses.

As an Omega, Halcyon kept short hair that reached her shoulders, signifying her mated status. Unmated Omegas kept their hair longer, not cutting it to their shoulders or chin until they were bound in a union with a mate.

Halcyon moaned when Thora hit a strained muscle at her neck. She had pulled it during her time at the barracks. She was surprised when Thora massaged the aching muscle and bent her head forward for better access. Nobody had paid attention to her body's needs in the past.

Thora withdrew her hand and remarked, "You tired from gone."

Halcyon knew that Thora meant her training at the barracks. "It's my duty." She sank under the water and rinsed the soap from her hair.

Thora stood up with the soap and returned it to the wooden shelf on the wall, placing it in the proper spot beside the other two soaps. She looked at Halcyon, who climbed the steps out of the bath. Thora retrieved the linen and approached with it.

Halcyon was offered the linen, but for the first time, she pushed it back into Thora's hands. "You." She was too tired to do the work herself, and she could admit to herself the desire to have Thora touch her, even if it was through a towel.

Releasing a low breath, Thora nodded and unfolded the linen, then proceeded to dry Halcyon. She was slow, methodical, and attentive as she cared for Halcyon's muscular body. At times, she seemed to pause and study a spot on Halcyon. Perhaps it was the scars that caught Thora's attention.

Halcyon opened her eyes after Thora finished drying her body and her hair. Thora collected the clean chiton and helped Halcyon into it. Last, they put on the girdle around her waist.

"*Þakka fyrir,*" Halcyon murmured.

Thora smiled at the gratitude and nodded. "*Ekki at þakka.*"

Halcyon was a few hands shorter than Thora. She found it suitable, as she had to gaze up at the blue sky, much like she did into Thora's eyes. Eventually, her attention was drawn down to Thora's discolored neck. Again, she touched the angry skin, then a low growl broke free from the back of her throat. She yanked her hand away and frowned at her natural, volatile response toward the pain inflicted upon her slave.

After picturing the possible fight between Thora and Euclid, a slow burn churned in Halcyon's stomach and climbed into her chest. She took personal offense to the fact that her mate damaged her slave, especially when Thora was innocent of the kitchen fire. To add to it, Halcyon viewed Thora as her slave, solely. She ruled the finances and property in their union.

Thora saw Halcyon's bitter expression and collected the smaller hand into hers. "It done," she said, attempting to close the door on the past.

Halcyon sighed and freed her hand. Thora was right that the incident between Thora and Euclid was over. But for Halcyon, it was fresh and required time to cool her temper. She moved toward the door. "Come." Tonight would be long and trying, especially for Halcyon. At first light, her mate would leave for the barracks, and this evening's dinner was her only social event with him.

Heeding the command, Thora carried the damp linen and the dirty tunic; both needed to be cleaned now. Halcyon stepped out of the bathing room and into the courtyard. She cast a glance over her shoulder at Thora, who canted her head in silent request. Halcyon indicated the items in Thora's arms. "Join me in the suite after you are finished."

Thora dipped her head, then promised, "I quick."

Halcyon smirked and said, "Good Alpha." She savored the pretty blush on Thora's cheeks, then left.

CHAPTER 9
Halcyon

Halcyon remained sprawled out on the long chair in the mistress's suite located on the second floor. Now that she had a moment to relax, she sensed the onset of her approaching heat. The earlier bath had done little to ease her increasing body temperature. Perhaps she should have taken a cold bath rather than a warm one. Glancing at the open window, she noted the late afternoon sunlight, which meant dinner would be served soon. Halcyon preferred Thora's cooking over Glauce's, but her nearing heat would curb her appetite for food. In the coming hours, she would hunger for sex and a worthy Alpha's knot. By nature, an Omega would try to select an ideal Alpha and fine-tune their pheromones to call to that perfect Alpha, who would answer by going into a rut for her.

Halcyon denied her Omega from making such an attempt.

With a groan, she covered her face, which had a thin sheen of sweat already. Her last heat was long enough ago that she was unsure of when. Halcyon considered why her heat had resurfaced. She told herself there was no logical trigger for her to have one after all this time. A firm but familiar knock at the door coaxed her out of her thoughts. Opening her eyes, Halcyon laid her gaze upon Thora—her trigger. Her Omega confirmed it with a broken mewl that was half strangled, half calling out.

Thora paused a few steps from her owner's chair. She swallowed hard enough for her throat to bob, then she took a deep breath. With stiff shoulders, she closed the gap between them and said, "You must drink."

Halcyon bit her bottom lip when Thora knelt in front of her and offered a full cup of water. Indeed her mouth was parched and the crystal clear liquid was a welcomed sight, almost as much as Thora herself. She accepted the water and drained the clay cup. After she returned it to Thora, she managed to speak. "Sit." She pushed up higher against the back of the chair and scooted to the edge, providing room for Thora.

At first Thora hesitated, but she placed the cup on the small table next to them and then took a seat. She covered her lap with both hands. Was Thora trying to conceal a possible erection? Halcyon banished the idea because she refused to let her heat trigger an Alpha into a rut.

Halcyon dragged her fingers through her hair and considered what they needed to discuss. "You are aware that I am going into a heat."

"*Já.*" Thora curled her fingers together. When she first entered the suite, her scent had been light, but it developed a depth that called to Halcyon's Omega. "You not mate with master." Thora's Greek was imperfect, but it was much improved and easier for them to talk.

"No." Halcyon glanced toward the window and studied the trees located behind the villa. After a sigh, she focused on Thora and said, "He may make another attempt."

"I stop him." Thora fisted one of her hands, then cleared her throat. "If you desire."

Halcyon warded off a jolt of excitement after Thora used the word "desire." She clenched her bottom lip between her teeth but forced herself to relax. "Yes, I wish for you to stay close. He seems leery of you."

"Leery?" Thora tilted her head, revealing the curious spark in her eyes.

"Cautious," Halcyon replied but the new word was still foreign to Thora. "A little scared." The simpler definition seemed to help, and Thora nodded. Halcyon's Omega wanted to ask Thora to protect her. However, Halcyon scoffed at the weakness and strangled down the request before it was too late. She was a hoplite and an elite bodyguard to one of the kings. She refused to ask anyone for protection much less her slave.

"I stay near," Thora promised with a rumble that sent a shiver racing down Halcyon's spine.

"He will leave at first light," Halcyon further explained. "I will rest in here tonight." She would lock the door behind her to ensure that Euclid couldn't sneak in and breed her. A few drops of guilt roiled in her belly, but she smothered it. Even though they were in a union, there was no legal requirement that she breed with him. It was an expectation, and like all such social contracts, Halcyon snubbed it. "You must sleep with your door open tonight and one ear listening."

Thora dipped her head in agreement. "Yes, mistress." She and Halcyon both looked toward the closed door of the suite when someone rapped on it. Thora rose and faced the newcomer, who was Glauce.

"Dinner is ready to be served." With a curious expression, Glauce looked between Halcyon and Thora. "Do you wish to eat in here, mistress?"

"No, I will join my mate in the courtyard." Halcyon swung her legs off the side of the long chair. "You and Cesare will have to serve us dinner. I will be there in a moment." She stood as Glauce murmured her agreement and left. Halcyon found cool blue eyes regarding her again. "You will stay in the courtyard with me."

"Yes, mistress." Thora straightened her back and waited for Halcyon to lead the way. She followed a few paces behind and went down to the courtyard.

Halcyon sat in her usual spot and waited for Euclid's arrival. She glanced to her left and admired Thora standing watch over her. For a beat, she preened like a lovestruck pup until she regained control of her Omega. A soft curse drifted under her breath.

"Hello, my mate." Euclid had come from the open gates of the villa. He was perhaps out at the stable after taking a short horseback ride. He took the other seat and remarked, "Your tutor for the barbar returned."

"Vitus," Halcyon supplied. She suspected he would take his meal in his room rather than interact with them. Once Euclid was gone, everyone would be more at ease. Well, except for the minor problem with Halcyon's heat. Searching her memory, she tried to pinpoint how many days her last heat lasted, but it was fuzzy. At best, it would be two days, then she could return to her normal routine.

Huffing low, Euclid became situated in his chair and commented, "It seems like a waste of coin to teach her to speak our tongue." He pointed in Thora's direction. "How long has it been? She barely speaks Greek and not well."

Halcyon stole a glance at her slave, who was fighting the curl of her lip. Thora understood every word Euclid spoke and his condescending tone. Halcyon cooled her own initial reaction and offered Euclid a smile. "Well, it's my coin after all." She leaned to one side when Cesare arrived with the initial plates of food. "I can squander it as I see fit." Her harsh retort won the verbal spar, silencing Euclid for the moment.

Glauce placed filled cups of diluted wine on the table and left a small pitcher. She backed up behind Cesare, who was taking the lead.

"Anything else?" Cesare looked between his owners, but his question settled on Halcyon's shoulders.

"No, Cesare."

Cesare shifted on his feet and placed his hands behind his back. "There is also a sweet bread with honey and fruit for after. Thora made it." He canted his head and waited for Halcyon's decision about the dessert. Halcyon was known for steering away from treats, but unlike the other slaves, Cesare was aware of Halcyon's weakness for sweet foods. "She made it to celebrate your return home."

Halcyon bit the inside of her mouth after swallowing down a bite of fish. For over a fortnight she had craved fish, but it was never offered at the barracks. It was much too expensive, especially to feed ravenous hoplites who wouldn't appreciate quality food. With a slight upturn of her lips, she gave in to her early heat-induced desire and replied, "Yes, please prepare it." From the corner of her eye, she caught Thora's chest rise. Damn Alphas and their egos. Halcyon wondered whether Thora had learned about her sweet tooth.

"Yes, mistress." Cesare hurried off with Glauce in tow.

Euclid had a slight frown, but he said nothing and ate his meal.

"The Carnea Festival begins in a day's time," Halcyon spoke up, attempting to redirect her mate's attention.

"Yes." Euclid had a more pleased look. The festival was one of his favorites for as long as Halcyon had known him. "Will you have time to join in the festivities?"

"I'll be on duty for much of it," Halcyon replied. She took a handful of olives from the bowl and placed them on her plate. "The movements of the Persian army are a concern." The topic seemed to capture Euclid's full attention. Over the entire meal, they discussed King Xerxes of Persia and his army, which had crossed into Greece back in the spring and marched southward. Everyone smelled war and blood in the air.

Thora remained silent but at attention, as if she were a guard herself. Several times Halcyon stole glances at her Alpha slave. In that moment, she realized that Thora had once indeed been a warrior and trained at some point in her life. There were certain stances, expressions, and subtle movements that soldiers tended to learn. Thora would have blended in with any Spartan hoplite, if not for her height and light hair.

"Have you changed your mind about mating?" Euclid asked when Glauce brought the sliced bread.

Glauce revealed rosy cheeks after Euclid spoke. She scampered off when Halcyon dismissed her.

"No." Halcyon owed him no explanation. She took a piece of the bread, smelling it. The fruity scent made her mouth water. Pieces of cherry stood out against the bread itself.

Euclid was undeterred for the moment and leaned against the table, closer to Halcyon. "Then you will let that barbar knot you."

Halcyon had taken a bite from the bread. She placed the piece onto her plate and eyed her mate while she chewed on the mouthful. He was jealous but also outmatched by Thora, who was a barbarian among the eyes of Greek society. In her homelands, Thora had perhaps been far more respected both as a person and a warrior. Even so, Thora's path in life was different now; a slave was at the bottom. A barbaric slave was even a notch below a Greek-born slave.

"No," Halcyon declared with finality. The power of her voice caused Thora to shift. "None will knot me." For Thora to knot her, she needed to go into a rut and grow a cock. Halcyon's heat scent might be calling to Alphas, but it required a special note in it to trigger a specific Alpha's rut. Halcyon believed she had full control of her Omega nature, keeping herself from triggering Euclid or Thora.

Euclid rumbled low. "You forget that it's my right to—"

"Mount me? I think not." Halcyon rose from the seat, abandoning her dessert. "We are Spartans, not barbarians." She flinched at what sting her words might bring to Thora.

Euclid stood, attempting to tower over her. His pheromones unfurled and slithered toward Halcyon. They were pungent and heavy, like chains wrapping around her. "Yes, and we have a duty to continue our people's legacy."

"Do not speak to me about duty," Halcyon snapped and fisted her hands. The increase of her voice prompted Thora to act. Halcyon felt Thora's Alpha pheromones rise like a tidal wave and push back against Euclid's own. Halcyon inhaled her slave's superior scent that was undeniable and heavy but warm too. Every tendril of Thora's pheromones poured into Halcyon, making it easier for her to breathe after choking on Euclid's scent. With a clearer mind, she fired off another warning to her mate.

"I may have pledged my life and body to Sparta, but I have not pledged my womb." Halcyon took a step closer, rounding the table. "And I certainly never pledged my body to *you*." Euclid would press her to mate, and she held her silence in the past. Not tonight, not when she was going into a heat that would mean pregnancy. This time she refused to bend. She was not like the rest of the Spartan females or Omegas. Halcyon was a hoplite and the Iron Edge.

Euclid showed off his teeth, but he retreated from his initial assault and looked at Thora.

Halcyon turned her head to the side and caught Thora's calm features. But in her blue eyes, a storm brewed and threatened Euclid. Thora took a step closer, yet remained positioned behind Halcyon. Her slight movement was enough to push Euclid back again. Halcyon returned her attention to her mate, amazed by his submission. Everything made sense to her now. Thora was a superior Alpha, who could outmatch and control other Alphas with her pheromones. Halcyon had heard of such powerful Alphas, but they were far more rare than even female Alphas themselves.

With a low huff, Euclid took a step to his right and said, "When you come to your senses, I will be waiting in our bed." He started around them, as if an invisible wall blocked him from Halcyon. He retreated to the upstairs in the last bit of sunlight.

Halcyon released a low breath while her shoulders fell.

"You okay?" Thora asked, remaining motionless but with concern written across her face.

"Yes." Halcyon faced her slave. She searched Thora's eyes, which had softened compared to earlier. "Thank you."

Thora bowed her head and peered over her shoulder toward the upper level of the villa. "He displeased." She looked at Halcyon again. "Like a cat who had their tail stepped on."

Halcyon snorted low at the joke and smiled when Thora beamed at her. "I agree." She found herself leaning into Thora's space, breathing in her wonderful scent. Shaking her head, she moved away and said, "I'll retire to the mistress's room." Not waiting for a response, Halcyon left the courtyard and headed upstairs, but not to the master bedroom. She returned to the suite reserved for her and other females. Once inside, she bolted the door to ensure no one could join her without permission, especially Euclid.

* * *

A strong knock at the door stirred Halcyon from her light sleep. She groaned from the elevated heat in her belly that she could do little about. Swinging her legs off the long chair, she stood and grumbled at the soreness in her body. The chair was fine for a few hours, but too hard for any meaningful rest. Once the heat fully manifested itself, she would fail to have any sleep. Another bang encouraged her to hurry across the moonlit suite.

She yanked open the door after unbolting it. "What?" she barked, until the tantalizing Alpha pheromones washed over her. "Thora," she breathed out in a husky voice. "It's late." Her attempt to glare was weakened by Thora's rather inviting presence.

"I sorry, mistress. I bring supplies for tonight." Thora indicated the items in her arms and hands.

Halcyon studied the various things, which included blankets, full waterskins, a linen, and a bowl of grapes. At first the blankets seemed ludicrous considering the sweat that coated her from head to toe. It was also late summer. Then her inner Omega reminded her that the blankets weren't for warmth but rather for nesting. As her heat strengthened, she would feel the natural urge to build a safe place for breeding. Many Alphas would overlook the importance of allowing an Omega to prepare a special space.

Thora was different.

Halcyon strangled her inner Omega's desire to whine at her Alpha slave's thoughtfulness. She instead forced herself to step aside. All of the items were important and necessary for the next day or two. Thora took the invite and placed the blankets on the long chair. The bowl of grapes went on the side table, while the water skins were slung over the back of the chair.

Thora returned to her owner's side and asked, "Chamber pot bring?"

Halcyon crinkled her nose at the idea of having one of the pots in the room with her. Her villa was set up with a specific room for the chamber pot. "No." She glanced at the open door and said, "I will relieve myself now." She would be fine until first light, after Euclid left.

Thora nodded and followed her owner out of the suite. Halcyon decided against ordering Thora to leave her. The unconditional protection created a wonderful hum inside Halcyon. Thora waited outside the chamber-pot room until Halcyon was done, then escorted her back to the suite.

"Inform me when Euclid leaves," Halcyon ordered after she entered the room. Then her eyes roamed all over Thora's tall figure. Even in the overhead moonlight, she caught sight of Thora's mild erection that she was hiding with her hands in front of her. Thora's growing cock was due to Halcyon's heat. The wonderful idea that she had triggered Thora's rut almost elicited a moan from Halcyon. To have a superior and gorgeous Alpha rut for her elated her Omega. She pictured Thora pleasing herself later tonight with Glauce asleep next to her.

"Yes." Thora took a step back and dipped her head. "Goodnight, mistress."

Halcyon grunted and forced herself to close the door despite her Omega's yearning for an Alpha tonight. "Goodnight." She sealed the door and bolted it, then pressed her back into it. She slouched heavy against the cool wooden door. Halcyon was determined to outmaneuver her heat, which wanted her to throw herself at Thora. Even with brewing a cup or two of the infertilis herb, the risk of pregnancy was possible. The safest option was to remain locked in the room until the heat ended.

Returning to the long chair, she studied the items that Thora had brought her. She smiled at her slave's consideration, then berated herself for being too soft. Looking at the small table, she spotted a piece of cloth with something wrapped inside it. Too curious, Halcyon unfolded the item and rumbled at the slices of cherry bread. "Damn that Alpha," she muttered under her breath, then bit into a piece. How could an Alpha, like Thora, be sweet and thoughtful?

One slice of bread was gone in a few bites. Halcyon grumbled at the thought of the restless night ahead of her while glaring at the long chair. It was a tight space even for someone of her smaller stature. She glanced across the room and decided to use a second chair. With ease, she managed to bring over another long chair and set them together to create more room. Then without consideration, she started to arrange the blankets in an inviting manner. After it was perfect, she crawled onto the long chairs and curled up in the middle of the blankets, which carried a mild scent of Thora. For a brief period, she rested well and at ease, until the heat took over.

The heat's pain began in the predawn hour, pulling Halcyon away from her sleep. She cursed at her misfortune and glared at the open window that allowed a soft breeze to come through. The slightest bit of sunlight penetrated the dark horizon beyond the villa.

After rising from her curled position, Halcyon used the linen to wipe clean the sweat from her face. She forced herself to drink from the waterskins, but a glance at the food triggered nausea. Slouching against the back of a long chair, she groaned and clutched her stomach, which twisted with lancing pain. For a beat, it settled and instead the throb between her legs became apparent. Halcyon rubbed her thighs together and bit her lip when slick coated the outside of her pussy.

"Fuck." Even though her last heat was long ago, Halcyon was well aware of the process and what she would have to do survive the next day or two. Without wasting time, she hiked up her chiton to her waist, propped up a leg, and inserted two fingers inside herself. Groaning, she moved her fingers a little and savored the wonderful burst of excitement in her gut. She hooked her right arm across the back of the chair and widened her legs for better access. Halcyon pumped her fingers in and out, causing slick to smear all over her pussy and thighs. She clawed the chair behind her head and rolled her hips against her hand.

Halcyon arched her head back and moaned. Her heat-riddled mind created a perfect fantasy of Thora and herself. Her gorgeous, blond Alpha slave was gentle and sweet on the exterior, but Halcyon could smell the fire hidden under the layers. She pictured Thora in charge, wrestling control away from Halcyon, who would fight and surrender. Thora would bend her over the back of the long chair and play with Halcyon's clitoris. Unable to last, Halcyon would beg to be fucked, to be knotted, and to be bred like a good Omega. Then when it ended, Thora would take her again and again, and again.

Biting back a cry, Halcyon jerked against the chair and drove her fingers in one last time, as deep as possible. It was barely enough to tip her over, but the climax washed over her. For an instant, she enjoyed the satisfaction and the brief peace from the heat's pain. She was aware that it was a respite and that the heat symptoms would overwhelm her again. At least she could function long enough to handle a few chores.

A firm knock at the door caused a breath to hitch in her throat. But it was locked, and whichever slave was at the door would never barge in. Halcyon stood and straightened her chiton, then she crossed the distance. Before she even opened the door, she inhaled Thora's alluring scent, which brought a terrible ache to her stomach. She swore at her weakened state but squared her shoulders and forbid herself to fall into Thora's arms, or onto her cock.

Cracking the door open, Halcyon took in her slave's candlelit features and asked, "What is it?"

"Euclid gone," Thora replied. Her nostrils flared while the blue in her eyes shrunk. However, she kept her distance and pheromones under control. "You eat?"

Halcyon curled her fingers against the open door and swallowed hard. "No." She suspected the scent of her heat and slick affected Thora, who started to rumble. "I need to wash up." She left the suite's door open so fresh air could clear it out.

Without hesitation, Thora shadowed Halcyon across the open-air walkway to the other side of the second floor. Similar to last night, she remained outside the chamber-pot room, then followed Halcyon to the master bedroom.

With a deep inhale, Halcyon drew in her mate's harsh scent, which struck her harder than a racing chariot. It would be impossible for her to stay in the master bedroom for long with his scent all over. Her distressed whined prompted Thora to ease closer to her. Clearing her throat, Halcyon warned Thora with a slight glare. "I'm fine." She willed her voice to remain neutral, but it was hard with Thora close to her. It would be safer if she ordered Thora to leave; however, her Omega overrode her better senses.

Halcyon needed Thora near her.

After a swallow, Halcyon went over to the washbasin and poured fresh water from the pitcher into the bowl. From the droplets around the table, it was obvious that Euclid had used it moments before her. The cool water eased the burning in her face.

Thora remained a few steps inside the room, waiting for Halcyon. By the time Halcyon returned to her, Thora's forehead had a sheen of sweat, and she cupped her hands in front of herself. Without needing to look or ask, Halcyon already smelled Thora's arousal. Before she could say anything, Cesare entered the master bedroom.

"Mistress," Cesare greeted in a warm tone.

Unprovoked, Thora growled low in Cesare's direction.

"Thora," Halcyon warned her, ending Thora's posturing Alpha display. A hint of Thora's distress clung to the air and cooled Halcyon's own reaction. She had a scowl, but her Omega was lathering in Thora's protective reaction.

"Sorry, Cesare." Thora fidgeted with her chiton while keeping one hand in front of her possible erection.

Cesare shifted from foot to foot and looked between the pair until he settled on Halcyon. "I merely came by to check on you. Is there anything I can do?"

"I will remain alone," Halcyon replied. "Perhaps tomorrow I'll be in a better state." She pursed her lips and ordered, "Continue the normal chores. I won't require any meals." Her attention jumped to Thora, who huffed low. "I have no appetite."

Thora remained quiet, but her displeasure reflected in her eyes.

Again, Cesare glanced between them, then cleared his throat. "Shall we check on you?"

"Yes, but send Glauce." Halcyon tensed from Thora's throaty sound and looked at her slave. "You understand why."

Thora met Halcyon's gaze before she lowered her eyes to the floor. Tension lines formed along her jaw.

Cesare gave an audible swallow before he dared to step into the conversation. "Perhaps it would be best if Thora worked in the stables today." He flinched when Thora raised her burning blue eyes to him.

Halcyon rubbed her brow, which was damp with perspiration again. She was running out of time. With a sigh, she looked up at her frowning slave. "Thora, Cesare makes a wise sug—"

"I sleep there too?" Thora snapped at her owner, then she looked away and shook her head.

Halcyon took a deep breath and curbed her mixed emotions that surged in reaction. On one hand, she wanted to reprimand Thora as a slave. But then her Omega ached to comfort her Alpha slave, who was responding to the heat pheromones in the air. "No. You will sleep in your room." She tilted her head in hopes to get Thora's attention. "You are well aware what my heat is doing to you. It will become worse before it's better."

"The fresh air will help," Cesare added in a hopeful tone.

"Fresh air is horseshit," Thora bit back, then huffed and took a deep breath.

"I see you've learned a cuss word too." Halcyon dragged her fingers through her dark hair and noticed the slight ache in her gut. "I must go." She looked to Thora and said, "Stables today." She turned to Cesare. "Manage the villa and Glauce."

"Of course, mistress." Cesare hurried off, as if escaping with his life.

Halcyon departed the master bedroom with Thora behind her. She paused in front of the steps that went to the ground floor. Thora would go down while Halcyon would return to the mistress's suite.

"I check on you," Thora said in a tight voice.

Halcyon fisted her hands and sensed a slight tremble in her whole body. "No."

"I punished no reason," Thora snapped.

Gritting her teeth, Halcyon struggled to hold on to her control, but she was close to cracking open. "Why must you be so damn stubborn on a day like today?" She bared her teeth at Thora, allowing the growing pain in her belly to spark her temper. "You don't have to clean the stalls. Find other work to do out at the stables."

Thora's defensive nature fell away, then she shook her head and took a step back, closer to the stairs. "Yes, mistress." She pivoted and descended the steps in a hurry. Her abrupt departure stole away her wonderful Alpha scent.

Whimpering, Halcyon bent over and clutched her stomach. "By the gods." She took a few deep breaths before she urged herself toward the suite. In the past, the heats were difficult but not to such a level as this one. If she managed to survive this heat, she would pray to Hera and thank her.

* * *

On the third day of her heat, Halcyon was uncertain about her fate or why the gods were being cruel to her. Any meaningful sleep had eluded her over the long days. She remained locked away in the suite, unwilling to emerge until her heat was done. In the past, her heat would last twenty-four hours, and once or twice she recalled it went a second day. However, the continued pain, raised body temperature, and burn under her skin crept into a third day. The heat was unrelenting and started to drive Halcyon closer to madness.

Long ago, she had torn off her clothes in hopes it would give her a measure of reprieve from the burning across her body. She had lost count how many times she attempted to dispel the pain in her gut by pleasing herself. Between the soreness of her wrist and the uselessness, Halcyon had given up and remained curled in the nest of blankets she made days ago.

At some point, someone tapped on the door. Glauce's delicate scent caressed Halcyon's nose, but she ignored her slave, who neared her. She remained balled up on the chairs, panting and sweating from her heat. Glauce spoke to her, and Halcyon attempted to respond, but her throat was tight and dry. Glauce darted off, sandals slapping and echoing in the room. The door groaned, then the sunlight was cut off.

CHAPTER 10

Halcyon

Halcyon's entire body jerked when the suite's door flung open and hit the wall behind it. The thunder was enough to slice through her heat-riddled brain. She raised her head from the safety of the nest and attempted to focus on the tall shadow coming toward her. The distinct and strong scent of an Alpha drifted under her nose. The smell was warm and inviting, calling to her Omega like nothing else could on this Earth. Halcyon worked her aching throat when the Alpha came into her view. "Thor…"

Thora stood by the chairs, eyes scanning over Halcyon. A mild yet harsh note entered her scent and brought out a whine from Halcyon. Thora rumbled, then bent down and whispered, "Come." She remained on the edge of Halcyon's nest, respecting the security it brought to Halcyon. Her blue eyes were bright in the sunlight from the nearby window.

Halcyon raised her body with her weakened arms. She groaned but pushed herself forward, crawling toward Thora. She crossed the border of the nest and neared Thora's waiting hands. The pain in her belly flared up, causing her to hesitate and clutch her stomach.

"I touch you?" Thora waited for permission and released a sigh when Halcyon nodded. She leaned closer and scooped up Halcyon from the chairs. Straightening, she lifted

Halcyon with her until they were upright. She maneuvered Halcyon until their fronts were pressed together. Without thought, Halcyon hooked her legs around her slave's waist. The amount of sweat coating her body caused Halcyon to slide through Thora's grip.

"Hold me," Thora ordered while she placed an arm under Halcyon's butt.

Halcyon encircled Thora's shoulders and clung to her. She was secured in Thora's arms and now enclosed by warm Alpha pheromones. They left the suite and came outside onto the walkway that wrapped around the second floor of the villa. The fresh air was a relief, but it did nothing to hide Thora's Alpha scent. Halcyon turned her head into Thora's neck and nuzzled in, closer to the location of Thora's scent gland. The strength of Thora's pheromones filled Halcyon, easing her pain to a bearable amount. But then the soft throb between her legs became more apparent.

Thora rumbled low while she walked around the second level. She descended the steps, but Halcyon ignored everything around them. Nothing else was more interesting than Thora's scent, soft skin, and sure hold. When they came to a brief pause, Halcyon withdrew her face from Thora's neck and blinked in an attempt to focus even a little. Before she could, they were descending again and somehow, then, cool water traveled up her body.

Gasping, Halcyon buried her nails into Thora's skin at the edge of the chiton's material. Thora hissed, but her grip around Halcyon remained constant. Then they were submerged inside the villa's bathing pool. Thora crossed the pool and sat on a stone seat, keeping them submerged to their necks.

The cool water was delightful against Halcyon's flushed skin. She was able to take deeper breaths, no longer panting like a dying animal. Moaning, she loosened her grip and slumped against her slave. The floral scent of the water mixed with Thora's tender Alpha smell and lulled Halcyon to sleep. She was unsure how long she slept for, but Thora's gentle movements brought her back.

Thora let out a soft grunt and moved again. The stone seat and wall of the bath were anything but comfortable. However, she had allowed Halcyon to sleep on her lap and in her arms.

"Thoruh," Halcyon rasped.

Freeing an arm, Thora twisted to her right and grabbed a clay cup from the floor. "Drink." She pressed the rim against Halcyon's lips and tilted the cup until the water flowed into Halcyon's dry mouth. Halcyon was greedy, taking large swallows. Once done, Thora returned the cup.

Halcyon cleared her throat and blinked a few times, regaining her bearings. The fogginess in her mind had lessened a considerable amount.

"How feel?"

"Better." Halcyon breathed in until her chest was tight with air. The heat had subsided for the moment, but it would reclaim her at some point. "How did you know this would work?" She gazed about the bath. It had never occurred to her that chilly water could soften her heat.

"Omegas in my village," Thora replied.

Halcyon focused on her slave. "They would do this?" She indicated the water around them.

"Yes." Thora tilted her head and studied Halcyon's features. The sapphire of her eyes was a thin ring now. "You has fever and suffering."

Halcyon sighed and seconded her slave's assessment of her heat. She frowned at the seriousness of it, which continued to linger in the background of her head. Even though her body's temperature was more bearable, her heat was an ember deep inside her. It would wait until Halcyon left the safety of the water, then reignite her. But maybe she could outlast it thanks to the reprieve the bath gave her.

"Glauce told you," Halcyon concluded.

"*Já.*" Thora tilted her head and explained, "She very worried and came to stable. Your heat too long."

Glancing past Thora's shoulder, Halcyon said, "It will pass soon." She swallowed, then pushed off Thora's comfortable lap. If she stayed any longer, she might attempt to grind her hips and rub her pussy against Thora's crotch. She was certain that Thora might have a cock now. All her Omega wanted to do was take it.

Thora sat straighter and watched Halcyon with a slight frown. However, she remained silent and still.

Halcyon collected one of the soaps from the long wooden dish near the edge of the bath. The few minutes of cleaning gave her a chance to organize her thoughts. Her mind processed at a slow rate due to the heat's grip. After ducking underwater, she worked the soap from her hair and returned the bar to the open spot between the others. From her position in the middle of the bath, she studied her quiet slave. "Thank you."

"You are welcome." Thora began to climb out of the bath. "You must eat while able."

Halcyon bit her bottom lip and considered the appearance of Thora's commanding nature after months of being more subtle as an Alpha. It wasn't unpleasant, especially while Halcyon's Omega ruled her mind and body. Halcyon was still the master of the villa.

Thora moved about the bathing room in her soaked chiton. She dried herself—at least what she could without removing her wet clothes. She tossed the large linen aside, then opened another in a silent offer to help her mistress.

With a sigh, Halcyon exited the cool water and prepared for the gradual return of her heat. Coming closer, she slipped on the stone floor and fell forward but collided with a soft body rather than the floor. She gripped Thora's extended arms and released a shaky breath.

Thora closed the gap between them, keeping her mistress upright. "You weak." Her brow knitted together, tighter than earlier. She used the fresh linen to dry off Halcyon, keeping one hand anchored to her mistress.

"I ate some grapes," Halcyon argued, but there was no bite.

Thora grunted, then wrapped the linen around Halcyon's midsection to hide her breasts and lower half. "Not enough." Without forewarning, she picked up Halcyon into her arms.

"Thora," Halcyon complained and gripped her slave's shoulder. She was ignored and instead carried out of the bathing room into the courtyard. The sun's warmth was refreshing against her face even though the air was humid. No one else was around, which made Halcyon ponder whether Thora planned it that way. Her reputation as both a hoplite and master were important, not her place in society as an Omega.

Thora went to the second level of the villa and returned Halcyon to the suite. "I come back with food." After she deposited Halcyon on the long chairs, she hurried from the room and left the door open. She was gone for a short period, and voices filtered up from the ground floor. Halcyon recognized Cesare's baritone.

Unsure what else to do, Halcyon decided to make a trip to the chamber-pot room and used a blanket from her nest to cover herself. When she returned to the suite, she sat in the middle of the nest and considered the mild pain deep in her gut. It was unusual for a heat to last beyond three days, so by tomorrow it would be gone. She was confident she could outlast it, then return to her normal duties. She squared her shoulders and looked to the open door when Thora arrived with two plates of food.

"That is enough for a small army," Halcyon remarked.

Thora raised an eyebrow. She had changed into a dry chiton while gone. After she gave Halcyon one plate, she set the other one on the table nearby. She checked the waterskins, which were low. Again she departed with the waterskins and empty grape bowl. By the time she returned, Halcyon had eaten half the food on her plate.

Thora offered a pleased rumble, and pride oozed from her. There was nothing greater for an Alpha than caring for an Omega, especially one in distress like Halcyon. "I leave now." She pivoted but was halted by Halcyon's hand on her wrist.

"Stay for a moment." Halcyon indicated the open space on the chairs, outside of her nest. The invitation was a bad idea, but her Omega refused to allow Thora to leave her. Thora could remain near Halcyon, a little longer.

Thora took the spot, sitting with one leg folded in and the other off the side of the chair. She cupped both hands between her thighs and watched Halcyon eat. "Your heat long."

"I know." Halcyon swallowed down a mouthful of barley that had cheese, olives, and tomatoes. The food filled her empty belly and would help her combat the heat's demands on her body. "It will be gone by tomorrow." She ignored Thora's doubtful expression. "Are you practicing with Vitus?"

"A little." Thora plucked at the hem of her chiton while her other hand continued to hide her possible erection. "It difficult to focus while you unwell."

Halcyon snorted low, catching the unspoken frustration. Similar to Halcyon, Thora struggled with the heat's effects and was perhaps having to please herself in hopes of staying in control. An Omega's heat attracted Alphas and broadcasted over a small area, calling to them but not always prompting them into a rut. Halcyon admired her Alpha slave's ability to hold an iron grip over herself. If Euclid were here, he would have succumbed to his Alpha nature.

"It'll end soon," Halcyon promised.

Thora offered a faint nod, then lowered her attention to the plate. "I glad you eat."

Halcyon pushed the spoon around in the small bowl of barley gruel. She met Thora's gaze and whispered, "Thank you for your care." Her appreciation was unusual, but Thora's devotion meant something to Halcyon. Hoplites were loyal soldiers, to their state and to each other. Halcyon respected such devotion that Thora showed her.

Thora smiled in return, then her Alpha pheromones unfurled around them. She smelled of spice and a bit of musk that indicated her arousal. Her scent attracted Halcyon, more than any Alpha had in the past. Thora seemed to sense the shift in Halcyon and rose from the chairs. "I must leave."

Halcyon clamped down on a groan from the spark of pain in her gut. Her Alpha was leaving her alone. After fluttering her eyes, she pushed back her Omega's desire to keep Thora close by. But her clitoris developed a dull throb.

"Glauce check you," Thora promised while she pulled the door shut, sealing Halcyon away again.

For a minute, Halcyon stared at the little bit of food on her plate. Her earlier appetite was fading, but she attempted to eat more. After she finished the slice of bread, she put the dirty plate under the other one on the table. Another sharp pain bolted through her stomach and up her spine. "Fuck," she muttered and collapsed in her nest. Reaching between her thighs, she coated her fingers in ample slick and started to rub her clitoris. Her climax was quick and brought a moment of reprieve until Thora's scent on the chairs caught her nose.

Halcyon gritted her teeth, then stretched out from the safety of her nest and rested her head near the spot where Thora sat earlier. She breathed in the distinct Alpha smell that excited her Omega. Thora's lingering scent would be all the comfort she would allow herself. In her mind, she chanted that tonight would be the last one. By sunrise, she would be free of her heat.

* * *

Halcyon was coated in sweat again. Her heart raced faster than any galloping horse. The blaze underneath her flushed skin had long ago clouded her mind. Every one of her muscles was curled with tension, as if prepared to fight. But most of her energy was spent. She was accustomed to feeling this way, but from training or combat, not a heat. Each new hour brought a higher level of agony that ate away at Halcyon's sanity.

Halcyon was a Spartan hoplite who earned the glorious title of the Iron Edge. She had bested many male Alphas in her time and was recognized for her prowess. No one questioned her strength or skills. Yet she had forgotten her biggest enemy—nature. The gods had reduced her to a whimpering mess by reminding her what she truly was on the inside—an Omega. Halcyon was retaught her most basic form, stripped of her layers of power, control, and greatness.

The night crept by slower than wine aged. The heat's ending was supposed to be near, but the symptoms didn't relent and instead clung harder to Halcyon. She expected to find relief, if not freedom, by first light. But the heat boiled deep inside her, unwilling to let her go. Her awareness of reality was close to being gone thanks to the bone-deep pain.

Halcyon broke open that night.

All she had left was her Omega identity. She gave in to it, even relied on it. With her Omega in charge, Halcyon rallied the last of her strength and cried out between her pants. Her call echoed in the room, and she hoped it reached beyond the door. Her throat was dry, but she ignored the developing rawness and called out again, pleading and hoping.

The door was nudged open, then bare feet raced across the floor. Glauce's familiar smell offered a measure of hope. Halcyon clawed at the chair's cushion and squeezed her eyes closed, fighting back tears. "Th…" She groaned from the hot bolt that ripped through her body. Glauce ran off before Halcyon could finish speaking. "N-No." Halcyon whined and forced her eyes open, taking in the open door. Maybe she could crawl. But the heat spiked again, paralyzing her.

Then the most amazing scent washed over Halcyon, giving her a spark of life. After a few tears fell, she opened her eyes to find blue orbs glowing under soft firelight.

Thora put the oil lamp on the side table, next to the full plate of food. She snared a waterskin that hung from a long chair. She uncorked it and pressed the tip to Halcyon's mouth. "Drink."

Halcyon did so, savoring her Alpha slave's presence and care. She gulped a few mouthfuls and spilled some on her bare chest. She gasped and toppled back into her nest. Now lower, her view aligned with Thora's crotch better. Under the chiton, she pictured Thora's cock, which would swell from

Thora's clitoris. Halcyon had heard various rumors about the size of female Alpha's cocks. There was a new and stronger scent that clung to Thora, pointing toward a rut. She all but salivated at the thought that such a superior Alpha wanted her.

Thora returned the waterskin, then touched her owner's damp temple and hissed. "You need bath again." She sounded prepared to leave, but she was rooted in place. In the lamplight, her pupils were blown now, and a slight glisten was noticeable on her forehead. Earlier her pheromones held sharp notes of concern; now they were being overpowered by arousal.

Halcyon licked her lips, basking in her Omega's ability to will her Alpha. There was only one thing that could sate her heat. She used her pheromones to enthrall her Alpha, who rumbled deep in response. Another bout of pain shot through her belly, reminding her to hurry. With ease, she further enticed Thora with her sweet Omega scent. "Undress."

Fisting her hands, Thora seemed to weigh the order, but her scent gave no indication of her disliking the idea. The rise and fall of her chest increased with each passing breath. Then her chiton developed a slight tent between her thighs. Thora didn't bother to hide it with her hands as she had before. Her hesitation both comforted and pained Halcyon all at once.

"Please," Halcyon whispered. Her plea was fragile and desperate. Their gazes remained locked for another moment. Halcyon released a groan when Thora responded by reaching for her chiton.

After disrobing, Thora was as bare as Halcyon and took a seat on the edge of a chair, not entering Halcyon's nest.

Between her legs, her enlarged clitoris had grown in length and droplets of slick glistened in the soft light. The headiness of her arousal poured off her and brought a gut-wrenching ache to Halcyon. Thora had indeed rutted for her.

Resting on her side, Halcyon clenched her sticky stomach and pulled her knees closer to her body. She whimpered low and trembled under the pain, but she managed to peer out at her slave, who could give her peace.

Thora whined low while her features darkened. She leaned closer and asked, "Can I…?" Reaching, she placed her fingertips at the edge of the nest and continued to respect Halcyon's security. Halcyon freed a hand, extended her arm, and clasped Thora's larger hand. She tugged with approval and released a sharp breath when Thora crawled forward, crossing the invisible barrier.

The invitation freed a level of restraint from Thora, who scooped up Halcyon. She lifted Halcyon upright and pressed her against the chair's back. Thora rested on her knees, between Halcyon's spread open thighs. She growled and pressed the head of her cock against Halcyon's soaked pussy. Gripping the chair behind Halcyon's head, Thora leaned in and cupped her owner's burning cheek.

Halcyon moaned from the pleasant sensation of Thora's cockhead kissing her clitoris. She prepared to move her hips and take what her Omega was desperate to have and own. But Thora's pheromones shifted, pushing back the haze in Halcyon's mind.

Thora searched Halcyon's eyes and seemed aware what her pheromones were doing to Halcyon. She was in control, of both Halcyon and the situation. She rubbed her thumb across Halcyon's cheek and whispered, "Yes or no?" Glancing down, she indicated how close she was to penetrating Halcyon.

Thora's request for consent scored across Halcyon's heart.

Euclid considered himself above consent, not requiring it from his mate, who he shared a union with. If he truly wished to have Halcyon, he took her. Tonight was the first time Halcyon was asked and given a choice. A chance to refuse and have her decision respected by an Alpha lover. The sting in her eyes became too much and a few tears raced down her cheeks.

"Mistress?"

Halcyon swallowed and nodded over and over. "Yes," she replied after a gasp. "*Já.*"

Thora released a strained breath, then brushed her thumb across Halcyon's lips. Her touch was gone, but she snared Halcyon's thighs next. "Up," she ordered and lifted both legs.

Halcyon hastened and rested her legs against her slave's broad shoulders. "Hurry," she pleaded and snared Thora's arms. Her entire body was coiled from a jumble of anticipation and consuming need. The throbbing from her swollen clitoris was unbearable, causing her to move her hips. But then Thora's cockhead shifted lower and nudged against Halcyon's opening. "Please, Thor—" She cried out from the sudden intrusion that stretched her open. "By the gods." She rolled her head back against the chair. After a brief pause, she whispered, "More."

"Yes, mistress," Thora said in a rumbly voice. This time, she was less cautious and plunged into Halcyon until she bottomed out. Halcyon's cry filled the room, then she gulped for air and sensed the heat loosen its grip ever so slightly.

"Fuck." Halcyon was full and grateful to have a beat to adjust to Thora's full size. "That feels much better." Thora and her cock were all that Halcyon's Omega needed since the onset of her heat. The stretch inside her was delicious and satisfying, even without an orgasm yet. She could have saved herself much sooner if she had taken Thora's cock at the start. With every bit of the hard length buried in her, she was certain of two things. First, her heat would end soon. And second, from the expression on Thora's face, Halcyon knew her slick cunt would keep Thora forever tied to her.

"Now I fuck you," Thora warned. Then she placed a hand under Halcyon's ass and hoisted her a little. She tightened her grip on the back of the chair and braced herself better. The hunger in her features was clear, revealing how much she wanted Halcyon. She pulled her hips back until her cockhead was close to Halcyon's opening. The first few pumps were slow and careful until Thora found her rhythm. Then the pace increased, coaxing louder moans from Halcyon.

"Yes!" Halcyon curled her head back and lost herself in the bolts of pleasure Thora sent through her body. Every smack of Thora's hips against Halcyon's ass was perfect and loud. She could feel her walls tighten and pull at Thora's thrusting cock. The girth was more than she was used to, yet she loved it. She didn't want it to end, but she was too wound up from waiting for days.

"You close," Thora murmured between grunts. She leaned over Halcyon and used the new angle to thrust harder into her mistress. "Tight. Very tight." Her plunges grew a bit frantic.

Halcyon clawed her slave's biceps. She attempted to bounce on Thora's shaft, grinding down on it with each drive into her. The wonderful sparks up and down her spine consumed her. Halcyon loved what Thora gave her, taking it all. She wanted it to last, but her walls started a light flutter. "Fuck, no," she hissed after a moan.

Growling in Halcyon's ear, Thora latched onto Halcyon's hips with both hands and pinned her against the chair's back. "Yesss," she ordered and rammed her cock in slower but much deeper. The shock wave it sent through Halcyon was overwhelming.

Crying out, Halcyon held on and took the punishing thrusts. Then the orgasm crashed over her, forcing her to lock around Thora's shaft on the next drive. She screamed and bucked against Thora until the climax left her a trembling mess. At first, she was uncertain whether Thora also orgasmed, but then a shot of wet heat splashed against her inner walls. Halcyon released a keening moan, feeling her Omega even more satisfied. Such an usual, gorgeous, and superior Alpha was breeding her and could give her a perfect pup. However, when Thora's slick seeped out between their bodies, she whined in protest and opened her eyes. That wasn't supposed to happen. Her Omega howled inside her chest.

Thora met her gaze and curled her lips back to reveal a pair of canines. "Better now?" She lowered them both back to the cushion, ensuring she remained inside her owner.

"Yes." Halcyon was panting, but the weight against her chest was gone. The wonderful smells of sex, arousal, and slick filled her nose and stirred her heat again. However, she was more clearheaded than any time before the heat ruled her. The fullness inside her was perfect, better than she expected it to be. Thora's weight pressed into her while her Alpha scent enveloped Halcyon. Her Omega wanted more, but for the moment, she could rest and breathe.

Thora loosened her arms and moved Halcyon's legs over her shoulders. Once Halcyon had her thighs pressed against Thora's side, Thora rested her forearms against the cushion under them and hooked her hands under Halcyon's shoulders. She turned her head toward her owner, then inhaled her honey-like scent. Thora nuzzled in closer, pressing her lips against damp skin.

Moaning, Halcyon turned her head away, offering her neck. She rubbed her knees against her slave's sides. "Thora," she murmured and dragged her nails across tense shoulders. Arousal started to burn under her skin again. "Please." She emphasized her plea with the movement of her hips.

Rumbling, Thora licked the very spot that Euclid had laid claim to ages ago. He renewed the mark on occasion, but his claim had weakened over the years. It seemed as if his mark did nothing to deter Thora, who latched onto it without warning. But she didn't break the skin, which would have overridden his claim.

Halcyon gasped, loud and sharp, then the fierceness of Thora's bite overtook Halcyon's entire body. She clung to Thora, stilling and holding on without any control. Thora had her.

Now that Halcyon was so compliant, Thora began to rock her hips and forced her buried cock in and out at a delicious pace. She increased the speed after the initial test thrusts. The girth of her shaft filled Halcyon to her limit while the wet slaps echoed through the room. Halcyon dug her nails into Thora's skin and attempted to cry out between her gulps of air.

Thora growled in response and pounded harder, causing the long chairs to squeak against the stone floor. She was unrelenting and passionate, but never violent. Every thrust sent fire through Halcyon's body, extinguishing her heat little by little. Thora grunted and rumbled with each hard plunge, never releasing Halcyon's neck. She was determined to split Halcyon in half.

Unable to last any longer, Halcyon bucked from the pleasure that spilled through her entire being. She screamed and dropped her legs away from Thora, who finished Halcyon off with a few hard lunges. Then Thora released inside Halcyon, filling her with a warm rush. She let out an embarrassing, keening moan that prompted Thora to let go of her neck.

"Good Omega," Thora whispered into her owner's ear. Her taunting praise echoed Halcyon's own from days ago. Halcyon tried to hold back a whimper of enjoyment, but it was too difficult. Thora jogged her hips and groaned as more of her wonderful slick entered Halcyon. "Fill you." She grazed the tip of her nose along Halcyon's ear. "Again and again."

Halcyon groaned after the wonderful promise. Such a gorgeous Alpha fucking her senseless was all her Omega needed right now. As she gazed about their immediate area, she realized that Thora had fucked her in the middle of her nest. She moaned in utter satisfaction and contentment. She was safe, cared for, and filled. There was one last thing that her Omega needed, and that was to have Thora knot her. A knot meant a pup, the heart of any Omega, including Halcyon.

CHAPTER 11

Halcyon

Thora shifted underneath Halcyon, who stirred awake from their brief nap. After Halcyon had climaxed the last time, Thora rearranged them on the long chairs so that Halcyon was curled up against Thora's larger frame. Thora was settled against the back rest of one chair, with their legs tangled together.

"How feel?" Thora asked in a groggy tone. She combed her fingers through Halcyon's dark hair, catching a minor tangle and working it free.

"Better than earlier," Halcyon replied. The heat continued to hum in the background of her mind and body. Her Omega demanded more, especially Thora's knot. However, the respite helped strengthen her. Not only did she want more, but she could now handle all of it. Stealing a glance, she confirmed that Thora's rut hadn't ended. The sight of Thora's flaccid cock was rewarding and pleasing.

"What you need, mistress?" Thora bowed her head and pressed her nose against Halcyon's neck. For once, she spoke Halcyon's title with such tenderness. "Tell me."

Halcyon groaned and melted into the tightening of Thora's arms around her body. "Your knot," she replied in a breathy voice. She sensed how Thora stiffened under her.

"Knot?" Thora repeated in bewilderment. She raised her head and pressed her cheeks against her owner's damp temple. "What a knot?"

Grinning, Halcyon calmed now that she understood Thora's hesitation was confusion rather than uninterest in knotting. "It's the ring at the base of your cock," she replied, but her explanation was lost in translation. After a chuckle, she clutched Thora's cock, causing her Alpha slave to jump under her. Halcyon circled the tip of her index finger around the base of Thora's cock and repeated, "Knot."

"Ah." Thora rumbled and nudged Halcyon's temple. "*Knútr.*"

Halcyon canted her head but kept her attention on the swelling length in her palm. "*Knútr,*" she repeated and shivered after Thora responded with a soft growl in Halcyon's ear.

"You drink herb water," Thora said while she grazed her palm across Halcyon's abs. "After." The command in her voice swept over Halcyon, more controlling than the orders she received as a hoplite.

"Yes." Halcyon would agree to anything her Alpha slave asked of her right now. She tightened her grip around the hardened length, needing Thora inside her again. The idea of taking the infertilis herb grated against her Omega. The possibility of pregnancy was guaranteed once she was knotted by an Alpha. It would also satisfy her heat, ensuring it would end.

"Good Omega," Thora whispered, then she started to maneuver them to a different position. It only took Halcyon a heartbeat or two to figure out her slave's idea. Together they rearranged themselves so that they faced the tall backrest of one long chair. Thora scooched the second chair away, causing Halcyon to peer over her shoulder toward her Alpha slave. With more space, Thora stood behind Halcyon and straddled the remaining chair.

Groaning, Halcyon realized their next encounter might be rougher than the last. Her entire body was alight from the pending fuck. She curled her nails against the backrest and whined like the needy mess she was. From the corner of her eye, she saw Thora's stiff cock that had a glistening tip and a flushed hue to it. Halcyon was dry-mouthed and aching with desire to be rutted into by Thora. "Please."

Thora closed the small gap between them, pushing her cock between Halcyon's ass cheeks. She gripped Halcyon's hips, stilled her rocking motions, and dipped her head lower. "Hold on," she advised before she freed a hand.

Halcyon moaned from the throaty warning that sent a shiver down her spine. She spread her legs wider, near the edge on either side of the chair. When Thora backed up, she dragged the head of her cock down, then grazed the shaft against Halcyon's soaked clitoris. She stroked her full length between Halcyon's pussy, smearing the slick all over. They moaned together, enjoying the pretense of what was to come.

"Thora, please," Halcyon begged again and leaned against the backrest. Her Omega writhed inside her, causing Halcyon to whimper. The heat pulsed from deep in her gut and made her limbs go weak. But then a blissful amount of pressure built up around her pussy's opening. She gasped, straightened, and whined with need. A tremble passed through her as the heartbeats ticked by. The pressure increased as Thora nudged the swollen head past the entrance. "Yes," she whispered in relief.

With her cockhead inside, Thora returned her hand to Halcyon's side. Her tightening grip was the only warning, then she fully hilted herself inside Halcyon.

"Fuck!" Halcyon was close to losing her balance, but she tightened her grip on the backrest and gulped for air. She let out a pleased groan from the fullness and the closeness of Thora. All the pheromones and arousal blanketed them. Without a single plea, Halcyon was given what she wanted so much. It even seemed as if a soft shudder passed through Thora.

Holding Halcyon steady, Thora started the frantic, heated ride to satisfy them both. She withdrew enough, then plunged back inside. The girth of her full length stole Halcyon's breath. Then the next thrusts grew faster, even a bit harder. Halcyon cried out when some went deeper than others. Each new thrust reminded Halcyon how much she was an Omega. How much she needed to be fucked and bred. Her earlier resistance to her heat had been shameful but not her keening whines that filled the room now.

"Good… Omega," Thora whispered between pants. She snared a handful of Halcyon's hair and forced her head to one side. Thora watched Halcyon's enraptured expression, responding with a guttural snarl. "Very good."

Halcyon gave a low cry after the praise. She was no longer the master, but rather the slave. Thora's Alpha scent enthralled her, and Thora's cock freed her Omega from years of enslavement. The sweet slapping of their joined bodies was bliss, sending shocks through her being. Already Halcyon sensed the closeness of her orgasm, unable to halt any of it because Thora ruled her.

"You want my knot?" Thora asked, slowing down enough to stall Halcyon's climax.

Halcyon growled, but it was a pointless fight. She gasped and whispered, "Yes."

"Tell me in Norsk," Thora ordered before thrusting back inside Halcyon, who cried out.

Cursing, Halcyon slumped against the backrest but held herself up. Thora was buried deep in her, stealing Halcyon's breath. She panted and tried to move her hips, but Thora halted her. She whined in protest until the warm Alpha pheromones compelled her. "*Já,*" she murmured. Thora's grip on her hair increased, warning her. "*Já!*"

Leaning forward, Thora rumbled and gave a delicate jog of her hips, just enough to graze the length of her cock against Halcyon's tight walls. "Try saying *líka*. It means please." The roughness of her voice sent heat racing through Halcyon's veins. Thora wouldn't be denied.

Halcyon groaned from the power of her Alpha slave, who was a rare blend of sweet and fiery. If she wanted Thora's knot, she had to appease her. But the unspoken truth was that Halcyon desired to please Thora. "*Líka,*" she said in a growly tone.

Thora smirked in triumph and drew her hips back until her cockhead rested at the entrance of Halcyon's aching pussy. She straightened and eased her grip on Halcyon's dark hair.

"See? You can learn Norsk. I am proud of you." Halcyon's groan brought a deep rumble from Thora. "Tell me again, then I give you everything you want."

"Fuck," Halcyon muttered and closed her eyes. She was desperate and hurt to have Thora locked inside her. After a painful exhale, she whispered, "*Líka*, Thora, fuck me."

"Knot you?"

"*Já! Líka!*"

Thora rammed her full length back into Halcyon. A piercing scream broke free from Halcyon, leaving her throat somewhat raw. Thora gave Halcyon zero chance to catch her breath, starting to drive into her with an unrelenting force. Halcyon held on, welcoming every thrust and plunge deep into her aching pussy. She may be a needy Omega, but she was made to handle a rutting Alpha like Thora. Her cries matched Thora's throaty grunts.

"More," Halcyon demanded, using her pheromones to tease Thora's Alpha. There was a thin veil of restraint behind Thora's hips. It unsettled Halcyon's Omega and urged her to free Thora. "B-Be a good Alpha," she ordered between pants. "And fuck me well." Her demand was met with a harsh huff of air near her ear. But then Thora did the unthinkable; she pulled out of Halcyon with the next stroke.

"No!" Halcyon howled and thought her heart might burst from her chest. However, when she drew in Thora's strong scent, the fight inside her died even though the panic lingered at the edge of her mind. Thora dismounted from the long chair, then snared Halcyon and swung her around to reposition her. Halcyon was forced to her hands and knees at the foot end of the chair. She curled her fingers around the edge of the chair and peered over her shoulder in time to see Thora straddle the chair again. Much to her relief, Thora realigned herself and sheathed the full length of her cock inside Halcyon. The fullness was perfect and the closeness soothed her Omega.

Thora performed a few gentle thrusts before she returned to their earlier pace, taking away any concern Halcyon had from before. The wet smacks of their bodies rang out. But Halcyon's cries grew louder as she took the force of Thora's drives. She sensed Thora towering behind her, over her, and in her. The desire burned heavy between them, pushing them both to take more from each other. Thora's girth somehow seemed bigger, but Halcyon realized it was the swell of a knot.

"Harder," Halcyon encouraged her slave. She wasn't disappointed when Thora bent over her and hooked an arm across Halcyon's chest. Thora locked Halcyon in place, pounding into her. The growing ring at the base of Thora's cock slapped against Halcyon's cunt. It was thick and perhaps more than Halcyon could handle. However, her Omega was more than determined to have it, all of it.

"Close," Thora breathed into her owner's ear. She seemed to sense the slight spasm of Halcyon's walls. Her efforts doubled, harder and faster. Halcyon trembled, then tensed as the initial wave of pleasure was set free. She split open, crying out into the dimness of the room. Thora snapped her hips once more and howled before bearing more of her weight onto Halcyon.

Halcyon fought against the prick of tears behind her closed eyelids, clinging to the chair for support. Every muscle coiled in her arms and legs while she held them both in place. Through the wash of passion, she sensed Thora's hips rocking against her ass. A new, larger pressure rolled against her pussy's entrance. "Too big," she murmured between choked breaths.

"You take me," Thora whispered and nuzzled Halcyon's ear when she turned her head. "Take my knot."

Groaning, Halcyon lowered her chest against the chair and raised her ass higher. The adjustment encouraged Thora's hips to nudge with more persistence. Their combined wetness smeared all around the knot, allowing it to work its way forward. Halcyon bit her lip, then nudged back onto the bulge against her entrance. She had to have it. Nothing else but Thora's knot would satisfy her heat.

"Good Omega," Thora praised and then snapped her hips without warning.

"Fuck!" Halcyon yowled from the brief sting, but it was overshadowed by the glorious stretch and completeness. With a few bucks of her hips, Thora drove them into another orgasm that released Thora's seed. Silky heat filled Halcyon, closing off the tiniest of gaps between them. She slumped forward until Thora's arm under her supported her. Her stubborn heat unfurled from low in her gut, cooling like a stormy afternoon in the summer. Halcyon's tight channel clamped around Thora's full length, knot, seed, and all.

Their union was final.

Thora grunted a few times between pants. Another spurt painted Halcyon's fluttering walls. After a soft groan,

Thora grazed her nose over Halcyon's ear and began to whisper in Norsk. Halcyon had no idea what her slave was telling her, but Thora's native tongue had become much less coarse in that moment. Each word held a sweet note and tugged at Halcyon's heart. Her Omega reveled in the Alpha's secret affection for Halcyon.

Halcyon shifted a little, which disturbed the tie between them. She whimpered from the mild burn around the opening of her pussy.

"Be still," Thora murmured in a gentle tone. She lifted herself off her owner, then helped up Halcyon, ensuring the knot wasn't pulled on. With Halcyon nestled in her lap, Thora scooted them to the backrest, leaned against it, and adjusted Halcyon against her body. "Better?"

"Yes." Halcyon nestled into her slave's arms and was further cocooned by Thora propping up her legs. She took a deep breath that eased her racing heart. With Thora locked inside her, Halcyon was content, if not happy. She had the gorgeous Alpha's seed, and they would produce a beautiful or handsome pup soon. Her Omega swelled with pride. Halcyon pictured her pup with golden hair, fair skin, and dark eyes like a Greek. Or perhaps their pup would have Halcyon's dark, wavy hair and Thora's magnificent blue eyes. Images of her future pup shaped and reshaped until Halcyon dozed off.

Thora's slow movements later stirred Halcyon. Around them, the early sunlight poured into the suite. Halcyon bit back a yawn and lifted her head from Thora's warm breast.

"Knot gone," Thora murmured in Halcyon's ear. She gripped her owner's sides and helped her lift off her cock, which had become soft. Her shaft slid out, grazing along Halcyon's inner walls. Halcyon groaned at first, then whimpered when the head of Thora's cock drew close to the end. Thora sighed in response and continued to break their union by pulling free.

Halcyon sat on the chair, between Thora's thighs. She frowned when Thora rose and left their comfortable space. "Where are you going?"

"Herb drink," Thora replied while she collected her chiton from the floor. "It not wait."

Halcyon gritted her teeth and held back a harsh remark about the infertilis herb drink. Lowering her eyes, she nodded and conceded to her slave's wise decision. However, the Omega inside her battled with her. With her heat weakened, Halcyon had better control of herself and regained her composure.

Thora cleared her throat after she straightened her chiton. She picked up a few blankets that had fallen away from Halcyon's nest. Next she butted the second long chair against the other so that Halcyon had more room again. Thora placed the blankets around the chairs and helped Halcyon repair the nest.

Blinking a few times, Halcyon worked away the burn in her eyes and finished fixing her nest. She was grateful to have it back but withheld from crawling into it, not wanting to advertise her weakened state.

"I return soon." Thora studied Halcyon for a beat, taking deep breaths. She was attempting to read Halcyon's mood through scents and pheromones, but Halcyon had a better handle on them now. Without another word, Thora departed and left the suite door cracked open.

Halcyon curled up in the nest and released a shaky breath. She was a damn hoplite, not a sniveling Omega. She was nothing like Selene, who often required Halcyon's strength after sex. At that point, Halcyon considered her sexual exploits with Selene for the first time in a few fortnights. Selene was a shadow in Halcyon's past now. After being with Thora, Halcyon was shaken to her core and felt a twinge of withdrawal due to Thora's current absence.

However, Thora returned and refilled the room with her strong yet comforting scent. Halcyon lifted from her curled up position and blinked away the fuzziness in her gaze. The distinct bitter smell of the infertilis herb hit her nose when Thora neared her.

Taking a seat at the edge of the nest, Thora held the full clay cup. Halcyon attempted to take it, but Thora drew it away and said, "*Nei.*" The Norsk word was somewhat familiar to Halcyon and easy to translate after Thora's warning. Halcyon frowned at her Alpha slave's continued control over her. "Closer," Thora ordered, grabbing Halcyon's hip and drawing her forward.

Unable to resist, Halcyon scooted and left the nest. She was pulled into Thora's lap, and they faced each other. She moaned at their proximity and melted under Thora's pleased smile. Halcyon couldn't hide how much she enjoyed fulfilling her Alpha slave's simple desires.

Thora adjusted one of Halcyon's legs, hooking it behind her. Halcyon did the same with the other leg and then settled into her new favorite spot. She studied the warm blue eyes above her before reaching up to play with a few blond strands. Thora's initial rumble softened to a delicate purr, but she broke the spell by bringing the cup to Halcyon's lips.

Grousing and muttering a complaint, Halcyon caved to Thora's insistence and swallowed a mouthful of the foul liquid. She did her best not to choke, but it brought out an unexpected and pained whine from her. Halcyon glanced away after her Omega's displeasure came out.

"It best," Thora murmured. Even though her voice was even, a spark of sorrow showed in her eyes that clenched around Halcyon's heart. "Drink all." She returned the cup to Halcyon's lips.

With a huff, Halcyon latched onto Thora's wrist and tilted her head back to guzzle the rest. She hated drinking the herb more than sucking on Euclid's cock. However, the herb served a purpose, especially in this situation. At least, it was crucial to her future to ensure there was no pup.

Why did it feel as though she was telling herself a lie?

After cursing her Omega, Halcyon pushed the empty cup away and frowned at the minimal space between her and Thora. Her heat may have dissipated but it wasn't gone. She eyed Thora's covered lower half and considered whether Thora's cock had receded back to a clitoris. From the slight bulge, she doubted it.

Thora set the cup off to her left, near the end of the chair. "Do you wish rest alone?"

Halcyon bit her bottom lip and mulled over her pending day. She needed more time to recover and perhaps would feel closer to normal by tomorrow. Thora had done her duty, as both a slave and an Alpha. There was no reason for Thora to remain with Halcyon. And yet, she was unprepared to let Thora leave her. They could hide away together in the suite for the rest of the day rather than separate. Halcyon warmed under the idea of fucking more between hours of being cared for.

"Mistress?" Thora tilted her head, while her warm pheromones eased Halcyon's wild thoughts. "You think much."

Halcyon glowered at her slave, who seemed to be perceptive and confident in her assessment. Although her annoyance bled away in a few heartbeats. Thora had teased her, displaying a new level of comfort. She had also come to Halcyon's aid multiple times over the few days. After a sigh, Halcyon slid her arm around Thora's shoulders and whispered, "Stay." She touched Thora's slave iron, recalling her unspoken oath to Thora.

Thora's tender smile cracked open Halcyon's guarded heart a little more.

* * *

By sunset, Halcyon was spent, in the most pleasant way possible. Thora had kept Halcyon satisfied and her pussy full. Halcyon lost track of how many times they had fucked, but she was certain they used every surface in the suite. The table especially became a favorite after Halcyon discovered it was useful for multiple positions, the best being bent over the table and fucked from behind. Thora never once disappointed her.

But the infertilis herb had become similar to spoiled wine, abrasive on her tongue.

"You eat," Thora murmured into Halcyon's sticky hair. She turned her attention to the window from their spot on the long chairs. Moments ago they had knotted on a regular chair on the other side of the room. Halcyon had ridden Thora's cock until the ring swelled at the base and indicated Thora was ready to breed Halcyon, properly. After rocking a few times, Halcyon slid it in and received a steady stream of release from Thora. Once they separated, Thora urged Halcyon to drink more of the herb that was now nearly gone from a waterskin.

"Must eat," Thora added after a stretch of silence. The determination was thick in her tone and prompted a slight grin from Halcyon.

"Stubborn," Halcyon muttered, but she moved her head in agreement. She suspected that Glauce had put together an evening meal for everyone in the villa.

"I return," Thora promised and slid away from her spot behind Halcyon. She put on her chiton. "Drink more." She indicated the waterskin that had the herb drink.

Halcyon huffed and watched her slave depart the room. She eyed the waterskin and considered its disgusting contents. Reaching over, she ran her fingers over the leathery material of the skin, but she withdrew from it. Deep inside, her Omega growled in protest and asserted more control. Halcyon left the chairs and went to the window. She took deep breaths of the fresh air, which cleared her mind. Already much of her heat was gone, and by dawn tomorrow she would be free of it.

By first light, she would be the Iron Edge again.

The return of her sanity and control should have excited her, not make her glower at the distant horse stable outside the villa. With a shake of her head, she peered over her bare shoulder and stared at the open door to the walkway. She half expected Thora to fill the opening, but she was still alone. Tomorrow they would be owner and slave again, not lovers. Thora had served her purpose with both pride and care. Halcyon was grateful for her slave's devotion. The heat had acted as a bridge between them, but it was gone. Now she hoped they could return to normal.

"Mistress?" Thora stood beside the long chairs and held a tray between her hands. Somehow she had returned undetected.

Halcyon approached and crawled into her nest while Thora sat on the end of the chairs. Thora handed over a bowl of food and kept the second one for herself. She placed the tray on the floor. There was still a small plate with two slices of sweet bread on it. They ate in silence. Halcyon caught Thora sneaking glances at her, probably to ensure Halcyon ate.

"You sleep in bedroom tonight?" Thora asked, raising a golden eyebrow.

Halcyon considered the idea since her heat was retreating. She studied her nest around her.

"We take," Thora said and pointed at one of the blankets. The idea of sleeping in a bed was appealing after several nights on the firm long chairs. After Halcyon nodded, Thora smiled in victory and promised, "Glauce and I ready it. Bath?"

"Yes." Halcyon wanted to hold on to Thora's scent on her body for longer, at least until first light. However, the linens on the bed would absorb their mixed smells and linger for days under Halcyon's nose. Such a reminder was unnecessary.

Thora nodded and returned her attention to the food. After the meal, she took the dirty dishes from the room and promised to ready a bath.

Halcyon considered the quietness of the room, which had once been filled with the sounds of their breeding. A slight flush burned in Halcyon's cheeks. She had never been quite so wanton with other lovers. Somehow Thora drew out a new side to Halcyon. Sighing, Halcyon slid off the chair and collected her forgotten chiton. She slipped it on and left the suite, heading to the chamber pot on the other side of the upper level. Afterward, she went downstairs and spotted Cesare, who was returning through the gate. He perhaps had worked out in the stable today.

"Good evening, mistress." Cesare kept a certain distance from her. "You seem… well," he finished in a curious tone. His nose flared a degree, indicating he picked up Thora's scent all over his owner.

Halcyon cleared her throat and nodded. "Yes, thank you." She bit back a grin when he shuffled from foot to foot.

"I assume Thora…" Cesare faltered and looked away from his owner. He pursed his lips, then murmured, "Took care of your needs?"

"Yes." Halcyon chuckled at his uneasiness. Even though they had known each other for many years, Cesare held a pseudo-yet-unspoken parental role in Halcyon's life, especially in her youth. He was well aware of Halcyon's active life in the bedroom, but he certainly never bore witness to it. However, her and Thora's recent exploits were rather loud and had most likely broadcasted through the entire villa. Halcyon felt a twinge of guilt, and yet everyone was aware of what Alphas and Omegas did together.

"Is there anything you require this evening?" Cesare asked, then a pink hue colored his cheeks. "That I can assist with."

Halcyon smirked and eyed him until his flush brightened. "No, Cesare." She relented and grabbed his shoulder when she passed him. "Just a bath, then my bed." Her hand fell away. Glauce darted out of the bathing room and carried an empty bucket between her hands. "Is it ready?"

"Almost, mistress." Glauce dipped her head and paused midway through her sprint to the well in the courtyard.

Halcyon slipped into the bathing room and found Thora putting an oil in the water to give it a floral scent. She let out a contented sigh and started to undress. "Can you retrieve a fresh chiton?"

"*Já,*" Thora replied in her native tongue.

With a tilt of her head, Halcyon said, "*Þakka fyrir.*" She reached for the chiton's strap on her shoulder but paused when Thora approached her.

"You may say '*Þǫkk.*'" Thora held a bucket in her right hand. "Less formal but okay to say."

"Oh." Halcyon considered the difference and nodded. "*Þǫkk,*" she repeated and softened when Thora smiled. A slight pulse started between her thighs, but she was able to ignore it.

"*Ekki at þakka,*" Thora said, then departed without another word or glance. She didn't return while Halcyon bathed. Glauce had returned to add one last bucket of steaming water to the bath, then she left too. Most likely Thora and Glauce were prepping the master bedroom.

The quietness of the bathing room and the fresh scents from the warm water were pleasant. After scrubbing her body clean of Thora's scent, Halcyon relaxed on the single stone step and considered her next days. At the start of her heat, she had sent Cesare with a message about her necessary time off. However, they would expect her to return to duty any day. Halcyon was due for guard rotation for her king. Part of her looked forward to returning to the normalcy of her daily life.

Heats were, after all, inconvenient.

CHAPTER 12

Halcyon

Halcyon dug her nails into the spear's wood and released a worried sigh as the public meeting continued in the council house. She feared the outcome of the discussions, especially for her king's safety. With a roll of her shoulders, she adjusted the bronze armor that clung to her sticky body. Even without her helmet, she was still warm under the early morning sunlight. Only moments ago she had completed her evening rotation as the king's bodyguard and looked forward to going home. However, her king requested she join him at the council house.

Nearby sat King Leonidas's wife, Queen Gorgo, and King Leotychidas, who jointly ruled alongside Leonidas. Often when there was war, Leonidas was the first to step forward, while Leotychidas tended to step back. For centuries, Sparta had two kings in order to ensure there was always a ruler available. One went to war and the other remained in Sparta.

"We must act quickly." Leonidas further urged the council to take a stand against Persia and its ruler, Xerxes, who everyone knew had a grudge against Greece for the death of his son. Like Halcyon, he stood on the stage before the seated elders, who were fanned out in the building. Higher up were female Omegas of various ages and stature in society.

"Yes, Leonidas is right," Leotychidas added, even though he didn't stand next to the other king. He puffed up his chest, as if he cared. Halcyon refrained from rolling her eyes, relieved she guarded Leonidas and not Leotychidas.

One elder, Dromeus, rose from his seat and said, "As you know, my king, it is the sixth day of the Carnea Festival. We would be smote by god Carnus, and even Apollo, if we engaged in any war activities during this sacred time."

Leonidas toyed with a ruffle in his chiton, an agitated tell of his deteriorating mood. He parted his lips, and a stormy expression over took his features. But his Omega mate clasped his shoulder, and that seemed to ease him, causing his Alpha pheromones to dissipate. He looked at her and gave a faint nod.

Queen Gorgo removed her touch and smiled at the elders. "Yes, the festival's laws are of utmost importance to all." She folded her hands in front of her. "And so is the safety of Sparta."

Dromeus was still on his feet. He often spoke for the whole of the council and continued to do so quite freely. "My queen, we do greatly appreciate the information you revealed from the tablets that Demaratus sent us, but we cannot act until after the festival."

"But we can prepare," Gorgo argued. Most Omegas in Sparta were outspoken compared to Omegas in other parts of Greece. Gorgo was as famous in the political arena as Halcyon was in the military. They were Omegas in body but Alphas at their core.

Dromeus hesitated after Gorgo's idea, but there were agreeing murmurs from either side of him.

"We can prepare our hoplites," Gorgo continued louder, gaining favor with both the elders and the Omegas above them. "Because Xerxes will come here. To Sparta, to our homes. And we cannot rely on Thrace or Corinth or even Athens to stop him."

Leonidas shifted in his sandals as the elders whispered among each other. The tide was turning in his favor, but he required more support. The recent reports showed that King Xerxes and his army were moving faster each day. It could mean trouble for Sparta if they waited and did nothing. He peered over his shoulder and exchanged a glance with Halcyon, who sensed her king's worries. An unspoken question lingered in his gaze. Halcyon offered a smile of confidence and promise. She would march anywhere with him.

A spark entered Leonidas's eyes, then he turned back to the council. With his chest raised, he called out, "Until preparations are complete, I and my three hundred hoplites will march north and meet King Xerxes and his army in battle."

For several heartbeats, a silence loomed in the building. Then a chorus of questions and demands fell from the elders. Many rose to their feet, but it was the female Omegas' claps from the back of the council house that overwhelmed the council's voice.

Gorgo studied Leonidas, then her pheromones shifted and held a proud note. He was an Alpha and a mate but a king first. Everyone in and outside of Sparta were well aware of Gorgo's support of her mate. They were an unbreakable couple.

After much of the clamor subsided, Dromeus made a final attempt to disarm the king's suicidal plans. He turned his full attention to the silent hoplite beside the king. "And will the Iron Edge march with her king?"

"With great honor," Halcyon declared with finality.

* * *

Three days had passed since King Leonidas made his decision to face King Xerxes. He ordered his three hundred elite hoplites to prepare to march on the dawn of the fourth day. Since then, the barracks throughout the city had been buzzing like hives. Not only had the king's order trickled down, but so did the council's command for war preparations. Every hoplite was organizing, training, and planning for a nasty, bloody war. King Xerxes had a vendetta against every last Greek.

Halcyon's time on duty was split between being at the barracks and guarding the king. All her equipment and weapons required inspection and repair, or replacing if they failed to pass. As one of the king's elite guards, she was given priority over other hoplites in the military.

On the afternoon prior to departure, Halcyon found herself, the king, and the commander in deep conversation about the plans. Earlier in the day, they'd been at the council house, apprising the council and citizens of their plans. Now they stood over a map of Greece, stroking their chins and weighing their options. The commander, Meles, made several suggestions about how to face King Xerxes and slow his enormous army. No one among them was under the illusion that three hundred hoplites could defeat King Xerxes.

Leonidas was confident several hundred other soldiers from other Greek city-states would assist them, but it hardly compared to the massive Persian force.

Like her king and commander, Halcyon's instincts told her that Thermopylae was the best location to make a stand. There was a narrow pass that they could funnel the enemy to, then hold them until the rest of Greece finished preparing for war. As Halcyon stared at the spot, she sensed the god of death's hand on her shoulder. For the first time, Halcyon swelled with pride at the thought of returning upon her shield, immortalized for her sacrifice to protect her people and her home. The brief thought of home reminded her that she needed to prepare the villa for her impending fate.

By that evening, Halcyon had returned to her home and handed off her repaired armor to Cesare, who would check over it in normal fashion. As she changed from her red chiton to a pale purple one, she looked over at Cesare. He was nearly out of the bedroom, arms loaded with military equipment.

"How does Thora fare?"

Cesare paused a step from the doorway and pivoted toward his owner. "She is well, but she is concerned why you avoid her after..." He looked away from Halcyon but mustered enough courage to finish his sentence. "After your time together."

Halcyon tossed her uniform chiton into the basket next to her. She took a seat on a stool and started to unlace her boots, exchanging them for her old sandals. "We are busy preparing for war." Between taking off boots, she looked over at Cesare. "I'm well aware of how slaves gossip." She never worried about Cesare talking about her personal life. However, he stayed abreast of city gossip, which included political ongoings.

Cesare nodded and said, "I have informed Thora of the pending war." He lowered his gaze, and a furrow worked its way across his brow. "I didn't make her aware of your upcoming march." Looking over, he held his owner's curious gaze. "I felt that information must come from you, all things considered."

"All things considered?" Halcyon peered down at her feet and finished putting on her sandals while she spoke. "She sated my heat, not marked me." Once done, she stood and approached Cesare. "Are you inferring I owe her an explanation of my duties as if she were my mate rather than my slave?" The slight heat in her tone caused Cesare to recoil a step.

"Of course not, mistress." Cesare adjusted the armor in his grip. He squared his shoulders, though, reaffirming his place as Halcyon's eldest slave. "But perhaps she has earned some consideration after her own sacrifices for you."

Halcyon responded with a soft rumble and folded her arms, forcing her biceps to stand out. "Perhaps." The idea that she owed Thora, or anyone, made her stomach twist in terrible directions. But Cesare had a point. Thora could have allowed Halcyon to suffer. Only the gods knew for how long the heat would have plagued Halcyon. If Thora had refused, then Halcyon would have been forced to call on Euclid. He would have ensured Halcyon never drank the infertilis tea.

After a tired exhale, Halcyon nodded and said, "I will give it some thought."

"You mean some overthought," Cesare joked, then took two hasty steps away from his owner.

Halcyon cursed Thora, who claimed her owner was an overthinker. Cesare most likely had warned Thora that their owner was a thinker. Now it seemed it was a joke among her slaves. "Why do I not rid of you all and get helots?" She swore again and followed Cesare out of the room.

"Because you may be the master of this villa, but we are the foundation of the home," Cesare replied, then he hurried down the steps with his armload. His claim was difficult to argue.

Shaking her head, Halcyon followed Cesare to the courtyard and offered Vitus a smile. He was reading from a scroll but lowered it when she joined him. "How are you, Vitus?"

"I'm well." Vitus rolled up the scroll and tied it closed with a leather thong. "I've seen little of you lately."

Halcyon relaxed in her chair on the other side of the table. "Yes, duty has had my attention." They didn't need to discuss her earlier heat, which everyone in the villa was well aware of. "But I've been wishing to discuss Thora's education with you."

"She is learning quickly," Vitus said. "She shows a natural talent at learning a new language. Perhaps even more than I."

Halcyon was unsurprised by the news. Her slave was unusual and special in many ways. "Then she will become the teacher." She recalled her own few lessons in Thora's native tongue. One of the most recent lessons had been in the suite. Halcyon pushed back the sweet memory, not wanting it to distract her.

Vitus laughed and placed the scroll on the table. "It's quite possible."

Halcyon prepared to make her request, but she hesitated when Glauce and Cesare arrived with a starter dish and wine. Once the slaves headed toward the kitchen, she returned to her earlier thoughts and said, "I wish for you to teach Thora how to read and write."

Vitus was between bites of olives and paused midchew. After he swallowed it, he said, "That will require more time."

"Yes, I know." Halcyon gathered a few olives and cubes of feta from the shared bowl. "Are you willing to stay longer?"

Pursing his lips, Vitus remained quiet for a beat, then he gave a firm nod. "Yes." He mirrored Halcyon's smile. "And not simply for the coin. I enjoy teaching Thora."

Halcyon battled with a distinct surge of sharp heat in her gut at Vitus's obvious like for Thora. She looked away and gathered herself, then forced a smile at him. "Excellent." She rolled an olive between her fingers and met his pleased features. Perhaps Vitus and Thora were spending too much time together; at least, Halcyon's Omega disliked it. Halcyon tamped it down and asked, "How much longer can you stay?"

"Two or three more months before I must return home," Vitus replied. "It could be enough time to teach Thora the basics, if we work every day." He folded his hands in his lap and studied Halcyon. "If Glauce and Cesare can take on more of her duties."

After consideration, Halcyon nodded and said, "They should be capable. Glauce has become more apt in the kitchen."

"It only took a kitchen fire," Vitus joked, without care. He then flinched and blurted out, "My apologies, Hal—"

"It's all right." Halcyon waved him off, then took a handful of olives and feta again. "I have come to terms with the kitchen fire. It was an accident." She brought an olive to her lips and muttered, "An expensive accident."

Vitus let out a low breath. To his left, Cesare came out with two plates of food, which he deposited on the table.

"Cesare, please have Thora come out here."

"Yes, mistress."

Halcyon and Vitus continued to converse until Thora arrived in the courtyard. She stood near Vitus, hands behind her back and full attention on her owner. Briefly Halcyon returned her slave's piercing gaze. In that moment, she remembered how much she adored Thora's blue eyes. Then Thora's rumbly voice refocused Halcyon, who blinked out of her stare.

"Yes, mistress?"

"Vitus and I have discussed your continued education," Halcyon informed with a stern tone. She glanced at Vitus, who enjoyed more of the olives and listened to the conversation. "We have made an arrangement for Vitus to remain here longer to teach you to read and write."

Thora kept her eyes trained on Halcyon. "Thank you, mistress." There was a certain coolness in her voice and even shards of ice in her gaze.

Halcyon could sniff out the irritation in Thora's scent. However, Halcyon had a household to run and duties to fulfill as a hoplite, not her slave's ego to coddle. "Vitus must return home in two to three months from now, no later." She sensed that Thora understood her enough. "You must learn quickly."

Thora nodded and glanced once at her tutor before she looked at Halcyon again. "Vitus return?"

"I'm afraid not," Vitus replied.

Sighing, Thora pressed her lips together until they were a fine line. She regarded Vitus and said, "I understand. There little time."

"More of your chores will be taken over by Glauce until Vitus returns home." Halcyon saw the pending protest, so she cut it off. "Unless you wish not to learn and remain an uneducated slave, like the others."

Thora snapped her jaw shut after the warning. Her irritation continued to seep into her pheromones, but she dipped her head in agreement. "Yes, mistress."

"Excellent. Now go eat before it is any later." From the corner of her eye, Halcyon watched Thora leave for the kitchen. She popped the remaining olives into her mouth and continued to talk with Vitus. Over the weeks, she had missed sharing meals with him. Vitus was both intelligent and respectful, a rare virtue in any breed of male. He somewhat reminded Halcyon of her sire.

After dinner, Halcyon went to the stable and checked on her horses. She gave her favorite horse, Cheimon, an apple, which lasted less than a minute. The stalls had been cleaned today, and the riding equipment was well organized against the wall. Everything was in order and pleased Halcyon. She suspected Thora had taken care of the stables today. Stable chores had been an early punishment for Thora, but in recent months it seemed to provide a physical outlet for her Alpha slave.

Upon returning to the villa, Halcyon went upstairs but paused a few steps from the entrance to her bedroom. All three slaves were in the room, working and chatting together. Coming closer, Halcyon pressed her shoulder against the wall and listened to their conversation. It wasn't unusual for her to eavesdrop on them at times.

"The Persians are savages," Glauce said.

"Savages?" Thora repeated in a bewildered tone.

Cesare huffed, a familiar sound to Halcyon. "Animals."

The sound of linens being shook out caught Halcyon's ear, then Thora spoke up again. "Like a Norsk," she said. "Like me."

Cesare chuckled, then there was a soft snap of metal. He seemed to be working on Halcyon's armor, checking over it. "Persians come from Hades. I do not believe a Norsk comes from there."

"It cold in my lands. Hades no live there."

Glauce gave a soft laugh and asked, "Do you miss the cold?"

"*Nei*," Thora replied, then she added, "*Já*." There was a forlornness to her voice that brought a sad sigh to Halcyon.

"Why do you talk about the Persians?" Cesare asked from a bit deeper in the room.

"Glauce heard more talk about war in the market."

"Everyone was talking about it." Glauce moved and shook another linen. She and Thora were perhaps remaking the bed for Halcyon. "They will not speak or declare war with the Carnea Festival." Each day Glauce and Thora went to the market for supplies. Halcyon assumed they had heard all the excitement and gossip about the war and the festival. "When I was there today, there was talk that word came from the former king, Demaratus, that the King of Persia marches toward Greece."

Halcyon had indeed learned it was true from her commander and her king.

"Demaratus! That treacherous king," Cesare said with venom, and huffed. "This morning I was at the council house again with Halcyon. The war will begin after the festival." He paused and then said, "The building where the city council meets, beside the market."

Thora gave an acknowledging rumble, then she and Glauce were moving again. There was a soft creak, perhaps one of them sat down.

Then Cesare spoke again. "Demaratus sent two blank tablets to Sparta last week." Halcyon recalled the tablets, which had contained secret information about King Xerxes's plans.

"That is strange," Glauce said.

"No," Cesare argued. "Queen Gorgo determined they were not, in fact, blank. There was wax concealing his warning message about the King of Persia coming into Greece."

Glauce gasped and asked, "He is here already?"

"In northern Greece." Cesare spoke with a grave tone. "Do you know where Thrace is?"

"*Já*," Thora replied. "I seen on map." After a pause, she asked, "Will Greece fight?"

"Of course. But only after the festival, and today is the last day." Cesare moved, which caused metal to tap against metal. "It is sacrilegious to fight during the festival," he told them. "Plus Sparta must first spread word, but with the Olympiad..."

After another creak, Thora argued, "Why games control Greeks?"

Glauce sighed this time. "The games are important."

"More than war?" Thora argued in a perturbed tone.

"Sparta will rally her hoplites before King Xerxes can march any farther south into Greece," Cesare replied. Halcyon tensed when Cesare mentioned King Leonidas's pending march. Would he tell Thora about Halcyon leaving?

"Then mistress will fight?" This time a slight growl entered Thora's voice. Even her scent started to drift out of the bedroom.

Cesare set the armor on the floor, then said, "She is a hoplite, a very special hoplite to the king, and she guards him. They call her the Iron Edge because she is strong like iron and sharply skilled like the edge of a spear." There was a drawn-out silence before Glauce broke it.

"I heard the story that she stopped an assassination attempt on the king."

"Yes." Cesare made a creaking sound, then was moving metal again. The familiar groan of Halcyon's trunk signaled the last of his chore. "That is when she earned the name the Iron Edge." He stowed the equipment into the trunk, then closed it. "But the title is linked to our past."

"How?" Glauce asked.

Cesare reclaimed his squeaky seat and replied, "The Iron Edge became the patron god of Alphas in Sparta after his death."

"His death?" Glauce echoed. Her voice held a curious note, then she shifted on whatever seat she had found.

"Yes. His name was Hopla." As Cesare continued the old tale, his voice grew lighter and even a bit warm. "Hopla was the Alpha of Alphas. Cold, hard, and strong. His nickname was Iron. No one could defeat him in battle, but many attempted to do so, and all died in vain. At one point, there was a terrible war between Athens and Sparta over a colony. An Illyrian king named Dardan decided to ally with Athens."

"Illyrian?" Thora asked the pair.

"Illyria. A region north of Greece," Glauce replied. "There are different kingdoms there."

"The Spartan king at the time sent Hopla to the colony, in hopes he could end the battle over the lands. At first, Sparta was beating the Athenian forces even with King Dardan's support." Cesare paused, perhaps for extra effect. Halcyon held back a chuckle after she pictured Thora's and Glauce's wide eyes. "Desperate to win, Athens pleaded with King

Dardan for more weapons and even warriors. But King Dardan had heard the stories about Hopla and saw no reason to waste such resources."

"What happened then?" Glauce asked in an excited tone. "Did the Spartans win?"

"Well, King Dardan had a sister named Eike, who was said to have sapphires for eyes," Cesare replied. Glauce murmured a comment, but Cesare continued with the story. "King Dardan decided his best weapon was his sister, who was an unmated Omega. He triggered Eike's heat with a concoction from a healer. Then one night when the Spartan camp was quiet, King Dardan forced his sister into the camp full of Spartan Alphas."

Glauce gave a low gasp.

"Every Alpha attempted to claim her, many of them battling among themselves. But it was Hopla who claimed Eike, and no others could contest him." Cesare took a breath, then his soft chuckle reached Halcyon's ear. "While Hopla mated Eike over the days, the Athenian force crushed the Spartans."

Thora responded with a low snort.

"After the battle was over, Hopla emerged with Eike as his mate. The Athenian warriors attempted to kill Hopla and retrieve Eike, but Hopla was able to flee with her."

"Poor Eike," Glauce said in a forlorn tone.

Cesare chuckled and argued, "Yes, she was caught in the middle. But it turned out Hopla was her true mate, and Hopla had in fact set her free from King Dardan."

"With his cock," Thora remarked and earned a soft smack, most likely from Glauce. Halcyon gritted her teeth at the idea of Glauce hurting Thora or worse, being playful.

"After the defeat at the colony, Hopla swore vengeance not for the defeat itself but for the mistreatment of Eike," Cesare said.

"Did he get vengeance for her?" Glauce asked.

"Yes, he did… by killing King Dardan in battle," Cesare answered. "After the failure at the colony, Hopla was even stronger, which many attributed to Eike herself." He moved, causing a creak that echoed through the room. "In Illyrian, Eike means 'edge.' So upon Hopla's death, he was remembered as the Iron Edge."

"It's a love story," Glauce concluded and gave a contented sigh.

Thora huffed, then said, "In Norsk we say, behind a great warrior is a greater mate."

"So why is our mistress the Iron Edge?" Glauce asked after a moment. There was a soft scrape of sandals. Someone was moving or standing.

"Many believe that our mistress is the Omega version of Iron." Cesare paused, then added, "She is merely waiting for her edge." He seemed to move, boards protesting under his feet. "Iron is strong but the edge of an iron sword is where one can take or give life."

Halcyon pushed off the wall, sensing the slaves' conversation was over. She headed for the chamber-pot room, needing a visit before the end of her night. Later she retired to the bedroom and was grateful that a lamp had been left burning for her. Tonight she needed a good night's rest. Tomorrow King Leonidas and his three hundred hoplites would march toward glory.

However, Halcyon found that sleep was difficult, and she was rather troubled by her pending future. She had trained from an early age to embrace such a fate. It was now upon her, but there was a strange conflict inside her. Halcyon grappled with it throughout the night until she decided it was useless. Leaving the comforts of bed, she prepared for her one-way journey.

It took about an hour for Halcyon to dress and organize her belongings for the march. She slung her satchel over her shoulders, the only extra item she would carry. After she put on her helmet, she left the room and went to the courtyard, where her spear and shield waited by the sealed gate. Cesare was awake and waiting for her.

"Good morning, mistress," Cesare greeted and smiled. Every time Halcyon departed for duty, he was there to wish her well and ask her to return home.

"It isn't quite morning," Halcyon argued under the light of the moon.

"No, but it will be soon." Cesare indicated the shield and spear. "I cleaned your shield yesterday."

"Thank you." Halcyon studied her favored slave's aging features and wished his story would never end, at least until her death. Then she recalled that this would be her last time speaking to him. Once she was gone, the villa and her wealth would be handed to Euclid, who would one day die and pass on everything to his nephew. Halcyon was comfortable with the arrangement since her family's legacy was coming to an end.

"I hope you return with your shield," Cesare said in a gentle voice and shifted closer to her.

"I will be upon it this time," Halcyon told him and watched the glistening of his eyes. She had meant her declaration to sound prideful and glorious. But her voice cracked halfway through, then she warred with the strange turmoil in her chest. As a hoplite, it was the first time she faced a battle with her fate. She pushed it aside and straightened her back. "I saw that you will be cared for."

Cesare rubbed his hands together in front of himself. He bowed his head and said, "Thank you, mistress." He cleared his throat and blinked a few times. "You'll be missed." He swallowed, and then his Beta pheromones pitched down. "I will miss you."

Halcyon remained quiet and still, then she gave a firm nod. "And I you." Before she could think of anything else to tell Cesare, footsteps caught their ears. They both pivoted toward the newcomer, unsurprised to see Thora. There was heat in her gaze, which centered on Halcyon.

"You should be resting." Cesare stiffened when fiery blue eyes settled on him. He cut his attention to Halcyon, who didn't buckle under Thora's cold regard.

Halcyon released a low breath, then ordered, "Leave us, Cesare." She kept her eyes on Thora and waited until Cesare was gone from earshot.

"You leave for war."

"Yes." Halcyon decided there was no reason to lie about her departure. Her slaves were aware that it was imminent, but Thora and Glauce were unaware of when or of the costs of war. She had hoped to leave without an emotional scene. Cesare understood that, while Thora did not.

"You die." Thora's voice threaded with a slight ruggedness from her accent. Then a rumble followed her next demand. "You must not go."

"And if I do not, then Persia will come here, to this villa." Halcyon indicated the courtyard and the rooms around it. "They will take all that I possess." She tilted her head and whispered, "Including you."

Thora shook her head. "Then we no stay." She fisted a hand at her side.

Halcyon balked at the idea of running from her enemy. Since a pup, she was trained to face danger and odds without restraint or fear. "I am Spartan." She hardened under the sheer foolishness. "It is my duty." Ending the conversation, Halcyon reached for the gate, until a strong hand held her shoulder, pulling her back.

"*Nei!*" Thora clenched Halcyon and asked, "Your duty to your home?" She ignored the warning in Halcyon's swirling, bitter pheromones. "Your duty to your slaves?"

Halcyon shrugged off Thora's hold. "I will have none of those duties if they are taken from me."

"Your life no value?" Thora's Greek was crumbling under her surge of emotions. The harshness in her pheromones stung the inside of Halcyon's chest.

"My life has no value if I cower here." Halcyon shook her head and argued, "You were once a warrior. You must understand this."

"*Já*, but I a warrior that stayed home with sword." Thora was flushed in the face, growling out her words. "I protected my home. Then it was all taken from me." She indicated her body and whispered, "I became slave."

Halcyon released a shaky breath and wrangled the rising Omega inside herself. This was her slave, not her mate. Even if Thora had sated her heat, she was the master of the household and also a hoplite. She parted her lips to speak, but Thora continued her argument.

"War takes, it never gives," Thora argued. In the moonlight, her cheeks glistened from a few tears that stained them.

"You are right." Halcyon struggled not to touch her slave, wanting to offer and receive physical comfort. She tried to ignore her Omega's need to soothe the person it perceived as her Alpha. They were owner and slave, even after a day of intimacy. She should have walked away, ended the conversation with a turn of her back. But Thora's low-pitched whine pierced deep into Halcyon's heart. "That is why I must stop the war from taking what I hold dear." She hoped Thora could accept her fate. "Before war tries to take you, again," she whispered.

Thora shook her head and sidestepped Halcyon when she tried to edge closer to the gate. "Stay."

Unable to hold back any longer, Halcyon snared Thora's hand into hers and held tight. "I must go and you must understand."

Thora growled low as her eyes shifted to the locked gate. She clenched and relaxed her jaw several times. "History repeats," she muttered and offered no other explanation. Taking a step back, she gave her silent acceptance.

Halcyon should have picked up her shield and spear, and left the villa. Instead, she found her fingers threaded through the red plume of her helmet. She dragged the bronze away from her face and held the helmet at her side. Halcyon moved with enough force that Thora caught her with both arms. Without care about duty or position, Halcyon pulled Thora's head down for their first and last kiss.

For months, Halcyon had fought off the urge to kiss Thora, too concerned about bearing the weight of what it could mean for them. The romantic act of sharing herself with Thora through a single kiss had always overwhelmed Halcyon. But this moment was her last chance to show Thora what she had freed inside Halcyon's heart. The gods could damn her for any consequences that may follow.

The instant their lips pressed together, Halcyon was undone and completed all at once. She pressed harder into Thora's warm body, then parted her lips enough to invite Thora into her mouth. Their tongues touched with a shyness that Halcyon found charming. But it dissolved under their desire for each other. Halcyon buried her nails into the back of Thora's neck, moaning and whimpering. Their tongues met with love and rage, both trying to keep ahold of the other.

Halcyon withdrew a scant amount, but she was pulled back in by the sheer attraction between them. It felt as if even the gods couldn't separate them. Their tongues danced again while their teeth scraped over swollen lips. Thora groaned this time, pulling Halcyon's tongue into her mouth. For an Alpha, Thora tasted sweet and yet strong. Halcyon wanted to kiss Thora until her last day.

Gasping for breath, Halcyon turned her head away and broke the heated kiss. She buried her fingers into the thickness of Thora's blond hair and whispered, "I am sorry."

For once, Thora whimpered, nuzzled into Halcyon's dark hair, and breathed in her scent. "I understand." She tightened one arm around Halcyon's waist while she cupped Halcyon's warm cheek. "We have other lifetimes." Then she released Halcyon, taking two large steps back.

The sudden rush of fresh air grazed across Halcyon's lungs. She tried to steady her wild heart while she watched with a frown as Thora left her. Thora's last words repeated in her mind, touching her soul. Halcyon parted her lips, prepared to ask Thora what she meant. But Halcyon already knew and could not bear hearing the truth from Thora. After a pained huff, she pivoted and gritted her teeth before unlocking the gate.

Halcyon swung open the iron gate, then put on her helmet and collected her spear and shield. She forced her trembling body forward, yet paused and peered over her shoulder toward the moonlit courtyard.

Thora was gone.

CHAPTER 13
Halcyon

Today was the first battle against King Xerxes and his vengeful army. Over six thousand Greek warriors held a blockade at the pass outside of Thermopylae against thousands upon thousands of Persian soldiers. Similarly, four hundred Greek triremes blocked the strait near Artemisium, facing over a thousand ships from Persia.

Like all Spartans, King Leonidas and his three hundred hoplites believed they were descendants of Heracles. On Thermopylae's beach, they became the impenetrable wall that blocked King Xerxes's raging flood until the rest of the Greek city-states could rally to arms. They would not allow Persia to take Greece and their freedom.

King Xerxes withdrew his men for only a few hours in the night, after hundreds were killed by the small Greek force. This gave Leonidas a chance to conjure up more creative ways to hold his enemy at bay. It also allowed his hoplites a chance to rest, clean their wounds, and eat before Apollo brought the sun over the eastern horizon.

Leonidas approached one of the campfires and took a seat beside Olus, their makeshift healer. Leonidas rubbed his beard and regarded Olus's patient. His dark eyes flickered under the firelight.

Halcyon returned her king's stare. She refused to admit her shortcomings today and even the days prior. Olus continued to stitch her right shoulder from a sword wound. She deserved the wound after being too slow and weak. Her bronze armor did its best, but it failed to fully break the barbarian's strike during today's battle. She gritted her teeth against the memory of her failure but relished killing the Persian enemy once she recovered from her error.

A slight burn started in Halcyon's left eye and forced her to blink. The persistent sting had started when an arrow clipped her brow. She had washed the blood from her face, yet it continued to bother her. The laceration on her brow was at least dry now.

"Last stitch," Olus informed Halcyon. He finished his work, then repacked his medical kit. Halcyon thanked him before he went to his next patient.

"You must go, Halcyon." Leonidas spoke with an imploring tone rather than giving a command. They both were well aware why Halcyon needed to return to Sparta before it was too late. But Halcyon didn't agree with Leonidas's assessment. "You shouldn't be here."

"I belong here," Halcyon snapped, then looked away and bit her lower lip.

"There is no chance of survival here." Leonidas's rich brown eyes lifted and scanned over the littered battlefield along the coastline. "It is important you live."

Halcyon adjusted her chiton over her injured shoulder, which Olus had also wrapped. The few moments of silence helped her gather her resolve. "I am a hoplite and your guard," she declared and caught his worried gaze. His pheromones were still gentle, but Halcyon already rallied her own. "I've sworn to remain by your side."

Leonidas reached across the gap and gripped Halcyon's knee. "And one of my finest—until the Fates told us you are now carrying the future." He tilted his head and lowered his hand. "Sparta's future." Before Halcyon could speak, he reminded, "There is no Sparta without hoplites."

Halcyon kept the arguments silent, loathing the king's wishes and cursing her own fate. Above all, she hated her weakened body, which had done nothing but displease her since she left Sparta nearly a month ago. Each morning, she was bent over the nearest bush, and today she was injured due to her slowed reaction.

"If I must order you, then I will." Leonidas shifted forward but paused before he stood from the rock. He sighed when Halcyon offered nothing in response. He departed and she watched him head over to Meles, who was eating a tasteless dinner. Next to Meles was Stesichoros, Halcyon's direct officer.

Halcyon dipped her head and rubbed the uninjured side of her brow. She was certain they were discussing removing her. Stesichoros would side with Halcyon, but even he was subject to the king's orders. As early as the age of seven, pups were taught the importance of following orders. Once pups became adults in the military, orders were second nature and heeded without question. It made the Spartan army effective in battle, more than any other Greek army. Meles and Stesichoros would carry out their king's command, and so would Halcyon. In the end, Halcyon's best option was to concede, square her shoulders, and depart with dignity rather than dishonor herself by sparring against Leonidas. He cared for Halcyon, like a daughter. Perhaps he cared too much, in Halcyon's opinion.

Today Leonidas had determined what was wrong with Halcyon. He had sniffed it out, like any Alpha with a strong nose. He was, after all, a sire himself. Over the years, he had grown quite familiar with Halcyon's normal scent, which had subtly shifted over the last month. Leonidas smelled the truth that clung to Halcyon.

Even now, she placed a hand against her bronze clad stomach that held a piece of Sparta's future. A measure of shame flooded her because that piece was tainted by barbarian blood. At least, the Spartans would believe so. To Halcyon, Thora had gorgeous features and a loving disposition. It'd been easy to fall for Thora. And Halcyon had fallen, on to her hands and knees. Now the price of her mistake was upon her.

How could she had let this happen?

Her Omega rallied inside her chest, protesting Halcyon's disdain. Year after year passed without Halcyon having any success at expanding her family. Her mother had died not long after Halcyon's birth. Then her sire raised her until she was ready for a union. After her sire died, Halcyon was only left with Cesare. Long ago, she accepted that her family had come to an end, which would be met with honor upon Halcyon's glorious death. However, her dreams were crumbling before her.

Again, the humiliation struck Halcyon harder than any of her enemies' blows today. She failed her king and Sparta. She was meant to die here in battle at Thermopylae. But instead, she would be sent away to safety and to an unknown future. Her Omega warmed to the idea of motherhood. Closing her eyes, she willed her inner Omega to be silent. Halcyon fisted her hand against her belly and seethed low.

Not quite ready to accept her disgrace, Halcyon went in search of a meal, weaving through the camp littered with bloody weapons, broken shields, and body parts. With a bowl of gruel in hand, she returned to the same campfire. A few other hoplites joined her, discussing today's battle including the famed Persian soldiers called Immortals. They joked about the mortality of Immortals in King Xerxes's army. Each hoplite boasted about how many Immortals they killed. But they all quieted when their king came to the campfire.

Leonidas excused all the hoplites except for Halcyon. Once they were alone again, he studied her long enough to cause her to squirm on the inside. They both waited to see who would crack first.

Halcyon drew her red cloak around her weakened body and stared at the dark waters to her right. The sea peacefully brushed against the sandy shoreline and eased her earlier anger. She stiffened when Leonidas spoke first.

"You're not a failure, Halcyon. There is no dishonor in this."

Halcyon shook her head once and declared, "The gods have cursed me."

Leonidas grew wide-eyed, then his pheromones blanketed around Halcyon, who wanted to hide from it. His comforting Alpha scent caused her to recoil, not wanting it to reach her Omega. Leonidas shook his head and argued, "The gods have given you nothing but gifts in your life, including this one."

"Not this one." Halcyon met the king's gaze. "It has weakened me. I'm half the hoplite I should be." But her own argument felt weak, even to herself. She ground her teeth together, wishing she was a true Alpha rather than one in spirit.

"You're more than one hoplite now," Leonidas declared, but his tone remained calm. "And that is what you must remember over these coming moons." He grazed Halcyon's arm, gathering her full attention. "I am proud of you, Halcyon. I must know your life will continue." He then cupped her flushed cheeks. "Go home, for me."

Halcyon searched her king's eyes, feeling the earnest in them. Over time, she had come to care for Leonidas as a person. He had become family to her. She came into his service as one of his hoplites about ten years ago, and she hated to be away from his side during battle. After a moment, she inhaled his warm Alpha pheromones that reassured her Omega. "You're using your Alpha to sway me."

Leonidas tilted his head, then his lip curled with a slight grin. "Perhaps." He then went serious and whispered, "Please, Halcyon."

Halcyon bowed her head and stared at the sand between them. He hadn't ordered her, but he would if necessary. Leonidas had asked her in a respectful and caring manner. Her survival was important to him, and that was worth honoring. Straightening, she nodded and said, "Very well."

Leonidas dropped his shoulders and released a deep huff. "Thank you." His sincerity chiseled away at Halcyon's wavering resistance. He stood and offered his arm. "Come. Visit with your brothers tonight."

Halcyon conceded because this was her last time with them. Her heart was heavy now that she had made her choice to return to Sparta, alone. Once back in the meager camp, she bonded with her brothers throughout the night until Stesichoros fetched her. She swore to her brothers that their song would be told back in Sparta. In the shadows of the narrow pass's privacy, Halcyon shared a long hug with Leonidas and accepted a folded message meant for Gorgo.

"Be safe on your journey home," Leonidas murmured into her ear.

Halcyon withdrew from the hug, but she left her hands on her king's padded shoulders, gazing deep into his earthy-brown eyes. "I will see you soon."

"Yes. Upon my shield." Halcyon suspected Leonidas had accepted his fate months ago and looked forward to his foretold destiny. "Please tell my mate and pup that I love them."

Nodding, Halcyon pressed her left palm against Leonidas's bristly cheek, leaned in, and kissed his other cheek. "I will not forget you, my king." She withdrew and cleared her throat. Without another glance, she continued through the pass to where Stesichoros waited for her. Halcyon shoved on her helmet, which had blood spots, dents, and a tear on the backside. She then retrieved her spear and shield from him.

"Two Thespian hoplites will escort you home," Stesichoros told Halcyon. "They have enough supplies for the journey." He gripped Halcyon's bicep and said, "You made a wise decision."

Halcyon wanted to argue that it was a dishonorable decision, against her oath as the king's guard. It would haunt her for many months despite the fact no one among the three hundred faulted her. Instead, her comrades had offered her congratulations. With a sigh, she looked toward the camp, seeing a few hoplites resting on the other end of the pass. Halcyon was saddened at her brothers' future deaths, but they would be honored.

"Halcyon, dawn is quickly approaching."

Stesichoros's warning cut through Halcyon's concerns. She sighed and looked at him again. "Thank you. We'll see each other in Elysium."

Stesichoros smiled and nodded. "Elysium." He traded a brisk arm shake with Halcyon, then he headed back to camp.

Forcing herself to turn away, Halcyon left through the rear of the pass and sought out the Thespians, who waited for her. She hefted her spear as the Thespians took her side, heading to the path that would take them south toward Sparta.

* * *

It was a long journey back to Sparta, even longer than from Sparta. Halcyon was unsure whether the trip would come to an end. Her declining health made matters difficult and slow. She refused to acknowledge her ailments to her companions, although Stesichoros had told them.

Each morning, Halcyon would steal away from the camp until she had space from the Thespians. Then she would crumble to her knees behind a tree or rock and allow her last meal to burn against her throat until she finished with dry heaves. The stench under her nose was revolting and made her loathe her body even more.

After several gulps of air, Halcyon would rinse her mouth and return to camp. She tried to choke down a breakfast and prayed it would remain in her stomach. What made matters worse was that her shoulder wound had swelled, and foul pus oozed from it. Her armor scraped the wound and irritated it further. Halcyon sensed a fever come over her a few days after leaving Thermopylae. The late summer's heat added to her body's stress. She reminded herself that she was a hoplite and continued the march to Sparta.

The Thespian hoplites spoke little during the trip south. Everyone shared concerns for the battles at Thermopylae and Artemisium. The Thespians knew they would return to the war, but only after the battle in the pass ended. They were certain that Leonidas and his hoplites would not survive the bloody battle much longer. Even for three hundred Spartans, it was impossible to hold off King Xerxes's infinite lust for revenge. But by then, the Spartan army would mobilize for battle.

Halcyon was plagued by guilt for leaving her king's side and her brothers; her return to Sparta felt like a true failure.

She tormented herself with what Sparta would think of her, so she attempted to think about other things, like her home.

As such thoughts passed, she wondered how Thora was faring. It had been over a month, and Thora's Greek would have improved further. Halcyon had reminded Vitus to continue schooling her each day. Thora's Greek education would give her an edge, especially if Halcyon had died at Thermopylae. Before departing Sparta, Halcyon had updated her will and included instructions for Thora to be freed. Thora would also receive a certain amount of coin and a letter from Halcyon. The letter held encouragement for Thora to return home, back to the Norselands. Halcyon was uncertain whether Thora had anyone waiting for her in the Norselands, but she suspected Thora's homelands would be better for her than remaining in Greece.

As Halcyon drew closer to Sparta, she looked forward to seeing her peaceful villa. She imagined the olive trees along the street to her home, and she could almost smell the blossoms. At the villa's open gate, Cesare would be there with his loyal, warm smile in place. Then Thora would stroll into the courtyard, wiping her hands on a linen towel from the kitchen. In her daydream, Thora was surrounded by a sweet air from baking. Halcyon returned Cesare's smile but reached out and touched Thora's pale cheek.

Distracted, Halcyon hit a stone with her foot and toppled forward, but used the spear to catch herself. Her warm vision of home drifted away and left Halcyon's skin hot and her heart chilly. She was far from home, despite her longing.

Like the Thespians, she hoped to be in Sparta within a day and a half, yet the distance seemed impossible.

After they stopped to make camp, Halcyon repacked her shoulder wound with salt. She noted the wound had split open wider, but she could do nothing for it. She ate little and collapsed into her bedroll, sure her fever had again spiked. The cool night aided her overheated body, which battled against the infection from her shoulder. At dawn, the Thespians roused her, and she mustered all her strength to put on her armor and pick up her shield and spear.

One Thespian attempted to take Halcyon's shield, but he was denied by the tip of the spearhead at his face. He backed off and gave a low huff. His Beta scent swirled with bewilderment, but he and the other soldier said nothing. They started the march, which forced Halcyon to move forward.

Sparta was closer with each step.

* * *

By the following day, the weary travelers had approached the fields that surrounded Sparta. Halcyon recognized the lands. Seeing the end in sight, she forced her ailing body to pick up the pace. The Thespians recommended they go to the barracks and find a healer. Halcyon ignored their ideas and instead headed home after entering the city gates. She ignored all the onlookers' strange and curious gazes. The Thespians remained at her side until she slowed near the entrance to Villa Honor the Beloved.

Halcyon's spear became a crutch as she entered her home's courtyard. She leaned against the wooden shaft, while the shield felt like a boulder tied to her. She attempted to call for her slaves, but her throat was dry. However, the Thespians' arrival had roused them.

Cesare came out of the supply room followed by Glauce. He stared wide-eyed at his owner's unexpected return. Glauce gave a sharp gasp and snared Cesare's arm.

"By the gods!" Thora was in awe after she entered the courtyard from the rebuilt kitchen. She hastened across the courtyard to her owner, who was about to collapse. One Thespian moved forward, but he halted when the unusual tall slave jumped forward first.

Thora caught Halcyon, but she remained bent forward because Halcyon was heavy with the armor and weapons. "Cesare, remove her shield."

Halcyon dropped her spear, which clattered against the courtyard's stone floor.

Breaking from his stupor, Cesare freed the shield, lowered it to the ground, and watched as Thora moved her right arm under Halcyon's bent legs. Thora clenched her teeth as she lifted up and adjusted Halcyon in her arms. She let the bronze helmet slide off, and it struck the ground to reveal Halcyon's stricken features. Thora's own features contorted and darkened, but she lifted Halcyon higher.

After a deep sniff, Thora announced, "She is injured. Cesare, find Giles, please."

Cesare rushed out of the open gate.

Thora ignored the two Thespians. "Glauce." She startled the young Omega, who was staring at Halcyon. "Boil a pot of water."

Glauce ran across the courtyard to the kitchen.

Thora exchanged a glance with the two Thespians and offered, "Thank you." She said nothing else and departed for the upper floor. She moved with great speed. The frantic heat in her Alpha scent kept Halcyon conscious. Part of Halcyon wanted to reassure Thora, but she had little strength to speak.

Thora entered the master bedroom and lowered Halcyon onto the bed. With care, Thora removed the short sword, greaves, and cuirasses, then the sandals last. She left Halcyon in her red chiton. "I return with supplies," she said and exited the room. Halcyon hoped Cesare would come soon with a healer.

The increasing commotion drew Halcyon's attention to the right. She narrowed her eyes until Glauce and Vitus came into focus. They carried in two large bowls of steaming water. After Vitus set the bowl down, he approached Halcyon and frowned at her. He was prepared to speak, but Thora's arrival redirected everyone's attention.

Vitus stepped aside but kept his worried features glued to Halcyon.

With Glauce's help, Thora removed the chiton. Thora's frantic pheromones unfurled in the room, causing Halcyon to whine low. She attempted to speak to Thora, but her voice came out rough and weak.

"Glauce, she needs water," Thora ordered, causing Glauce to bolt out of the room. With a wet cloth, she started to clean Halcyon's shoulder wound. Even though her touch was gentle, Halcyon jerked from the pain. Each time Thora removed a piece of salt, it felt as if a dagger were being drawn out of her body. "I am sorry," she whispered to Halcyon.

Whimpering, Halcyon attempted to use her pheromones to convey her understanding and even appreciation. The pain to her shoulder was bearable, but it would also soon drain her. Glauce returned and offered her water. The cool water raced down her throat and spread through her overheated belly.

Glauce used a cloth to wipe the sweat from Halcyon's brow and face. "She has a fever."

"I know." Thora had a stern expression, focused on removing the salt. She paused when Cesare barreled into the room.

"Giles is coming!" Cesare looked from Halcyon to Thora. "What can I do?"

Thora shook her head but never broke her attention away from Halcyon. "Everyone must leave." Her scent held a degree of agitation and protective heat. "I will stay to help Giles." She jumped when the next shard of salt brought a cry from Halcyon.

Halcyon clutched a fist against her bare chest and whispered, "Thora."

Pausing, Thora held her owner's gaze and said, "There is one piece left. Ready?"

"*Já,*" Halcyon murmured, then she felt Thora's hand cover hers. She spotted a tear falling to Thora's cheek. There was little she could do to comfort Thora. But she promised to do so later, if she survived the infection brewing inside her. The last piece of salt was deeper than the others, requiring a harder tug. Halcyon cried out against the lancing pain, then blackness claimed her.

CHAPTER 14

Halcyon

Halcyon lost track of time as she roused for brief periods. Thora was there, offering her water each time. She did her best to sip from the cup, but it was difficult. On occasion, Thora would rub Halcyon's throat, coaxing the water farther down. Other times, Halcyon was awakened by Giles prodding at her shoulder wound. When she tried to look at the wound, the strain tired her out and forced her back to sleep.

Then at one point, Halcyon heard Cesare's familiar voice, stirring her. A wooden creak caught her ear before she could open her eyes. Above her, Thora and Cesare studied her with tired and concerned features. Her slaves were far too devoted. Other slaves would be praying for their master's death.

"You must drink," Thora said in a gentle tone.

Halcyon groaned and shifted her arms underneath, then took a sharp inhale from the flash of pain in her shoulder. After a curse, she slumped against the bed.

"Slow." Thora assisted her owner, raising her.

Halcyon panted from the amount of effort it took her to move with help. She swallowed and looked between Cesare and Thora. Cesare handed a cup to Thora, who proceeded to steady the rim along Halcyon's lips. The task to drink was trying, but the water was refreshing.

"Gentle," Thora whispered and dipped the cup back before the water overwhelmed Halcyon. She set it on a table to her left. Then she helped Halcyon settle back into the comforts of the bed.

"My eyes deceive me," Halcyon whispered and gazed about her surroundings. Her voice strained from disuse. A few of her memories were foggy, but she hadn't expected to make it to the villa.

Thora gathered Halcyon's smaller hand into her own. "You are home but must rest more." With her free hand, she wiped Halcyon's brow with a cloth.

"How long?" Halcyon asked.

Thora paused and clenched her lower lip between her teeth. Her canines showed in the daylight.

"You came home three days ago, mistress." Cesare held his owner's gaze and gripped the bed frame.

Halcyon blew out a low breath and grumbled to herself. She attempted to get up, but the searing pain took her breath away. A firm hand on her good shoulder halted her next attempt.

"Giles insisted that you rest," Thora said, her voicing taking on authority. Even Cesare shifted from side to side when Thora used her pheromones to quell Halcyon.

"I have slept enough." Halcyon needed to visit the council house and report their king's plans, but her weakened body gave out under her. King Leonidas was perhaps dead, bleeding out on the sands of Thermopylae with all his loyal hoplites, except Halcyon.

"You are weak," Thora reminded, then her jaw tensed. No one would be able to command Thora. Halcyon was at her slave's mercy. Thora returned to wiping Halcyon's skin clean but glanced at Cesare. "Bring the broth and bread."

Cesare heeded the command and left the room. Halcyon grunted at his willingness to follow Thora's orders without question.

"You have been the master of my villa in my absence," Halcyon murmured and spread her fingers when Thora brought the damp cloth closer.

"*Já.*" Thora glanced up at her owner and added, "I have kept it nice for you."

Halcyon managed to roll her eyes, but she indeed trusted Thora's intelligence and skills. In a short period, she had learned that Thora liked order. The kitchen's equipment was always clean and neat after being organized when Thora first arrived in Villa Honor the Beloved.

"The healer will return today," Thora said and continued her mission to clean Halcyon's body. "He is uncertain how you are still alive." Her eyes lowered to the hidden wound under the thin sheet. "Your fever broke last night."

Halcyon pursed her lips and considered the information. She tried to lift her uninjured arm when Thora came to it, but it was grueling. Thora shot her a scowl in warning. "You stayed here all night," Halcyon concluded. "Every night."

"*Já.*" Thora peeled the thin sheet away from Halcyon's nude form and continued her administrations. "One night I carried you to the bathing room and held you in cool water." She peered up at Halcyon and added, "You were hotter than when you were in heat."

Halcyon remained quiet and searched her mind. There wasn't a single fleeting memory of being submerged in the bath. The fever may have killed her if it weren't for Thora's care. After a minute, she cleared her throat and studied Thora's focused expression. "Your Greek has improved again."

Thora paused, letting the damp cloth sit on Halcyon's knee. "It has been over a moon since you left us." She went to a bowl of water and moved the cloth through it.

"Yes." Halcyon was amazed by Thora's ability to adopt the language once she was given the tools to learn. She was grateful that the barrier between them was down. "You are no barbarian."

After a snort, Thora wrung out the linen, then continued to clean Halcyon. "Your eyes are open now."

Halcyon flinched from the coolness in her slave's tone. "*Nei.*" Her use of Thora's native tongue caused Thora to hesitate. "They were never closed." She shifted her legs but groaned from the expenditure of energy. "I have always seen you for who you are, not what."

Thora finished wiping Halcyon's legs and feet, then placed the cloth in the water. "Why call me barbar?"

After a sigh, Halcyon tilted her head to the side and studied her slave's tense profile. "I was referring to everyone else."

Thora rolled her eyes and folded her arms. "I speak Greek, but everything else is barbar." She indicated her body, which was the opposite of a Greek. Pointing out her face, she added, "My ascent too."

Halcyon narrowed her eyes and attempted to discern what Thora meant by "ascent." Then it came to her, making her chuckle until the pain cut her short. "You mean accent."

Rumbling, Thora loosened her arms and said, "*Já*, I mean accent."

Halcyon smiled for the first time in over a month. In secret, she loved Thora's unusual accent and wondered if it would disappear over time. She hoped it would remain. Closing her eyes, she murmured, "You are Norsk." The weight of her exhaustion started to pull against her being, then she slipped into a light sleep. But Thora's gentle touch brought her back.

"You must eat," Thora urged in a warm voice. In her hand was a small steaming bowl.

The idea of eating sounded exhausting, but Thora was right. Cesare was on the other side of the bed now, and he helped Halcyon sit up a little. Earlier the light bedsheet must have been pulled back over Halcyon. Thora fed her owner, going at a careful pace. She glanced at Cesare and asked, "Can you retrieve more water?"

Cesare nodded and took the pitcher from nearby. He left without a word.

Thora set the bowl on the side table and tore free a piece of bread. She offered it to Halcyon, who ate it slower than normal. "Why have you returned home?" The concern was written in her features.

"I don't wish to speak of it," Halcyon replied with a bite. She looked away when Thora frowned at her.

Thora released a low breath, then picked up the bowl and said, "I understand." She finished giving the broth to Halcyon and withheld from talking again.

Halcyon struggled with the prickly ball in her throat after her harshness with Thora, who always cared for her. When she was first placed in this bed, she had promised to console Thora, but instead she was digging a hole. Halcyon's regret swelled in her chest until it was unbearable. After her last mouthful of broth, she said, "I'm sorry."

Thora focused on her task of tearing bread apart. "You do not have to talk about why you returned." She offered a piece. Her lack of persistence was strange and left a pit in Halcyon's stomach.

"I prefer when you push me," Halcyon admitted aloud, for the first time to either of them. Thora had challenged Halcyon at the beginning, then they found common ground. Later their care for each other shined through in subtle ways. Thora was stubborn, and when she applied it to Halcyon, it warmed Halcyon's heart.

Holding the bread short of Halcyon's lips, Thora tilted her head and stared at her owner before she spoke again. "I prefer when you tell me what is in your head." She pressed the food against Halcyon's lips, handing it over. "Silence breeds doubt in me."

While chewing, Halcyon considered her slave's insightful words. They'd always been able to speak through body language, but the verbal communication closed the distance between them. There was a lot they had to learn about each other. Thora gave her another piece of bread, which was enjoyable and felt heavy in her belly.

Cesare returned and set the water pitcher down near the dirty bowl. He picked up the bowl and gave a relieved sound. "There were three hoplites who came to see you yesterday."

"I sent them away," Thora added.

Halcyon should have been annoyed, but Thora was looking after Halcyon's best interest. Her Alpha slave seemed to have developed a protective streak. Regardless, she was in no condition to speak to the hoplites, even if her sense of duty ridiculed her for being weak.

"It is time to rest." Thora adjusted Halcyon until she was comfortable in the bed. The movements caused a slight wave of nausea to wash over Halcyon, but it faded after she settled into place.

For once, Halcyon conceded and closed her eyes, but she opened one when dishes clanked together. "Thora?" When her slave hesitated, she said, "*Þǫkk.*"

Thora smiled in return and grazed her fingertips along Halcyon's bicep. "*Ekki at þakka.*" She took a step away, hands filled with dishes. "I will wake you when Giles arrives." Then she left.

* * *

After sunset, Thora stirred Halcyon awake and announced that Giles was here. But first, Thora helped Halcyon sit up and lowered the sheet to expose Halcyon's upper body. She then gave Halcyon a chance to drink some water. Once set, Thora left to retrieve Giles. In the silence of the room, Halcyon had a chance to consider what had happened to her since her arrival home. She could have died from her shoulder injury, but Thora had done everything possible to ensure her survival. Again, Thora had put Halcyon first.

The nearing footsteps alerted Halcyon. She looked over at the doorway and watched Thora escort Giles into the room. There was a heavy air around Thora, who took a position off to one side near the foot of the bed. Giles smiled at Halcyon.

"How are you feeling, Halcyon?"

Raising a dark eyebrow, Halcyon huffed and replied, "As if Zeus struck me with one of his bolts."

Giles's smile grew wider, but he went serious and nodded. "But you are healing." He placed a satchel on the table next to the bed. Leaning over, he studied the wound, which intrigued Halcyon too. The skin around the wound had regained color rather than remaining white, which would have indicated the spread of the infection. The scab no longer smelled or leaked pus. At some point, the wound had been resewn. Giles most likely removed Olus's initial work, recleaned the wound, and stitched it again.

"I'm happy with your progress." Giles retrieved a few items from his satchel, placing them in Halcyon's lap. He started to clean it and attempted to be gentle. "You were able to fight off the infection."

Halcyon flinched from Giles's administration. A sheen of sweat coated her body by the time Giles finished. She slouched against the cool wall behind the bed.

"In another week, we should see much more improvement." Giles tucked his items away and wiped his hands clean on a linen. "I'll continue to visit each day."

"Thank you." Halcyon shifted her head against the wall and asked, "Have you given a report?" The military would expect details from Giles, especially since she didn't visit her assigned barracks for medical assistance.

"Yes, I went to the nearest barracks and gave details about your ailments. They're aware." Giles closed up his bag, then took it off the table. "Please continue to eat and rest. When you're strong enough, you should begin to walk, but I don't suggest any lifting."

Halcyon nodded and said, "Thank you, Giles."

Thora followed Giles from the room.

Alone again, Halcyon considered her path to healing. She'd suffered worse battle wounds in the past, but this one was far more taxing thanks to her other condition. The exhaustion in her body was bone deep and wanted to pull her to sleep for days, if not weeks. She closed her eyes and waited for Thora's return, knowing she would come back.

"Mist…" Thora's voice sounded distant. "Halcyon?" she called in a firmer tone. The use of her name shook Halcyon from her sleep. Thora let out a low sigh and said, "I will bring you dinner soon. Is there anything else you require?"

"Yes. I need to relieve myself." Halcyon attempted to ignore the heat in her cheeks. By the gods, they had fucked, knotted, and gave into their basic instincts together. However, it was another matter to handle her new personal situation.

Thora smirked, but she relented after a beat. "I can take you to the chamber-pot room, then put one in here for later."

"That'll do." Halcyon fisted her hands when Thora wiggled her arms into place around her. When Thora lifted her, she groaned in pain and slumped against her slave's larger frame. In short order, she found herself being lowered to the chamber pot in the neighboring room. She had no idea how Thora managed to lower them both so far down.

"I return." Thora stepped out and gave a semblance of privacy to Halcyon, who rolled her eyes. It was an embarrassing situation, but Halcyon had few options. After she was done, she attempted to stand, which was difficult but not impossible. She leaned against the wall and let out a heavy breath that seemed to alert Thora.

Without a word, Thora picked up her nude owner and returned them to the bedroom. She was slow when placing Halcyon back in the bed. She adjusted the sheet back over Halcyon, then collected a torn piece of linen and dipped it in water. Thora focused on cleaning the wounds along Halcyon's face.

"Gifts from the battle," Halcyon murmured. She closed her eyes while Thora cared for her. Tomorrow would be a chance to better assess her own body. Every muscle was sore. Her side hurt, which might indicate a damaged rib or two. The injuries would require time, and patience.

"Perhaps a bath tomorrow," Thora whispered after she was done applying a salve to the facial and arm wounds.

"Yes." Halcyon opened her eyes and studied her slave's worn features. "Have you slept in your room lately?" Thora didn't answer and instead closed the salve jar. "Thora, you must sleep in a comfortable place." She glanced at the wooden chair pushed against the wall. "My fever is gone, so there is little worry now."

Thora rumbled and cleaned her hands with the damp linen. "I—"

"*Lika.*"

Thora fell silent after Halcyon's plea in Norsk. After a beat, she nodded and said, "I will rest in my room." She took a hesitant step toward the hallway. "Dinner will be soon."

Halcyon allowed Thora to retreat. With no energy left, she fell asleep in a minute and didn't awake until dinner was brought to her. Both Glauce and Thora helped her eat, and Cesare came up later with a piece of honey bread. The homemade food tasted better than what she ate during the march and battle. The flavors danced on her tongue, reminding her how alive she was. The extra treat of honey was even better.

One by one, her slaves filed out of the room until only Thora was left. Earlier Glauce had placed a bell on the table in case Halcyon needed help at night. Halcyon waited for her slave to speak first, sensing something on her mind.

"Is there anything else?" Thora asked and edged closer to the bed's side.

"No, but thank you." Halcyon fought a yawn.

Thora reached but slowed and pressed her fingers against Halcyon's forearm. "I am happy you returned home." Halcyon looked away, unprepared to allow Thora's joy to curb Halcyon's strife. Thora withdrew her hand and huffed at the subtle rebuff. She extinguished the lamp on the side table. "Goodnight, mistress."

Halcyon was left to wiggle herself back down into the bed. At least she was able to convince Thora to sleep in her room tonight. By first light, they both would be in a better state.

* * *

"I can make it to the steps," Halcyon snapped after Thora grabbed her hips before her third step from the bed. The sun had risen about an hour ago, washing the bedroom in sunlight. She had already eaten after Glauce brought her a meal. While she ate, Thora and Cesare had taken care of filling the bathing tub downstairs. Glauce took the dirty dishes away when Thora arrived in the bedroom to collect Halcyon, who declared she would try to walk on her own.

Thora rumbled and released her owner, then took a step to the side. "Your mood matches your smell."

Halcyon shot a glare at her outspoken slave. "Perhaps it was a mistake to teach you Greek." She clung to the bottom of her chiton, then took more steps forward. Her legs had a slight tremble, but she had control. Once she made it to the steps outside, she paused and waited for Thora. Her balance was off, and she didn't trust herself.

Coming closer, Thora picked up Halcyon and cradled her. They descended the steps in quick succession, and then Thora lowered her to the tiles of the courtyard. Together, they went to the bathing room and entered the herbal-smelling space. It was a welcomed smell—Thora was right. Halcyon smelled bad. Thora had done her best to keep her owner clean, but it couldn't compare to an actual bath. With care, Halcyon worked to remove her chiton.

Thora closed the door, then went to the bench where the linens rested. She picked up a fresh, folded linen and brought it to the in-ground pool.

"Thora, bathe with me."

Stiffening, Thora eyed her owner and weighed the request. She dropped her shoulders when Halcyon touched her wrist. "I will help you." Untying her chiton, she removed it and dropped it next to Halcyon's red one.

Halcyon did her best to keep her eyes above Thora's chest. However, her imagination pictured the soft golden patch between Thora's legs. With Thora's rut long over, her clitoris had returned to normal size, albeit a larger one than an Omega's. With ease, Thora carried Halcyon down into the water and allowed Halcyon to slip away.

Thora went to one side and organized the soap and cloth for them. Halcyon enjoyed the epsom salt water that soothed her injured body even though her shoulder wound still stung. She leaned against the wall of the bath and admired the delicate brown that speckled over Thora's shoulders and arms. "Come sit by me."

Thora did so and relaxed next to her owner. A soft thrum rolled in her chest, indicating her contented mood.

"Your Greek has improved greatly."

Thora rested against the wall, too, and stared across the room. "We started to read and write the day after you left." She was quiet, then looked at Halcyon and whispered, "My chores and learning have helped keep my mind busy."

Halcyon grasped Thora's deeper confession. Halcyon's absence from the villa had weighed heavy on Thora. While at battle, her slaves had waited for the inevitable—Halcyon's corpse to arrive at the villa on top of a shield. However, the Fates had altered her destiny and created a new future. Without thought, Halcyon placed a hand against her belly and frowned at the idea of everything changing for her. Too many questions lingered in her mind, causing a thread of distress to bloom in her chest. Thora's slight movement broke Halcyon's wandering thoughts.

Thora retrieved the soap, lathered the cloth, and came back to Halcyon. She offered to wash her owner, who gave a faint nod. Halcyon's skin cleaned up the quickest, but her thick and matted hair required extra attention. Later it would need to be untangled, after Thora put oil in it. For now, the remnants of the blood and grime from the kills at Thermopylae were cleaned away.

After Halcyon was done, Thora bathed herself, then they left the bathing pool and dressed together. Halcyon approached the sealed door, but she could barely pull on the ring. Thora jerked the door open and allowed Halcyon through first. As they reached the stairs, Halcyon lifted her leg to the first step, but her knees gave out under her. She fell back into Thora, who caught her and lifted her. "Hades!"

Thora adjusted Halcyon and said, "No one sees." They were alone in the courtyard. In short order, Halcyon found herself in the cleaned bed. "Rest," Thora said. "I will bring a meal soon." She placed the mat over the window and left the room.

An hour later, Thora returned with a small plate of food, causing Halcyon to wake. Glauce joined her and refilled the clay cup on the table. Thora sat down after handing the food to her owner. Halcyon enjoyed the meal that Thora had made her. The honey-coated olives were a new treat.

"Did my mate stay at the villa while I was gone?" Halcyon asked.

Thora's distant expression fell away. "*Já.*" She tilted her head and said, "He stayed for about a fortnight and returned to the barracks two days before your return." There was a heavy silence, then she rumbled and asked, "Shall I send Cesare to fetch him?"

"No." Halcyon placed the empty, dirty plate on the table next to her. "He prepares for war." Her reasoning sounded hollow even to her ears. However, Thora refrained from asking questions. She held a cup of water between her hands and considered a different topic. "Are all your people similar to you?"

"Not all."

Halcyon had a slight grin. "Perhaps taller."

Thora tilted her head at the slight tease. "Some are." She went to the table that had the salve and removed the wooden lid. "I must rewrap your wound." The covering had been removed when Halcyon took a bath.

Sighing, Halcyon peered over at her healing shoulder, then set the cup on the table. She was a little better today and hoped tomorrow she'd have enough energy to visit the council house.

Thora untied the chiton over the injury and allowed the chiton to fall away from the shoulder. With the skin exposed, Thora started to coat and wrap the wound. "Does it hurt?"

"Less than before." Halcyon hid any discomfort as Thora applied the salve, training her eyes across the room. "Tomorrow I will venture out from the villa."

Thora responded with a displeased sound and eyed her owner. "It is too soon." She ignored Halcyon's cold stare. "You failed to climb the stairs, an easy task."

"Tomorrow I will," Halcyon repeated with finality. "You will accompany me."

"Yes, mistress." Thora often agreed in Norsk rather than Greek. To hear the clipped agreement created a mild sting inside Halcyon. After Thora finished re-covering the wound, she put away the salve and said, "Your scent has changed."

Halcyon narrowed her eyes at her perceptive slave. The shift in her scent was a telltale sign, and Thora seemed sensitive to Halcyon's scent, which was a concern. With a lift of her chin, Halcyon remarked, "It was the bath."

Thora set the jar on the table and gave a low huff. She opened her mouth a little, then hesitated and snapped her jaw shut. Halcyon sensed the slight shift in Thora but was unsure what it meant, for her or them. "I will wake you when Giles arrives."

Halcyon remained rigid until Thora left, then turned and sank into the bed again. She hoped after her nap that she could relax in the courtyard until dinner. The white walls of the bedroom were tiresome. Tomorrow, she swore to leave the bed, rise like normal, and tell the story about King Xerxes and

King Leonidas. But still the exhaustion in her bones remained stronger than her.

CHAPTER 15

Halcyon

Halcyon was brought to her knees, losing against her wrenching stomach. Partially digested food rose and burned against her throat. She lost her breakfast after eating it half an hour ago. As her stomach settled, she caught hurried footsteps from outside the bedroom. She remained seated on the wooden floor, clutching her weakened stomach, unsurprised by Thora's arrival.

Thora knelt beside her owner and demanded, "What is wrong?" The alarm was written across her features while she inspected Halcyon with gentle touches.

"It's nothing." Halcyon brushed off the concern. "Leave me." She remained seated close to the chamber pot that had been brought to her room the other day. The pot had been emptied earlier this morning. After breakfast in the courtyard, she had come to the bedroom to change from a chiton to a peplos before going to the council house. However, she was forced to detour to the chamber pot.

Thora ignored the order and raised Halcyon's head, studying her damp features. "You should remain here and rest further."

"I have rested plenty." Halcyon was harsh and felt guilty after a moment. Thora cared for Halcyon, too much.

"You are unwell." Thora placed her hand against Halcyon's forehead, but the fever was long gone. She frowned and murmured, "Why are you sick again?"

"I'm well enough," Halcyon said with heat. She started getting to her feet, but she needed Thora's help. "I must go to the council house today." Halcyon took a deep breath, and most of the nausea passed.

"I will accompany you," Thora said. Yesterday Halcyon had informed Thora that they would go together. But now Thora was imposing herself, if the power of her pheromones were any indicator.

When off duty, Halcyon often went alone, but at times, Cesare joined her. This would be the first time that Thora accompanied her. After a slight nod, she went to the trunk, sat, and started to put on her sandals. She also made certain to collect Leonidas's letter for his mate. Thora departed the bedroom and met Halcyon in the courtyard. She held out a cup, which was half filled. Halcyon smelled the herbal contents, then she rinsed her mouth out with it. After Thora returned the cup to the kitchen, they left the villa at a slow pace.

The walk to the market passed in silence, but they made it before the meeting started at the council house. They entered from the side and took a seat near the stage. Behind them, over a hundred council members and citizens sat in the stone seats that lined up the slope. A few times, Thora looked over her shoulders and scanned the entirety of the building.

Halcyon saw Thora's interest in the amphitheater-style structure where the council had held meetings for many years now. She leaned in close and whispered, "I'll speak at some point, but you must remain seated here."

Thora nodded.

Halcyon straightened and centered her attention on the small stage as a few members gathered before the entire council. She listened to their talks about the war with King Xerxes. Twice she glanced at Thora, who was rather captivated by the council meeting. She wondered if Thora's people held such councils in their villages.

"Halcyon," Gorgo called out from the side. Her dark hair was curly and longer than Halcyon's own. A stunning golden necklace matched her arm bracelet. She smiled when Halcyon stood.

Halcyon traded a few words with her queen and handed Leonidas's letter to her. Behind her, she felt Thora's hard stare in their direction. Gorgo was a beautiful Omega who captivated everyone. A thin line of jealousy threaded itself through Halcyon at the thought of Thora being attracted to Gorgo. After a brief conversation, Gorgo promised to visit Halcyon at the end of the meeting. A council member called for Halcyon.

Halcyon descended the steps and joined the council on the stage. She was instructed to speak about what had transpired in Thermopylae. She recounted the entire tale and explained King Leonidas's plans to the council. After the speech, Halcyon encouraged the council to immediately send the army, and then she returned to her seat.

After half the day had passed, the council ended with plans to mobilize the army now that preparations were done.

The march to Thermopylae would take only a handful of days. There they would meet King Xerxes head-on, without any restraint.

As the councilors filtered out of the building, Halcyon climbed to her feet. Thora followed her example and remarked about Halcyon's weary manner. She stayed close as they entered the aisle. Their exit was cut off by Gorgo. Halcyon smiled at her queen and mustered her strength to talk.

"Halcyon, I won't keep you long."

Thora shifted to the side and gazed upon Queen Gorgo. There was a heaviness in her pheromones that hadn't been there a moment ago.

Halcyon gave a slight bow and said, "I'm nearly recovered."

"After all these years, that is unnecessary." Gorgo waved off Halcyon's formality. "I wanted to thank you for speaking to the council today."

"Of course."

Gorgo studied Halcyon's worn features before she homed in on the shoulder wound that poked out from beyond the peplos. "And I thank you for your service at Thermopylae."

Halcyon's full lips turned down. "I hardly fought, my queen, and for that, I am ashamed by my return." She found it too easy to expression herself to Gorgo. Perhaps it was the comfort of another Omega.

Gorgo reached forward and grasped Halcyon's good arm. "My mate would not have sent you home without good cause." No one was aware why Halcyon had been sent back, but many gossiped about it. Halcyon had noticed the peculiar looks when she arrived at the council house and then the subsequent whispers that followed her.

Halcyon swallowed and replied, "It's my own failing." If she had been more cautious and restrained her inner Omega, such a poor future would not have befallen her.

Gorgo bit her bottom lip. "Perhaps one day soon, you'll explain such to me." After a gentle squeeze, she released Halcyon.

"Perhaps." Halcyon was drained from the day even though the sun had passed the midway point only an hour ago. She would need to rest soon. "Have you received any word about King Leonidas?" After Gorgo's headshake, she dropped her shoulders and rumbled in displeasure. Everyone was aware he was dead; the eventual announcement was a formality. Still, Gorgo was a widow and would have to raise their six-year-old pup alone.

Gorgo switched topics and looked to the right at Halcyon's slave. "And who is this unusual Alpha?" A measure of intrigue lingered in her voice and features. Thora may be a slave, but she had captivated Gorgo.

Halcyon understood Gorgo's interest and held out her hand to Thora. "Queen Gorgo, this is my slave, Thora." There was little point in hiding the fact that Thora was hers rather than a helot. An elite group of Spartan citizens were wealthy, and Gorgo was no exception.

Gorgo regarded Thora for a quiet moment, then focused on Halcyon again. "Where did you find such a slave?"

Halcyon hid her uneasiness, but she had known Gorgo for a long time. It was no secret that Halcyon's sire had made his fortunes in Athens and brought them to Sparta. After a sigh, she answered, "From Telamon." She suspected Gorgo was familiar with the slave trader.

Gorgo stared again at Thora. "Where is she from?"

Halcyon attempted to answer but was cut off.

"I am Norsk."

Gorgo raised an eyebrow, then a playful grin creased her lips.

Halcyon peered over her shoulder at Thora, giving a nonverbal warning. However, Thora was undeterred, if the puffiness of her chest was any indicator. Halcyon was too exhausted to further reprimand her slave. She looked at her queen again. "As you can see, she has learned our language."

"Yes," Gorgo replied in a thoughtful manner. She turned her amused features onto Halcyon. "And I can also see she has an independent spirit, like her owner."

Shifting on her feet, Halcyon concluded it was best to end their conversation. She bowed in silent request. "My queen."

Gorgo responded with a soft chuckle, but she relented. "I expect an invitation once you are well enough, Halcyon." With a smile, she departed and went back down the steps.

Halcyon watched her queen leave, and she noticed how Thora did the same. "Come." Together, they started the walk back to the villa. Halcyon sensed that Thora was closer to her than normal, probably concerned about Halcyon's well-being. She grumbled, but it wasn't worth an argument. "What did you think of the meeting?"

Thora had a thoughtful look and replied, "It is different from the Norsk way."

Halcyon tilted her head in interest. "How so?"

"We are led by one."

Halcyon understood. Spartan culture had two kings, but they were often balanced by a council. In many Greek city-states, the government was controlled by the people. Sparta had a special system compared to the other parts of the country.

"There is no council," Thora said.

Halcyon slowed as she approached the open gate to the courtyard and waited until Thora was at her side.

"It intrigued me."

The hint of appreciation in Thora's words showed how she enjoyed the Greek culture. Halcyon would take her again.

Thora frowned at her. "You should rest." The authority had returned to her features and her voice. She followed Halcyon into the courtyard, which was quiet, but Glauce and Cesare were never far.

"You have said that many times to me of late."

"Only out of concern," Thora said. "You have yet to heal." She eyed the shoulder wound with open worry. "I must change your dressing."

"Giles will be here soon." Halcyon was pleased by Thora's administration to her health and well-being since her return from battle. She suspected, between Giles and Thora, she had recovered sooner than most. "But I should relax." Thora was right, as usual. Thankfully Thora wasn't one to gloat about her perceptive nature, and that kept Halcyon calm.

Thora followed Halcyon upstairs to ensure she made it. In the bedroom, Glauce was cleaning and putting new sheets on the bed. Thora instructed Glauce to prepare a meal. Halcyon smiled at Thora's command over the house slaves, including Cesare. She was grateful for Thora's ability and willingness to take charge of the villa. Halcyon trusted her.

After Halcyon took a seat on a stool, Thora undid the peplos from Halcyon's injured shoulder. After she re-dressed the wound, she helped Halcyon change into a fresh chiton and asked, "Do you wish to eat here?"

Halcyon weighed the options and replied, "In the courtyard." The fresh air was nice and more enjoyable in the evenings when the sun was low.

"I will return to wake you."

Halcyon nodded, then lowered onto the bed and fell asleep as Thora's footfalls faded away. She slept for the next few hours until Thora roused her. She went to the courtyard, and Thora emerged with several plates of food. Halcyon eyed the honey-coated olives. Thora was about to return to the kitchen, but Halcyon stopped her.

"Join me."

Thora squinted at the unexpected request. She peered toward the kitchen's entrance and curled her fingers into the hem of her chiton. The spike in Thora's pheromones told Halcyon how unsure she was.

"I prefer company when I eat." Halcyon withheld from confessing that she desired only Thora's company this evening. Vitus ate with her on occasion, but he'd also befriended local Spartans with his charm and would dine with them at times. At that moment, Glauce arrived with the wine and a set of dishes. "Glauce, fetch another plate and cup after you finish pouring my wine."

"Yes, mistress." Glauce smiled at Thora, who aired her uneasiness. After a giggle, Glauce hurried off to retrieve another setting.

Halcyon collected the bowl of honey olives and popped them into her mouth. "These are very good. Have you tried them?" Using her pheromones, she further invited Thora to the table.

Thora shook her head, then slipped into the empty seat.

"Then you must." Halcyon handed her the bowl.

Thora inspected the honey-coated olives before eating one. She blinked a few times and cleared her throat. Halcyon chuckled at her slave's startled expression. Glauce brought a plate and filled a cup for Thora. Once they were alone again, Thora spoke up.

"We do not have these in Norsk." Thora pointed at the bowl of honey olives.

Halcyon placed different items on her plate. "What did you often eat?"

"We ate much fish, fresh and dried," Thora replied. "Also cow and pig and other livestock."

"I enjoy fish," Halcyon said. "When it is affordable." Tonight they were fortunate to have fish, but Halcyon's first bite had an off-putting flavor. She frowned at the fish on her plate and switched to the figs.

"Are there figs in the Norselands?"

Thora shook her head. "I like the fig. It is much better than the olive." She ate one before she picked up the bowl of gruel. A contented hum left her after the first mouthful.

Halcyon chuckled and smiled. "I can't imagine my life without olives."

Thora remained quiet and focused on the food. She tore up slices of barley bread and coated them with the olive oil and herb dip. The air around her was heavy, causing Halcyon's Omega to stir.

"Tell me your age," Halcyon attempted, leaning closer to her slave.

"I will be twenty-four this winter."

Halcyon grinned in triumph after confirming the truth. "I will be thirty-four this summer." She fought a blush when Thora smirked at her.

"I knew you were older. You have gray hair." Thora pointed at the spot along her owner's temple.

After a chuff, Halcyon rolled her eyes and argued, "It's from my time as a hoplite." Yet she fussed with her hair, in a failed attempt to hide the fine silver strands. She exhaled and took a sip of her fruit drink. "Do you miss home?"

Thora remained quiet and hesitated from eating the next slice of bread. After a sigh, she met Halcyon's gaze and replied, "I have learned to accept my place in Greece."

Halcyon had a thin frown and dropped her shoulders. "I'm afraid Greece may never fully accept you." Her statement was colored with sadness from the truth. It was also a reminder of the decisions Halcyon had to face. She gritted her teeth and forced back the upswell of trepidation inside her. There was no reason to face it right now.

"It does not have to accept me."

Halcyon pursed her lips after Thora's rebuke. Similar to Greece, Thora may never accept Greece back. Most Greeks were arrogant and saw themselves as Zeus's children compared to the rest of the world. Halcyon had experienced a measure of such unacceptance in her youth when her sire moved them to Sparta. She was an outsider until she proved her worth to Sparta. With a sigh, she took a piece of bread and decide to change topics. "Tell me what your name means."

Thora had a slight grin, which lightened her dismal features. "It is Norsk for…" She bit her lip and looked up to the sky. "When there is rain and light in the sky. The sound that the storm makes?"

"Thunder."

Thora had a wider grin and nodded. "That is my name."

Halcyon grunted, then chuckled and rumbled low. The name was appropriate for her slave, who had a distinct personality rather than a meek one. Thora's prior owners failed to contain her, while Halcyon learned it was simpler to win over Thora's loyalty. However, that was only after Halcyon first emphasized her place as the master of the villa. Euclid was second in charge after Halcyon, but Thora had asserted herself above him.

"And what of your name?" Thora drank some wine.

Halcyon shook her head. "My name means peace and calmness."

Thora choked on the wine and put the cup on the table, coughing several times until her throat cleared itself.

"Did I amuse you?" Halcyon flashed a faint grin.

Thora shook her head and cleared her throat. "I apologize, mistress." She took a sip of the wine, then tried her throat again. "You are a hoplite."

Halcyon shrugged and crossed her legs. "It is a slight naming error on my sire's part." She remembered her sire's tale about her name. "A Halcyon is a bird who once was a female Omega."

After a tilt of Thora's head, Halcyon told the story about how her namesake had a mate named Ceyx, who lost his brother. Ceyx boarded a ship and went in search of his brother, but like his brother, he lost his life at sea. Upon his death, Morpheus came to Halcyon in her sleep and told her that Ceyx had died. Overwhelmed with grief, Halcyon threw herself over a cliff but was turned into a beautiful bird by the gods. Halcyon flew to her mate's corpse that floated on the seas and swept him up with her wings. Ever since Ceyx's death, Halcyon kept the seas and winds calm for a fortnight after the winter solstice in honor of her dead mate.

At the end of the story, Thora grunted low but remained quiet and ate a few cubes of cheese. A soft rumble sat deep in her chest and called to Halcyon, who wanted to ignore it.

"Why is the villa named Honor the Beloved?" she asked her mistress.

Halcyon's answering smile was bittersweet. "My sire named it after my mother. Her name was Maria." A slight roughness entered her voice. "Maria is a Latin name for beloved."

"Oh." Thora had a thoughtful expression, then she offered a warm smile. "It is a good name for the villa."

Halcyon mirrored her slave's smile. She tried the lamb next and hoped it had a better flavor than the fish. "Tell me about your lands, your life before becoming a slave." She placed several pieces of lamb on a large piece of bread and handed it to Thora, who was surprised by the gesture.

Thora nibbled on the food as she spoke about her previous life. "The Norsk life is a simple one. We farm, fish, and fight on occasion." She seemed content and more comfortable than earlier.

"Fight with whom?" Halcyon asked. She cut more meat and placed it on another slice of bread for herself. Her first bite left her uneasy, but the flavors were familiar after all.

"Clans fight each other for resources, land, power, or even Omegas."

"Have you fought?" Before Halcyon's departure for Thermopylae, she had learned tiny secrets about Thora's past as a warrior. At least, Thora appeared to have training in the art of fighting.

Thora swallowed her mouthful first, then replied, "I have when necessary." She met Halcyon's curious gaze. "For my mate's honor and to protect my pup."

Halcyon stiffened from the jolt that went through her entire frame after the mention of Thora's pup. Did Thora have an Omega mate waiting at home along with a pup? Part of her suspected not if Thora had rutted and knotted Halcyon. It wasn't impossible for a bonded Alpha to rut outside of their union, but it was less common. "You are in a union, then?" The crack in her voice was too obvious.

Thora stayed silent and stared at Halcyon, trying to read her owner. After she made a soft noise, she replied, "I was until our clan was attacked by neighboring clan." She looked away and murmured, "He was killed along with my pup. I was taken and sold into slavery."

Halcyon had suspected that may have been Thora's path to Greece. The story pressed against her heart and stirred her Omega. "Your mate was an Omega?" A male Omega was as rare as a female Alpha, but it was unsurprising that a female Alpha would be mated to one.

Thora shook her head and picked up a piece of lamb. "*Nei*." She chuckled after Halcyon's eyes widened at her. "My mate was an Alpha." After eating the lamb, she took pity on Halcyon and said, "I birthed our pup."

Halcyon was at a loss. Her mind went in hundreds of directions at the idea of two Alphas together. Thora was a female and, as such, had the ability to become pregnant. But it was an unusual situation for two Alphas to form a union. One oddity was the fact Thora bore no claim mark on her neck. A part of her wondered whether her relationship with Thora worked because of Thora's former union to an Alpha. Many in Sparta commented about Halcyon's Alpha-like personality.

"May I ask what the name of your pup was?" Halcyon refrained her Omega's desire to touch Thora. As much as she wished to learn about Thora, she would respect Thora's decision to decline her requested.

"Bjørn," Thora whispered and revealed the glisten in her eyes. "In Norsk, it means bear." She lifted her gaze to the sky and blinked a few times.

Halcyon smiled despite the fact she hurt for Thora, who lost one pup. She placed a hand on her stomach and pictured how the pup might look one day. With a soft huff, she banished the pleasant images that weakened her. Releasing a breath, she said, "Tell me more about your family. Do you have any siblings?"

"*Já.*" Thora smiled, chasing off the sadness in her eyes. "I have eight siblings."

"Eight!" Halcyon placed a hand against her chest. "The gods bless your mother."

Thora laughed and set her plate on the table. She rested her hands in her lap, becoming more relaxed with Halcyon. "Five of my siblings survived to adulthood." She pursed her lips and stared at her hands. "Of the five, two were enslaved when I was."

Halcyon's eyelids fluttered for a beat, then she shook her head at how much Thora's family had suffered. "What of the three remaining?"

Shaking her head, Thora exhaled and met Halcyon's gaze. The dip in her pheromones indicated her somber mood. "I assume they live. My older brother was mated and had a pup." She cleared her throat and whispered, "I was the third oldest, but my sister between me and Arne passed away from fever."

Halcyon dragged her fingers through her hair and withheld a delicate whine for Thora's sake. She cleared her throat and said, "You must miss them."

Thora remained silent and stared across the courtyard. The heaviness in her scent tugged at Halcyon's heart.

"What of your parents?" Halcyon asked.

Thora grasped her slave iron and turned it along her wrist. "Mother was alive when I was taken, but my sire died in battle."

Halcyon flinched and wished she could change Thora's past. But she wasn't a goddess, and the Fates could be cruel. The discussion was difficult and brought up ugly memories for Thora. "I'm sorry. I chose a poor topic."

"*Nei.*" Thora regarded her owner and whispered, "I do not mind. It has been many years since I spoke of my family and homelands."

Halcyon chewed on her bottom lip, then asked, "How long ago were you taken from your homelands?"

"Over three years ago," Thora replied. "I was transported from my Norselands to Greece. It took six months." She pursed her lips, and her eyes became distant. "The slave trader sold me to a master in Athens, where I stayed for year and half. Then I was sold to Telamon, until you purchased me."

"Did Telamon touch you like he did Glauce?"

"*Nei,*" Thora replied in a growly voice. "He was scared of me."

Halcyon snorted low and smiled to herself. "It takes an Omega to subdue you, not a Beta or another Alpha." A smirk curled her lips further.

Thora rolled her eyes, but a soft laugh escaped her. "It would seem so," she revealed in a warm voice.

"What is life like in the Norselands?" Halcyon asked, in hopes to move to a happier topic. She wanted to learn about Thora's previous life and how it compared to Greek life. Halcyon had experienced the various lifestyles within Greece but not outside her nation.

With ease, Thora spoke about her life at home. There were minor similarities between the Norsk and the Greeks, at least when it came to warfare and power. However, the everyday cultures were rather different. Thora explained how her homelands had grand mounts, lush plains, a lot of coastlines, and many water inlets. The weather was hotter in Sparta and seemed to have little relief. By winter it would cool off, but Thora insisted the Norselands were much cooler and had snow. Halcyon had never seen snow.

Cesare's arrival in the courtyard ended their conversation. He regarded them both and offered a slight smile to Halcyon. "It is getting late, mistress."

Halcyon eyed Cesare, who shifted on his feet from her hard stare. She attempted to hide her good mood and forced Cesare to sweat her mock annoyance. That was until Thora ruined her fun.

"It is late." Thora stood after seconding Cesare. The sun had set about half an hour ago. Earlier Glauce had lit the various lamps in the courtyard. Once Vitus returned, Cesare would lock the iron gate for the night.

Halcyon narrowed her eyes at the pair. "As I recall, I am the master of this villa."

"*Já.* Of course, mistress," Thora teased and ignored Halcyon's sour expression. She turned to Cesare and said, "I will help our mistress to bed."

Cesare deferred to Thora's order and scurried off before Halcyon could halt anything. How was it possible that Thora had taken over the villa and slaves to such a degree?

Halcyon glared at Thora, who remained unbothered by the look. "We must discuss this."

At first, Thora was unfazed by the coolness in Halcyon's tone. Then Thora offered a hand. "Your bedroom would be best." Thora fought a smirk that pulled at the corner of her lips. "Rather than the openness of the courtyard." She had pushed one of Halcyon's buttons, the need to have privacy. Cesare and Glauce would overhear their discussion.

Halcyon huffed and considered refusing the hand in front of her. With grace, she took it and was helped to her feet. For an instant, the weariness in her body almost pushed her back into the seat, but she ignored it. There was no room to be weak in public, or in front of Thora for that matter. The journey to the upper floor became a climb. Thora was behind her for every step to the bedroom.

Once in the room, Halcyon dropped to the trunk with a soft thud and dragged a hand through her hair. The curls of the strands gave way to her fingers, and she cursed her body for its brittleness and for being an Omega. She prepared to lean down, but Thora knelt in front of her and handled freeing the sandals.

"You make it difficult to reprimand when you care for me," Halcyon whispered.

"Do you not trust me to run your villa while you heal?" Thora asked after she took off the first sandal.

Halcyon did trust Thora, and Thora alone. "It seems you have taken charge since I left," she replied, then found crystal blue eyes on her. The richness of them softened Halcyon. The temptation to lean forward and kiss Thora overwhelmed her. She forced her gaze away and said, "I'm still the master of this villa." She grumbled at how many times she had to remind her slave.

"*Já*, you are." Thora finished with the second sandal, setting both aside. "You are the first to ever force me to kneel." The incident had been months ago and felt somewhat distant to Halcyon. However, the significance of her ability to force Thora, a superior Alpha, to heel sank in. "And you are the first to ever make me rut," she added in a soft yet husky voice.

"That's impossible," Halcyon argued and cursed the blush that overcame her. The Omega in her was so pleased by the news. Thora seemed far too experienced to have gone through her first rut. However, if Thora's former mate was an Alpha, then she had plenty of knowledge on what to do.

Thora grunted and wrapped a hand around the back of Halcyon's muscular calf. "My mate was a male Alpha. Do you believe I would rut for him?"

Halcyon fidgeted, then stiffened after her strange motions. The warmth of Thora's hand started to lull her. She raised her chin and ordered, "This ends." She stood, broke the contact, and stepped around her slave.

"When you are well again."

Halcyon stopped and half turned toward Thora. How could her slave infuriate and arouse her at the same time? She wanted to snap at Thora, but the remainder of her energy was enough to go to bed, not fight. Thora approached Halcyon's side and towered over her. They both remained silent, still, and tense. Thora's chest rose and fell with great effort, indicating she had scented Halcyon. The battle to stay calm was hard for Halcyon. She didn't want Thora's Alpha mind to come to any conclusions about her recent physical changes.

After a delicate huff, Thora broke away and left Halcyon to her privacy. Even though she was gone, her musky pheromones lingered around Halcyon. Without thought, she breathed in the comforting scent of her Alpha slave. She whimpered low and wrangled the desire to call Thora back. Her Omega would have to learn the consequences of her poor decisions in the past.

CHAPTER 16

Halcyon

Halcyon dove under an arrow that swiped past her face. She attacked her opponent with a thrust of her spear, which pierced him in the gut. With a grunt, she wrenched it deeper into him, driving him back into another Immortal soldier. A sword came at her from the left, but she raised her shield to block it. The Immortal was determined and slammed his sword against her shield again. Another arrow came toward her, forcing Halcyon to release her spear. She stumbled away, then fell onto her back after she tripped on a body.

The Immortal chased her, yelling something in his native language. He raised his sword and brought it down. Again, Halcyon used her shield to protect herself, then kicked at his ankles and pushed him back. It was enough time for her to climb to her feet, but she had to protect herself from another sword swipe. She unsheathed her blade and came at him. They traded blows in the middle of the battle. The sand under her became both firmer and wetter, warning her that she was too close. The roar of her brothers convinced her that this was their last day. She would see Elysium soon. But first, Halcyon would kill as many Persians as possible.

With a howl, the Immortal beat against Halcyon's shield and attempted to break her defenses. He had backed her into the water a few steps and would drive her deeper into the water if necessary. Halcyon roared back at him, then slammed him with her shield. The Immortal landed on his back, but he jumped to his feet without hesitation. The redness in his face was more than blood; it was fury for being overpowered by a female Omega.

Halcyon yelled at him, then slapped the front of her shield with the flat of her sword. Her challenge rallied him and herself. The Immortal sprinted toward her, prepared to ram all his strength into her. From under the bronze helmet, Halcyon revealed her bloody teeth in a fierce smile and launched forward when he took the bait. After two wide steps, she dropped to one knee, let go of her sword, and tensed her upper body for the impact. The loud slam of the Immortal warned her, then Halcyon cried out and lifted up and over.

The Immortal hollered when he was hoisted into the air and launched toward the sea. He hit the water with a loud splash that caught Halcyon's attention. She scrambled for the hilt of her dagger. The Immortal's brief thrashing in the water signaled that he was close to recovering. Halcyon freed her dagger, adjusted her grip, and then flung it around toward the Immortal. She prayed to the gods that her accuracy was true.

For a beat, the Immortal stood motionless before he toppled into the water again. Blood flowed from his neck and mixed with the salty water. Halcyon panted for a beat, then stood and howled her victory.

"Halcyon!"

A strong voice cut through Halcyon's dreamscape. She flung open her eyes and snared the attacking person by the throat. Halcyon snarled at her enemy, who grappled with her.

But then the familiar scent cut through her battle haze. The person's outline started to take shape along with the rest of the area. She wasn't on the beach anymore.

"Thora!" Halcyon released her slave and hurried out of bed when Thora stumbled back. Cursing and panting, she hastened to Thora, kneeling down next to her.

Thora coughed several times and cradled her bruised neck.

Halcyon went to the small table by the bed. She grabbed the cup of water, trying to not splash it. She fell to her knees in front of Thora and ordered, "Drink." She watched Thora gulp down the water in a few swallows. "You know not to touch me when I sleep." The moonlight from the open window provided little light to inspect Thora's neck. It wasn't long ago that Euclid had attacked Thora and bruised her.

"I have learned why," Thora said after she placed the cup on the floor. She sat on her butt and patted her chest between a few more coughs.

Halcyon pushed the sticky strands of hair off her own forehead. She returned the cup to the table and picked up the lantern, which she lit. With a heavy sigh, she set the lamp aside and checked Thora's neck. The redness started to fade, but anything more long-term might not show until tomorrow. "Can you breathe okay?"

"*Já,*" Thora replied in a rasped voice. She rubbed the spot after Halcyon withdrew her hands. "You were having a bad dream and stirred the entire villa."

"I know." Halcyon continued to feel the effects of the nightmare. Her heart pounded against her chest, but the rush in her blood hummed a little less. "You're safer to throw my helmet at me than touch me."

Thora huffed and dropped her hand from her neck, noticing her owner's playful smile. "I will do so next time." She stood. "I hope you sleep better than before." She started for the door until Halcyon's husky voice called to her.

"Stay tonight." Halcyon flinched at the implications of having Thora stay with her. "In my bed," she added when Thora's jaw loosened. "It's the least I can do after I strangled you." The peace offering could open other doors, if Halcyon wasn't careful. Deep inside, her Omega needed to make amends to Thora.

"And what if you strangle me again in our sleep?"

Halcyon tasted the humor in the question. "I will not."

After a deep breath, Thora bent down and picked up the lamp. "Glauce will notice my absence."

"I imagine she noticed your absence during my heat," Halcyon bantered, then returned to the bed. She waited for Thora to make her choice.

Thora grunted and placed the lamp on the table. She extinguished the flame and proceeded to walk around the foot of the bed. Halcyon did her best to remain neutral when Thora climbed into the bed next to her. Yet Thora's company sparked a ball of heat low in her gut. Thora was a gorgeous Alpha and had captivated Halcyon from the first day. "Thank you," Thora whispered in the darkness.

"For choking you?"

Huffing low, Thora stretched out, then she settled into a spot next to Halcyon. "This is much more comfortable than my bed."

"You sleep on the floor," Halcyon stated. She closed her eyes and basked in the closeness of her slave. She wanted nothing more than to turn toward Thora and touch her. Such enticing thoughts were dangerous, so she buried them. "Goodnight, Thora."

"Goodnight, mistress."

Halcyon turned onto her right side and had quieter dreams instead of nightmares about the battle at Thermopylae. By morning, she found herself alone and suspected Thora had risen before daybreak. After dressing in a yellow chiton, Halcyon started for the courtyard until the constant nausea increased and forced her to race to the chamber-pot room.

"Hades," Halcyon growled, hating mornings. Her weakened body brought her to her knees before the damn pot. Halcyon tried to be quiet, but the sounds had alerted Thora. The soft slap of sandals echoed in her head.

Thora was at her side and assisted Halcyon, wiping her face clean. She remained kneeling beside Halcyon and studied fatigued features. The sharpness in her pheromones were a giveaway about her worry.

Lifting her head off the wall, Halcyon rasped, "I'm okay."

"I realize now." Thora placed her hand against Halcyon's good shoulder. "You are with pup." The brightness of her eyes took on a glow. "With our pup."

Halcyon stiffened, then glared at Thora. Her heart lurched against her chest before it drummed harder. She tried to ignore the building buzz in her veins. Her Omega wanted the gorgeous Alpha to know and recognize the growing pup as theirs. However, Halcyon was a female hoplite who had to uphold her status as a Spartan.

"That is why King Leonidas sent you home." Thora placed the linen on the floor and looked at Halcyon's stomach. "I suspected yesterday about why you have been so sick and craving strange things like olives with honey." She lifted her gaze until their eyes met. "Then last night when we slept side by side, I noticed how different your scent has become over the days."

Halcyon's stare was hard, perhaps even bitter. She began to pant at the grave reality of her situation. She failed to find a rebuke or any firm denial. It was impossible to deny scents and pheromones, and more so when it was the Alpha who impregnated her. From the start, Thora was sensitive toward Halcyon. With a developing pup, Thora would become more attuned each day.

"I have not spoken about this to anyone." Thora kept her voice low. The warm invitation in her scent called to Halcyon. But then Thora frowned. "You are unhappy about a pup." She held a touch of bewilderment in her features. "This is a gift from our gods."

Halcyon shook her head and clenched her hand. "There is a great war burning for our freedom. And this *thing* has weakened me to the point I cannot wield my spear." Halcyon's voice trembled from her rage.

"It is *our* pup! *Not* a thing," Thora hissed. Then her scent went sour, causing Halcyon to almost recoil in shame.

"It's a curse that has taken me from my duties," Halcyon said with a growl. Her pounding heart grew louder in her ears. She wanted to cave into Thora's protective Alpha nature, but Halcyon's mind forbade her.

After a deep breath, Thora shook her head and murmured, "There can be no hoplites without pups. The gods could have ended your life at the tip of a spear, but they gave you a pup and a future far beyond your own." She raised her hands and cupped Halcyon's flushed cheeks. "You are a hoplite, and soon you will bear another. It is a blessing."

Halcyon lowered her head and refused to accept her slave's points. She was a hoplite, pregnant or not. However, the pup was a minor inconvenience that would grow into a burden. To add further social shame to Halcyon, the pup would be only half Spartan. If the pup was born with dark hair, then there was a chance it wouldn't be ridiculed by the Spartans.

After a low huff, Thora shook her head and glowered at her owner. "My three-year-old pup was murdered in front of me." Her eyes glistened while her voice grew rough. "A curse is to carry my dead pup's murder for the rest of my life."

Halcyon closed her eyes after the ugly confession. She tried to hold her mouth shut, but she whined and bent forward after a wave of dizziness hit her. "Thoraaa..."

Thora latched onto her owner and held her steady. "It will pass," she whispered in a gentler voice. The tenderness of her touch and the strength of her scent soothed Halcyon. Her Alpha slave was close, ensuring her security.

"I wish for this to cease." Halcyon leaned into Thora, taking more comfort.

"It will improve," Thora whispered, then a thread of amusement entered her voice. "It is only for nine months." She received a low grumble.

"I will place you in charge of the pup," Halcyon said in warning. The threat was hollow and sounded like a tender promise. At one time, Thora had been pregnant and raised a pup. Thora's experience brought a level of reassurance to Halcyon.

Thora smiled and brought her head closer to Halcyon's own. "I shall enjoy that." A grin tugged at her lips. "I will teach the pup about Norsk ways." Her lack of "our" caught Halcyon's attention.

Groaning, Halcyon started to straighten, but she kept one hand on Thora. "The gods forbid that I have another Norsk-minded person in my household."

Thora chuckled, then became stern. "Perhaps fresh air in the courtyard will help." She refocused Halcyon, and they stood together. They exited the room and started down the steps. Thora kept a close eye on her owner.

"I'll go to the council house this morning." Halcyon faced her slave after they made it to the ground floor. "You will join me."

"*Já.*" Thora took a step toward the kitchen and said, "I will bring you breakfast and a mouth rinse." Her departure left a small gap inside Halcyon. Glauce emerged from the kitchen and offered the rinse. A little later, Thora arrived with breakfast for her owner and greeted Vitus.

"Good morning," Vitus said to Thora. He had taken the empty seat next to Halcyon. "You look well."

Thora indeed had a different air about her. "Would you like a plate?"

"Please." Vitus smiled. "Thank you." Thora left again but soon returned with food for him.

Vitus dined and chatted with Halcyon. This had been his first chance to visit with Halcyon since her return from Thermopylae over a week ago. A few times, Halcyon caught his stare at the wound across her left eye. For an hour, she and Vitus discussed Thora's advancements with Greek. A lot had been covered in a short period. Halcyon was proud of her slave for her accomplishments and developments.

Thora's return to the courtyard prompted Halcyon to leave for the council house. She bid Vitus goodbye, then headed through the courtyard, out the gate, and onto the streets. Thora followed behind her to the market where the council house was located.

Similar to yesterday, many seats at the council house were occupied by citizens. There were murmurs about an official announcement of King Leonidas's death. Halcyon's stomach churned, then she dipped her head when a Thespian messenger stepped on stage. With a stiff back, he made the devastating pronouncement. King Leonidas was dead. A great uproar ensued until the council wrangled in the crowd. King Leotychidas was the only citizen to hold an indifferent reaction.

Then the talks were renewed on how large of an army to send against King Xerxes. By early afternoon, the decisions were made and the army leaders given final orders. Within days, the Spartan army would march north to face the Persian king and his large army.

Halcyon was relieved by the outcome because it meant her king's sacrifice was not in vain. She prayed his soul would make safe passage to Elysium. As people left the building, she watched Gorgo speak with different councilmen. Halcyon suspected Gorgo expected her mate would return upon his shield any day now. Such truth stung Halcyon, whose own mate was preparing to leave for war. She decided it was best to visit Euclid before he started his march.

"Mistress?"

Halcyon broke from her thoughts and ordered, "Wait here." She left Thora, then went down the steps. She met Gorgo halfway and chatted for a few minutes. Gorgo smiled at the dinner invite from Halcyon and accepted it. Halcyon ignored the buildup of a knot in her belly. She'd had plenty of dinner guests in the past, but tonight the Queen of Sparta would come to her villa. After returning to Thora, they left for home and along the way, she mentioned, "Queen Gorgo will be joining me this evening."

Thora made a slight sound of acknowledgment but nothing else. She continued to follow her owner through the streets of Sparta.

Halcyon bristled at her slave's relative silence. Thora was talkative by nature, and her pheromones were the loudest. The hint of displeasure in Thora's scent was a signal that she didn't approve of Gorgo's visit. However, Halcyon didn't require Thora's approval. She raised her chin despite Thora's inability to see the motion. She passed through her villa's open gate and said, "I plan to relax for a while so that I am pleasant company."

Thora paused near the doorway to the supply room. "I will wake you before she arrives."

After a nod, Halcyon continued through the courtyard and went up to the second level. She let out a breath once she was alone in the master bedroom and had a chance to think. Thora's wonderful scent called to Halcyon's Omega and seemed to pull at her more than when they first met. She contributed it to her pregnancy and the natural desire to be close to her developing pup's sire. But the pup's sire was a slave, who was considered a barbarian by Spartan society. Halcyon scrubbed her face with soap and water from the washbasin, hoping it would wash away her mood. With a sigh, she stripped off her chiton and sandals, then went to bed. A wave of exhaustion overwhelmed her the moment she lay down.

When the sun hung midway in the western sky, Thora roused her owner and checked over the shoulder wound. Giles had visited yesterday and confirmed that Halcyon was well on her way to a full recovery. He would stop in next week. Until then, Thora was instructed by Giles to clean and wrap the wound twice a day. Meanwhile the various wounds on Halcyon's face would heal on their own and needed little attention.

"Did you sleep well?" Thora asked after a long stretch of quietness.

Halcyon nodded and continued to hold the sheet over her bare chest. Part of her wondered what Thora thought about Halcyon's pregnancy. Their earlier discussion had been brief. Thora had voiced support for the pregnancy, but the pup's future was another matter. Halcyon had several options on how to handle the pup, including methods to force its death inside her womb. Her entire frame trembled after the idea passed through her mind. She freed a hand from the sheet and put her arm across her stomach.

Thora paused and took a deep inhale of Halcyon's wild pheromones, but she held her tongue. She tied off the wrap on Halcyon's shoulder and went closer to the table. With a linen, she cleaned off her hands after using a salve on the wound.

"*Þǫkk.*"

After placing the refolded linen on the table, Thora regarded her owner and said, "I enjoy when you speak my language."

Huffing, Halcyon curled her fingers deeper into the sheet against her chest. "I can't speak Norsk."

"You have desire to try at least." Thora sighed, then added, "I must finish preparing dinner."

Alone again, Halcyon considered Thora's constant devotion and how little it took to please Thora. People in Sparta required much more to be happy. A villa, slaves, horses, fine foods, and status. Halcyon was guilty of such unnecessary desires until battle reminded her how life was a gift. Dropping the sheet, she touched her stomach with both hands and pictured what she may look like in the coming moons. Would her ab muscles disappear or become distorted around the growth of her stomach? The mental pictures were surreal, so she hid them deeper in her mind.

After dressing, Halcyon went downstairs and to the master's suite. She was pleased to find that the room had been arranged back to her preference. Already Thora or Glauce had set up a table with cups, a pitcher of wine, and a bowl of grapes. Halcyon took a handful of grapes and savored their sweetness on her tongue. She returned to the courtyard, sat, and waited for Gorgo's arrival.

About half an hour passed before Gorgo announced her arrival at the open gate. Cesare escorted her to Halcyon, who rose from the seat and invited Gorgo to the bench by the fountain. Once settled, Halcyon smiled and said, "Thank you for joining me this evening."

Gorgo smiled and bowed her head. "I was greatly pleased by your invitation." She let her smile slip and said, "I have been concerned about your health." There was an undertone of knowledge in her soft words. Halcyon forbid herself to bite Gorgo's unspoken offer to lend an ear. She further suspected that King Leonidas might have revealed to his mate why Halcyon was returned home. It would be his final effort to protect Halcyon's honor.

Halcyon composed her reply, but she held her silence as Glauce arrived and announced that dinner would be soon. Halcyon told Glauce that she and Gorgo would dine in the master's suite. Glauce hurried back to the kitchen. Halcyon escorted Gorgo across the courtyard and into the large suite. Gorgo was drawn to the Athena statue, marveling at it.

Thora entered and carried a single cup, which she delivered to Halcyon. She turned to Gorgo and asked, "Wine?"

"Yes, please."

Thora went to the table and organized a cup of wine for Gorgo, who returned her attention to the statue. Halcyon raised the filled cup to her nose and sniffed the fruity flavor. There was no alcohol, rather it was an apple juice. She rumbled at Thora's consideration, loud enough to capture Gorgo's attention. Halcyon smiled and sipped the juice.

"Who is the sculptor?" Gorgo asked and reached around the medium-sized statue when Thora handed her a cup. "Thank you."

Not responding, Thora exited the suite. However, her heady Alpha scent lingered in the air. Halcyon ignored the prickles on her skin that Thora brought on. She cleared her throat and answered Gorgo's question. Next they went to the wall fresco of Aphrodite.

"Who is the artist?" Gorgo asked while she studied the fresco before them. Aphrodite wore a buttery yellow toga and was midmotion of clipping a red rose from a bush. Her long dark hair was half up and half tumbling over her shoulders.

Halcyon trailed her eyes over to the fresco and smiled at it. "An artist from Athens named Olus."

"It is beautiful."

"Thank you," Halcyon replied, also appreciating the beauty of the artwork. She loved having a few luxuries in her home such as the frescoes and sculptures.

Gorgo shifted her attention to Halcyon. "You did not answer my earlier question."

Earlier in the courtyard, Halcyon had skipped over Gorgo's inquiry about her health. To do so a second time would be impolite. "My wounds have healed well." She directed her queen over to the long chairs in the center of the room.

"Almost fully healed?" Gorgo checked and spread out her legs on the chair.

"Yes." Halcyon detected a curious note in both Gorgo's tone and scent. But Gorgo's next question cemented Halcyon's suspicions that Leonidas may have told Gorgo why Halcyon returned to Sparta.

"No other ailments?" Gorgo asked.

Halcyon drank more of her juice in hopes to buy enough time. After she lowered the cup to the chair, she met Gorgo's gaze and replied, "No other ailments." A pregnancy wasn't considered an ailment by healers, but it was a condition. Not a positive condition in Halcyon's opinion, at least for her.

Letting go of the discussion, they shifted the conversation to the recent politics, especially the war. Many were pleased with the council's decision to send forth the Spartan army. The last time Persia attacked Greece, the Spartans had joined the battle too late. This time, King Leonidas would be remembered as the first Greek to face the Persian army.

They were soon interrupted by the arrival of the meal. Halcyon watched Thora place several plates of food on the table. She and Glauce filled the empty plates with food, then

Glauce served one each to Halcyon and Gorgo. Thora handled refilling Gorgo's and Halcyon's cups. Earlier Glauce had brought in a second pitcher, which was probably filled with juice rather than wine. In her own subtle way, Thora had a controlling streak that was natural to Alphas. She didn't exhibit it in an unhealthy or even violent manner like some male Alphas. In this case, Thora was aware of Halcyon's pregnancy and ensured alcohol was far from Halcyon's lips. Glauce finished tending to Gorgo and left with Thora, who had stiff shoulders.

"She is quieter than the last time I met her," Gorgo remarked when they were alone again.

Halcyon pretended to be unbothered by Gorgo's intrigue of Thora. "She is focused on her duties." She first tried the smoked goose meat. "As she should be." After a swallow, she asked, "How is Pleistarchus?"

Gorgo smiled upon hearing her son's name. "He is well and grows every day." Then her smile crumbled. "I have not told Pleistarchus about his sire's death." After a pause, she murmured, "I will tomorrow."

"I am sorry." Halcyon liked Pleistarchus. Even at his young age, he had a good head on his shoulders. He was, after all, the union of Gorgo and Leonidas. Pleistarchus was also next in line to become king, but a male family member would act as regent for him until he was old enough.

"In the spring he will begin training," Gorgo informed.

"Yes, I thought his seventh birthday was soon." Halcyon recalled the day when she entered Sparta's rigorous training program at the age of seven. They were difficult and demanding days, but she was a better person from having gone through them. After Gorgo's nod, they continued to converse well into the evening. Glauce returned with the sweet dish and lit more candles in the room. She refilled the cups before she departed.

Halcyon was uncertain about Thora's lack of appearance and would question her later. She remained focused on Gorgo, who intrigued her from the first time they met years ago. She had always admired Gorgo's strength, especially when it came to politics. Halcyon had steered away from the politics because a hoplite's lifestyle was simple and logical. She loved it. But Gorgo's will to hold power in the political games was an amazement.

Later, Halcyon walked Gorgo to the gate and called for Cesare to accompany them back to Gorgo's home. Together, they crossed through the city until they came to a large home, and a helot opened the gate.

"Thank you for tonight," Gorgo said.

Halcyon offered a smile. "I enjoyed your company." Her sincerity brought a smile from Gorgo. Halcyon had a nice visit with her queen, finding that she needed the social time. She suspected Gorgo appreciated being kept busy while she waited for her mate's body upon his shield. "Perhaps tomorrow evening you can join me again."

Gorgo's eyes glowed after the offer. "At the same time?"

"If you wish." Halcyon bowed her head in respect.

Gorgo reached and grazed her fingertips over Halcyon's jawline. "I will see you then."

"Goodnight, my queen." Halcyon straightened and smiled while Gorgo slipped into the entrance of her villa. She and Cesare headed back home, both quiet.

Once back at home, Halcyon bid goodnight to Cesare, who handled locking up the stable and villa. She detoured to the kitchen, which was clean and dim. Going upstairs, she noted that both female slaves were in their shared room. The warm glow from the master bedroom invited Halcyon. She dragged her fingers through her curly hair and stared at the bed. As nice as the evening was, it exhausted her too. But before she could prepare for bed, a warm scent drifted under her nose and soothed her Omega.

"I change your bandage," Thora murmured after she came behind her owner.

Halcyon bit her bottom lip, keeping back a moan. "I thought you were asleep." She turned her head sidelong, gaining a partial view of Thora's profile. Part of her wanted to lean back in hopes Thora would hold her. She tensed her shoulders, fighting off the desire.

"I have been waiting for you." Thora stepped around Halcyon and went to the table by the bed. "Sit."

Halcyon huffed at the order, but she went to the trunk and took a seat. She undid the chiton from her injured shoulder and allowed it to fall away. If her breast was exposed, she didn't care. Nor would it bother Thora.

With the salve, linen, and fresh bandage, Thora took care of replacing the old wrap with a fresh one. She was meticulous and delicate, checking Halcyon's features for any signs of discomfort. "The wound is much better." The small talk was enough of an opening for Halcyon.

"Yes." Halcyon canted her head to the side, gaining a better view of her slave. "You were quiet tonight." Thora offered a narrowed gaze and a slight head shake of denial. "Are you jealous of Queen Gorgo?"

Thora focused on tying off the bandage. She remained on her knees, cleaned her hands, and looked at Halcyon. "You ask many questions."

"I'm a curious Omega." Halcyon reached for her first sandal, but Thora shoved her hands away.

"You are a thinker." Thora worked the sandal's straps while they spoke. After Halcyon's huff, she paused and met Halcyon's stare. "You are known for sleeping with other Omegas."

Halcyon pressed her hands flat against the trunk and glared after her slave's attempt to redirect the conversation. "Then you are jealous."

Thora pulled off one sandal and went to the next one. After a beat, her pheromones grew heavier, then she yanked the strap a little harder than necessary. "*Já.*" She removed the second sandal and set it by the other one, then looked up at Halcyon again. "How can I not?" Her argument was sound, in every way.

Halcyon would turn green if Thora became involved with another slave, like Glauce. Early on, she had wondered if Thora and Glauce would form a relationship. When Halcyon threatened to return Glauce to Telamon over the kitchen fire, a jealous piece of her saw it as a chance to separate Thora and

Glauce. However, Thora's protective response over Glauce wasn't romantic interest. It was closer to pack mentality, which included Cesare. Still, the idea that Thora could form a romantic bond with a slave or helot created deep, unpleasant feelings in her. The major difference between her situation and Thora's own was that Halcyon held power over Thora's personal life.

After a deep breath, Halcyon faced her own fear and asked, "You and Glauce—"

"*Nei*," Thora cut off, then shook her head. "She is younger sister to me."

Halcyon allowed a line of tension to unbuckle inside her heart after the confirmation. She could separate them if they were together. However, such control over Thora would destroy any peace or hope between them. Nor did her Omega like the idea of distressing the sire of her pup. Leaning a little closer, she whispered, "Stay with me tonight." She grinned a little. "I'm already pregnant."

Thora raised an eyebrow after Halcyon's suggestive invite. For a beat, her eyes dropped to Halcyon's chest, which was semi-bare from the loose chiton. Her attention darted back to Halcyon's expectant features. "I am not rutting." She stood and took the items to the table but kept hold of the soiled bandage.

With a shake of her head, Halcyon attempted to recover from Thora's rejection and speedy escape. "Thora—"

"Goodnight, mistress." Thora was gone before Halcyon could stand.

"By the gods," Halcyon muttered and played with her hair. She stared at the quiet doorway and wondered if Thora had been here at all. Thora's lingering scent was the only confirmation that she hadn't daydreamed their strange interaction. After a tired sigh, she decided it was best to sleep than pursue her slave, who seemed to need space. Their attraction for each other had always been strong. Tomorrow she could think more on Thora's rejection and what it meant for them.

CHAPTER 17

Halcyon

After entering the bathing room, Glauce bowed to her owner, then carried in clean clothes and checked that a dry linen was ready too. She paused when Halcyon spoke to her.

"Glauce?" Halcyon was comfortable in the bathing pool. "Where is Thora?" She had risen close to dawn and had yet to see her Alpha slave. Every morning Thora would check on Halcyon, even assist her. Thora wasn't one to be aloof, so she was certain Thora was avoiding her.

"She is with Vitus this morning," Glauce replied in a meek tone. She turned and revealed the slight color in her cheeks. Either it was a lie or Glauce was embarrassed by her owner's nudity. After she shuffled on her feet, she asked, "Is there anything else you need, mistress?" Their relationship remained tarnished by the kitchen fire and Halcyon's subsequent threat to return Glauce to Telamon. One day Halcyon would find the heart to mend it but not today.

Halcyon waved off Glauce, who took her leave from the room. After a sigh, Halcyon pushed aside her concerns and decided that she was too sensitive to Thora. Today would be spent with Euclid before he left for war, then Gorgo would visit for an evening meal together.

The morning had begun like the others, with Halcyon's head in the chamber pot. However, Thora had not come to her aid, and she waited alone until the sickness passed. This morning's bath had helped soothe the aches of early pregnancy, but it was only temporary.

After her bath and dressing, Halcyon went to the kitchen in hopes to inform Thora about Gorgo's visit tonight. She frowned at Glauce by herself at the oven. The morning lesson with Vitus seemed to run longer than normal. But Halcyon had ordered both Thora and Vitus to learn as much as possible before Vitus returned to Rome.

"Is Thora still with Vitus?"

Glauce shook her head and looked from the baking bread to her owner. "No, mistress. She is at the market."

Halcyon grumbled and gave a faint nod. "Inform her that Queen Gorgo will be here this evening." It wasn't unusual for Thora to handle picking up supplies from the market, especially if Glauce was tending to the bread today.

"Yes, of course."

Halcyon went in search of Cesare next and located him in the shed, performing maintenance on the tools. He set down a large old blade called a kopis. The weapon was once a blade of war, but Halcyon had retired it and gave it to Cesare to use around the villa. There were certain plants that required a heavy blade to trim them back.

Cesare was seated on a cracked massive clay pot. He placed the blade across his lap and set the oily rag on top of it. "Good morning, mistress. How are you?"

"Well. You?" Halcyon noted his long stare. Cesare knew her well and probably sensed Halcyon's pregnancy to a degree. However, he was also smart enough to not inquire about it and to wait for Halcyon to discuss it first.

"Well too." Cesare tilted his head and waited for whatever his owner required of him.

"Have you seen Thora?" Halcyon was curious whether Cesare would have the same answer as Glauce. At least then she could learn whether or not something was amiss.

"Briefly, mistress. She went to the market to collect goods." Cesare pursed his lips a little, then asked, "Is something the matter?"

"No." Halcyon wrote off the eerie morning as Thora's avoidance. They would face each other at some point and maybe the space would help Thora. "I will be spending the day with Euclid." Before she could say more, Cesare was on his feet and started to put away the blade. Halcyon halted him and ordered, "You will stay here."

"But, mistress, you should have company." Cesare had a spark of determination that he often hid around his owner. Halcyon was certain that Cesare was aware of her pregnancy if he was willing to overstep his reserved role.

"No." Halcyon's rejection ended his attempt. "I'll visit Euclid alone." She half turned and placed a hand on the doorframe of the shed's open door. "I'll return early afternoon or so. Queen Gorgo is dining with me tonight."

"I'll inform Thora," Cesare promised.

Halcyon glanced at him over her shoulder and caught the concern in his features. She didn't have time to console him or any of her slaves. Their worry over her pregnancy was unnecessary. The unborn pup was her concern and hers alone.

The walk to Euclid's assigned barracks seemed longer than normal. For a moment, Halcyon had to reorient herself in the streets. The barracks' shade and coolness were a blessing. Halcyon visited with her mate for some time, and they discussed many things about their war with King Xerxes. By midday, Halcyon took her leave and wished Euclid glory in battle. She hoped to see him again, but they kissed for perhaps the last time.

Halcyon never revealed her pregnancy to Euclid.

* * *

In the midafternoon, Halcyon visited the council house and listened to the latest politics, but she didn't stay long. The walk home was tiresome, due to the marching hoplites leaving the city. Halcyon recognized several faces under the helmets, and she wished her brothers well. She would pray to Ares and Athena for them.

At home, the kitchen was busy with Thora and Glauce's preparations for an evening meal. Halcyon retired to the bedroom and managed a short nap until Cesare woke her. After Halcyon freshened up, Gorgo arrived at the villa, bringing a special dessert. Since sunset wasn't for another hour, they enjoyed the courtyard and chatted. Only once had Thora appeared, delivering wine for Gorgo and an apple juice with pomegranate for Halcyon. Before the meal was ready, Halcyon directed Gorgo into the master's suite where they would be more comfortable.

Cesare finished lighting the lamps in the suite. He gazed over at Glauce and Thora when they came through the open doors. He noted their full hands, so he hastened to them and distributed the dishes. Similar to last night, Thora put together plates of food from the larger dishes, then Glauce delivered one each to Gorgo and Halcyon.

Cesare took a step back, toward the door. "Anything else, mistress?"

Halcyon received a full plate from Glauce. "No, but thank you, Cesare." The response prompted all three slaves to exit the suite. She sighed at Thora's continued avoidance, but it would have to wait until Gorgo left the villa.

"You treat your slaves well."

Halcyon hummed, unsure whether it was true. She was better than other masters and mistresses, but she could still have a heavy hand.

"How did your slave Thora learn Greek?" Gorgo asked after a brief silence.

Halcyon tried the grapes first and toyed with one between her fingers. She considered a safe answer that would protect Thora and herself. "Perhaps from her previous owner." After she popped the fruit into her mouth, she watched her queen's features for any disbelief.

"She is bright for a barbar."

Halcyon bit the inside of her mouth to contain her harsh retort. She had taken offense on her slave's behalf without any thought. In that moment, Halcyon realized she wasn't the only person protective over the other. Her Omega nature bristled to the point that she almost growled—at her queen. She shifted on the long chair, then peered down at the plate in her lap. After a deep breath, she forced a smile in Gorgo's direction. "Yes," she said in a monotone.

"I wish I had such intelligent slaves." Gorgo popped a torn piece of bread into her mouth. "Perhaps I will have you select my next one."

Halcyon peered up and smirked. "Perhaps."

Gorgo chuckled and ate the last morsel of bread. "I have enjoyed these last two evenings with you, Halcyon." She had a lovely smile that stood out like her kohl-rimmed eyes. Like most Greek females, she had applied chalk to her features to give herself a paler appearance. Last night, Gorgo hadn't used any makeup, but tonight she was regal and vying for Halcyon's attention.

After a swallow, Halcyon offered a warm smile that Gorgo returned to her. "I, too." She crossed her legs. "I have hoped to distract you from thoughts of your mate."

Gorgo grew solemn at the mention of Leonidas. "I..." She cleared her throat, but her voice was weak. "I expect his shield any day."

Halcyon thought of Euclid, who could be marching to his own death. "I am sorry, my queen."

Gorgo had picked up her wine, but she stretched out her other hand and rested it on Halcyon's covered knee. "We both understand what our mates must do, as we must do for Sparta." She pulled her hand away. "You understand better than any."

Halcyon felt the lingering warmth against her skin from Gorgo's tender touch. She wanted to push the sensation away but was drawn deeper into it when she met Gorgo's honey-brown gaze. She parted her lips, but her words failed her when her Alpha slave's wonderful scent caught her nose. Halcyon turned her attention toward Thora and Glauce, who must have entered the suite a moment ago. Glauce handled Gorgo while Thora went to her owner.

"Anything else, mistress?" Thora had taken the plate from Halcyon's lap.

Halcyon swallowed but composed herself before she spoke to Thora. "No." She shook her head and said, "But…"

Thora had pivoted away, then hesitated and raised an eyebrow at her owner. Her eyes were an icy blue rather than inviting and warm. "*Já?*"

Halcyon faltered after receiving the cold response from Thora. But she shoved aside her concerns because they were in public after all, owner and slave. "Queen Gorgo brought sweet bread earlier. I'd like it cut up and brought out to us."

Thora rumbled and responded with a faint nod. She and Glauce took several dirty plates but left the grapes and pitchers on the table. Later Glauce returned with the dessert, handing out pieces on linen cloths. For most of the visit, Glauce came and went from the suite and attended to their needs. Gorgo inquired about how Halcyon came to be a hoplite. Like many in Sparta, there were different stories about how Halcyon had earned her way into the army. While Halcyon spoke about it, Gorgo was gripped by every detail and asked several questions. Somehow the hours passed faster than Halcyon expected them to.

"You are tired, Halcyon." Gorgo had a handful of grapes in her lap. She plucked one free from the vine and continued to eye Halcyon for a long moment. At first, it seemed as if she might open the conversation to Halcyon's unspoken pregnancy.

After a deep breath, Halcyon straightened from her slumped position against the long chair's back. A slight warmness entered her cheeks after her weariness had been caught. She shook her head, which broke away the sleepiness. "I have not been myself of late."

Gorgo chewed on the grape, slow and steady. After she was done, she pushed off the chair's back, scooted down it, and touched Halcyon's lower thigh from across the distance between them. "You have recently returned from battle. You're still healing from your wounds." With a downturn of her lips, she whispered, "Now your mate has been sent to war."

After a slight flinch, Halcyon tensed her jaw together. Many would assume that Halcyon was pregnant with Euclid's pup once the news came out. Even now, Gorgo's sympathy had to be for Halcyon's future, which Gorgo would assume meant raising his pup without him. Euclid's possible death would be seen as a great honor to Sparta; however, his absence from his pup's birth would be mournful. Halcyon placed a hand against her belly, then yanked it away. Again, her cheeks warmed over. "Euclid and I accepted the risks of our duties when we became hoplites."

"Yes, I imagine so." Gorgo's eyes shone with sorrow, then her grip tightened on Halcyon's leg. Her lower lip quivered a little, and her Omega scent carried a heavy note. It held concern and comfort that tugged at Halcyon's Omega. "Birthing a pup without your mate would be cruel," she whispered.

Halcyon regarded her queen for a quiet minute. Gorgo's attempt to use her pheromones on Halcyon started to work, coaxing Halcyon to put down her guard. However, Gorgo's words registered and brought a rumble from deep in her gut. Supposedly their gods looked down upon pups born without their sire present. People believed it brought a lifetime of bad luck to a pup. But the sire of Halcyon's pup was alive and well, not facing certain death.

"Then it's good fortune that I'm a hoplite rather than not," Halcyon said in a curt tone. The gods did smile down upon hoplites, especially Spartan ones. Her greatness as the Iron Edge outweighed Euclid's possible lack of presence at her pup's birth. But the concern was pointless because Euclid wasn't the sire. She drew her leg away, breaking their contact. Gorgo may be the queen, but Halcyon was the master of her villa. Gorgo's effort to persuade Halcyon to be vulnerable left a strange taste in Halcyon's mouth.

Gorgo withdrew and then cleared her throat. Her pheromones retreated, too, signaling a shift in the room. "Halcyon, I'm sorry." She was alert, even breathing a little harder.

Halcyon worked her jaw and used her anger like a shield. "Leonidas disclosed in his letter why I returned to Sparta," she declared.

"Yes."

For a moment, they stared at each other, then Halcyon scooted to the edge of the chair and hung her legs off the side. "I'm not ready to discuss my illness at—"

"It's not an illness," Gorgo interrupted in a harsh manner. "How could you see your preg—"

"No." Halcyon shook her head and halted Gorgo's rebuke. "It's merely a condition, a temporary one." She watched Gorgo's features shift from concern to anger over the growing argument. However, this was Halcyon's personal life and her domain. "I prefer that it remains private."

Gorgo's eyes widened at the news. "Do you plan to hide away in your villa for the next nine months?"

"If I must, then yes." Halcyon refused to have people gossip about her pregnancy, much less make people aware of it. Once the pup was born, everyone would expect to see the pup and even bless it. But then they would become aware that Euclid wasn't the sire and shun the pup. Spartan society was cruel and cold, more so than their gods.

Gorgo opened and closed her mouth a couple of times before she looked to the open doorway to the courtyard. Thora had appeared without a sound and studied them both before she went to the table, pretending to check on the food. Gorgo turned her attention to Halcyon and remained quiet while the air between them thickened.

Thora carried the pitcher of apple juice over to her owner and asked, "Is there anything I can bring you, mistress?" She held Halcyon's gaze, then her Alpha pheromones pierced the tension between the Omegas. Gorgo shifted back and forth on the chair.

Halcyon grew a touch smug at her slave's ability to affect Gorgo. Thora's scent was enticing for Omegas and made other Alphas envious. And Halcyon held claim over Thora, not only as a slave but as her lover. Thora's status as a slave worked as a perfect front because Halcyon was well aware that if Thora wanted to be free, she would find a way. Thora was determined and stubborn, willful even.

Silencing her thoughts, Halcyon offered her empty cup and replied, "No, but thank you." Her appreciation had nothing to do with Thora's inquiry but rather Thora's arrival. She wondered if Thora sensed Halcyon's minor distress or if she happened to have excellent timing.

Thora canted her head a little and met Halcyon's gaze for a beat, then she focused on refilling the cup. "It is getting late, mistress." She withdrew the pitcher and added, "Giles will be here at dawn tomorrow, and then you have an appointment afterward."

Halcyon hummed at her slave's ability to pick up on Halcyon's needs. Giles was expected tomorrow morning, but not quite at dawn. The appointment later was with Iason, who handled Halcyon's race horses in Athens. Sparta may not be much of a place for businesses, but it didn't halt Halcyon from continuing her sire's legacy as a seller of fine horses. "Yes, I recall." She looked to Gorgo and said, "Thora can fetch Cesare soon."

Gorgo had scooted back to her original spot on the long chair. She folded her hands in her lap and remained composed rather than bothered by the change of events. "Yes, that would be nice."

With a nod, Halcyon turned back to Thora and said, "Have Cesare meet us in the courtyard in about half an hour."

"*Já*, mistress." Thora returned the pitcher to the table, then went in search of Cesare.

Halcyon could have ordered Cesare to escort Gorgo now rather than later. The delay was a subtle invite for them to make amends rather than say farewell on an unpleasant note. After a brief silence, she stretched out on the long chair again and said, "I hope we haven't damaged our friendship." About ten years ago, Halcyon had joined the elite guard of King Leonidas and in turn developed a friendship with Gorgo. This was their first time spending it alone together.

"No." Gorgo was an Omega of careful decisions and words. She was also reasonable. "Certainly not." After a sigh, she swept a loose strand of dark hair behind her ear. "I overstepped. Leonidas told me in confidence about your pregnancy. He asked me to support you, especially when it came time for you to face the military."

Halcyon turned her attention away and weighed Gorgo's concerns. She was unsure what the military would do once they learned about her pregnancy. They may offer her temporary leave or discharge her. As an Omega, she was expected to raise her pup until they were seven years old, then afterward the government would take charge.

"But it is much too early," Gorgo added in a delicate tone. After Halcyon focused on Gorgo again, she spoke more. "I apologize for pushing you to speak about this when you're not prepared to do so."

Dipping her head, Halcyon accepted the apology and offered a smile. "I know it comes from a place of concern."

"And care," Gorgo added. "I will honor what decisions you make, Halcyon."

"Thank you." Halcyon allowed the weight to slip off her shoulders. It was a comfort to have the Queen of Sparta as an ally when it came to facing the military. They spoke for a little longer, discussing King Xerxes's latest movements. However, Gorgo cut their conversation short when Halcyon spoke less and slouched against the chair.

"I should return home." Gorgo stood from the chair. "So you can rest."

"My apologies for being a bore," Halcyon said, displeased with herself. Everything about her body was weak.

"There is no reason to apologize." Gorgo started for the courtyard with Halcyon beside her. "You require more sleep in your state." She was careful with her word choices.

Halcyon sighed, knowing that Gorgo was right. "This is not the fate I saw for myself when I marched to Thermopylae."

"We can never be sure what the gods have in store for us." Gorgo paused beside the water fountain. She faced Halcyon and smiled at her. "Thank you for tonight. Again, I apologize for—"

"It's done," Halcyon insisted. She offered her hands, which were collected by Gorgo. Behind her, she sensed someone's attention on them but ignored it.

Cesare emerged from the upper floor, went to the closed gate, and waited.

"It'll be my turn to invite you over soon," Gorgo promised. She leaned in and kissed Halcyon's cheek.

Halcyon rumbled and decided it would be nice to visit Gorgo's villa. It had been many months since she last went there. "I'd enjoy that."

Gorgo withdrew, revealing her smile. "Perhaps next week." She let go of Halcyon's hands, then said, "Goodnight, Halcyon."

"Goodnight." Halcyon watched her queen leave with Cesare, then she turned around and regarded Thora, who stood in the kitchen's entrance. Sighing, she crossed the distance and wondered if Thora would further attempt to avoid her.

"It is late," Thora said once Halcyon was close.

"Do you require more space from me?" Halcyon asked and folded her arms.

Thora pushed off the doorframe and took a step toward Halcyon. They were separated by a hand or two. "You think slow."

Halcyon huffed and narrowed her eyes at Thora. "You are stubborn." She edged nearer and tightened her arms so she wouldn't touch Thora. Her attraction to Thora was endless and could break Halcyon's control. "It's unlike you to avoid me."

"I required space, but I have not been far."

Halcyon couldn't deny that Thora wasn't nearby. She dropped her arms and adopted a more open posture in hopes to break down Thora's defenses. "What have I done now?" she asked in a soft voice. A tremble passed through her. She tried to hide it, not wanting to appear weak in front of her slave. But it was hard when it came to Thora.

Thora huffed and regarded Halcyon before she closed the small gap. "Nothing."

However, Halcyon sensed that Thora was either lying or not ready. She refused to push it again, at least for now. If she knew Thora enough, it had to do with her pregnancy and the future. Thora was aware that Halcyon wasn't inclined to discuss it. They were at an impasse at the moment. In the meantime, Halcyon wanted a distraction, as sweet of a distraction as she could find. She placed a hand against the outside of Thora's larger one. Their touch sent a charge through Halcyon. The contact was alive and exciting, stirring heat between her legs.

"Come to my bed," Halcyon whispered, trying again.

"I am not rutting." Thora withdrew her hand and took a side step, but Halcyon blocked her. Thora rumbled in displeasure and eyed her owner.

"I'm well aware." Halcyon pressed their bodies together. She bit her lip to hold back a moan from the feeling of having Thora against her. Her earlier weariness was gone, replaced by hunger. But her mind cleared when Thora frowned at her. Halcyon placed a gentle hand on Thora's hip and mulled over Thora's hesitation. "I don't require a cock to have pleasure. You know this."

"*Já*," Thora murmured. She broke their eye contact and grumbled. "But I am not like you." She focused on Halcyon, revealing the uncertainty in her gaze. "I am not like an Omega."

"I've heard how female Alphas are a little different." Halcyon leaned in more and was hopeful when Thora grabbed her hip. "Have you been with another female?"

"*Nei*," Thora whispered, as if confessing a secret. "Only ever with my mate."

"Oh." Halcyon smiled at the prospect of being Thora's first. "You experienced your first rut with me." She reached up and cupped her slave's flushed cheek. All around her Thora's scent became richer and spicy. "You took such good care of me," she whispered. Their closeness was calling to Halcyon. She rubbed her thighs together, feeling the slick coating her pussy. "There is no reason to be scared now." Deep inside, her Omega wanted nothing more than to assure her Alpha lover first and foremost.

"My rut was driving me," Thora reminded in an uneasy voice. Yet a distinct hum was coming off her. Like Halcyon, she seemed to want the same thing and wasn't scared off like last night.

"I know." Halcyon caressed Thora's cheek and smiled. "This time, let me take care of you." She was certain that once Thora understood how they could have sex, Thora would desire it again and again. "I want you," she confessed, unable to deny it any longer. "*Líka.*"

Thora groaned, then leaned down and captured Halcyon's lips. They moaned into each other's mouths, toying with one another in the heated kiss. Both were too determined to have the other, and they stumbled a step into the courtyard. Thora pulled back and growled while catching Halcyon's hips to keep her from falling down after their battle of wills. She bit at Halcyon's neck. "*Já, já… já,*" she repeated between nips, then her words spilled over into whispers of Norsk.

Halcyon had no idea what her lover said to her, but the language was as rough as Thora's grip on her ass. She moaned loudly from the jolts of pleasure racing through her body. "Bed. *Now*."

ᚲHAPT� 18

Halcyon

Thora and Halcyon were tangled together, stumbling into Halcyon's bedroom under the welcoming lamplight. Halcyon tilted her head to the side and moaned louder when Thora's teeth scraped across the most sensitive spot on her neck. She wanted nothing more than to have Thora ravish her all night. The heat underneath her sticky skin hummed louder and quicker each minute. Halcyon nudged it back enough, recalling her promise to take care of Thora tonight.

With a soft growl, Halcyon spun them around and shoved Thora, sending her back toward the bed. She grinned at Thora's bewildered expression. She closed the distance, pressed against Thora, and used her pheromones to soothe her slave. "I said I would take care of you tonight. Let me." She grabbed Thora's ass and squeezed, hard.

"I am not used to receiving pleasure." Thora leaned forward and cupped Halcyon's cheeks. "You may not like what you find under this chiton."

Halcyon rolled her eyes and argued, "I've seen what is under this chiton before."

"Not like this," Thora murmured.

"Whether you're rutting or not," Halcyon whispered, brushing their lips together, "you're truly gorgeous." Thora's scent shifted and became gentler, telling Halcyon that Thora believed her. Halcyon wanted nothing more than to prove her words true. She would show Thora how gorgeous she was. With a surge, they tumbled back into the bed together and became entangled again. Halcyon was on top, dominating her Alpha slave.

Thora returned the fierceness of Halcyon's kiss. She was full of fire and set Halcyon ablaze with a hurried frenzy. Halcyon urged them onto the bed the rest of the way, then she tugged and pulled on Thora's chiton between their unstoppable kissing. Similar to their first kiss, Halcyon wanted it to last until the sun died, but she had made a promise. Together they tossed Thora's attire to the floor, then Thora helped Halcyon do the same with hers. The lack of clothing was more than relief, it was bliss. Halcyon groaned in pleasure when her bare skin made contact with Thora's warm flesh after too many weeks. However, she caught Thora's interest in Halcyon's newest battle wound.

Thora rubbed the pinkish skin near the healing shoulder wound. "You could have died."

"You saved me," Halcyon said, without hesitation or thought. It was true that Thora protected her from the infection and fever. Then without any consideration, her Omega took control and spoke for her. "You saved *us*."

Thora jerked, then switched her focus to Halcyon's features. She parted her lips, but Halcyon's confession seemed to have stolen Thora's voice.

Halcyon cursed her Omega, then shoved it back down. She captured Thora's lips again, banishing the earlier conversation's heaviness. Thora threaded her fingers in

Halcyon's unruly hair and started to grind her hips against her lover.

"*Já,*" Halcyon whispered after she moved downward. Thora's arousal filled the air, adding to the mix of their pheromones. It was dizzying and perfect. She twisted and grinded until she had Thora's collarbone under her lips. She licked and nipped at delicate flesh, earning hearty moans.

"*Fukka!*" Thora gasped and clawed her owner's back. She murmured another curse in her native tongue, then sucked in a breath when Halcyon came to her right breast.

Flicking her tongue, Halcyon teased Thora's nipple before she grazed her lips over and sucked. She palmed Thora's other breast, which spilled from her small hand. She savored every single moan from Thora, but then she rolled the delicate, rosy nipple between her teeth. Thora's soft cry sent a hot jolt through Halcyon's wired body. She switched to the other breast and lavished it.

After a growl, Thora hooked one leg underneath Halcyon's ass and lashed an arm across her back to hold them together. She rubbed her pussy even harder against Halcyon's hip, smearing slick all over. Halcyon grinned at her successful attempt to rid Thora of her earlier shyness. Even without a rut, Thora was still an Alpha at her core and would respond to an Omega desiring her. Halcyon wanted to stay here longer, but she also wanted to have all of Thora.

"Halcyon," Thora murmured after a throaty groan. There was only one other time Thora had used her owner's name. Similar to last time, Halcyon allowed it to pass and refused to admit how wonderful her name sounded with Thora's accent. "*Lika*," she added with a hint of desperation.

Halcyon was kissing and clenching skin between her teeth, finding her way farther down. Thora's body was more than gorgeous in that moment, it was Elysium. Every curve earned a chaste kiss, while supple flesh was bitten with desire. Thora loosened her grip on Halcyon, who neared her prize. Indeed, Thora had no cock that she could use to penetrate Halcyon again. At least, not that way. Yet her prize was still an eyeful.

Uneasy for a moment, Thora covered her pussy and hid it from Halcyon's curious gaze. She sat up on one elbow, panting and gulping. "Hal—"

"You *are* going to remove your hand," Halcyon ordered and followed it with a growl. The slight pull of her lips revealed her canines in a final warning. Earlier she had attempted being comforting, but now she battled Thora's insecurity with firmness. There was no reason to shield Halcyon from what she wanted so much.

Thora remained still, if not stiff. A slight tremor ran through her and passed into Halcyon, who held her silent snarl. Thora was the Alpha, but Halcyon had her own power that could extinguish Thora's strength. Similar to the first time Thora knelt for Halcyon, she bowed out of their current confrontation and eased her hand away. She released a strangled breath when Halcyon responded with a pleased moan.

Halcyon was rewarded with a view of Thora's beauty. Slick glistened throughout the mound of light curls. But what captured all Halcyon's attention was Thora's clitoris, which protruded beyond the pinkish folds of her pussy. The gods designed Thora's clitoris the same as Halcyon's, except it was larger and swollen full. If Thora's rut restarted, her clitoris would grow and extend, more than enough to satisfy Halcyon in a different way. But even without the rut, Thora was stunning and made Halcyon's mouth water. Halcyon disliked giving oral to both Euclid and Selene. Thora, however, was irresistible on every level, and Halcyon craved to please her Alpha. Even now, Thora's alluring scent invited Halcyon in for a taste.

"Gorgeous," Halcyon murmured before she brought her lips closer to Thora's rosy-pink clitoris. She grazed her lips, testing Thora's response. Already the heady taste tickled her senses and made it hard to resist. But she basked in Thora's hearty moan. With certainty, Halcyon slid her lips over the protruding, puffy bud that demanded attention.

A few curses spilled from Thora, then she moaned and fisted the sheet. She remained half upright and bent to one side. Her stare was fixed on Halcyon, who adored the audience.

Halcyon snaked an arm underneath Thora's thigh and latched onto Thora's hip with her other hand. She planned to play with her lover and test how long she could last. Dipping her head lower, she drew Thora's clit deeper into her mouth and brushed the flat of her tongue against the sensitive pearl.

"*Fukka*," Thora cursed and dug a heel into the bed. She grew louder when Halcyon dipped her tongue underneath the hood and toyed with the very tip hidden there. Thora jumped twice, then a third time, and gasped for air. "What you…" Her question plummeted into Norsk, harsh yet desperate, and Halcyon answered with sucking rather than words. Thora's moans carried through the room, if not beyond the walls.

Halcyon spoke with her tongue, tracing and flicking. It wasn't long before she learned what made Thora shudder and curse, or what might send her lover over the edge. Halcyon had no plans to give Thora gratification quite yet; she wanted to taste more. For the first time, she found immense pleasure in giving it to someone else. It seemed that Thora had moved beyond her insecurity, confirming it with a slight gyration of her hips.

"More," Thora pleaded breathlessly, then whined low enough to tug at Halcyon's heart. "*Serða mér,*" she demanded with a little heat. Even without translating, Halcyon knew what her lover wanted from her. "*Líka.*"

Unable to ignore Thora's need, Halcyon shifted lower and used the tip of her tongue to flick the pulsing bud that poked out. She held tighter to Thora, who tried to buck and push into Halcyon's mouth. Then the strain from sitting up caused Thora to topple back and cry out. Halcyon was determined, pleasing Thora's clitoris with every stroke and brush. She wanted Thora to come more than anything else in that moment. The increasing moans filled her ears, then Thora jerked and stiffened for a beat. Thora's next cry shifted into a howl that reached across the entire villa.

Halcyon withdrew and kissed along Thora's inner thigh, and noticed the claw marks on Thora's upper thigh from her own grip. Peering up, she grinned at how fast Thora's chest rose and fell. Her Omega wanted to move and comfort Thora, but she wasn't done.

Panting, Thora covered her chest and trembled a few times. She gulped air and groaned in delight. Her pheromones swirled and rested heavy in the space around them. After another deep breath, she sat up and placed both hands behind herself. "I have never…"

Halcyon chuckled and kissed Thora's skin again. "I know." She suspected Thora's mate was much like Euclid, selfish and shallow. Many male Alphas were, by nature. Halcyon had no idea that female Alphas were quite the opposite. "I know how overwhelming it feels the first time." She flashed a playful grin.

With a tilt of her head, Thora responded with a sly smile and her voice deepened when she spoke again. "And this is the best pussy you will ever have."

Blinking once, Halcyon mentally stumbled over her lover's huge boast, then she roared with laughter. Thora's humor and Alpha confidence were gorgeous. She was caught off-guard by Thora's clever remark, but she had spoken the truth. They laughed together, then Halcyon was certain she sensed another thread bind her closer to Thora. "Yes, it is." With a hungry smile, she asked, "Ready to continue?"

Thora cleared her throat, then a blush dusted her cheeks. "Can we try again?"

Halcyon raised an eyebrow and started to stroke Thora's hip. "Repeat what we did?" She chuckled at her lover's obvious enjoyment. "*Já*, if that's what you wish." After all, tonight was about Thora's needs.

"I wish try different," Thora said but frowned, maybe due to her choppy Greek or her inability to explain herself.

"Show me?" Halcyon asked, hoping to guide Thora forward.

"*Já.*" Thora nodded, then hooked a hand behind Halcyon's head and drew her back to her clitoris. "Take me, again."

Halcyon had a wonderful view, discovering Thora's clitoris was swollen and ready again. There was something to be said about an Alpha's stamina compared to a Beta's. Without hesitation, she brought the lengthened clitoris into her mouth and savored the distinct taste that was her lover. She waited to see what Thora had in mind this time, pleased that Thora had taken charge.

"Keep your tongue there," Thora instructed, then she raised her hips off the bed and performed a test thrust. She groaned and paused, watching Halcyon out of concern. Halcyon was fine and squeezed Thora's hip in confirmation. Euclid wasn't half as considerate as Thora, and Selene was never allowed to take or use Halcyon.

Halcyon held on and waited for Thora to use her mouth. Another gentle thrust caused Thora's large clitoris to rub against Halcyon's lips and tongue. She signaled for Thora to add more speed. Thora followed the silent command and rocked her hips at a cautious pace, finding her rhythm. She moaned and rumbled while she watched Halcyon take her.

Thora dug her fingernails a bit deeper into Halcyon's scalp and whispered, "Good Omega."

Halcyon melted under the praise and sucked on the next thrust. She was rewarded with a beautiful cry from Thora. Then the pumps became more frantic and faster. Halcyon did her best to hold her position and please her lover. The shakiness of Thora's hand at the back of her head told Halcyon that they were close. Thora bucked her hips once, then a second time, driving harder on the next one. Her entire body stuttered before she gave a growly cry. For a moment, she remained anchored to Halcyon, then she fell back into the bed.

With a heavy gasp, Halcyon pulled away and wiped clean her mouth. Rather than staying, she climbed up part of the way and rested half of herself on Thora. She placed an arm across her lover's sticky abdomen and nuzzled into salty skin.

After a heavy exhale, Thora returned a hand to her lover's tussled hair and massaged her scalp. "*Þokk.*" She rested her other hand on Halcyon's upper back and drew small circles.

Chuckling, Halcyon raised her head, then balanced her chin on Thora's stomach. "We're not finished."

"You require sleep," Thora argued and played with Halcyon's hair.

"After I'm finished with you." Halcyon grinned and kissed the warm skin under her lips. Thora seemed prepared to argue, but she forbade it. "Or you can leave now." Underneath her, Thora became rigid, then the silence ticked by with weight. She was certain Thora was considering the best decision, to be together more or to let a pregnant Omega rest.

"Time is up," Halcyon ordered and started to get off her slave. Two large hands latched onto her sides and halted her departure. She raised an eyebrow.

"I will stay."

"Wise decision," Halcyon teased, then scooted up and kissed Thora with renewed fire. Her dark hair fell around them until Thora pushed it back. They kissed without fear or guilt, taking what they could of each other. Their hips rolled and danced together, finding an enticing rhythm that smeared their slick on the other. Halcyon groaned from the silkiness of Thora's clit against her. She was tempted to grind harder and find release, but it would have to wait.

"Spread your legs," Halcyon whispered between kisses and snaked a hand down. She shifted to the side and grinned at Thora's responding whine. Then a silky heat coated her fingers. Already Thora's clitoris was hard again and demanding attention. But first Halcyon urged two fingers inside Thora, slipping past her opening.

"*Já,*" Thora called between gasps. She twisted her head back, exposing her neck to Halcyon. Without hesitation, Halcyon dug her teeth into the tender flesh offered to her.

Halcyon nudged her fingers deeper, relishing her moment to have Thora for once. The hugging of her fingers was exquisite. Once fully inside, she raised her head and admired Thora's awed expression and the upward curve of her body. Thora was a free spirit, but in that moment, she was a slave to Halcyon's touch. Halcyon suspected she herself had worn the same look when Thora had bent her over and taken her with Thora's cock.

"Such a gorgeous Alpha," Halcyon praised and smirked after Thora's rumbly moan. She lowered back down and took Thora's nipple between her teeth. Drawing her fingers back, Halcyon listened to the whimpers and moans around her. Each one was perfect and caused Halcyon's heart to fall more. She drove her fingers in again, curling them at the end this time. Thora was louder and bucked against Halcyon's hand.

"More," Thora pleaded and clawed at Halcyon's ass, forcing their bodies closer.

Without hesitation, Halcyon met the demand and started to thrust inside her lover. With each pump, she ensured her upper palm rubbed against Thora's beautiful clit. Thora continued to grind against Halcyon's skillful hand. Her cries became faster, matching the speed of their fucking. Halcyon kissed and bit her lover's breasts and held on while she drove her fingers harder, deeper. Thora was close, shaking and frantic, but she seemed unable to find the release her body needed. Halcyon ached to give it to her lover, to take and give it all. She adjusted her thumb, finding Thora's swollen pearl, which was covered in arousal and aching with need.

Thora jolted when Halcyon massaged her clit. "*Fukka! Já!*" Her hips rolled with demand and new speed. She cursed again and bowed her back upward, causing Halcyon to lift herself away with her injured side. But Halcyon kept pace and gave her heart in the final hard thrusts. She was relentless and Thora took all of it. Then there was a beat of silence other than the drumming in Halcyon's ears. Thora remained stiff and hung on to the edge of ecstasy until Halcyon pushed her fingers in and curled them.

The initial howl tumbled into an emotional scream that stole Halcyon's breath. Thora tumbled back to the bed and fought for air while her body twitched in different directions. Halcyon kept her hand still while the walls spasmed around her fingers. Then her hurt shoulder sent bolts through her back. She panted and toppled onto Thora, who attempted to grab her.

"N-No," Halcyon said, requiring a minute to rest her shoulder. She focused on the wonderful feeling of Thora clenching her fingers. Thora panted and trembled a few times, then started to shift toward Halcyon, who withdrew her fingers.

Thora turned toward her lover and pressed her nose into Halcyon's hair. She took a few deep breaths and murmured something in Norsk.

"What are you saying?" Halcyon asked and peered up at her lover.

Thora replied in Norsk, unwilling to translate it.

Halcyon shook her head and cupped Thora's burning cheek. "So stubborn." She kissed her slave, slow and loving.

After they withdrew, Thora whispered, "I said it is time to sleep."

"Liar," Halcyon argued and narrowed her eyes. She didn't press it. "The lamps—"

"Let me." Thora climbed out of bed, but she faltered and leaned against the frame.

Halcyon smirked at her handiwork and asked, "Anything wrong?" She earned a huff followed by a weak growl. She chuckled when Thora pushed off and went to each lamp, cutting off the oil to the wick. The room was left in a soft glow of moonlight from the open window. Thora crawled into bed and rested on her back. Halcyon turned onto her side, facing away from her slave. As her body relaxed, she sensed the exhaustion fill her from head to toe. Her mind started to slip, but Thora's movement stirred her enough that she became aware of the warm skin pressed against her back.

Thora hooked an arm across her owner's waist, then wiggled her other arm under the pillow. The heaviness of Thora's Alpha scent wrapped around Halcyon. The wonderful security of being in Thora's arm was the last drifting thought in Halcyon's mind.

Halcyon slept well through most of the night. She awoke in the same spot, safe in Thora's arms. In the silver darkness, she considered her future that wasn't meant to happen to her. As a young Omega, she had pledged her body to Sparta as a hoplite, not a bearer of pups. She dedicated her life to the military, looked forward to battle, and wished to die with honor. Weeks ago, she had been so close to a hoplite's greatest achievement. Now, she watched as it turned to ash in her palms.

Thora had impregnated Halcyon and cut short her greatness.

To blame and hate Thora would be easy, even expected of Halcyon. However, Halcyon recognized Thora's devotion, her care, and her continued support. Halcyon had asked to be knotted and Thora had consented, both understanding the risks but wanting Halcyon's dangerous heat to end. Thora ensured that Halcyon drank the infertilis herb, which had failed to work. In the end, Halcyon's biology was mightier than the herb. And perhaps it was also the strength of Thora's seed that outwitted the herb.

Thora shifted in her sleep but kept a hand over Halcyon's bare stomach. A soft thrum echoed deep in her chest and brought comfort to Halcyon. For a moment, Halcyon pretended they were mates in love, and expecting a beautiful pup soon. The fantasy was sweet and tempting despite the coldness of reality. The barriers in front of them were too big to scale. Their pup's sinful biology would be a curse in Spartan society.

Soon Halcyon would have to be the one to make the heartbreaking decision for them all.

A slight sting began in Halcyon's eyes. She cursed her Omega for disarming and weakening her. After a deep breath, she regained control and tried to rest more. Her busy mind refused to let her sleep, so she turned in Thora's arms. Halcyon nuzzled into the crook of Thora's neck and whispered nonsense. She ran her hands up and down Thora's side and back.

After a moan, Thora tilted her head back and revealed her mercury-blue eyes. "Sleep."

"I can't," Halcyon murmured and started to nibble on Thora's ear. She earned a deep rumble that sent a shiver down Halcyon's back. In a heartbeat, Thora's pheromones unfurled and enthralled Halcyon. She ducked her head lower and tasted the spiciness of her lover's Alpha scent.

"If cannot sleep, then I can tire you." Thora chuckled when Halcyon groaned against her neck. The prospect of being taken again aroused Halcyon. Thora growled in response and started to roll them until Halcyon pushed against her shoulder.

"Wait." Halcyon grinned when Thora gave her a peculiar look. "I want to feel your clit against mine." She watched how Thora's eyes became more blown, then Thora kissed Halcyon with heat and passion until they both were panting.

"*Já*," Thora agreed. "Show me." She tried to bite at Halcyon's neck, but Halcyon avoided her and smirked at Thora's disappointed features.

"Lie back." Halcyon pushed Thora into the bed, and then she climbed on top. Thora rumbled and gripped the sheet underneath, as if containing her urges. Halcyon admired the Alpha below her and inhaled the distinct smell of their mutual excitement. But she hastened to adjust their position until she had Thora's one leg extended and the other bent forward. Halcyon straddled her lover's pussy sideways, then lowered herself until their clits touched.

Thora held her breath the more Halcyon pressed against her.

"Breathe," Halcyon ordered in a hoarse voice. She struggled to control her own breathing after feeling Thora's larger clitoris against hers. Once or twice she had done this position but found it uninteresting until tonight. Thora's pussy was wet, and her clitoris seemed to harden underneath Halcyon. "Fuck. There's a lot of slick." She latched onto Thora's knee for balance, then began to rock.

"*Skit*," Thora cursed and lifted her head. She stared with dark, hungry eyes and watched every motion of Halcyon's hips. "You look beautiful."

Halcyon blushed, if it was possible with her already flushed cheeks. She placed her other hand against Thora's stomach and ground harder. Thora's clit was much more swollen, making it easy to ride. Shocks of pleasure set off deep in Halcyon's belly. A thin sheen of sweat coated her skin the longer she rode Thora. "I need more."

Thora obliged and held on to Halcyon. She moved her hips and matched her lover's pace. They exchanged moans while they rubbed their slick pussies together, driving their clits against each other. Halcyon became more frantic to take, to release, and to scream. Thora's silky pussy was perfect and massaged against hers with feverish demand. The frantic strokes of pleasure pulled them both into a primitive dance.

"Fas-ter," Halcyon snapped between ragged breaths. They were close to coming together, on each other. Halcyon wanted to feel every bit of it. With a few more snaps of her hips, the intensity of the orgasm washed over her. Halcyon bucked against Thora, crying out. A few more jolts crashed through her when Thora rocked against her. Then Thora yelled, deep and raw.

For a heartbeat, Halcyon knew Thora was *hers*.

Gasping for air, Halcyon lost her strength and struggled to stay upright. She was grateful when Thora sensed her mild distress and helped her lie down beside her. Resting on her back, Halcyon closed her eyes and savored the bliss humming below her skin. For once, her mind was quiet and at peace.

Thora reached for her pussy and touched herself for a moment. "I enjoyed it."

Halcyon turned her head toward her lover. "If you are a good Alpha, I might let you ride me next time." Thora smirked at her, making Halcyon's clit pulse some.

"I *will* ride you next time." Thora rolled onto her side, facing Halcyon. "Now, get on your stomach. We are not done."

* * *

At predawn, the birds' morning song filtered into Halcyon's consciousness. The bedroom was washed in delicate hints of gray and yellow light that signaled the start of Apollo's chariot ride. Halcyon took stock of the soreness in her limbs from last night's pleasures. She half expected her stomach to revolt, but it remained settled for once. At least she was allowed some relief from the morning sickness, for now.

Halcyon shifted and felt Thora move against her. As a slave, Thora had early duties to handle before sunrise. Either Thora ignored them or slept through them. Cracking open an eye, she discovered Thora regarding her and considered whether to comment on Thora's neglect of her work. In truth, Halcyon preferred waking up next to her slave after spending last night together.

"You should sleep longer," Thora murmured and ran her fingers through Halcyon's hair.

Halcyon shut her eyes and weighed the idea. She, too, had duties to handle. Then her stomach made a loud noise. Sex had left her hungry in other ways. But first, she needed to bathe and remove Thora's scent before venturing beyond Villa Honor the Beloved. She expected Cesare and Glauce to remain discreet, and even trusted Thora to keep them in line. It wasn't unusual for Spartans to bed their slaves, but it was frowned upon to advertise it in public.

Thora traced her fingertips along Halcyon's curves, over muscles, and across soft skin. She rumbled and lowered her head close to the side of Halcyon's head. With her nose, she traced the outer part of Halcyon's ear. "You tasted perfect last night."

After a soft whine, Halcyon cupped Thora's cheeks and whispered, "You were the first to taste me." She had refused the attempts from Selene, who gave up after a few times. Euclid viewed giving oral sex to an Omega as beneath him. "*Þǫkk.*"

"*Ekki at þakka, ást.*" Thora trailed her fingertips up Halcyon's thigh, then withdrew her hand. In a hurry, she moved out of the bed.

Halcyon frowned at the quick departure, but Thora did have chores. She wondered about the new word that Thora said at the end of her response to Halcyon's gratitude. With a shake of her head, she prepared for her day and put on her chiton from yesterday. She went to the washbasin as Thora headed to the open doorway. Halcyon dried her face and was startled to see Thora still in the room. From Thora's furrowed brow, she knew they might butt heads.

"What will happen to our pup?" Thora moved away from the doorway and neared Halcyon. Her earlier mood in bed made better sense to Halcyon.

"I'm undecided." Halcyon almost choked on her own lie. She wasn't ready to accept what had to be done much less tell Thora.

Thora towered over her owner, who held her ground. "You are thinking over it." She narrowed her eyes and demanded, "Tell me what you are thinking."

Halcyon tilted her head back and held Thora's gaze as it grew dark. She fisted her hands at her side and said, "I think you have mistaken last night as mating rather than a meaningless fuck." Thora retracted as if struck and caused Halcyon to wince in response. Her Omega ached inside her chest after her cruelness. Several comforting words hung on the tip of her tongue, but she refused to let them out. She couldn't afford to live in a fantasy where she and Thora could raise a pup together. Each new day with Thora brought on deeper feelings, tempting her. Halcyon wanted to ignore the fact that her Omega had managed to fine-tune her heat pheromones to attract and trigger Thora to respond. They had an undeniable attraction to each other, but in the end, they were both slaves to the Spartan system.

Thora raised her chest and curled a hand at her side. An icy mask fell over her features, and a coolness entered her voice. "Tell me." Her pheromones swirled and whipped around Halcyon, who cracked open a fraction. "Tell me what will happen to *my* pup."

Halcyon flexed her fists and blew out a throaty huff. She at least owed Thora the truth. A truth that would create a rift between them. With a raise of her chin, she swallowed against the forming bile in her throat and whispered, "After the pup is born, I will surrender it to the government." A heavy silence filled the space, except for the pounding of her heart.

"They will be a helot," Thora murmured in a rough voice, and then she started to pant. She shook her head and whispered, "*Nei.*" She flashed her teeth and argued, "Let me raise them as one of your house slaves." The idea had crossed Halcyon's mind, but it was far too difficult for Halcyon.

With a slight shake of her head, Halcyon said, "I can't allow it." She refused to spend the rest of her life having her pup be a servant to her and possibly Euclid. To be a stranger. To be a secret. And to watch on in silence while Thora raised their pup. But if her pup was a helot, then Halcyon could live on in utter ignorance.

"Then surrender both me and the pup to the government," Thora urged and seemed prepared to touch Halcyon. She dropped an open hand back to her side and whined low when Halcyon shook her head. If Thora and the pup became helots, there wasn't any chance that they would remain together.

"I will not allow you to become a helot." Halcyon was selfish when it came to Thora, from the first day their gazes met. She would never allow another to own Thora, much less the Spartan government. Halcyon would rather free Thora first than make her a helot.

"But you will allow our pup to become a helot?" Thora demanded in a raised voice. Her eyes glistened with shards of anger and deeper pain. "How can you be this heartless?" She bared her teeth, and her pheromones boiled with intense heat.

Halcyon shook her head at Thora's growing rage about the horrible situation before them. "This is the safest option. You will learn to accept it." She stepped around Thora, needing the space before the argument became a fight. After a few steps, her wrist was snared, so she pivoted back, but her arm remained extended between them.

"How can I live alongside you after what you will do to our pup?"

After a swallow, Halcyon lifted her chin and remembered one of her greatest lessons as a hoplite. From an early age, she was taught how to live through pain, how to carry on, and how to battle until her last breath. She nodded once and ordered, "You'll have to find a way to *survive* alongside me." With a firm shake of her wrist, she freed herself and added, "Our story isn't one about love." She headed for the doorway but paused and looked back at Thora, who had tearstained cheeks.

"Greeks prefer tragedy."

CHAPTER 19

Halcyon

The late summer day went on without another incident between Halcyon and Thora. They avoided one another as if they had the plague. Halcyon kept her shoulders squared throughout the day until she found herself kneeling in front of a chamber pot. She should have known better than to hope the sickness would leave her alone for one day. Again, she wished that Thora was at her side.

Halcyon's Omega twisted and clawed against her mind and heart. Deep inside she battled with the images of handing over her little pup to the government. Perhaps Thora's idea of raising their pup as a house slave in the confines of their villa was better. Even though Halcyon couldn't claim the pup as hers, she could at least keep them safe from the ugly fate that awaited them as a helot. As Halcyon sat on the floor in the chamber-pot room, picturing her pup being taken by the government, she began to hyperventilate. She boxed away pictures in her head and took deep breaths until her heart rate was normal again.

For a beat, she hoped that Thora would rush in and console her. Halcyon wiped the sweat from her brow and reminded herself that her hurtful actions had pushed Thora back. But she was certain that Thora would work through their differences once Thora accepted Halcyon's way. She was certain they could move forward, again.

Picking herself up from the floor, Halcyon leaned against the counter, then took the oil lamp that provided the light. She stepped out of the tiny room and breathed in the night air, which was sticky and humid but was at least a little cooler than when the sun was up. She gazed toward the entrance to her room and the short walk felt like a league. She was tempted to call for one of her slaves, but she pushed herself forward. The sheer amount of weakness the pregnancy brought on was appalling.

Once she staggered into her room, she set the lamp on the table by the bed, then started to prepare for her night. The sun had set about an hour ago, and often Halcyon would remain awake to handle a few duties dealing with her business in Athens. Tonight, though, it was too great of a feat. Her body melted into the bed, and she spared enough energy to extinguish the lamp. Exhaustion claimed her in minutes.

At dawn, Halcyon's churning stomach woke her. She purged what little food and bile contents were left in her and then sat on the floor by her trunk. Leaning against it, she tried to steady her breathing and remind herself that her situation wasn't indefinite. Once the pup was born, she could return to her normal routine.

Then leather sandals smacked against wooden steps at an alarming pace. The rather light footfall couldn't be Thora's. Halcyon dragged herself onto the top of the trunk before someone found her curled up on the floor. Glauce barreled into the room, waving the shredded ends of a cloth. The early morning light showed the lines of distress across her flushed features.

"Mistress!"

Halcyon folded her hands in her lap and kept a stoic appearance, ignoring the trembling in her body. "What is it?"

Glauce handed over a scrap of cloth, which had strange letters written on it. She wrung her hands together and whispered, "She is gone, mistress." While Halcyon studied the cloth, Glauce continued to explain what happened between yesterday and this morning. "Last night Thora went upstairs first while I finished cleaning the kitchen. She said she was tired. When I came to the room, she was asleep already." Glauce faltered and shifted from foot to foot. "She was gone when I woke up." She pointed at the scrap linen in Halcyon's lap. "It was all she left."

"Did she take supplies?" Halcyon asked, struggling to keep her voice indifferent. "Anything from the kitchen or supply room?"

"I-I don't know, mistress." Glauce bowed her head, as if prepared to be lectured.

"Please check and also send Vitus to me," Halcyon ordered and shooed her slave from the room. Once she was alone, she blew out a breath and dropped her head into her hand. The linen held a hint of Thora's scent, which pulled at Halcyon's Omega. She looked at the scrap cloth again and frowned at the Norsk letters. The letters were bold and strong, much like Thora's personality.

Thora had left, presumably to return to her homelands.

The Norsk note did nothing to ebb the flood of feelings inside Halcyon. She clenched her lips between her teeth before she murmured, "She left me." Halcyon closed her hand around the cloth and used her techniques to mentally prepare for battle. She closed her eyes and took several deep breaths that helped her steady her mind. The sweatiness of her palms was easy to ignore but not the thundering of her heart. Distant footsteps drew her back to the present.

Vitus hurried in and called, "Halcyon?"

"Here." Halcyon stood from the trunk, relieved her legs were sturdy again. "Can you read this?"

Vitus took the linen and held it out between his hand. He shook his head, then turned it over and frowned more. "I am unsure what it says on the one side." After a huff, he whispered, "But I believe this is an apology." He looked from it to Halcyon. "*Fyrirgef.* She has said it to me whenever she makes a mistake."

Halcyon received the cloth and stared at the single Norsk word. She turned it over and wished she could read what Thora had scratched on the other side. It was a full sentence in smaller print compared to the apology.

"Has something—"

"You leave in the next day?" Halcyon asked in a stern tone.

Vitus hesitated, but he nodded after a moment. "I leave tomorrow." He appeared uneasy and frowned at the linen folded up in Halcyon's hand.

"That is all." Halcyon refused to discuss further what happened to Thora. Already her heartbeat was erratic and her muscles coiled with tension. Her Omega screamed at her to track down Thora, and she wanted to heed the natural instinct. Thora was hers; she was *theirs*. After a shaky breath, she said, "Thank you."

Vitus pursed his lips, then nodded and started out of the room. But he faltered in the hallway and returned to the opening of the bedroom. "Halcyon?"

Halcyon was near the washbasin after she tucked the cloth inside her chiton. She looked toward him and raised an eyebrow. With skill, she kept her distress locked down and features neutral. "Yes?"

Vitus cleared his throat. "Early on in our reading lessons, I showed Thora how to read maps." He hesitated when Halcyon narrowed her eyes. "She asked if I had other maps, larger ones. I only had one other that I brought with me from Rome." He laced his hands in front of himself in a submissive stance that eased Halcyon. "It showed the routes in Gaul that Roman merchants travel for trade."

Halcyon lifted her chin but tamped down on the sudden fire in her chest after Vitus's confession. He could not have known Thora's plans, she reminded herself. She had even briefly shown Thora a map of Greece and the surrounding countries.

"Yesterday I began to organize my belongings, and I noticed the map was gone." Vitus's eyes fluttered a few times before he insisted, "I intended to ask her of it before I left."

Halcyon schooled her breathing and turned her head away. "That is all, Vitus." The bite in her voice was more than enough to send him out. A thread of guilt sat in her belly, but right now she had much to consider. First she tried to clean the bitterness in her mouth using mint, then she washed her face in hopes it would cool the violent heat under her skin.

"Mistress!" Cesare barreled into the bedroom and hunched over. He labored over his breaths but managed to speak. "Thora is gone."

"Yes, I am aware." Halcyon tossed the drying linen onto the table next to the washbasin. She approached him and touched his shoulder to garner his attention. She did her best to not allow Cesare's distress to rattle her.

"Th-Th-ere's two…" Cesare took another deep breath, then straightened and placed a hand on his heaving chest. "There are two hoplites at the gate. They requested to speak to you."

Halcyon dropped her hand from Cesare and groaned at the possibility that it was a superior officer from the barracks. She was King Leonidas's last guard, but she was tied to the military regardless. Her time away was excusable due to her injury, but they would expect her return to duty any day. The simple thought of putting on her armor exhausted her. "I will speak to them."

"Yes, mistress."

"In the meantime, ready my horse and another and enough supplies for about five days." Halcyon ignored Cesare's hopeful gaze because she needed to focus on her upcoming visit with the hoplites. She preferred to send them away and focus on her heart's mission to find Thora. Beyond the lands of Sparta, Thora was at great risk once someone spotted her.

Regardless of her slave iron, Thora was clearly an outsider from head to toe and would be attacked upon first sighting.

"Come find me when you're done," Halcyon ordered and headed for the courtyard on the ground floor. Cesare was on her heels and followed her to the gate where the visitors waited to be greeted or sent away. After Cesare slipped past them, she welcomed them to her villa.

The male Alpha on the right was dressed in full uniform but didn't carry his spear or shield. His one weapon was his short sword sheathed at his hip. He removed his helmet and revealed his round cheeks, dark hair, brown eyes, and thin beard. He was familiar to Halcyon, but she didn't know his name.

The other male was named Xanthos. He was older and dressed in a red chiton and sandals. He also carried a blade at his side, the only indication of his status in the military. He oversaw the particular barracks that Halcyon was assigned to.

"Hello, Halcyon," Xanthos replied after her welcome. "This is Myron."

Myron didn't smile, but he nodded.

"We wished to speak to you about your recovery and return to duty," Xanthos said. He had a milder scent than most Alphas, which was common as they aged over the years.

"Yes." Halcyon pivoted and said, "Please sit with me in the courtyard." She often handled business matters in the master's suite, but it would appear strange to her fellow comrades if she took them there. She escorted them to the open area, near the fountain. After a brief dance of sitting arrangements, Halcyon and Xanthos took a seat in the two chairs at the table. Myron elected to remain standing off to Xanthos's side.

"As I was saying, we're here to inquire about your return to duty." Xanthos folded his hands in his lap and sat rigid like any trained hoplite. "The healer, Giles, reported that you have recovered well."

"Yes," Halcyon agreed and kept an even tone. Their unexpected visit had set her heart into a gallop, but she showed a stoic expression. "There is only a minor strain in my shoulder." She would need to stretch out the affected muscle before she could return to intense training. However, the thought of training and exerting her already tired body was unpleasant to her. "I have nearly regained my strength."

"That is excellent news." Xanthos nodded while Myron rumbled low. "Perhaps then it would be best if you returned to duty at the start of the month." It would give her about a fortnight until she was due to put on her armor.

"And what of my assignment?" Halcyon asked, tilting her head to the side. With King Leonidas's death, her position as his guard was in question. Another person would assume his role as one of the two kings, but it would take time. The next king would choose who he wanted assembled in his guard.

"King Leonidas's death has brought about change. There will be many meetings at the council house to decide the new king." Xanthos paused and cleared his throat. "As you know, one of the requirements of the king's guard is that the hoplite has an heir." The tradition was long-standing in Sparta. The military wanted assurance that an elite hoplite such as the guard would one day have a replacement. "King Leonidas authorized for you to circumvent this requirement."

Halcyon remained passive rather than let out a growl. She had Leonidas's full support when he chose her. Her distinguished title as the Iron Edge also played a key role in her ability to become a guard. Xanthos was forewarning that such events may not repeat again with the new king.

He shifted and prepared to speak, but Glauce arrived in the courtyard.

Halcyon looked between Xanthos and Myron. "Would either of you like drink or food?"

"No, but thank you," Xanthos replied first.

Myron shook his head and attempted a smile that was lackluster. He continued to remain like a statue, albeit a listening one.

Halcyon waved off Glauce, who probably had breakfast ready for her. She was famished and even shaky after throwing up this morning. But her visitors would leave soon. "Then I will return to regular duty?" The earlier topic about her questionable place in the king's guard was too delicate at the moment.

Xanthos didn't answer this time and looked to Myron, prompting him to speak for once.

Myron turned to his right and met Halcyon's gaze. "I would like to offer you a position as a polemarchos," he said with a puff of his chest. "Your long experience in the king's guard warrants you such a position." The slight stench of his increased pheromones caught Halcyon's nose.

Halcyon was calm even though the new position was a high one in the army. She would be a military leader in charge of five hundred seventy-six hoplites. The position was a promotion, but it wasn't considered as honorable as being one of the king's guards.

"It requires consideration," Xanthos said, causing Myron to deflate.

"It is a great honor to be offered the position," Halcyon said, looking from Xanthos to Myron. "Do I have time to consider?" With the war against King Xerxes in motion, changes in the military would take time. But death did bring openings in the ranks.

"Yes," Myron replied. "Perhaps once you have returned to duty, you will have made a decision."

Halcyon accepted the unspoken grace period and smiled at Myron. "Yes." She looked to Xanthos and asked a few questions about the war. The Spartan military was mobile, and units had started to depart the city. Orders were being sent to Spartan provinces, who were sending their own forces. Xanthos confirmed there were six units left to depart Sparta, while three would remain in the city as a defense. Many didn't expect King Xerxes to make it to Sparta, but it was better to be prepared for a hostile attack.

"We must depart," Xanthos announced after their discussion. He stood and shook arms with Halcyon, who also exchanged arms with Myron. She escorted them from the villa, promising them an answer by the start of next month.

Now alone in the courtyard, Halcyon considered her plans to handle Thora. She needed to pack a few clothing items and gather her sword, coins, and a map or two. Vitus could remain at the villa with Glauce to ensure everything was secure and safe until her return. It was difficult to say at what time Thora left the villa, but Halcyon's horse would travel faster than Thora. While seated in the courtyard, Glauce appeared and served Halcyon breakfast.

"Thora took food and skins from the supply room," Glauce reported.

Halcyon studied the plate and bowl of food for her meal. Her stomach responded to the wonderful smells. "Do you have an idea how long the supplies may last?"

Glauce fidgeted with the hem of her chiton. "About five days, mistress." The food wasn't inadequate for a trip to the Norselands. Thora didn't have any coin to purchase more or owned hunting weapons. After Halcyon's nod, Glauce took a step back but paused and added, "She also took a kitchen knife and the reed pen."

Halcyon had gifted the pen to Thora. A kitchen knife wasn't a hunting blade, but it was useful regardless. She was grateful that Thora had taken supplies rather than leaving empty handed without any chance of survival. Thora was smart, and so very stubborn.

"Is there anything else, mistress?" Glauce asked, shifting from foot to foot.

"No." Halcyon tried to eat the bowl of fruit with patience.

Glauce took a few steps away but turned back and said, "Mistress, we've had our differences."

Halcyon lowered the bowl to her lap, studied her meek slave, and remained silent. For once, she sniffed out a bit of confidence in Glauce's scent. She was intrigued by what sparked the change.

"I-I'm certain that you care for Thora as I do." Glauce held her hands together, producing white knuckles. "What might be troubling you, Thora would help you with, if you ask her." She swallowed, then looked to the side and whispered, "Her hearts runs deep for you." Without another word, she hurried back to the kitchen.

After a sigh, Halcyon stared at the remaining fruit and weighed Glauce's advice. The young Omega had taken a leap of faith to speak openly to Halcyon. She respected Glauce's developing strength that was perhaps inspired by Thora. Somehow Thora had an ability to inspire people to find their own power. While she ate, Halcyon considered what routes Thora may take to head north toward her homelands.

"Mistress." Cesare emerged from the gate. He had saddlebags in each hand. "The horses are ready. I'll place your saddlebags in your room."

"Yes, then pack your things." Halcyon brushed her hands clean, then took a sip of fruit juice. "Did you ask Glauce to prepare food supplies?"

"Yes, I'll check with her." Cesare started for the kitchen.

"Be ready to depart in an hour," Halcyon ordered and heard Cesare's confirmation echoed back to her. She took a piece of bread and went upstairs to her room. She took large bites of the slice while she gathered her belongings for the journey. Almost ready, the one question was her armor. The fitted bronze armor would denote her as military, giving her an edge. But the weight of it would deplete her already weakened energy level. In her mind, the benefits of the armor's status outweighed her own fragility. With determination, she put on the cuirass and greaves but decided to leave the helmet lashed to the side of a saddlebag. With a sword and dagger on either side, she felt prepared to leave the villa.

Down in the courtyard, Glauce waited and then informed her that Cesare was at the stable with all the supplies. Halcyon ordered Glauce to locate Vitus and have him meet her there. It didn't take long to check Cheimon's tack, then Cesare was joining her outside the stable.

Vitus arrived that moment and took a gulp of air after running from the direction of the villa. "Glauce said you wished to see me."

"Yes." Halcyon and Cesare hauled themselves onto their horses' backs while she asked Vitus to stay longer. He was agreeable about delaying his journey back to Rome. She promised him that they would be gone two to five days at the most.

Halcyon glanced at Cesare, who struggled to get comfortable in the saddle. "Can you no longer ride?" Many years ago, she had taught him how to ride because he had once accompanied her on military campaigns or operations. Once she joined the king's guard, she spent most of her duty in Sparta.

Cesare grumbled and cursed but settled into place. "I am old, mistress, but not dead."

Halcyon laughed, touched by his loyalty to her. "Let us go, then." She tugged on the left rein and started the journey. Beyond her villa, she and Cesare rode through the streets of Sparta and steered around the carts and people. Once beyond the city, the maintained road later became swallowed by the beautiful landscape.

Halcyon had long ago retained a mental map of the region after many marches to Corinth and Athens. Regardless, she double-checked their location on the map when they took short breaks. The summer was brutal today, but various trees along the way offered relief. At one point, Halcyon studied the regional map with great intent. If she were to find Thora, she had to think like her slave, who was smart and clever. Thora wouldn't travel on the roads, at least not during the day, or go into villages. Thora's very appearance and stature made her stand out like the Minotaur. But she may follow the roads from a distance, then use them at night when few were out. Even at night, the roads still posed a threat with bandits.

If she and Cesare were to locate Thora, then their last chance was at the Diolkos along the Isthmus of Corinth. There were only a few spots that allowed traffic to cross the portage road along the isthmus. However, it would take them four and a half days to ride to Corinth. Her hope was to catch up to Thora before the portage road, if they were fortunate to be following her trail.

At a fast pace, Halcyon traveled northeast as Apollo rode across the sky and shone light on the beautiful lands. Cesare rode behind his owner and kept a careful eye out for trouble. After many hours, Halcyon became stiffer in the saddle. The breaks for them and the horses helped, but it was a difficult ride.

When the sun hung low in the sky, Cesare pressed his horse to catch up. He was unusually quiet for much of the ride. Once alongside Halcyon, he slumped forward against the horse, as if quite stricken. "Mistress?"

Halcyon's attention was lost among the sea of hills that formed the peninsula. She broke away from her visual survey and raised an eyebrow at Cesare.

"It is late," Cesare said in an exhausted tone, "and these old bones of mine..."

Halcyon had been so preoccupied with her thoughts that she had missed Cesare's weariness, but she couldn't deny him or even herself. After a nod, she smiled and said, "Not much farther."

Cesare was soon rewarded with a welcoming stream beyond a line of pistachio trees. With cautious movements, he dismounted from the horse and sighed once his feet touched the ground. After a glance to the west, he looked to Halcyon and mentioned he would collect firewood. Halcyon took care of their horses.

Well before sunset, Halcyon and her slave were comfortable beside a fire. Few words passed between them as they shared a meal of dried meat, nuts, and uncooked vegetables. The small fire was enough to keep them warm, but it would be a cool night. Long ago, Halcyon was trained to snuff out campfires during the night. A fire could attract bandits.

Cesare wished Halcyon goodnight, then retired to his furs. Halcyon remained beside the campfire. Earlier she had removed her armor and left it by her bedroll. She was wrapped in a fur that blocked out the evening chill. She watched the gentle dance of colors from the sunset. It was a slow end to a difficult day.

Somewhere across the Grecian lands, Thora basked in the same sunset but perhaps farther north. Halcyon vowed to find her slave, who had abandoned her and their pup. But the harsh truth was that Halcyon had driven off Thora. If she failed to locate Thora, then Halcyon would have to face a future that would break her. At an unknown point, Thora had claimed Halcyon's heart.

Total exhaustion crept through Halcyon. She collapsed into her bedroll and managed to get the furs over her shoulder before she fell asleep. Above her head, she kept her sword and dagger hooked to her side in case there was a problem. Cesare carried the old kopis from the toolshed. Through the night, she stirred a few times and relieved herself. The morning birds woke her to the new day, and she found the campfire lit back to life. Halcyon was grateful for the warmth and reclaimed her seat by the fire.

Cesare busied with making a light breakfast for them. He was a decent cook when on the road and made do so that their bellies were full for the morning. A few minutes before he served the meal, Halcyon left camp and fought a round of morning sickness. Cesare had yet to question Halcyon about her constant illness, but she suspected he knew the truth. He offered her a worried glance when she returned and attempted to eat.

The morning meal passed in silence, and then the pair broke camp at a steady pace. The horses were tacked and soon the journey continued north, toward the Isthmus of Corinth. Each hour burned into the next one until the beautiful mountains of Mainalo rose in a soft green wave. Nestled below the mountain range was the busy city of Mantineia, which also served as Halcyon's navigational aid. From here, they would turn northeast toward the isthmus.

For a reward, Halcyon took a break in the city. They walked their horses to the market and hitched them near a stable, then sought out supplies for their continued journey. Halcyon spent far too much time bartering over food. Mantineia was known for its wine and honey mead, but she steered away from it. Yesterday she had noted that Cesare had filled the skins with water or juice rather than wine.

By the late afternoon, they had departed the busy town and continued northeast on the only route off the peninsula. The sun's afternoon heat warmed their backs during the ride. Every hilltop and valley rolled in a constant tide of terrain. They would arrive at the isthmus in two to three days. If their timing was right and the Fates willed it, they would arrive before Thora and be able to halt her. They were perhaps already ahead of Thora, thanks to the horses.

Cesare traded few words with his owner. At dinner, he fussed with Halcyon about taking care of certain chores. Halcyon wanted to argue, but she had little strength left. Her pregnancy and the fast-paced travel were taxing. After sunset,

Halcyon sat in comfortable silence and sharpened her bronze sword in her lap. With each stroke of the whetstone, she was able to soothe the turmoil in her.

Thora was gone, but not lost.

How could Thora leave—leave her? They had arguments, but Halcyon had believed she and Thora could work through their differences. She was certain their fight over the pup's future had chased off Thora. But had there been more to it? Halcyon rubbed her brow after she recalled how harsh she'd been with Thora during their last morning together. Pretending to not care for Thora was an impossible task.

Halcyon wanted Thora in her life.

Tonight, she struggled with the frantic need to locate Thora immediately. If a Greek citizen crossed paths with Thora, they would have legal right to claim Thora as their slave. It was difficult to reclaim a runaway slave, who would be considered lost property. Even so, Halcyon would pay a ransom for Thora. But then there were the thieves, who would use Thora in unspeakable ways, then leave her decapitated body on the roadside.

Pausing, Halcyon blew out a shaky breath and returned to running the whetstone along the angled blade. She had driven Thora off by cutting her out of their pup's fate and future. Halcyon believed she was doing what was best for all of them. Sparta would never accept a pup with mixed blood and foreign features. It was acceptable for an uncle to mate his niece, but it was unspeakable to have a pup with a barbarian.

Growling low, Halcyon cursed the people of Sparta for their double standards. She may have been raised and groomed by Sparta, but she was well aware of the government's twisted views. Yet Halcyon had devoted her life to the system and almost gave her life to it. Putting the sharpening stone down, she touched her stomach and considered the developing pup inside her. Once the military learned of her pregnancy, they would oust her through forced retirement. Like Halcyon, the military turned a blind eye to Halcyon's true nature as an Omega.

After a rumble, Halcyon took a cloth and wiped the blade, then packed everything away. She said goodnight to Cesare and crawled into her bedroll. Rolling onto her side, she gazed off toward the moonlit landscape and stared at the pistachio tree at the crest of a distant hill. As her eyes grew heavy, she thought she saw slight movement beside the tree, but her tired mind was useless at this stage. She dozed off in a few heartbeats.

CHAPTER 20

Halcyon

Before Apollo could even mount his sun chariot, Halcyon was yanked out of her bedroll by hands that were calloused like her own. She stumbled in the darkness, but she saw two dirty faces pass hers. There was an awful, uncleaned stench that was mixed with Beta pheromones. She was thrown onto her knees while Cesare's yells filled her ears. A rusty iron blade tip pressed into her lower neck and stilled her movements.

"What is a lone Omega doing traveling with only a slave?" a bandit asked.

Halcyon cast a glance to Cesare, who was held at dagger point by two other men. Cesare's old kopis was kicked away by one of the bandits. Altogether they were dealing with four bandits, who probably considered these lands their territory. Three of them were male Betas, while the presumed leader was a male Alpha. She returned her dark stare to the Alpha, glaring along the length of his ugly sword to his marred features above her. "We are headed to Corinth to see family."

The Alpha weighed the answer, then huffed low and indicated the armor to their side. "Yours?"

Halcyon gritted her teeth and drew her fingers closer to the hidden dagger's hilt at her waist. She had only a slim chance to save herself and Cesare. Her heart lurched at dying out here by worthless bandits.

"It is hers," another bandit confirmed. The bandit had midnight hair in long strands braided behind his back and wore a tattered leather cuirass. He was inspecting her well-crafted armor and indicated the adjustment in the bronze cuirass for a female's breasts.

"A female warrior," the leader bandit mocked, then flexed his grip on the sword hilt.

"These markings are of the king's guard," the dark-haired bandit further revealed. He dragged his fingertips along the stamp engraved at the right shoulder. His two comrades who held Cesare captive started talking low. He stood up and suggested, "Sciron, she could be worth a nice ransom."

The Alpha, Sciron, smiled and revealed his few pretty teeth. "Iros, tie her." He kept his sword trained on Halcyon.

The dark-haired bandit, Iros, moved away from the armor. He reached behind his back and unhooked a length of coiled rope. He went behind Halcyon and growled low in warning at her. With him much closer, she confirmed he was indeed a Beta. "Don't make trouble." He knelt, took her right wrist first and then reached for her other wrist.

Halcyon tore the dagger free from the sheath at her hip, grazing her own flesh against the tip of the leader's sword in the process. The twinge of sharpness against her skin fueled her as she spun to her left and swung her dagger up. With skill, Halcyon drove the dagger into Iros's neck, and blood poured from the wound. His dying gurgles were music to her ears.

Sciron was awestruck, but he recovered and lunged at her. He missed and blew past her. He turned with the sword pointed at her. His large body blocked Halcyon from obtaining her own sword. Halcyon had her hands raised and the bloody dagger at the ready. She backed up and stepped around Iros's body.

Sciron bared his teeth, then ordered, "Kill the slave, Pratinos."

Pratinos was on Cesare's left, and he drew the blade tight against his neck. Cesare's initial scream cut across Halcyon's heart. Pratinos went slow, cutting through the skin until Halcyon yelled at him.

"Stop!" Halcyon crumbled under the threat to Cesare's life. She tossed the bloody dagger to the ground and surrendered to the bandits; jaw clenched.

Sciron smiled with his broken yellow teeth, but it turned into a sneer. He lunged forward with the blade overhead. He struck his fist against Halcyon's jaw and took her down to her knees. Sciron jammed his right knee into her chest, the force of it knocking her onto her back.

Cesare's distant holler echoed in Halcyon's head. She groaned, and dizziness swept over her. A thread of panic charged through her when Sciron drew back his foot. She shielded her stomach with her arms before he kicked her. Halcyon whimpered from the bolt of pain, but her arms took the brunt of it. She saw Sciron prepare to kick again, and she cringed at what it would do to the life forming in her belly.

"Please!" Cesare tried to move, but Pratinos tightened the blade to his throat. "She has suffered enough." His plea carried a slight whine.

Sciron growled and huffed. "Hardly—compared to my dead friend." Even if he knew Halcyon's value as a ransom, murder and hunger shone in his eyes.

She warred with her weakened body, demanded her muscles to lift her and fight back, but after the hits, she struggled to sit up. All her attention was drawn to his rusty blade that reflected the moonlight. For the first time in her life, Halcyon faced true fear. Not for herself, but for the unborn life in her belly. Her Omega instincts told her to protect her pup, and she prayed to the goddess Rhea—her first ever plea to the Mother of the Gods.

From the twinkling skies, Rhea listened to a mortal's appeal for motherhood, and she responded with thunder across the valleys. Her beautiful voice came out in a powerful yell and rolled through the campsite. A single word in a strange tongue to the Greek ear. Then a golden bolt cut through the darkness and collided with Sciron.

Halcyon gasped after Sciron was slammed to the ground beside her. She tingled with hints of strength and peered over her shoulder at the downed bandit. Even in the dark night, Halcyon made out the golden strands of her savior. "Thora," she whispered in awe. Like Halcyon, the two bandits beside Cesare were dumbstruck by Thora's arrival as if she were a goddess.

Quick to recover, Halcyon crawled over to her bloody dagger and fingered the hilt. She stole a concerned glance at Thora, who remained on top of Sciron's back.

Thora was bulkier and several hands taller than Sciron, and she raged with Alpha pheromones. She growled between clenched teeth and rolled them so that he was on top. Sciron yelped and struggled against Thora, who swung a bit of rope around his neck. Sciron choked and clawed at the thick coil across his throat while the stars twinkled above him.

At the same time, Halcyon snatched her bloody dagger, flipped it, and held it by the blade end. She rolled onto her back with her right arm retracted. In a heartbeat, she aligned her aim and threw the dagger at Cesare's captor. Pratinos screamed when the blade plunged into his right eye. He dropped his own dagger from Cesare's throat.

The last bandit watched his comrade fall to death and reversed from Cesare. He had no weapons beyond his rough fists. After a glance at his dying leader, he danced on his bare feet a few times, then bolted from the campsite.

Halcyon watched him flee, then she turned her attention to Thora and Sciron. She flinched at the sudden silence in the camp. Sciron was limp against Thora, but he was tossed off. His eyes were wide open toward the gods above them.

Thora dropped the rope and hurried to her feet. After a visual scan of the campsite, she went to her owner's side and dropped to her knees. "Halcyon?" There was a distinct strain in her voice that left Halcyon trembling in Thora's arms. After a deep breath, Halcyon relaxed against Thora and allowed concerned hands to check over her.

Cesare appeared on the other side of Halcyon. "Are you hurt, mistress?"

Halcyon flinched at Cesare's gentle touch against her face. "I am fine." From her kneeling position, she saw the thin line of blood on Cesare's neck from the bandit's blade. She rose from the ground and groaned from the growing soreness in her body. Thora's hand was against her lower back. Secure around her two slaves, Halcyon lifted her gaze until her eyes locked on Thora. For several silent moments, they exchanged unspoken thoughts and feelings after being apart.

"I will remove the bodies," Cesare said and withdrew himself from the tense situation growing between Halcyon and Thora. However, Thora broke away and assisted Cesare with hauling the bodies away. Halcyon said nothing and was grateful that Thora wouldn't allow Cesare to handle the foul job alone.

Halcyon decided to handle restarting the fire, needing the distraction after what happened earlier. The fire wouldn't attract any new bandits after they put an end to the current ones. Bandits tended to have their own territory that they patrolled until another group of bandits chased them off or absorbed them. Seated by the rekindled campfire, Halcyon had a few minutes to collect her thoughts and consider Thora's stormy arrival. If it weren't for Thora, she would be kidnapped and Cesare dead. With a heavy sigh, Halcyon rubbed her brow and finished cleaning her dagger.

After the bodies were removed, Thora mentioned she would return with her supplies. She disappeared under the moonlight and returned about half an hour later. After she set a rucksack by Cesare's bedroll, she took a seat on the ground between Cesare and Halcyon. Everyone sat around the camp in tense silence. Nobody dared to speak first, because it was Halcyon's right as their owner. After a long quietness, Halcyon shifted on the fur-covered boulder and said, "Thank you for saving us."

"Yes," Cesare agreed and stretched out an arm to touch Thora's bare knee. "Thank you."

"You are welcome," Thora replied, glancing between the pair. Her features appeared calm, but Halcyon caught anxious hints in Thora's pheromones when they drifted under her nose. Earlier Thora had been full of thunder and wrath when the bandit was beating Halcyon.

"Mistress," Cesare said, "I will gather more firewood."

Halcyon flashed a grateful look to Cesare. She indicated the hatchet beside her saddlebags. Once Cesare's footfall faded, she turned to Thora and held out Thora's scrap cloth that had Norsk words on it. "What does this say?" The edge in her tone warned Thora not to lie or skirt around the truth.

Thora released an exhale and replied, "It is an old saying from my people." She stared at the cloth. "It says, 'The dog always chases the rabbit.'"

"And who is the rabbit?" Halcyon asked, preferring to ignore the irony of her pursuing Thora these past few days.

Thora gave a pointed look, then she replied, "It means a person should always chase their dreams. Sometimes the dog may catch the rabbit, but the rabbit is also clever and smart and escapes the dog." After a pause, she added, "They are connected."

Halcyon huffed and studied the cloth, attempting to translate the words from Norsk to Greek. The letters were foreign to her. It was the second time she'd seen Thora's handwriting. Despite the purpose behind the note, she would hold on to it and the lesson she learned from Thora.

"But sometimes a connection is not enough," Thora whispered in a drained volume, as if to herself. However, Halcyon heard it and chose not to bite on the suggestion. If they shared a connection, then Halcyon wasn't prepared to voice it.

After returning the scrap cloth into the folds of her chiton, Halcyon swallowed and redirected the conversation. She regarded Thora for a quiet minute before she asked, "Wh-hy?"

Thora slouched a little, then turned her attention to the flames in front of her. She played with the leather strap of her sandal and rumbled low. "I am sorry I have upset you." Her response wasn't an answer and prodded Halcyon's internal wound.

"Upset me?" Halcyon huffed and stared over at her lover, who regarded her now. "That is a mild word for it." The storm of emotions was finally unleashed inside her after Thora's apology pierced her. For a beat, they stared at each other, and the painful silence reminded Halcyon of all the things left unsaid between them. Here and now with Thora could be her last chance to speak with her heart. "You have hurt me!" Her grief-stricken yell made Thora flinch. She exhaled a shaky breath after voicing her pain. "You left me," she whispered in shock, wishing her voice didn't rattle.

Halcyon was always aware of the possibility that Thora might leave her. There was nothing in life one *must* do except die, as her sire once told her. However, she had wrongly assumed that Thora would stand by her, even through the devastation that the pregnancy might bring. A simple Norsk note wasn't a goodbye, it was a dagger plunged into Halcyon. Thora had struck Halcyon in a manner that she hadn't expected of Thora.

The rush of feelings became louder in Halcyon's head. She had faced many battles and won, but tonight this one would change her. Halcyon wanted Thora to return to her. She could force Thora through numerous methods. But then what? How could they ever trust each other again?

Thora had to choose with her own free will.

With a heavy huff, Halcyon blinked back the heat in her eyes and said, "But I know I drove you away." She had played a large part in their unraveling. Her bottom lip quivered as the recent events and arguments started to bang against her skull. She placed a hand on her chest, over her thundering heart, and struggled with her next breath. "I am so sorry." Her apology brought out a pained whine from Thora.

"I did not want to do this," Thora said in a trembling voice. Her cheeks were stained with tears that reflected in the firelight.

Halcyon's next breath hitched, caught at the back of her throat. She fought against the raging emotions in her. Part of her wanted to scream at Thora, for leaving her. Another part demanded Halcyon sit in silence and pay the price for her failure. She could bite her knuckle raw. "It is the pup."

"Y-Yes." Thora visibly swallowed. "I do not want to watch our pup be banished to a cruel life, beaten and raped, then murdered later." More tears fell. "I have already watched my first pup be murdered." She shook her head and dragged her fingers through her reflective hair. "I had no voice in the matter of our pup."

Hanging her head, Halcyon closed her eyes and allowed the harsh truth to strip her bare. She and Thora had conceived the pup together, but she took away Thora's rights over the pup.

"But it was more than the pup." Thora untangled herself from the bedroll and knelt in front of Halcyon. She rested a hand on Halcyon's leg. The trembling from her palm prompted Halcyon to lift her head. "Your passion for me frightens me."

Halcyon clenched her jaw and struggled to not recoil from Thora. Again, Thora's words sliced through Halcyon's armor and drove the air from her lungs. But Thora tightened her grip on Halcyon's leg.

"M-My mate cared for me," Thora explained. "Our union was a convenience for my family." She wiped her eyes with her other hand and choked on her next word. "He was beautiful, but I was never attracted to him, not like…" Her jaw remained loose. The redness around her blue eyes brought a thin layer of agony to Halcyon. "Not like I am to you. It terrifies me." She searched her lover's features. "And I can feel how attracted you are to me."

Halcyon looked away and fought to get enough air in her lungs. She dragged her fingers through her disheveled hair and wished her mind were clearer. The tightness in her chest made it harder. "I-I am selfish when it comes to you."

Thora snorted.

"I want you in my life," Halcyon confessed, allowing some of her cracked armor to fall away. "You have become an important part of me." How could Thora not understand how important she was to Halcyon?

Thora rubbed her hand against her lover's tense leg. "We were new and exciting in the beginning. We could not speak, not like now. I became lost in it, especially when I went into a rut." She sniffed and shook her head a little. "I carry guilt for what I have done. You are in a union, and I feel I have betrayed my dead mate."

"Thooora," Halcyon intoned. She dropped her shoulders and leaned forward on the rock, getting a hand in delicate, golden strands. "I am sorry I contributed to your guilt. But you *will* make peace with yourself." She hadn't realized Thora's own weight. There wasn't any way that Halcyon could banish Thora's guilt as much as she desired to. "My union is one of convenience as well." After a pause, she whispered, "We made our choices. I don't believe there are mistakes in life." She lifted Thora's head until their eyes locked. "Love does not make mistakes."

Thora's chest shook with a delicate sound. Her features fractured a little while tears slipped free again. "If love makes no mistakes, then why were we given a pup? One that you plan to sentence to a horrible life."

Halcyon gritted her teeth and asked her gods to give her the ability to be strong. Their pup's life was already damned before they were even born. Deep inside her, she hated Sparta for taking this from her after she had given so much to Sparta.

"I'm being logical about their future." At least she attempted to convince herself she was being logical.

"You care for my life, but not our pup's?" Thora stood and demanded, "How can you be colder than my homelands?"

Halcyon growled at how their conversation was slipping again. Thora was too blind about their pup's fate. Day after day, she reminded herself that she had to surrender the pup when the time came. Thora's constant objection made it more difficult. "How can you think our pup will ever have a happy life?" she demanded and hopped off the boulder when Thora walked away.

Thora spun around and snapped, "Being a slave is better than a helot." She approached her lover and used her pheromones to push against Halcyon's rising ire. "But you deny me from raising our pup. Why?"

"No," Halcyon whispered, more to herself. She went around to the other side of the campfire and started to pace from side to side. "We can't keep the pup," she muttered in a drained tone.

Thora hastened around the campfire but kept space between them. "Because you wish to not ruin your status as a hoplite." She flashed her teeth and argued, "You think if the Spartans figure out that our pup is yours that you will lose your status." Halcyon fisted and uncurled her hands while Thora hypothesized the reasons. "You will sacrifice our pup for duty."

Halcyon came to an abrupt stop and faced her slave. Her head hurt and her eyes throbbed from the endless argument. She was tired. So tired. All she wanted was to end their fight and curl up in Thora's arms.

"After the pup is born, sell us both to someone in Athens," Thora demanded in a growly voice. "Then you can forget about us and be hoplite again."

Halcyon snarled and clenched her hands at her side. "*No!*" She was unable to withhold her Omega nature anymore. Every natural instinct unfurled inside her and shoved aside her rational thoughts. "If we cannot raise our pup together, then neither of us shall." She returned to walking back and forth, growling low. The developing life in her belly was her and Thora's pup, meant to have both parents. Halcyon hissed at the idea of Thora raising the pup alone while she returned to being a mindless hoplite, pretending she didn't care for either of them. Her next step brought her right into Thora's larger frame.

Thora snared Halcyon's wrists and asked, "What do you mean?" Halcyon gave her a bewildered look. "What do you mean by neither of us shall?" She softened her grip on Halcyon, who shook her head. "*Líka.*"

Halcyon closed her eyes and whispered, "I cannot bear to watch you raise our pup without me."

Thora was quiet and studied Halcyon, who reopened her eyes. After a gentle rumble, she released Halcyon's arm and cupped her cheek instead. "If everything perfect, would you want to raise a pup with me?"

"Yes, more than anything else." Halcyon cracked open and grabbed onto Thora's sides for comfort. "I can handle losing the pup, but I cannot handle losing you. I do not have feelings for it as I have for you." She twisted her fingers in Thora's chiton. The material wrinkled the harder she turned it. "But each day, it feels like it's becoming a little bit more of a lie that I must tell myself." The unshed tears stung in her eyes. "I-I…"

Thora bowed her head and encircled Halcyon's waist. "Please keep talking to me," she whispered near her lover's ear. "I am listening."

"I-I can feel myself wanting this pup more and more." Halcyon leaned her forehead against Thora's breastbone and inhaled her spicy Alpha scent. Her tongue grew looser as she confessed her dreams. "I want you both." She leaned into Thora and let out a sigh when strong hands worked her knotted back muscles. "But we are in Sparta, a-and I gave myself to Sparta decades ago. I vowed to die a glorious death and now this pregnancy could change all of it." Raising her head, she met her lover's concerned features. "It frightens me."

"Becoming a mother is a big change. I do understand." Thora tightened her arms and searched Halcyon's eyes. Her blue gaze was sharp and cut away at the last of Halcyon's armor. "But no government owns a person."

"Tell that to the thousands and thousands of helots," Halcyon whispered and turned her head to the side. She stared at the fire, watching the flames move together.

"The helots outnumber the Spartan citizens," Thora argued.

"But the citizens have the weapons." Halcyon let out a tired breath and closed her eyes. She considered what the future could look like if she kept their pup. There could be a way to co-parent the pup. However, once their pup was older, they would ask too much and desire to know their background. The pup would carry her and Thora's blood, unable to resist the call to fight back against restraints. "This is impossible," she murmured and screwed her eyes shut when the burn started again.

Thora nuzzled her lover's hair and tightened her arms. "There may be another answer if it has time to show itself." She exhaled low, then offered a warm thrum that calmed Halcyon's nerves. "There is much time between now and the birth."

Halcyon considered her slave's more patient attitude toward the problem. She was never patient, being well reminded by her own sire. There was a solution to every problem in life—until today. Halcyon was at a loss on how to move forward without someone being hurt or worse. Her heart wanted to have and raise Thora's pup, together. But there was no real-life route to such a dream.

Her beautiful dream was a heartbroken fantasy.

Yet, Halcyon clung on to hope—and on to Thora. She raised her head after a deep breath. "Please come back," she pleaded in a soft voice. Their story wasn't finished, it couldn't be. Halcyon dread the thought of Thora leaving and traveling any farther. Thora would be caught out here, then murdered. But earlier Halcyon sensed Thora accepted such a fate, wanting to face death rather than face another loss of a pup.

"If you don't wish to be lovers, I would not ask it of you," she added. "What you can give of yourself will always be enough for me." Halcyon buried her nails into Thora's chiton.

If they had more time together, they could work through their missteps. "I want you in my life, Thora."

Bending down, Thora settled her forehead against Halcyon's and rumbled with more vigor than before. Halcyon could feel the dull hum of pain between them, but it didn't overshadow the natural pull they shared. They weren't ready to talk more about the depth of it. For now, their unspoken connection was what could keep them bound to each other.

"Halcyon," Thora murmured, then grazed her lips over her lover's brow. The earlier tension in her body seeped out and then her scent eased. Halcyon let out a shaky breath and raised her head when Thora straightened. "I will return to the villa with you, if you wait longer to make your final decision."

Halcyon tilted her head back and regarded Thora. She sensed her weakened grip on the idea of banishing their pup fall away from her. Once gone, it left a dark opening in front of her, perhaps both of them. What if there was nothing to fill it? Thora's idea was all she had to hold on to, so she nodded. "I will wait, then we will decide."

Thora started to smile until her eyes reflected the same warmth of the fire.

"Why are you smiling?" Halcyon developed a wrinkle across her brow.

"You said, 'We will decide,'" Thora replied, smile brighter still.

Halcyon realized her mistake. However, the error nestled inside her, sprouted a fraction, and felt more like a start of a different life than her old one. Somehow the weight of deciding their pup's future was less scary with Thora's support.

If there was a way to have both Thora and the pup, then she was willing to listen and try. After a nod, she returned her lover's tender smile. "Together."

"*Já, saman.*"

Halcyon echoed the new Norsk word. But their verbal agreement to work together was tarnished by the slave iron on Thora's wrist. To Halcyon, the slave iron was a barrier to their future. It was one that would have to wait though. After a yawn, she spotted Cesare and started toward him when he stumbled from the armload.

Thora broke away and crossed the distance in a few wide strides. She took most of the firewood from him and tutted at him. "We do not need much firewood." They placed the wood near the fire, stacking it.

"Mistress, do you think more bandits will arrive tonight?"

"No, we will be fine for the rest of the night." With the current bandit gang eliminated, it would be a few days before another group replaced them in the area.

"We should sleep," Thora said to the group. All at once, everyone settled into their bedrolls without further conversation. After Cesare rolled to his side and put his back to them, Halcyon managed to join her bedroll with Thora's, and they snuggled together under their shared furs.

Halcyon basked in the comfort and security of having Thora back. They had much to work through in the coming months, but Halcyon was grateful that Thora agreed to return. Tonight's conversation with Thora had taken a burden away from Halcyon, who had finally voiced her deep fears and true desires. She wanted Thora, and she wanted the pup regardless of the price. There was no immediate resolution, but Thora was right that time might present a solution.

Curling more against Thora, Halcyon allowed her imagination to play with her secret fantasy of her and Thora raising their pup. Her Omega keened inside her chest, confirming this was what Halcyon wanted in her future. Spartans and their social traditions could fuck themselves. Halcyon had given plenty to the government, to the military, and to the country.

⟨HA⋗TⵟR 21
Halcyon

Halcyon looked up from the desk when Cesare entered the master's suite. She placed the quill in the inkwell and waited for Cesare's explanation.

"Good morning, mistress." Cesare crossed the room and held out a sealed scroll. "This was delivered a moment ago." The wax seal indicated it was from the council house. "Vitus is preparing his belongings." A week ago, he, Halcyon, and Thora had returned to the villa after Thora's attempt to run away. They all had eased back into their normal routine, except Halcyon didn't go to the barracks to perform her hoplite duties. She had a few days left before she had to report, or make a decision.

"Please tell him I wish to see him before he departs."

"Of course." Cesare bowed a little, then left the suite.

Halcyon moved aside the letter she was writing to Iason, who managed her race horses in Athens. In the coming months, she would travel to Athens, rent a small villa, and go over the stables and ensure the facilities and business were in proper order. Iason was an excellent manager, but Halcyon liked to visit twice a year. There were times that the buildings required maintenance, and Iason could be too frugal.

Breaking the yellow seal, Halcyon unrolled the small scroll and studied the bold handwriting at the top. She read over the brief but important details contained in the scroll. But it was the signature at the bottom that would change one person's life. Perhaps it would change a few lives once Halcyon acted upon the scroll's permission. After a deep exhale, Halcyon rolled the scroll and used a leather string to tie it closed. She set it to the left, then heard the nearing footsteps to the master's suite.

Vitus entered and stood behind the chairs in front of the desk. "Good morning, Halcyon."

"Good morning." Halcyon indicated for Vitus to take a seat, then she relaxed in her chair. "Are you prepared to travel?"

"Yes, and thank you for the supplies." Halcyon had ordered Glauce to prepare food and water for Vitus to take on his journey back home.

Halcyon was more than pleased with Vitus's efforts to teach Thora. He had also helped around the villa when it was necessary. She would miss him, even though she refused to voice the truth. "You must send word when you arrive home."

"Yes, of course." Vitus smiled, but he became somber and said, "I have enjoyed my time here. Thora was an excellent student."

"You taught her well," Halcyon complimented, offering a smile.

Vitus shifted in the chair and an uneasiness lingered in his scent. "Thank you." He dipped his head for a beat, then he cleared his throat and folded his hands in his lap. "I was hoping that I may stay in touch with Thora, with your permission."

Halcyon recognized the friendship that Vitus and Thora had built together. She was grateful that Thora could forge her own relationships with others. "As long as Thora agrees, I don't see why not."

Vitus beamed. "I'll check with her before my departure."

Halcyon nodded. "Speaking of." She sat forward and leaned her arms against the desk. "I have one last parting gift for you." A slight grin creased her lips when Vitus narrowed his eyes. "This morning, I informed Cesare to ready a horse for you."

Vitus opened and closed his mouth a few times. Shaking his head, he held out a hand toward Halcyon and argued, "I can't accept such a gi—"

"You'll accept it," Halcyon cut off in a firm tone. She grabbed a sealed scroll from the left corner of the desk and held it up. "Otherwise, I'd hate to have to keep this letter of recommendation."

After a soft sputter, Vitus wiped away his shocked expression and blew out a heavy breath. "Thank you, Halcyon. All of this was unnecessary."

Halcyon wanted to convey her great gratitude toward Vitus. He had helped bring Thora out of the shadows by giving her a Greek tongue. Without his teaching, her relationship with Thora might have developed slower, if not at all. However, deep inside she was certain she and Thora would have found their way even without a common language. Regardless, she was in debt to Vitus for his help.

"I appreciate all that you have done here." Halcyon stood, went around the desk, and handed the letter of recommendation to him when he rose.

"Thank you." Vitus accepted the scroll, then held out his arm in offer.

Halcyon gripped his arm for a moment. But she yanked him forward and exchanged a brief hug with him. She chuckled at his awed features. "Be safe on your journey home."

"I will." Vitus started for the open door and paused steps away from the opening. "I wish all the best for you, Thora, and the pup." He darted off before Halcyon had a chance to reprimand him.

Halcyon shook her head at his last bold statement. His kindness spread a warmth around her Omega heart, which she used to ignore in the past. But her pregnancy was changing her outlook on life and the future. At least, it was easier to blame the pregnancy rather than believe she herself had changed at all. However, she suspected that after her pup's birth, her life wouldn't return to how it once was.

After a contented sigh, Halcyon returned to her desk and finished her letter to Iason. She took care of a few other duties on her list. But the scroll from the council tugged at her attention. She couldn't ignore it anymore. Halcyon took it and decided to complete her silent promise from months ago.

It was time for a new chapter.

The courtyard was quiet, but a little noise came from the kitchen. Halcyon started there and wasn't surprised to find Glauce making barley bread for the next few days. She scanned the room but failed to find the person she wanted most. "Glauce, have you seen Thora?"

Glauce jumped and spun toward her owner. She covered her chest with a flour-coated hand and let out a sharp breath. "Mistress." She shook her head, then pointed toward the courtyard. "Thora said she was going to make more cups."

Halcyon nodded and pivoted back toward the courtyard, but she hesitated and said, "Thank you."

Pausing, Glauce looked up from the kneading and flashed a shy smile. "You're welcome, mistress."

Halcyon crossed the courtyard and found the door to the supply room open, where she heard the soft sound of the pottery wheel turning. She stood in the entrance, leaned against the frame, and admired Thora's seated position in front of the wheel.

Thora's back was toward Halcyon. The wheel on top of the table spun at a constant speed while Thora molded and shaped a piece of clay. On occasion, Thora's clay-coated hand would spin the table to keep it moving. The window on the opposite side provided plenty of light. To the right, a long, narrow table had seven cups resting on it, ready to go into the oven later.

"Hello, mistress," Thora greeted without ever stopping or looking over her shoulder.

Halcyon suspected her scent had drifted under Thora's nose after a minute. She pushed off the doorframe and approached her slave's side. "After you are finished with that cup, meet me in the courtyard." Thora gave her a sideways glance. Halcyon said nothing else and left, allowing Thora to concentrate on her task. It was also far too tempting to stay and admire Thora's skilled hands. The wait was short. Thora joined her owner in the courtyard but didn't bother to sit as Halcyon stood from the bench. She eyed the rolled-up scroll in Halcyon's hand.

"Please tell Glauce we're going to the market," Halcyon ordered her slave. Thora split away from her while she went to the open iron gate. When Thora rejoined her, they started on their way to the market. The day was less humid than it had been the last few fortnights, signaling the upcoming change in the seasons. Halcyon looked forward to cooler weather, especially as her pregnancy continued to develop.

The market was busy. Both citizens and helots filled the streets, but unlike other Greek markets, no one bartered or paid for supplies. The Spartan government provided and distributed the necessary items for citizens to live. However, there were select merchants who sold luxury items if any citizen could pay in coin. Sparta's iron monetary system was close to worthless to other city-states. Similar to Halcyon, other wealthy citizens hid within Spartan society.

Halcyon exchanged a few greetings with familiar faces. Most were other Omegas who were citizens and had met Halcyon at previous symposiums. Glancing over her shoulder, she confirmed that Thora shadowed her. They cut across the market to the northwest corner, where the soft tap of metal grew louder the closer they came. The familiar strikes tingled along Halcyon's hands and fingertips. It was a sound that reminded her of duty and brotherhood. Ahead of them, the blacksmith's forge emerged among the other buildings.

Underneath a thatch roof, Halcyon entered the open space of the blacksmith's shop and watched the muscular Alpha pound against bright orange metal. Behind her, Thora stood over her shoulder and watched the smith. Several minutes passed before the blacksmith finished his work and plunged the blade into a quench. He held the crude blade inside the filled bucket, using a pair of tongs.

"What do you want?" the blacksmith asked and glanced over at Halcyon.

Thora puffed up until Halcyon used her Omega pheromones to settle her. After a grumble, Thora folded her arms and remained silent.

"I have orders." Halcyon raised the scroll and waited for him. "Platon." Her tone was tight and held a measure of warning.

Platon grumbled and placed the cooled blade onto a workbench. He removed his leather gloves and tossed them next to the blade and tongs. After he neared Halcyon, he snatched the scroll from her hand and proceeded to untie it. "I know who you are." Platon held the meat of the scroll in his left hand and used his other to uncoil the document. He frowned and looked up at Halcyon, then over to Thora.

"Do you have time now?" Halcyon asked, but her question left no room for refusal.

Sighing, Platon closed the scroll and replied, "Yes, Iron Edge." He tied off the scroll and tossed it back to her. "Let me organize my tools."

Halcyon waited and met Thora's curious stare. She wanted to explain the pending event, but it was better for

Thora to watch it unfold before her. Otherwise it would merit a lengthy discussion that could wait until later. After a beat, Halcyon noticed that Thora had shifted closer. Her Alpha's protective nature warmed Halcyon. Out of instinct, she placed a hand against her stomach, which appeared the same to most, but inside, she was aware of the changes.

"Come over here, slave," Platon ordered and indicated the workbench.

Thora glanced at Halcyon, both out of concern and for confirmation.

Halcyon nodded and whispered, "*Já.*" She waited until Thora stood in front of the workbench, then she edged closer but to the side. She knew better than to get into Platon's way when he was working. He was a well-respected blacksmith for a reason.

"Does this barbar understand Greek?" Platon asked and huffed low.

"She understands enough," Halcyon replied, unwilling to divulge Thora's advanced skill with Greek. "Tell her what to do, and she will." Her explanation was also an unspoken order to Thora to do as told.

Platon rubbed his large jaw before studying Thora, who outmatched him in height. He was forced to tilt his head back and meet her gaze. "Grab the workbench, like this." He demonstrated it.

Thora did so, but with her left arm.

"Right arm, barbar," Platon snapped and folded his muscular arms that were exposed beyond his leather apron.

Thora switched and rested her right wrist on the workbench. She mimicked how Platon had gripped the edge of the table. Her pheromones were neutral, but Halcyon sensed her slave's apprehension, so she used her scent to ease Thora. Despite the uncertainty of the situation, Thora seemed willing to go along with whatever the scroll had ordered to be done.

Platon moved a few items to the workbench next to Thora's arm. He first took a square metal piece that was close to the width of Thora's wrist and arm. He snared Thora's slave iron and ordered, "Keep your arm against the bench while I'll pull on this." He tugged on the iron bracelet with one hand and then slid the iron plate between the bracelet and Thora's arm. He released the slave iron, which rested on top of the plate now.

Thora rumbled and flexed her fingers against the edge of the workbench.

"Now stay still," Platon ordered and picked up a tool. He took a position on the opposite side of the table from Thora. He placed the tool's serrated teeth at one side of the slave iron. With slow precision, he drew the saw's blade across the bracelet with single and slow strokes. After a notch formed inside the iron, he nestled the blade into it and started to saw away.

Halcyon remained off to the side and admired Platon's commitment to cut away at the bracelet. She fingered the scroll in her hands, thankful she was able to secure it. Without it, a blacksmith would never remove a slave iron and risk being punished by the government.

Platon released a grunt after cutting through the bracelet. He caught himself from hitting Thora even though the metal plate would have protected her. Scooting down the work bench, he lined the saw on the left side of the bracelet and repeated the same process. After much sawing and a few huffs, he won the easy battle and sliced through the iron bracelet. The middle piece twisted down and hung on by a mere thread of iron. Platon tossed the tool to the side, grabbed the sawed piece, and wrenched it loose from the rest of the slave iron.

Thora panted a little, remained still, and stared at the bracelet that was sawed open. She looked from it to Halcyon, who offered a small smile.

Halcyon came to her slave's side and tugged on her arm, which came free from the workbench. She dropped the scroll onto the table and cradled Thora's arm with both hands. They held each other's gaze, both attempting to comprehend what this meant. Platon grunted at the pair, then walked off.

Grateful for a semiprivate moment, Halcyon first removed the metal plate and tossed it aside. It clattered against the table a few times. She hooked her fingers through the bracelet and started to turn it so that the new opening came to the side of Thora's wrist. "The first moment I saw you, I silently promised you that I would free you one day." Halcyon removed the slave iron and held it up between them. "It's done now."

Thora stared at the bracelet, which had the markings for the Spartan government. Before coming here, she would have worn a different one for Athens. The city-states kept detailed records of the slaves by using the slave irons, which were numbered and recorded. The slave record was kept by each council house in a city-state. In Sparta, the council held the authority to abolish a slave's bonds to the government. In other city-states, the slave's owner had the ability to set their slave free, or not.

"*Þakka fyrir*," Thora whispered and revealed the shine in her eyes.

Halcyon swallowed against the slight pain in her throat. "You're welcome," she replied and held her shoulders square. She wished they were back at the villa, alone. She raised the slave iron higher and asked, "Do you wish to keep this?" Halcyon was prepared to toss it, but it wasn't her decision anymore.

Thora plucked it from her former owner's fingers and turned it. "I will keep it."

Halcyon nodded and stole a glance at Platon, who watched them from the corner of his eye. He was wise to keep his mouth shut. After she picked up the scroll, she went around Thora and said, "Thank you, Platon." She received a brief nod from him. Turning to Thora, she asked, "Ready?"

"*Já*," Thora responded and followed Halcyon out of the blacksmith's shop. In her hand, she carried the former slave iron.

Halcyon had plenty of chores to do at home, yet she was unprepared to return. She scanned the different stalls in the market, then slowed when she realized Thora continued to follow her. "You must walk alongside me now." She halted and frowned when Thora paused behind her. "Do you not wish to walk alongside the mother of your future pup?" Her ploy worked well.

Thora rumbled and joined Halcyon when they continued through the market. With each step, her scent grew stronger and clung to Halcyon like a cloak. Perhaps her teasing about their pup had worked too well.

"Do you mind if we rest for a moment before we return to the villa?" Halcyon hated to show her weakened state. She was learning to accept the changes her body was going through from the pregnancy. With a sigh, she reprimanded herself for still viewing it as a weakness. Her body was growing a pup, who required enormous amounts of energy from Halcyon. It was difficult to retrain her mind, but Thora was there to help her.

"Of course." Thora indicated the shaded benches under a few trees at one end of the market. They headed there until Thora detoured to a fruit and vegetable stand.

Halcyon waited off to the side and heard pieces of Thora's conversation with the merchant. Thora seemed to have built up a rapport with him. After another moment, Thora turned and revealed the few items cradled in her arms. Halcyon's mouth watered at the grapes and apples. They made it to a familiar bench and sat next to each other.

"Here." Thora pulled a handful of grapes free from the vine and gave them to Halcyon. The fruit provided a source of juice, which was refreshing in Halcyon's parched mouth. Thora ate one of the apples and continued to hand over more grapes. Closer to her knees, the broken slave iron rested in her lap.

"*Þǫkk,*" Halcyon said after Thora gave her the last of the grapes. "These taste divine."

Thora smiled between bites of her fruit. "Do you remember when we last sat here together?"

"Of course." Halcyon smiled at her and slipped back into the memory. She and Thora could barely speak due to the language barrier. How much had changed over the summer. "It feels as if it was another life."

"Yes," Thora murmured before a soft thrum started in her chest. "I was a slave." She touched her now bare wrist, then gave the last apple to Halcyon and leaned back against the bench. Halfway through her apple, she picked up the bracelet and turned it through her fingers. "You freed me."

Halcyon tilted her head and swallowed a mouthful of apple. "So I did." She gazed about the market, which continued to be busy. Many of the people were slaves who went from stall to stall to collect supplies for their masters. "Now you have a better chance of returning to your homelands." She turned her attention to Thora and added, "If that's what you still wish to do."

"*Nei.*" Thora shook her head and took a bite from her apple. She chewed on it while a thoughtful, if not wistful, expression crossed her face. A soft thunder began deep in her chest and called to Halcyon's Omega. "I would have returned to the Norselands with or without the slave iron."

Halcyon accepted that truth months ago. Thora remained at the villa out of her own decision-making, not because of her enslavement. "You could have escaped your slave owner in Athens and returned to your homelands then. Why didn't you?"

Thora took a final bite from the apple, then tossed the core at the base of the tree behind them, for an animal to forage later. "At the time, I felt there was no reason to return. I had lost everything. And I did not know where to go." She sighed and picked up the bracelet. "We talked about why I left your villa."

"Yes." Halcyon finished her apple and pitched it too. She enjoyed the last sweet bite in her mouth and weighed the ever-changing future ahead of them. Thora was free to go and do as she pleased, so long as she didn't step on any Greek citizen's foot. A freed slave had opportunities, especially in Athens. "What will you do now?" The question was heavy for them both.

"I will stay," Thora said in a firm, certain tone that startled Halcyon. When she looked at Halcyon, every fragment of devotion shone in her blue eyes. Halcyon loved that Thora could be stubborn about her and them. Life here in Sparta would never be easy, not for Thora or their pup. Even though Thora was free, she would forever be viewed as a barbarian, an outcast without any rights as a true citizen. Yet she was willing to make that sacrifice so she could remain with Halcyon and their pup.

"If you will allow me," Thora added in a weak voice, dissolving the strength in her.

Halcyon whimpered and placed a hand on Thora's leg. "You are always welcome at the villa. You know I wish for you to stay." She withdrew her hand when a few people walked past them. "With my pregnancy, it'll become more of a challenge for me to manage the villa." She wiped a thin layer of perspiration from her brow, thankful for the shade. "I trust you to run my villa." Thora had done so with ease when Halcyon marched to Thermopylae. "I'll also give you weekly pay."

"*Nei*," Thora argued. "I do not want your coin."

Halcyon grinned at Thora's refusal, then she leaned in and whispered, "What if it's something other than coin?" Somehow she would find a way to give Thora a minimum amount of money as payment for her work. However, she suspected the offer for much more enticed Thora's Alpha tenfold. Or she might have overstepped, thinking back on their discussion in the campsite a week ago.

Thora raised an eyebrow and rumbled deep enough to send a shiver down Halcyon's spine. "Perhaps a spot in your bed every night."

Halcyon bit her lip to hold back her automatic agreement. She wanted nothing more than to have Thora in her bed. They would fuck, cuddle, and sleep together until Apollo completed his endless pursuit to draw the sun across the sky every day. However, there was still one last detail that affected such an arrangement. Euclid would return one day, but Halcyon had no idea whether he would return carrying his shield or return with his shield carrying him.

"I can't make a promise now," Halcyon said and let out a sad sigh.

"I understand why."

"But…" Halcyon leaned in again and used her sweet pheromones to entice her lover. "For now, we can spend most nights together, if you'd like."

"*Já*," Thora murmured and leaned in too. She withdrew after a beat and rumbled again. "Tonight, I want to thank you for freeing me."

Halcyon shook her head and attempted to deny the gratitude, but Thora's spicy scent wrapped around her. She choked on her refusal and considered how Thora might thank her tonight. Her clitoris throbbed when a few pictures of Thora between her legs flashed through her mind. In a last-ditch attempt, she gasped and argued, "I didn't free you for sexual favors. Nor do I wish for it to fester your guilt."

"I know. I am making amends with myself." After a pause, Thora nodded once and declared, "This is my choice." She reached up and grazed her fingertips down the length of Halcyon's arm. "I want to show you all of my gratitude, if you will have it."

After an instant nod, Halcyon gave in and started to rub her thighs together. They hadn't been together in several nights, not since before Thora left the villa. The disconnect in their sexual relationship left a dull ache in Halcyon's heart. Being together would bring them closer again.

Thora withdrew her alluring scent and allowed Halcyon to breathe. They were in public after all. She straightened and returned to toying with the bracelet. She shook her head and whispered, "It seems strange after all these years."

"You spent more years being free than enslaved," Halcyon reminded. "You'll adjust again." She relaxed against the bench, discovering a bit of weariness but also enjoying the burn between her legs. The wait to be with Thora tonight would be well worth it. No one else could touch her like Thora. "We should return home." However, neither of them moved from their comfortable spot under the pistachio tree.

"What will you do about your duty?" Thora asked in a soft voice. Soon Halcyon would start to show, unable to hide her pregnancy. During the ride back to the villa from the northern part of the territory, Halcyon had told Thora about the promotion in the military. "There are only a few days left until you must return to the barracks." There was an undertone of concern in her words. She had already voiced her dislike for Halcyon returning to duty while pregnant. In the end, it was Halcyon's final decision.

"I have given it much thought," Halcyon said and canted her head to have a better view of Thora's stony profile. With a sly grin, she prepared to enjoy Thora's next reaction to the news. "I'm writing a letter of retirement."

Thora's head snapped toward Halcyon. "What?" Her eyes bulged, then she breathed harder. "*Nei*, you cannot leave your position." The inflection in her accent grew the faster she spoke. "They have given you a promotion. If you leave, then—"

"Thora," Halcyon cut off and touched her lover's knee. Thora faltered and went silent while her shoulders slumped. "I want to raise our pup. I cannot be a hoplite and mother at the same time."

"*Nei*," Thora murmured and ran her fingers through her hair. "This is not you."

"It's not the old me," Halcyon argued. She gathered Thora's closest hand into hers and squeezed it, hard. "It will be a change, but it's the right one. I have given Sparta many years of service."

Thora glanced about them, then leaned in and asked, "What if you regret your decision?"

"How much longer can I go on?" Halcyon asked. She was in her early thirties, which was unusual for Spartan hoplites, who often died in combat in their twenties. The smartest and strongest ones lived longer, but they were few. Part of her felt she was on borrowed time. The gods were giving her a pup at a late age when most Omegas already had four, six, or more pups.

After an exhale, Halcyon withdrew her hand and waited for two slaves to pass by them. She tilted her head back and watched the storm inside Thora, who fixed her blue stare on Halcyon. "Do you want me to return to duty?" Somehow, she could find a way to take leave during the last months of her pregnancy. It would be difficult but possible, especially in her new position.

"I want you to be happy."

"Then do you believe this won't make me happy?" Halcyon countered and raised an eyebrow. She wanted Thora's honest opinion. From early on, she recognized Thora's innate ability to sense what may be right or wrong, a good outcome or an ugly one.

"I worry you will miss using a sword," Thora replied. "A warrior never truly puts down their weapon."

Halcyon concurred with her lover's assessment. There would be a piece of her that would miss being a hoplite even though the new freedom would take away the difficulty of duty. But here in Sparta, she couldn't be a mother and a hoplite. They were night and day, never able to coexist at the same time. "I'd rather remain at home, raising and protecting our pup."

Thora sighed and rubbed her brow before she made a sound of displeasure. They were both aware that their pup would require extra care due to Thora's distinct features. Their pup could inherit any of Thora's Norsk qualities, which would contrast against a Greek. At the moment, there was no solution to how best to raise their pup in Sparta, but Halcyon tried to be patient. She believed staying close to home was one way to shield their pup from the harshness of Spartan society. If the pup was a male Alpha, Halcyon would be required to hand over her son by the age of seven to the government for training.

Glancing around them again, Thora frowned at how more people came and went near them. She let out a soft growl and asked, "Can we discuss this at the villa?"

Halcyon was in agreement and stood from the bench. "Let us go then, my rabbit," she teased and urged Thora to walk alongside her. Their trek home was quiet, if not a bit uneasy. An occasional waft of Thora's musky Alpha scent caught her nose, comforting her too. The iron gate of her villa were a welcomed sight. They entered the shaded courtyard, and Thora told Halcyon to sit. Too worn to argue, Halcyon sank onto the bench beside the water fountain. She was grateful when Thora returned with a cup full of diluted apple juice.

Thora took the empty spot next to her lover and fiddled with the slave iron. She eyed Halcyon for a beat, then cleared her throat and said, "I have had a thought about our pup's future." Shifting to her left, she pressed her thigh against Halcyon's knee. "It is an idea and may seem"—she hesitated and pursed her lips—"stupid."

Halcyon frowned at Thora's uneasiness and placed a firm hand on Thora's thigh. "Tell me. I will listen." Thora was far from unintelligent.

After a nod, Thora took a deep breath and said, "It will be dangerous to raise our pup here. Athens would not be much better." She chewed her lip and stared at the slave iron in her hands. After she set it in her lap, she looked at Halcyon and whispered, "But the Norselands would be a safe home."

Halcyon blinked.

"Safe for all of us," Thora added, then sighed and remained quiet.

Thora's idea sparked a million thoughts in Halcyon's head. She had spent most of her life in Sparta, given much of herself to the city-state. She owed Sparta nothing, not even more loyalty. But the thought of leaving the familiarity for strange lands stole her breath.

"In my homelands, we do not look upon physical differences as a curse or that the person is less." Thora shook her head and said, "Not all Norsk are as light as me. There are those with darker hair." She touched the few loose strands of hair around Halcyon's nape. "Though no one has hair with beautiful curls or waves like yours."

Halcyon huffed at the gentle tease, which helped dissipate her shock. "Life in the Norselands sounds much simpler than here." From Thora's previous descriptions, there seemed to be no luxuries in life. Not that Halcyon minded after sleeping on the barracks' floor plenty of times or using the crude facilities when on duty. Sparta was far less refined compared to Athens, where everyone overindulged. Yet, Spartans still had quite a few privileges.

"*Já*, it is simpler but not much less than Sparta." Thora grew less hesitant about the topic and spoke faster, causing the rough edges of her accent to come out again. "There are power struggles between leaders and clans at times. But life is quiet for the most part." She grinned. "An Omega with a sword is common in my homelands, especially those with pups."

After a snort, Halcyon narrowed her eyes at her lover and said, "You are attempting to win over my hoplite nature."

"*Já*." Thora became serious, though, and released a sigh. "It is a lot to consider. I would understand why you would not wish to live there."

"I…" Halcyon fell short as she continued to reel over the suggestion. Her mind tried to picture a life there, but she didn't know the Norselands. She had to trust Thora's knowledge, experience, and upbringing as a Norsk.

"You do not have to decide now, if ever." Thora shrugged and picked up the slave iron from her lap. A long silence filled the space between them.

"If we went, I would prefer to travel after the pup is born." Halcyon smiled when Thora regarded her again. "I would also need time to organize my business affairs."

Thora worked her jaw a few times, but the spike in her pheromones said everything.

"It's not a stupid idea," Halcyon whispered. "And we will consider it." After she patted Thora's leg, she stood and headed toward the stairs. "I am going to nap. It's been a long morning." All the tension from this morning had drained her. A nice nap would make her more tolerable and clear-minded.

* * *

"On your hands and knees," Thora demanded of her lover. Her rumbly voice was a thick line around Halcyon's Omega heart, tugging and pulling at her. Once Halcyon was settled into the position, Thora shifted behind Halcyon and stroked her lover's soaked clitoris.

Halcyon cursed and dropped her head, her dark hair falling around her. "Thora, please." She hadn't been taken from behind since her heat. The position excited her as much as it did the last time, but a strange tightness lingered in her chest. She did her best to ignore it, which became easier the longer Thora massaged her clitoris.

"Good Omega," Thora praised and kissed Halcyon's back. "You are slick for me." She bit delicate flesh along Halcyon's side. There was a certain tenderness to the nips followed by pleased rumbles. "Do you want slow?" She teased Halcyon by nudging the tips of her fingers past Halcyon's entrance but then going back to her swollen bud.

"*Nei!*" Halcyon groaned and fisted her hands into the bedsheet. "Fuck me." She wanted to be taken by her Alpha. Deeper still, she wanted to be claimed by Thora, but she kept a cork on her dangerous desire. "By all the gods, please fuck me!" Two fingers plunged inside her, stealing her breath. Her sharp cry echoed beyond the bedroom.

Thora curled her fingers, working them. An excited burst rippled through Halcyon with each movement. Thora groaned when Halcyon whined and rocked her hips. Then there was a distinct shift, signaled by the heaviness of Thora's Alpha pheromones. After more movement, she lashed an arm across Halcyon's chest and growled in warning. Thora drew her fingers out, then plunged back into Halcyon's pussy.

Halcyon cried out from the bolt of pleasure sent through her. She panted between needy whines that would encourage her Alpha. "More," she whispered after a gasp. Thora responded with another thrust that went just as deep. The pace increased with each drive of Thora's fingers until they reached a perfect tempo.

Thora grunted and snarled near Halcyon's ear. Her front started to press against Halcyon's sticky back. As she drove faster, the wet slap grew louder and encouraged them to drive the other madder. "Good Omega," she hissed. "*My* good Omega."

"Yes," Halcyon agreed without thought. "Yours."

Thora huffed and declared, "*Mine.*" She nipped Halcyon's ear, coaxing a loud moan from Halcyon. "*Minn,*" she declared in Norsk. Her fingers plunged and curled, hitting the electric notes inside Halcyon's Omega. "You are going to give me the most beautiful pup."

Halcyon choked on her next moan after Thora's whisper. Her Omega made a keening whine. "Y-Yes." She cried out from Thora's next thrust. "*Já já,*" she repeated with each drive that caused her walls to clench a little more. The earlier tightness in her chest grew, but Halcyon became more lost in Thora's power over her.

"Deep inside, you always wanted my pup," Thora murmured and nuzzled Halcyon's cheek. "That is why you went into heat." She growled, then panted and plunged harder into Halcyon. "You went into heat for *me.*"

Falling to her elbows, Halcyon howled low and raised her ass in silent demand to be taken. She was on the cliff of something more than an orgasm. Thora was close to taking it all. "Yes!" Halcyon buried her face into the sheet and took the punishing thrusts to her pussy. "Yes!" She let the truth spill out, freeing her from the bindings around her heart. "Thora!"

With a final drive, Thora split Halcyon open in the most gorgeous and terrifying way. Her curling fingers released a riptide of pleasure that stole the last of Halcyon's strength. Halcyon screamed, raw and harsh from the orgasm. The pressure behind her breasts uncoiled in that instant, striking her in the heart. Her cry cracked, then turned into a sob that shook her entire body.

"Halcyon," Thora murmured in confusion and worry. She spoke her lover's name with her rugged accent, how Halcyon loved it. The headiness of her Alpha scent shifted to a softer weight and cloaked Halcyon from emotional turmoil.

Halcyon gulped for air while tears burned down her cheeks. She hadn't cried since she was a pup, and not in front of another since her father. Whimpering, she tried to hide her face in the sheet, but it was hard to breath. Her body trembled from both pleasure and distress.

Thora eased her fingers free, then covered Halcyon's body with her larger frame. They both eased down to the mattress and waited for the storm inside Halcyon to pass through her. Thora murmured different words in Norsk, and nuzzled and kissed her.

Halcyon curled her hands around Thora's forearms and held on while she recovered from the shattering climax. How had she lost such control of herself? She prided herself on being reserved and stoic, not a crying mess. But Thora breached all Halcyon's barriers one at a time, then helped put her back together with each tender whisper and loving kiss. Halcyon trusted Thora, with her heart.

After several deep breaths, Halcyon regained control and started to run her fingers along the length of Thora's forearm. She whimpered when Thora nuzzled against her temple and rumbled in her ear. Her lover's warm body had kept her secure while she had settled down.

"Are you okay?" Thora asked and combed her fingers through Halcyon's hair.

"Yes." Halcyon turned her head to the side and earned a couple of kisses to her tearstained cheek. "I'm sorry."

Thora hushed her and replied, "I understand why." She grazed a foot along the back of Halcyon's calf. "You are safe here." To emphasize her point, she tightened her arms around Halcyon.

Halcyon closed her eyes again, holding back a few fresh tears. "I know," she responded in a shaky voice. "*Þǫkk*."

Again, Thora combed away Halcyon's hair and nudged her jaw with her nose. "I promise I will always stay, if you will have me."

Clenching her jaw, Halcyon considered how Thora had left her and chosen the Norselands over her. The journey to the Norselands held a great deal of risk, especially for Thora, who had known that. However, Thora made the attempt because Halcyon drove her off. Halcyon had been blinded by her own fears and even selfishness. Without doubt, Thora was devoted to Halcyon and had earned Halcyon's loyalty in return.

"*Nei*," Halcyon murmured. Then she started to move, able to turn over when Thora lifted her body. She settled onto her back, reached, and stroked her lover's flushed cheeks. "We are no longer owner and slave." She threaded her fingers through golden strands and whispered, "We are lovers… perhaps friends now." She revealed a warm smile. "Soon we will be parents." Holding each side of Thora's head, she drew their foreheads together and said, "I'd like to be your mate one day."

Thora jerked back and stared wide-eyed at her lover. "Mate?" She was short on breath, and a layer of panic entered her voice. "As in…"

"Exchange bite marks," Halcyon whispered, still smiling. "Not tonight or tomorrow, but in the future." First, she had to dissolve her union with Euclid, one way or another.

When his fate was revealed, she and Thora could move forward. "If you would have me as your mate." Halcyon admired the pure shock on Thora's features.

Thora sputtered once, then dragged her fingers through her hair. "Mates," she murmured and started to smile. "*Já*, I want to be your mate." The tremor in her voice indicated that it was more than a want, perhaps a need. Halcyon felt the same deep draw toward Thora. "When the time is right."

"Soon," Halcyon promised, then guided Thora closer for a kiss. She moaned from the sweet feeling of Thora's tongue grazing across hers. No one else's lips tasted like Thora's or could send jolts through Halcyon's body. She may live in her villa, but she was alive in Thora's arms.

Thora had a radiant smile after the kiss.

"You are aware that *you* rutted for *me*?" Halcyon teased and dragged her nails over Thora's back. Thora's earlier pillow talk about Halcyon's heat returned to her mind. She loved Thora's Alpha nature coming to play in their bed.

Thora chuckled and swept some of her hair to one side, getting it out of their way. "*Já.*" She traced a finger along part of Halcyon's exposed collarbone. "I will rut for you again." Bowing her head, she flashed a toothy smile and rumbled. "I will fill you with my seed again, knot you, and have another pup."

Halcyon groaned and rolled her eyes. "You damn Alphas are all the same." She ignored Thora's laugh and poked her in the side. "You only think with your knot."

After a snort, Thora argued, "I remember you asking me for my knot." She smirked and raised herself higher. "After you used your pheromones to trigger my rut."

Halcyon growled after the taunts. She had asked for Thora's knot, again and again. It had been the best fuck she'd received in her life at the time. But she wasn't about to inflate Thora's Alpha ego at the moment. Instead, she targeted Thora's sides with nimble fingers and hit all the ticklish spots.

Thora howled in response and attempted to snare Halcyon's wrists. They struggled and fought, but Thora held back. "You are pregnant." She hissed when Halcyon found a rather sensitive spot down by her hip. Between a rising tide of giggles, she declared, "I do not want to hurt you!"

"Bad luck then." Halcyon seized her opportunity to torture her lover. She was amazed how easy it was to overpower someone bigger than her. Their laughter filled the room until Halcyon rolled them to the other side of the bed. Due to her greater strength, she was able to hold down Thora's arms and use her muscular thighs to pin Thora's legs. "Much better," she teased, but her grin slipped the longer she admired Thora's beauty. In Halcyon's opinion, Thora was more beautiful than Aphrodite, but it went deeper than skin. Thora's personality and heart were gorgeous.

"Why do you stare?" Thora asked in a gentle voice.

"I am admiring," Halcyon replied and mirrored Thora's growing smile. "Like I was on the first day I saw you." She released Thora's arms, which encircled her. With a featherlight touch, she traced Thora's lips and promised, "Now maybe I can spend the rest of my life loving you."

ЄPILOGUЄ

About One Year and One Month Later
Thora

After giving Cheimon a carrot, Thora rubbed his ear and told him to be good. Next she patted her second horse and offered her the last carrot. "Þǫkk, Whetstone," she said to the gray-coated mare. She and Halcyon were gifted Whetstone by her brother about a moon ago. A wonderful welcome-home gift after being gone for many years. He and Thora's other siblings were shocked when she arrived at the clan's door. What had further sparked excitement was that Thora had a mate and a newborn pup. The celebrations lasted for a fortnight.

The welcoming had been a blessing after she and Halcyon had left everything behind in Greece and traveled to the Norseland in a five-week period. Before they left Sparta, Halcyon had put all her affairs in order. First she sold her horse-racing business in Athens but ensured Iason retained his job with the new owner. Then Halcyon freed Cesare and Glauce and gave them each a hefty wage until Villa Honor the Beloved was sold. Cesare had been distraught about the news and in distress about a future without Halcyon in it. She had organized an arrangement for Cesare, who could live in Athens with Glauce. Despite Halcyon's best planning, Cesare refused Halcyon's offer, while Glauce accepted it.

In Athens, Glauce had a small home and would be able to find work or open her own business. Athens was much more progressive compared to Sparta. Athenian slaves were known to become doctors or business managers, earn a wage, and pay for their own freedom. Halcyon insisted that Glauce would be comfortable and happy there. Thora had cried and hugged Glauce several times when they left her in Athens. Glauce had become family to Thora, who hoped they would return for a visit, one day.

The one person Thora did not miss was Euclid. He had gone to battle against the Persian army and died at the Isthmus of Corinth where the Greek allied forces built a defensive line against King Xerxes. Weeks after his death, his body was delivered to Sparta on his shield. Halcyon had wept one day in Thora's arms over his death, then she handled his funeral to honor him. After his passing, Halcyon rarely spoke again of her former mate. About three months later, the Spartan military attempted to recruit Halcyon despite her retirement and pregnancy.

Halcyon refused them.

Tucking away the memories, Thora left the building and searched for her mate, who would be finishing up at the training field. Already the winter's cooler air was noticeable and was an old friend to Thora. As the sun crept closer to the horizon, the day's brief warmth escaped into the orangey sky. The leafless trees started to morph into silhouettes of fingers that reached toward the emerging stars. In the distance, the clang of metal and wood became louder.

Thora adjusted the leather gloves on her hands and smiled at the familiar figure standing in front of the rows of warriors. For a beat, she admired her mate's proud stance. As she drew closer, Thora's scent drifted on the breeze and caused a tiny head to poke out from behind Halcyon's furry neck.

Halcyon remained focused on her task and began to walk the line of warriors. She paused and barked out an order in Norsk. On her hip, she carried her favored short sword from Sparta.

Thora stopped at a distance and admired both her mate and pup. Radiant blue eyes peeked over the top of the brown fur and remained locked on Thora. After a chuckle, she smiled and continued toward her family. A small hand came out from the carrier, and tiny fingers pointed at her.

Turning her head sidelong, Halcyon spotted Thora from the corner of her eye, but she remained focused on her duty. She paused when Thora neared her.

Without hesitation, Thora reached into the carrier and lifted her daughter free. "*Hei, Hjǫrdís.*" She kissed Hjǫrdís on the cheek, finding it both cold and coated in snot. "*Hei, ást.*" A soft flush colored Halcyon's face after Thora's tender greeting.

"Hello, gorgeous." Halcyon exchanged a quick and warm kiss, but she snapped at one of the warriors on the training field. Her Norsk was choppy, and yet she never failed to get her point across to the trainees. She hollered another broken order that was followed without hesitation.

Thora chuckled at her mate's iron grip on the warriors. She suspected their clan would have the best force in the region within a year. The chieftain had been thrilled to learn that

Halcyon was a warrior from Greece. Thora and Halcyon had barely warmed their new bed in the longhouse before the chieftain roped Halcyon into teaching his warriors.

"We're almost finished," Halcyon said in Greek.

"Should we wait?" Thora replied and nuzzled into Hjǫrdís, who squealed and grabbed at Thora's hair. Like her sire, Hjǫrdís had straight hair, but it was dark similar to a Greek.

"*Já*," Halcyon replied and smiled. "*Líka*." She broke away from her family and walked between the warriors, who were practicing against each other in pairs. At times, she gave instructions to a trainee on how to improve or adjust.

Thora enjoyed her few minutes with her pup, having missed her today. She breathed in Hjǫrdís's distinct scent that carried fragments of Halcyon and herself. They were unsure whether their daughter was an Omega or an Alpha. Her breed wouldn't come to light until Hjǫrdís reached a certain age, which was years away. Halcyon had her guess, but Thora didn't care either way. Hjǫrdís was healthy and happy, as life was meant to be.

"*I missed you*," Thora told her daughter in Norsk. "*I rode out to the great lake and helped bring back a large cart of fish.*" Hjǫrdís cooed at her sire and tapped her heels against Thora's stomach. "*Do you want to help dry them tomorrow?*"

Hjǫrdís raised up her arms, then dropped them onto Thora's bicep and chest. She blew out her lips and pulled on Thora's coat.

"*I thought so.*" Thora chuckled and hefted her daughter a bit higher. Together, she and Hjǫrdís watched Halcyon wrap up the drills with the warriors.

"*Tomorrow we work with shields,*" Halcyon informed the group. Several warriors clamored and hooted.

Thora smiled at her mate's ability to teach their clan how to fight and protect, a far cry from how their days started out with the clan. Their first moon was the most difficult, but each week it became easier. Thora and her pup had been embraced by warm arms. The clan had attempted to welcome Halcyon, but she remained standoffish with everyone at first. Thora was well aware that her mate was less social and would require time to integrate. The language barrier added another hurdle. Thora had done her best to teach Halcyon more Norsk during their journey north. However, Halcyon declared she was better speaking with swords than languages. Thora agreed after she witnessed how well Halcyon handled the warriors.

Halcyon exchanged a few words with one of the last warriors. She slapped him hard on the back, then she headed to Thora and Hjǫrdís.

"It looks like it went well," Thora remarked in Greek. They continued to communicate in Greek, which gave Halcyon a break from stumbling through Norsk.

"I'm happy with their progress."

"So is the chieftain." Thora switched Hjǫrdís to her other arm and noticed how she smacked her lips. Sunset was dinnertime, especially for Hjǫrdís. She adjusted Hjǫrdís's fur hat, ensuring her ears were kept warm. "He is beaming." She and Halcyon strolled in the direction of the longhouse set in the center of their village.

Halcyon shook her head and revealed a small smile. "It's nice to be contributing to the clan."

Thora smiled at her mate's sweet confession. It was the first true indicator that Halcyon was finding her way with the clan. "Then you do not regret leaving Greece?"

Reaching out, Halcyon halted Thora and faced her. For a beat, she studied Hjǫrdís, who regarded her back. "*Nei.*" She pressed a hand against Hjǫrdís's back and met Thora's shadowy features. "I know I don't quite fit in." She indicated her face, then added, "But everyone treats me equally."

Thora bounced Hjǫrdís against her side. "You fit in, in the most important ways." She leaned down and kissed her mate. She moaned at the affection from Halcyon, who opened her heart more each day. Hjǫrdís interrupted the kissing with a low, needy whine.

Halcyon chuckled. "It's feeding time." They continued toward the longhouse. She unbuttoned her jacket which earned her a strange glance from Thora. The air was too chilly to be shedding layers. "I have been feeling warm all day."

"Are you sick?" Thora asked, a thread of panic setting in.

"*Nei, nei.*" Halcyon huffed and drew open her jacket wider. "I feel fine otherwise."

Thora frowned, but their conversation was cut off by the stomping of boots. She heard her name called by a familiar voice. "*Hei, brother.*" They stood a short distance from the longhouse's glowing entrance. At that moment, Hjǫrdís fussed louder and pulled on Thora's coat.

Halcyon reached and said, "Here." She took Hjǫrdís and looked at Thora's brother. "*Hei, Kóri.*" She excused herself from Thora and Kóri, needing to feed Hjǫrdís.

Thora noted her younger brother's pout and asked, "*What is it?*"

"*I wanted to tell Halcyon about the news before she went into the longhouse.*"

Thora shook her head and touched her brother's arm. "*What news?*" From the excited hum in his pheromones, she deduced it was good news at least.

"*The chieftain plans to give her a neck-ring!*"

Thora went wide-eyed and sputtered once. "*You kid!*"

"*No!*" Kóri beamed and hooked the back of Thora's neck. "*I told you he would give her one!*"

Thora worked her jaw a few times until she found her voice again. "*This is great news.*" She had been unsure whether the chieftain would give Halcyon a neck-ring because she wasn't born a Norsk. Clans had no qualms with foreigners joining them through a union with a Norsk mate. But the tradition held that neck-rings were given to Norsk-born people who joined a clan. The chieftain's decision to buck tradition and accept Halcyon was a great honor and show of love.

"*Do you think your mate will be excited?*" Kóri asked. Everyone referred to Halcyon as Thora's mate despite the fact they were unmated—for now. None one could contest Thora and Halcyon were mates to each other in their hearts.

Thora considered Halcyon's possible reaction, then grinned at her brother. "*On the outside, it may not seem like it, but she will be happy.*"

Kóri returned his sister's smirk, seeming to understand what Thora meant. He was much like Thora, outgoing and well-liked by everyone. At first, Halcyon had kept her guard up with Kóri, his mate, and their two pups. But she did the same with Thora's other brother, who lived with them in the clan. This past month, Halcyon had made strides in opening up to the two brothers. The high sense of community and family was a strange idea to Halcyon, who had no siblings and lost her mother at an early age.

"*Where's Sveinn?*" Thora asked and continued the walk to the longhouse. "*Is he back?*"

"*Yes.*" Kóri followed alongside. "*He said the hunting was successful.*" Their younger brother was unmated, but it wasn't unusual at his age. "*They killed three elks.*"

Thora rumbled in appreciation. They neared the front of the longhouse and entered into the busyness of the large home. The building was tall with an A-frame roof meant to dissuade snow buildup. Inside it was warm and inviting, and loud with all the chatter from the clan members. At the entrance, a few different looms were set up, and each had work in progress. There were also several spindle sticks set up for spinning various fibers.

As Thora and Kóri passed the work area, they started to unbutton their jackets and become more comfortable in the warmth and brightness of the longhouse. People greeted them from either side. At the center, a fire pit was built into the ground. It provided warmth, light, and a cooking source. Already several people worked to put together a meal for the clan. Beyond the fire pit, there was a one-step elevated platform where the chieftain and his mate sat during clan meetings or meals. Lining the left and right walls were bed platforms that could be used as tables. A few benches were placed here and there.

The longhouse was the largest one Thora had seen so far. The one from her childhood had been crude, and often leaked. The one in her early adulthood was better but similar to the first; it was temporary because her clan moved from place to place. However, this new chieftain had more influence and power. It showed in the longhouse's structure, which was more permanent and warmer, with luxuries like a wooden floor rather than packed earth.

Kóri nudged Thora, gave her a nod before he broke away, and went to his family on his right side.

Thora beelined to her mate, who was seated on their shared bed that was meant for a small family like theirs. Halcyon was humming while Hjǫrdís breastfed but looked up when Thora sat next to her. Without hesitation, Halcyon narrowed her eyes and asked, "What?" She continued to use Greek, which often worked to their benefit when they needed a private conversation in the longhouse.

Blushing, Thora spilled the news before it was too late. "The chieftain is giving you a neck-ring this evening." She chuckled at Halcyon's big eyes.

Halcyon shook her head after a beat. "Where did you hear such nonsense?" She turned her attention back to Hjǫrdís and cooed at her daughter.

"Kóri."

Halcyon glanced over at Thora's brother, who was helping his mate with their pups. She huffed and muttered, "He's lying."

"Kóri does not lie." Thora leaned forward and loosened the laces of her boots. She waited for Halcyon to take in the news.

"I'm not Norsk."

"I know." Thora kicked off the first boot, then the other one. She put on a pair of leather slippers that were tucked under their bed. "But it seems the chieftain sees it differently." Straightening, she looked at her mate's dubious expression. "This is a great honor."

Halcyon dropped her shoulders and stared at Hjǫrdís.

"Do you not want to accept it?" Thora asked in a delicate tone. She sensed her mate's insecurities about fitting in with the clan. Even though Halcyon could be aloof, she was persistent in her quiet ways and seemed to be finding her place. To go from being the master of her own villa to the outsider in a clan had been a huge change.

"I do." Halcyon met Thora's gaze and revealed a forlorn smile. "I do want to accept it." She let out a breath and shifted Hjǫrdís a little. "It's unexpected and kind of him." After tilting her head, she watched Hjǫrdís.

"The chieftain adores you. I think he would take you as a daughter if he could." Thora grinned at Halcyon's low snort. They both knew it was true. "Sometimes we have deep, unexplainable connections with certain people in our lives." She paused when Halcyon regarded her. Her words had hit a chord, for them both. Thora had felt such a connection when she first saw Halcyon. They hadn't discussed it, ever. She assumed such an honest conversation would make it too real, especially for Halcyon. But Thora wanted to toe open the door in hopes Halcyon would voice her heart. Decades of training as a hoplite made it difficult for Halcyon to be vulnerable.

"When we feel that pull, it is hard to ignore it, and all we wish to do is give ourselves to that person," she whispered. Thora waited for her mate's response and used her Alpha pheromones to temper any anxiety that Halcyon might feel.

"Are you still talking about the chieftain?" Halcyon eyed her mate, but her attention was drawn back to Hjǫrdís, who was done nursing. She adjusted and relaced her shirt, re-covering her breast.

"In part, yes." Thora suspected the chieftain felt a connection toward Halcyon. It wasn't by any means like her and Halcyon's bond.

Halcyon sighed and said, "He does remind me of a younger Leonidas." She had a smile again and placed Hjǫrdís in her lap. "I'm fond of him." A brief silence fell between them until Hjǫrdís made a few playful sounds. "She still needs to eat tonight."

"She is nursing a lot less," Thora said, accepting that the earlier conversation was closed for now. "I will handle feeding her." She pulled her pup over to her lap and laughed at Hjǫrdís's kicking antics. Bent forward, she nuzzled into

Hjǫrdís's hair and breathed in her soft scent that made Thora's heart swell. Beside her, she heard Halcyon's happy hum.

"Would you want another pup?"

Thora jerked upright, blinked, and stared at her mate. "Another pup?" She breathed a bit harder and hated how her voice squeaked on the last word.

"Yes, another pup." Halcyon removed her boots next and switched to her slip-on leather shoes.

Thora opened and closed her mouth while a furrow worked across her brow. "Do you want another pup?"

"I asked first," Halcyon countered and wagged a finger. She rose but turned to Thora, leaned down, and grazed her nose along Thora's cheek. Her scent was heavy and thick like honey, creating a burn between Thora's legs. "You can think about it." Rising, she winked at Thora and said, "I'm going to wash up before the chieftain corners me."

Thora watched her mate depart, then snapped her jaw shut after the shocking question. She wanted another pup or two or three. However, she hadn't expected Halcyon to want any more after Hjǫrdís. Their daughter had an easy disposition and was sweet, but that didn't guarantee more pups. Swallowing, Thora tried to mull over Halcyon's view about another pup. However, her Alpha brain was stuck on the wonderful scent emanating from her mate. Halcyon always smelled sweet, like an Omega, but tonight it coated Thora's tongue. She was forced to shake it off for the moment. Hjǫrdís needed her time and attention.

"Evening, Thora."

Snapping her attention up from her daughter, Thora smiled and greeted, "Good evening, Cesare. How was your day?"

Hjǫrdís squealed in delight when Cesare neared them. She held out her arms.

"Hi, Hjǫrdís." Cesare held out his arms. "Do you want Uncle Cesare?" He glanced at Thora and replied, "It was a nice day. A little chilly." He earned a chuckle from Thora.

Hjǫrdís kicked her feet and sputtered her lips together.

Thora grinned and allowed Cesare to take Hjǫrdís. "We are going to eat. Right, my little one?"

Cesare laughed at Hjǫrdís's next squeal. Halcyon had argued multiple times for Cesare to remain in Greece. He refused every time and argued that Halcyon was his only family. Somehow, Cesare beat Halcyon's stubborn nature and traveled with them to the Norselands. Similar to Halcyon, Cesare had become a vital component to the clan. He was a hard worker and spent most of his time helping care for the livestock, especially the horses. At times, he would assist Halcyon on the training field.

Thora stood and handed off her pup to Cesare. Together they went to the fire pit. In short order, they had huge plates of food and enjoyed a meal together. Halcyon joined them halfway through and tried to help feed Hjǫrdís, but Thora brushed her off. When they were done, the longhouse was busy with chatter and laughter. Toward the end of the meal, the chieftain called for order and went over today's events along with tomorrow's plans. He then called for

Halcyon to ascend to the platform. Thora gave her an encouraging smile, which seemed to help.

The chieftain stood beside Halcyon but addressed his clan. His heavy voice boomed through the longhouse. He was every bit the Alpha and radiated with confidence and power. The clan adored him as a leader and honored him like a king. After his speech, he turned to Halcyon and held out a neck-ring. "*Will you accept my torc and join our clan?*"

Halcyon was rigid and stoic, as if she were on duty back in Sparta. The slightest of smiles cracked her hoplite mask. "*Já,*" she replied in a loud voice. A cheer from the clan followed her acceptance.

The chieftain smiled and even glowed as he stepped forward. He raised the neck-ring that had a head of a wolf at each end. He slid the opening past her neck, then turned it until the two wolf heads settled on her collarbone. "*Beautiful,*" he praised in Norsk. Taking her hand, he lifted their arms and called out, "*Halcyon the Iron Edge!*" The clan chanted her name and title.

Thora admired her mate on the platform with their chieftain. She puffed out her chest, to the point it ached a bit. As an Alpha, pride was natural to her, but it deepened whenever Halcyon made strides. With Hjǫrdís in their lives, Thora had all the more reason to be a prideful Alpha.

The chieftain called for more mead and ale to celebrate Halcyon's new position in the clan. He clapped her hard on the back and followed her off the platform. Everyone was elated and congratulated Halcyon. Once she made it to Thora, she received a warm kiss on the lips and a wet nuzzle from Hjǫrdís.

"I am so proud of you," Thora whispered in Greek to Halcyon.

"*Þǫkk*," Halcyon murmured and remained close to Thora. She appeared ready to take Hjǫrdís, but several more people wanted to shake arms. Then the alcohol started to flow. Halcyon forwent it, but Thora drank a partial horn, not wanting to insult their leader. The celebration continued for several hours, but Halcyon had an excuse and took Hjǫrdís to bed.

Thora chatted with Cesare and her two brothers longer and enjoyed their usual banter. In the coming days, they hoped to travel to a neighboring clan and visit their sister, who was mated to a Beta. She wanted to talk longer, but her heart pulled her toward her family. After a goodnight, she weaved through the longhouse and joined her mate on the platform bed. Under the furs, the three of them snuggled together while the longhouse grew quieter.

Halcyon burrowed deeper into Thora's body, with Hjǫrdís secured in her arms. Hjǫrdís was closest to the wall, ensuring she couldn't roll out of bed by accident.

Thora nudged the back of Halcyon's head and murmured, "I love you."

"I love you, too, my gorgeous Alpha."

Thora smiled. Today's hard work on the lake settled into Thora's bones, and she was fast asleep.

* * *

Thora jolted awake when her hand was forced between two burning thighs. She detected the thick wetness that coated her fingers and fought back a moan. Raising her head, she peered down at her mate in the dimness of the longhouse. "Wha…" Halcyon covered Thora's mouth with her other hand. Thora drew in Halcyon's heady pheromones and they rushed to Thora's core. Halcyon smelled sweeter than honey and called to Thora's Alpha.

Halcyon was going into heat and would trigger Thora's rut soon.

Thora's heart leaped into a gallop. She pulled Halcyon's hand away and said, "We must go to the mating hut, *now*." Yet she remained still and considered the needy grind of Halcyon's hips against her palm. "I can—"

"*Nei*." Halcyon closed her eyes and bit her lip. "Not with Hjǫrdís here."

Thora nodded and jerked her hand free, growling at the separation. "I will alert Cesare, Kóri, and Gulla." She climbed out of bed, dressed in haste, and took Hjǫrdís, who fussed at her. But there was little time to prepare. Gulla stirred first and elbowed Kóri to get up. Gulla took Hjǫrdís and tried to soothe her before anyone else woke up.

Kóri tumbled from the bed he shared with his mate. He kissed her on the cheek once, then started to dress as fast as possible. Thora woke Cesare next, then hurried out of the longhouse, forgoing her jacket. All her focus was on preparing the mating hut so that she could take care of Halcyon. She sprinted across the village and shouldered open one of the huts. The cold, damp air greeted her, which wouldn't do. Stumbling around in the dim light, she attempted to organize logs and kindling in the fire pit at the center of the hut.

Kóri rushed into the hut next, a lamp in hand. He set it down nearby, lighting up most of the hut. "*Halcyon was getting ready.*" After he scrubbed his face, he went about checking the barrels for food and water.

"*I think we'll need more firewood,*" Thora told her brother. She took a short stick and held it inside the lamp.

"*I'll get some.*" Kóri hurried off with leather log bags in hand.

Cesare arrived next, asking what to do. He checked over the bed area and announced there were enough blankets. He promised he'd bring them hot meals later. Thora shoved the burning stick underneath the stack of firewood, lighting the kindling below it. She then asked Cesare to retrieve a few furs from her and Halcyon's bed in the longhouse. They carried their joined scents, which would be better for nesting. Cesare rushed off.

Thora's mind was racing as she pictured the next couple of days. In the past, she and Halcyon had discussed truly mating when she went into a heat again. But they hadn't talked about another pup until tonight.

Wiping the sweat from her brow, Thora checked that the fire would stay lit. Kóri returned and started to stack the firewood. "*Where is Halcyon?*" she muttered.

"*She's outside.*"

Thora frowned at her brother and left the mating hut, ensuring the door was closed so the hut would warm up. The cold bit at Thora's exposed skin, leaving prickles across her back. In the dark, she scanned for her mate and located the one lone figure halfway between the longhouse and the hut.

Thora crossed the frozen ground, but slowed when she realized what had captured Halcyon's attention.

"They're stunning," Halcyon whispered. All her attention was affixed on the night sky where bright green wisps danced against the starry backdrop. A few razor thin clouds drifted between the emerald flames.

Coming closer, Thora went behind her mate and encircled Halcyon, drawing them together. They were dressed in only tunics, trousers, and untied boots. But Halcyon's increased body temperature kept them comfortable. In warm silence, they watched the orchestra of colors above them. It was the first time that Halcyon had witnessed the Bifrǫst.

"How long will they last?" Halcyon whispered.

"Minutes… hours." Thora smiled at the wonder in Halcyon's voice. She hoped the Bifrǫst lasted for a little while so that Halcyon could capture it in her memory. They would see them again over the winter, but the first experience was always the best one. "Are you certain you do not regret leaving Sparta?"

"*Já.*" Halcyon placed her hands over Thora's larger ones. "I'm happy for the first time. This wasn't the path I planned to follow because I didn't know I could have it. But you gave it to me."

Thora smiled at the genuine honesty in her mate's response. They both were happy, as individuals, as mates, and as parents. They weren't bound through a union, but tonight it would change after their long wait for Halcyon's heat. Thora had rutted several times over the past year. But Halcyon hadn't gone through another heat due to recovering from pregnancy and breastfeeding. With the heat setting in, the opportunity to claim Halcyon as her true mate was within her grasp. Once they completed their union, Thora was certain her heart might burst.

"This is the perfect way to celebrate the start of our union," Halcyon said in wonder, tilting her head back farther. "It's as if the gods are blessing us."

"*Já.*" With a strong thrum in her chest, Thora admired the luminescent streaks above them. "The Bifrǫst is a gateway between our world and the gods' own."

"I believe it." Halcyon rested her head against Thora's chest and hummed a sweet sound. "One day when I die, will I go with your gods or mine?"

Thora chewed on her lip and wondered the same thing. The idea that they could be separated in the afterlife terrified Thora. After a deep breath, she replied, "I am not sure, but we will go together." Silence passed for a moment, then the Bifrǫst faded away as if the gods carried them back to Asgard.

Halcyon turned inside her mate's long arms and hooked her hands behind Thora's neck. "Together?" A thin smile tugged at the corner of her lips. "Are you referring to our connection again?"

Gathering her courage, Thora broached the subject after failing to get a response earlier tonight. "*Já.*" She watched Halcyon's features, waiting for any denial to form. "We have a connection." The drumming in her ear grew louder even though she was confident about their deeper meaning to each other. Halcyon was loving and passionate, but she didn't allow many to see those qualities. Early on, Thora savored the nights when Halcyon showed her vulnerable side. Since Hjǫrdís's birth, Halcyon let down her guard much more but only for her family.

"Mmmm." Halcyon rubbed her thumb against a delicate spot along Thora's neck. "Like the Fates brought us together." She leaned against Thora again and wet her lips. The new torc necklace rested on her neck, reflecting how much she belonged with their clan.

Thora considered the idea, then shook her head. "*Nei.*" She dipped her head lower and whispered, "I mean that we are woven together."

"That's quite romantic," Halcyon whispered and trailed a hand forward. She traced Thora's bottom lip with her thumb. Her wonderful scent enthralled Thora, making it next to impossible to think. "You're talking about true mates."

Thora gave a rumbly agreement. "Do you think it is true?" Hot energy burned between them, pulling and pushing them together. She was torn between carrying her mate to the hut and claiming her finally or continuing their crucial conversation. Both their hearts were bare.

Halcyon grazed her lips across Thora's cooler ones and murmured, "*Já.*" She withdrew a fraction and regarded Thora. "Your name is written all over my heart," Halcyon whispered to her mate. "You were in all my past lives and will be in all my future ones." An emerald glow reflected in her dark eyes from the return of the dazzling Bifrǫst. "I may have set you free, but it was you who saved me from a life of servitude and an unhappy union." Her tears started to fall, coating her cheeks.

"I was drawn to you the moment I saw you. I could never love another as I do you."

"Hjǫrdís?" Thora asked in a teasing manner, but her voice cracked from the weighted surge in her chest. Her attempt at humor did nothing to dissuade Halcyon from speaking what was in her heart.

"Our pup is a different kind of love." Halcyon gazed deeper into Thora's eyes, seeming to touch Thora's soul. "I love Hjǫrdís deeply and cannot imagine my life without her now. But one day she will outgrow us, and when that day comes, I know you will still be here by my side."

"*Já*, always," Thora said, unable to hold back her own tears. Over a year ago, she had attempted to run away from Halcyon, from their connection, and from a situation that she believed might break her. Thora expected to find her final ending at the tip of a stranger's blade while on the run. But the Moirai had another fate in mind for her. Or perhaps true love was much bigger than the gods. After reconnecting with Halcyon, Thora vowed to stay by Halcyon's side, through the darkest moments and the best ones. The loving dog had caught the frightened rabbit, ensuring their mutual dream came true.

"I love you so much, Halcyon," Thora choked out and held her true mate closer. "I am forever yours."

"And I am yours," Halcyon whispered between whimpers, then she drew Thora down for a salty kiss. But behind the tanginess was the sweet, everlasting love between them. "You are the Edge to my Iron." Her eyes glowed an iridescent green under the Bifrǫst above them. She sealed their lips together and handed over her heart to Thora in their kiss.

Thora did her best to remain upright, moaning and whining toward the end. Halcyon stroked her mate's cheek, smiled, and said, "Now, my love, it's time for you to finally claim me."

THE END

About the Author

Lexa Luthor is an avid writer and reader of the Omegaverse trope especially F/F pairings. In her books, each main character(s) is a strong-willed female, who navigates difficult situations but always ends up finding love with their mate. Every tale has a twist and is gripping, sexy, and even a bit adventurous.

When not writing, Lexa enjoys binge watching television shows like Game of Thrones, Gentleman Jack, or The L Word. Her other favorite hobbies are playing cornhole, rooting for the Kansas City Chiefs, and laying around the pool in the summer. At times, Lexa finds time to read romances (both dark and fluffy) and great sci-fi books but nothing else can beat a steamy, downright erotic F/F romance with biting, knotting, and slightly possessive love.

Visit her website at LexaLuthor.com for more information and be sure to sign up for her newsletter for the latest release information, bonus material, and freebies.